# BLACK WIDOW

# NICKY SHEARSBY

SRL Publishing Ltd

# BLACK WIDOW

NICKY SHEARSBY

SRL Publishing Ltd
London
www.srlpublishing.co.uk


First published worldwide by SRL Publishing in 2023


Copyright © NICKY SHEARSBY 2023

ISBN: 978-19150731-4-3

1 3 5 7 9 10 8 6 4 2

A CIP catalogue record for this book is available from the
British Library


SRL Publishing is a Climate Positive publisher removing more
carbon emissions than it emits.

SEL Publishing Ltd

London

www.selpublishing.com

First published as ebook by SEL Publishing in 201_

Copyright © NICE Publishing 201_

The author has asserted their right to be identified as the author of this work in accordance with the Copyright, Designs and Patents Act 1988.

ISBN 978 1 85776 7

SEL Publishing Ltd, Yvonne van der Heijden and other trademarks owned by SEL Publishing Ltd.

The book is a work of non-fiction based on the life and experiences of the author. In some limited cases names of people, places, dates and sequences or the detail of events have been changed to protect the privacy of others. The author has stated to the publishers that, except in such minor respects not affecting the substantial accuracy of the work, the contents of this book are true.

A CIP catalogue record for this book is available from the British Library.

SEL Publishing Ltd makes every effort to use papers that are natural, renewable and recyclable products and made from wood grown in sustainable forests. The logging and manufacturing processes conform to the environmental regulations of the country of origin.

# 1

I have no idea how long I sat next to my sister's grave that morning, trying and failing to ignore the fact I was surrounded by police officers — flashing lights, radio chatter, strangers in authority. Although I'd waited all morning for this to happen, the entire thing threatened to dislodge my composure once and for all, sending me spiralling over the edge of some cavernous drop I wasn't even aware I'd reached. I closed my eyes, wanting the events of the previous evening to be nothing more than the deluded workings of an overactive imagination. I did not dare look at my fingernails. Despite much scrubbing, much swearing, I suspected traces of blood could still be found there, mocking me, ready to expose all.

I deserved what was coming next, of course, what I'd set in motion. I wasn't stupid. Yet, I equally wasn't convinced I could turn and acknowledge these people, even if I wanted to. The concept of what such an act would provoke was willing to poison my thoughts — carnage, chaos, pandemonium, resulting in disastrous consequences I had nowhere to place. Last night's unavoidable actions would shortly see me confessing to all, blurting out details of my murderous deeds to those who did not care for my welfare, or appreciate my fragility. Although everything heading my way was purely of my own volition, none of it sat comfortably with my logical thinking. It was a fitting yet unfortunate notion that this day would forever now signal a pivotal change I wasn't convinced I was ready for. It was a shame — for everyone involved.

I glanced towards my niece, Eva, thankfully asleep in her buggy, blissfully unaware of the activity around us as two plain-clothed police officers calmly picked their way across the damp morning grass towards us. Their overly shined shoes threatened to become as tainted as the overgrown headstones that peppered this place — all of it left to the mercy of nature, my chaotic mind included. I hoped Eva would remain in her dreams, unaffected by what was about to happen. This event might therefore never interrupt her life as it was inevitably destined to determine the rest of mine. I sighed. There was nothing I could do about that now. *Shit.*

'Miss Adams?' My name sounded too formal as it emerged from a stranger's mouth in a polite manner unbefitting of this moment. He behaved as if he knew me already, able to address me with confidence. He had *no* idea who he was talking to. I nodded, getting to my feet, fully understanding why they were here, uncomfortably aware of a destiny they didn't.

'My name is DI Lewis. This is DS Cavendish. Would you mind accompanying us to the station, please?' the officer requested. 'We were told you might be here. We would very much like to speak to you.' They had questions. They assumed I had the answers. I stared at these men, their simple request nothing more than several they would make today, just another day, another crime. What would they say if I told them I wasn't in the mood for questioning? *No, thank you. Not today.* I was glad I could not read their faces, determined they would not unravel mine.

I swallowed, nodding my head, offering a smile I didn't mean, hoping they wouldn't realise how fake it probably looked. They had the audacity to glare at me as if the blood I'd recently spilt was still on my skin, staining my clothing, damaging my appearance, never again able to wash away with ease. Yet, I couldn't tell if such an ugly suggestion was merely a misplaced thought lodged in the back of my ridiculously unhinged mind, or if they could see the real monster I'd become. I wondered how long they would hold my gaze if I stared at them long enough, offering a flat smile, a knowing wink. What thoughts would be allowed to wander freely through *their* minds if I were to brush a stray fingertip across their controlled composure? Would they feel so calm in my presence then? It was their job, of course, to remove the unhinged from society, the damaged, the criminally insane. Yet, how do you begin to uncoil the mind of a freak? How would they uncoil mine? What did they see when they looked at me?

Ironically, if events had occurred in a contrasting way, if I had taken a different route, metaphorically speaking, this day might have become nothing more than an innocent, potentially pleasant moment for all. This unassuming cemetery was more than capable of creating well-needed solace, shielding me from thoughts I wished to keep firmly inside my head. This tranquil setting could have easily retained my niece's carefree slumber, my sister's grave nothing more than a comforting connotation to my swiftly unravelling senses. However, that was not how things were set to pan out for me today.

If this were a movie, the entire scene might have played out in slow motion. The evil villain receiving her just desserts, a justified comeuppance befitting of the unhinged person they had in their possession. Heavy hands resting on trembling shoulders, a flash of metal as unyielding handcuffs brushed immovable skin, blinding blue flashing lights set against a cloudless sky. I could see it now. As it was, this otherwise peaceful morning was lost to the reality of actions none of these people could possibly understand.

I had brought this all on myself, I know, inadvertently guiding the police to this very location, fully expecting the fallout from a deed I could never undo. The fact I assumed I was still in control was entirely misplaced. *How pathetic.* Yet, was I ready for what lay ahead? Ready for the next painful stepping-stone of this obscure endurance that I, at one time, called my life? No. Not a chance. And, if I was honest with myself; I probably never would be.

It was a shame I did not have the genuine ability to acknowledge the officers at my side, my thoughts already left to wander unchecked for too long. I thought of my poor Mum, forced to suffer in silence for a daughter whose mind had already tipped the scale of balance sometime earlier, her fragile granddaughter a mere by-product of actions wholly unmitigated. I swallowed, allowing strangers to press my torrid skull into a police car as they lifted Eva into another, the rest of the world finding this moment unimportant, yet those few seconds so very critical to *me*. It signalled the first day of the rest of my life. The first of many to come that would see the truth of Stacey Adams revealed in all her resplendent finery.

\*\*\*

The journey to the police station was slightly imposing on my day, yet my entire body was too numb from events of the previous evening to fully appreciate what was happening. I'd initiated this thing entirely on purpose, making the very phone call that had triggered this moment in the first place. I closed my eyes, screams I assumed must have emerged from my untethered mouth at some point over the last few hours, still littering my deranged thoughts long after my voice had silenced. What *did* these people see when they looked at me? A killer? A victim?

I was led along a narrow corridor, not unlike my perceived mind. Dark, questionable, no windows here that might otherwise allow a glimmer of light to filter unchecked, nothing but closed forgotten thoughts behind closed forgotten doors — cold hands gripping my forearms in pursuit of a truth still too painful for me to admit openly. I probably should have been afraid. I might very well have been, too, had I retained the capacity for such an emotion. As it turned out, I couldn't feel a goddamned thing.

'Thank you for coming in today, Stacey. I assume you know why we have asked you here?' A suited female police officer was speaking, too calmly for my liking, although she did not smile or offer any upbeat tone that might have confirmed such a reassuring presence. She was plain-clothed, probably a detective, an inspector, a DCI even. Dressed in a black trouser suit, crisp cream blouse, she appeared quite the stern image of authority. The police had done their job well. I was in custody. *Precisely where I belonged*. Not that they knew such a truth yet. I was only here to answer their questions, tick boxes, shed well-meaning light on the scene that had no doubt made them feel quite ill to recall. It was this poor woman's job to uncover the real me, the unfortunate murder I'd ultimately failed to disguise.

I nodded, my voice eluding me. I had nothing to say. Nothing that would make much sense to these people anyway.

'My name is DCI Moor,' the suited woman offered, placing a folder onto a laminated tabletop as she took a seat opposite me. *Of course she was.* Such privilege I'd yielded, warranting the attention of a *senior* officer. I refrained from rolling my eyes as she regarded me for a moment, obviously pondering my potential involvement, the probable existence of unpleasant photographs sitting inside her blue folder — the blood I'd spilt still fragmenting behind my fingernails, in my hair, in my mind. Evidence. *Proof.* Everything they needed to lock me up, throw away the key, forget this day ever happened. Those photographs would not have made enjoyable viewing, I know, yet it was hardly my fault. I wished she wouldn't keep giving me such a pointed look. I sighed, scratching an itch on my neck. Did it make me look guilty?

Although the detective couldn't possibly appreciate what I'd done, there was nothing to expel the sickness that grew in my belly, a sharpness in my chest cavity that forced much-needed air from my lungs. Had things played out differently, I'm confident today *would* have become just another day. It could have been a rather pleasant morning.

'I understand you made two phone calls at approximately eight o'clock this morning,' DCI Moor stated, tapping an index finger against the cheap cardboard wallet, staring beyond to the hidden contents as if she was unsure when, or if, to reveal them. 'The first was to a Mrs Janet Finch. I believe she is a cleaner for the couple who own the house.' She checked her notebook, probably reading my sister and brother-in-law's names for verification purposes. 'The second was to a local taxi firm.' DCI Moor raised her eyebrows, obviously curious by the taxi request. 'Mrs Finch tells us she was dismissed recently due to lack of funds. Is that correct?'

I nodded.

'She also confirmed Mrs Cole passed away a few weeks ago.' DCI Moor glanced at me, narrowing her eyes, thoughts left to linger in a mind that had no idea why I'd chosen to call Janet Finch instead of them. I didn't nod or offer any response. I had nothing to comment on the subject of my sister. 'Why did you call the cleaner, asking if she could come to the house this morning? And why, just moments later, did you call yourself a taxi?' She placed a printed sheet on the table, confirmation that they had all the information. There was no point in denying my actions. 'Where were you going, Stacey? And why were you at the local cemetery?'

I couldn't help offering a shake of my head. I didn't mean to appear so shut off, so callously calculated, so cold. I wished she would get to the point. Say what she had to say. Get it over with. We both knew what she was thinking.

'Please help me build a picture so we can understand your involvement.' She pressed her lips together, seemingly wanting to chew her bottom lip, uncertain if I had anything to do with the tragic scene that presented itself to them this morning. 'There appeared to be no attempt to cover what happened at the house. It won't take us long to piece it all together. There is plenty of evidence at the scene, fingerprints, amongst other things.' I knew what she meant. My fingerprints weren't the only evidence I'd left behind. DNA and bodily fluids were hardly readily disguisable. I hadn't exactly covered my tracks. Jason had made damned sure of that. DCI Moor continued. 'The poor woman received quite the shock, as you can imagine. Can you tell us what you know?'

I shrugged. Poor Janet. She was a good woman. One of the few decent people I'd met in my short, pathetic time on this godforsaken Earth who didn't make me want to scream in protest. Or at least, she seemed a good person on the two occasions I'd met her, one of those times being my sister's funeral. Yet, that was hardly an appropriate day for frivolity or for getting to know her better. Again, not my fault.

'It was the easiest thing I could think of at the time,' I muttered.

'The easiest thing?'

I nodded.

'Regarding?'

'The mess you saw in the hallway.' It was hardly something anyone could have missed. My fingerprints were everywhere. Jason's blood, my blood. Semen. *A mess.*

DCI Moor sat back in her seat, surprised by my choice of words. 'So you admit you *saw* the body?' She was writing something in her notebook, already putting words into my mouth, forming an opinion. There was no point in acting the shocked victim. Anyone could see I wasn't.

I nodded again, the image of Jason's brutalised corpse still swimming painfully in my brain. I did not for one second assume I would ever get it out of my head.

'Can you help me understand how the body came to be in such a location? Because I'm curious, Stacey, why you would refer to a dead man as a "mess"?'

*Because he was a fucking mess by the time I'd finished with him, that's why!*

I glared at DCI Moor, knowing this thing wasn't going to be as easy to gloss over as I would have hoped. I hadn't meant to kill him, although who would believe that? His death could not be classed as a mere accident, that's for sure. I was unhinged, granted. Yet, my crime was hardly unprovoked. The man had hurt me, irrefutably. However, it barely appeared self-defence in nature, more self-preserving, self-fulfilling, and entirely self-sacrificing, in the end, thanks to that selfish pig of a man, who I would have, at one, time done anything for.

DCI Moor sighed. 'Stacey, at this stage, we are simply trying to piece things together, place the whereabouts of the victim before he came to end up in that hallway, trace his movements. I know this must be a shock to you. Did you find the body there?'

I nodded. It was only a half-lie. I actually found him this morning, precisely where I'd left him before going to bed last night. I couldn't bring myself to touch him, let alone move him. I was impressed I slept as well as I did, to be honest.

She stared at me, a knowing look in her eyes. 'So why did you not simply call the police straight away? Why did you first call the cleaner, then call yourself a taxi instead of waiting at the house for the police to arrive?'

I didn't reply. Would "no comment" help either of us? Did I need a lawyer?

'What were you even doing at the house?'

'I live there.' *Lived* there. I glanced at DCI Moor. 'I've been helping out. Since my sister passed.' Why the hell did I assume the detective would care about such things now?

DCI Moor nodded. 'We need to confirm the current whereabouts of Jason Cole. Do you know where Mr Cole is, Stacey?' She already knew. They all did. They merely needed my confirmation.

I wanted to smile, my lips already attempting to turn up at the corners as she spoke. It was hardly appropriate. The poor deluded woman had no firm idea who the victim was as yet — those innocent smiling photographs lining the walls of his house not even remotely resembling the lump of pulverised flesh left behind on his now damaged wooden floor. I assumed she had her suspicions, merely needing confirmation, my clarification. It was unfortunate that Jason did not have any tattoos. If he did, Janet would have already identified her employer by now, the very question of his whereabouts completely unrequired. The poor bastard was probably now lying in a lab somewhere, a mere John Doe, his dental records of no use to anyone.

'I assume *Jason Cole* is currently on his way to the morgue,' I offered coldly, wanting to laugh. Why did I sound so sarcastic? It was a fitting end for him, I concluded, although an end I found no actual comfort in thinking about now. They could hardly blame me for the man's actions last night and what he subsequently made me do to him in the end.

'So, you're saying the body is, in fact, that of Jason Cole?' DCI Moor was writing again, her face expressing nothing of her thoughts, her emotions.

I nodded. She was good at this. Well done, DCI Moor. Well done.

10

# 2

My throat was so dry I felt it might choke me, giving me away once and for all, spilling my guilt across this table with little regard for anything. Not unlike Jason's splattering blood patterns, it seemed. I tried not to appear shaken by such a thought as I stared towards the far wall, but I could still hear the sound his head made as it split wide open. *Jesus Christ.* The detective nodded to one of her officers, offering a silent communication. The guy rose to his feet and left the room — confirmation pending that the lab was no longer required to check potential DNA of the unknown victim, his face no longer a face at all, his once considered beautiful lopsided grin permanently wiped from the world, from my memory. His DNA wouldn't have been on record anyway. He had little involvement with the police until today. It was an unfortunate fact. For him.

'Can you please tell me what happened? How do you know it was Jason Cole?' For the first time, the detective looked at me with sympathy, as if she believed I'd simply found the poor bastard like that, unable to deal with the incoming shock that now entirely rendered me incapable of rational interaction. He wasn't wearing much that would have identified him anyway, his wedding ring already in his sock drawer, forgotten, waiting for me to sell at the first opportunity, swap it for a new one. Did they assume I might have recognised him by the size of his penis? I couldn't answer. I didn't wish to be reminded.

'Stacey, why *did* you call the cleaner instead of the police?' DCI Moor repeated, sounding quite anxious now, slightly irritated. 'She claims you asked if she could go to the house. She said there was nothing in your voice to assume anything was wrong, simply that you had a problem that needed taking care of. A *mess* that needed tidying up.' She emphasised the word "mess" again, concluding that she believed I must have already known the body was there before Janet arrived. Apparently, I sounded calm on the phone. Too calm.

I stared at DCI Moor. I wasn't calm. I was completely numb. There was a big difference. However, I knew they would uncover the truth eventually, nothing for me to do now but confess, my fingerprints and DNA littering the scene, Jason's semen probably still inside me, on his kitchen table, and, despite many efforts to scrub them, remnants of his skin and blood still behind my nails.

'He attacked me,' I breathed, needing them to understand. My voice was unsteady, emerging slightly deranged as if it belonged to someone else. I closed my eyes, recalling his last breath against my cheek, his probing, unwanted hands between my legs, his twisted words in my ears. I couldn't dwell on the fact I'd brought this entire thing on myself. The fact Jason had ultimately become what he was because of *me,* was now irrelevant.

'He attacked you?' DCI Moor wasn't expecting such a revelation. To discover I was directly involved, in the house at the time, able to provide much-needed assistance, seemingly came as a shock to her. As far as she was concerned, Jason was the victim, attacked brutally, *fatally*.

12

His cold corpse now nothing more than evidence they needed to confirm a violent interaction they probably believed had been accomplished by a man.

I nodded. 'Yes. He raped me, actually. He was trying to do it again. I had to stop him.' It was true. I didn't want such a painful memory in my head. I had honestly loved Jason. I was devoted to him. I believed he felt the same way. Everything I had done, I did for him.

'Can you tell us what happened?' the detective was quieter now, patiently waiting for an admission to a crime, my words crucial to this entire case. *Pivotal*. Did I see who attacked him? Had someone come to my rescue? How did I get away? Who else was there? Unanswered questions churned the air to dust as the detective sat stone-faced opposite me, the room threatening to suffocate us all, my sullen features giving nothing away of the truth. I was waiting for her to ask the one question teetering on everyone's lips. *Who swung the golf club directly into Jason Cole's face?*

'I *killed* him,' I muttered, knowing she would be unprepared for my response. Nevertheless, it was futile denying the truth. My DNA was everywhere, already collected by some guy in a white paper suit. I waited for her look of surprise. Shock even. None came.

'*You* killed him?'

*I just told you I did. Are you deaf?* I wanted to scream but I nodded instead, keeping my mouth firmly shut. I'd probably said enough.

'You *bludgeoned* his face until it was unrecognisable?'

I nodded again. Did she believe such a small-statured female incapable of a violent frenzied act? The man was deranged. I had to make him stop. Make it all stop.

'Stacey, the man's jaw was caved in so far we found teeth embedded in the back of his skull. Teeth on the floor,

13

teeth in the wall. His skull was shattered, the top of his spine was protruding from his neck.' I appreciated that DCI Moor was struggling to cope with the idea that, in apparent self-defence, during a would-be rape attack, I would go to such lengths, create such resulting catastrophic injuries. She didn't want to believe that I could be so callous. To be honest, neither did I.

I closed my eyes. 'I know exactly what he looked like,' I confirmed. There was no need for a complete reconstruction now, thank you very much. I did what I had to do. It was all Jason's fault. It was as simple as that.

'Stacey, why didn't you simply get away from him? Run away, call for help?' She knew that if I had hit him with a golf club, he would have released me long enough for me to run.

I glared at the poor deluded detective in front of me, her job to uncover the truth of crimes committed, ensure criminals got precisely what they deserved, the CPS in control of them all, the courts offering the final word. She didn't want to ask the "whys" behind the crimes she investigated, uncover hidden pain that lingered beneath actions of potentially dangerous human beings. She wanted to tick boxes, close cases, move on — enjoy the occasional promotion on her way to retirement, a gold watch set to conclude it all. It all sounded so utterly dull.

'He pushed things too far.' It was true. He pushed me way further than I ever assumed I would be prepared to go.

'Pushed things too *far*?'

'Yes,' I snapped, unable to stop my outburst, prevent the increasing irritability that threatened to uncover everything about me in one swift, flawless motion. The previous night was still raw in my mind, his probing touch fresh on my skin. I could still feel the heat of his breath, his obliterated flesh against my closed fist.

'Care to elaborate?' DCI Moor was tapping her pen. I wanted to snatch the thing from her grip and throw it across the room.

I shook my head. *No.* I did not wish to relive any of what had happened last night, or over the previous few weeks, come to think of it.

'Can you tell me the events that led to such a moment? The moment you *killed* him?' She was staring at me intently, her tone blank, her eyes unseeing. She still assumed I was lying somehow, covering for someone else. Why was I so surprised?

I shook my head again. *No.* I didn't want to think about it. I didn't need the image in my head. Ghosts and demons lived there now. I knew they would never leave me, left to haunt my dreams forever. I couldn't change any of that. Maybe I didn't deserve to. I pressed a hand over my pregnant belly, my unborn child innocent in this increasing turmoil.

DCI Moor noticed, glancing at my abdomen, connecting dots she had no idea how to join. It did not mean she had the answers. 'We can do a pregnancy test including checks for sexually transmitted infections if you are at all worried,' she offered. It was kind of her to offer. *Stupid bitch.*

I smiled flatly, shaking my head. 'It's okay. I know I'm pregnant,' I swallowed something that tasted nasty, rancid. 'It wasn't because Jason raped me.' Although, the definition between rape and what I had allowed him to do to me over the last few weeks was seemingly the same thing. It was quite ironic. Was I so deluded that I hadn't noticed Jason's unrequited demands? Sex that wasn't sex at all, but acts of violence to satisfy a man out of control.

'Okay,' DCI Moor nodded stiffly. 'So, is Jason the father?'

'Would it make a difference if he was?' I snapped,

irritated, bored now. This was getting us nowhere. 'I thought he loved me. We were planning to build a life together.' It was true. I had wanted nothing else. Now I hated myself for believing such utter bullshit. For believing his pathetic, weak lies.

The detective nodded again. 'It's okay, really. But Stacey, we do need you to tell us what happened, in your own time.'

I could see Jason now, lying semi-naked on the floor of his hallway, penis still slightly erect, mocking me, provoking my untamed reactions, boxer shorts around his ankles failing to soak up the blood I'd willingly spilt. *So much blood.* DCI Moor opened the file and took out a selection of photographs. An unrecognisable corpse met my gaze, his body strewn across the floor as if I'd spread him out for effect. Small pieces of numbered yellow plastic scattered around the space, pinpointing areas of significant interest. Splatter marks against the wall, bloodied teeth on the floor, the golf club I'd willingly slammed straight into his cheating head coated with my blood-soaked fingerprints next to his dead body, confirmation of it all.

'I am showing Miss Adams a selection of photographs,' the detective confirmed for the little flashing light on the table next to us. Was the woman waiting for a shocked look to appear across my unreadable face? Did she wish to see my reaction, confirm or discard my words? I glanced her way, our eyes meeting for a split second. *I have already witnessed it all, thank you very much.* There was nothing she could show me now I hadn't already seen with my own eyes, unavoidably creating carnage they would need to clean up on my behalf. The problem with this woman was she had no idea *why* I had to do what I was forced to do, what I had already previously done — the very event that led us to where we were right now. The reason behind it all.

I blinked, glancing momentarily at the blood-red images in front of me. *The devil made me do it.* I had no other explanation.

'Does any of this look like self-defence to you, Stacey?' It was an honest question. I knew the answer. No. Of course, not. We both knew she had seen her fair share of rape victims in her line of work. I did not look like one of those women. I did not fit the profile. Rape victims lashed out. Of course, they did. They will hit back if at all possible, scratch, claw, potentially make use of a free golf club in order to get away as quickly as possible. To *run*. My actions were not the responses of a terrified victim. DCI Moor knew this as well as I did.

'Was that the reason you called Janet Finch? Were you planning on evading the police? You must have known the body would be found and thought you would simply point us to the location without wishing to hang around and be caught.'

I shook my head. No. That wasn't the reason. That wasn't how it was.

'Did you kill Jason Cole because you wanted to protect yourself from his advances, or was it a pure, frenzied attack undertaken for some other reason? Did you have an accomplice? What are you trying to cover up? Who are you trying to protect?' She tapped an index finger against an image of Jason's non-existent face. 'Because, I have to tell you, Stacey, self-defence doesn't look like *this*.' She glared at me, black eyes burrowing a hole into mine, wanting a peek inside my out-of-control mind, witnessing the potential trigger that could have led to this encounter with a man, seemingly much stronger than I.

She was right, of course. Self-defence was indeed an invalid reason I was failing to hide behind. In my deluded disguise, I assumed I would be safe inside the pretence I was trying to get away from his advances. It wasn't true. Jason was dead long before I could bring myself to stop hitting him over the head, making mincemeat of his flesh, wiping his features from the face of the earth. The DCI knew this. They all did. The mere presence of the attending forensic pathologist would have confirmed this truth.

One blow would have knocked him out. Two, potentially ensuring he suffered a significant traumatic brain injury, probably life changing. Three would have killed him. No question. I had hit him seven times. *Seven*. Each blow was more intended and forceful than the one before, each swing of the golf club meant to cause irreparable harm nobody could have done a damned thing about. He had brought the entire thing on himself. There was nothing to be done about any of it now. I was beyond anger. I think I always would be.

I shook my head. 'I guess it was a combination of both. I had to get him away from me. I couldn't leave things the way they were between us. And no, I did *not* have an accomplice.' I was more than capable of achieving such results alone. Unfortunately.

'Leave *what* between you?' DCI Moor seemed past caring now if I had help or not. She glared at me as if I was dirt she couldn't scrape off her shoe fast enough.

'He cheated on me. He cheated on his wife, my sister.' I thought about Emma, lying cold in her grave. Of a previous event I was forced to endure, long ago now, her death a historical event — Jason Cole the very reason behind it all.

'So you attacked him brutally simply because he cheated on you? Cheated on his wife?' The detective wasn't convinced. I knew how she felt.

'Amongst other things, yes.' There were many reasons hiding in the shallow recesses of my brain.

'Hardly worthy of such a savage death though,

wouldn't you agree? Did he rape you, Stacey, or is that accusation merely a way of deferring blame for what *you* did, onto him? A man who can no longer defend himself against your accusing words.' She no longer believed I was the victim in all of this. How ironic. I was actually the only victim left standing, apart from my parents, of course, Jason's parents, poor little Eva. I could not overthink such a travesty. I could not be held responsible for everyone else's emotions.

I nodded. I had allowed him to rape me, unintentionally, of course, yet undeniably. And on more than one occasion. However, I allowed such a vile act to lie hidden amongst the dark shadows of pretended love. A love I honestly believed he felt as deeply as I did, despite a profound realisation Jason loved only himself. It was hardly significant now, scarcely necessary to recall such details.

'It doesn't matter now,' I glanced at DCI Moor, my thoughts unravelling at a heightened pace.

'*Rape* doesn't matter? Or the fact Mr Cole is dead?' The detective seemed taken aback by my throwaway comment. Rape and death always matter. It's why she endures her job, puts up with the shit. Everything matters. DCI Moor is obviously very passionate about such things. *Deluded bitch.*

'I don't know what else to say?' I muttered. I honestly didn't. I had nothing left inside me that mattered anyway. I could say nothing now that would not lead them to the wrong conclusion. Or was it the right one? I no longer knew.

'You can begin by telling me the *real* reason you killed an innocent man, Stacey.' DCI Moor was staring at the photographs that had been purposefully left on view for my careful consideration.

'Innocent? Is that what you think he was?' I narrowed my eyes, this woman beginning to annoy me, my mouth beginning to chatter. *Innocent.* I could think of far more fitting words to describe the man. Bully. Bastard. Bullshitting, lying *son-of-a-BITCH*. I allowed a grin that must have told its own story.

'You tell me?' DCI Moor was still tapping her pen.

'Jason was anything but innocent, DCI Moor, *that* much I can tell you.'

'So you believe he deserved to die?'

I nodded, my mind unravelling too fast, this room too small, too hot. It was the detective's fault. 'They all do, in the end. Don't you agree?'

I was smiling. I couldn't help it. The last few hours had tipped me over the edge, so to speak, poured salt into an open wound, brought suffering to the surface of a deep lake of emotions I'd tried and failed to keep well and truly buried. I must have looked like a psychopath, grinning unprovoked. I certainly felt like one. The detective didn't need to dig further or ask additional questions to unspoken answers. She had what she needed — my confession. Everything else could be left to the evidence currently being gathered, and shrinks they would probably deem me worthy of.

DCI Moor sighed before writing something in her notebook and nodding to the officer by her side. 'Okay,' she paused before adding, 'Stacey Adams, I am arresting you for the murder of Jason Cole. You do not have to say anything, but it may harm your defence if you do not mention, when questioned, something which you later rely on in court. Anything you do say may be given in evidence. Do you understand?'

I understood. There was no point denying the truth. *I killed Jason.* Although I had not enjoyed doing such a thing, it was a simple fact, no matter what DCI Moor might choose to conclude. I loved him, yet I did not expect any of these people to understand. They would not appreciate the secret, deluded reasons forever hidden now in the back of my festering mind. DCI Moor was not looking for the "why" to my crime, only the confirmation that such a crime had happened in the first place, and I was the one responsible for the victim's ultimate demise. She would be happy to deduce her ultimate conclusion, close her little blue folder, tick boxes.

Despite my willing confessing, my mind now quivered in misspent anticipation as to what would happen next. From a police interview room to a prison cell, no bail would be offered to this demonic monster, no further attention given to the murderer in the room. I assumed the question lingering on everyone's lips, including DCI Moor's, was: *Do leopards have the potential to change their spots?* She looked at me as if she couldn't entirely fathom what had happened to such an innocent-looking female for her to end up in a police cell on a murder charge. I simply wondered if pigs had the potential to fly? Is a person capable of change? I had no idea. I guess that was entirely up to the courts to decide.

# 3

Barely in my darkest moments did I ever presume the words of an arresting statement would be aimed directly towards me, and *never* under such unprecedented circumstances. Yet neither did I determine I would ever find myself in a situation that might lead to this event in the first place. It was down to my unavoidable emotions that I was here now. Hardly my fault, I know. It was precisely because of the people I loved that I had found myself in such a harrowing situation — their actions leading directly to this moment. Yet, none of these people seemed capable in their small-minded ways to appreciate what I'd been through. It wasn't *all* about Jason. I was, however, fully aware that my inability to avoid such an explosive reaction to Jason's exploitations might appear entirely disproportionate to what these people ordinarily considered normal. Rational. Sane. Who beats a person until his face no longer looks recognisable? *Me.* I do, apparently. When pushed hard enough.

After taking my DNA, blood samples, fingerprints, DCI Moor left me to ponder my revelations in a police cell while she gathered evidence, organising the paperwork needed to officially charge me with murder. I'd already wavered my rights to a solicitor. What good would that achieve now? I'd confessed, blurted it out like a total bloody lunatic, too angry for judicious thinking, too emotional for anything else. I assumed it would work in my favour at some point, my voluntary confession. Secure a shorter sentence.

There was no need for someone in a goddamned suit to tell me such facts, adding to spiralling legal costs the British taxpayer was ultimately responsible for. I'd watched plenty of television to know how this thing worked. It mattered little that I hadn't yet felt it necessary to divulge the reasons behind my actions. Such truth wasn't important right now, certainly not to the detective. She had her man, or in my case, woman. I'd confessed. They would shortly have the evidence required to prove it to the CPS. That was enough for the Newbury Police. Enough for us all.

I wished I could eavesdrop on the private conversations taking place beyond earshot, away from my unwanted presence and potential revolt. What were the police saying in secret? What was DCI Moor thinking? More importantly, what had they told my parents? They would be at home, the kettle on, a cup of tea required to steady my mum's unravelling nerves. Eva would be playing on the kitchen floor, as usual, my niece oblivious to everything.

Five hours and two cups of tea of my own later, I was led back to the interview room to the firm sight of DCI Moor holding the paperwork she needed to confirm my guilt. I was expected to sign a simple piece of paper so she could stamp a box that deemed me a murderer, forget I existed, get on with her day. They would take me away in handcuffs, file away this heinous case, be done with it forever, be done with me. Jason was nothing more now than an unfortunate dead body the mortuary staff would need to release back to his parents, a funeral pending, their grief undeniable. No trial would be needed, no jury required to prove or disprove my guilt, confirm any potential innocence.

'Well, it seems you had quite the evening last night, Stacey,' DCI Moor said with a sigh, as if her latest findings concluded my crazed status. It was almost as if she believed I'd somehow *enjoyed* myself. I knew what she meant, of course. I already understood Jason's death could never be disguised easily. I couldn't hide from it. Run away. *Lie*. She was holding proof of my terrible deed, my confirmed fingerprints on the golf club, Jason's blood and skin behind my nails, my DNA all over *him*. I refused an internal examination. I didn't need the humiliation. I would never be able to prove rape now anyway. The man was dead, too late for him to pay for his crime. The fact he *was* dead and therefore already paying for his crime, failed to resonate with me as the detective charged me officially with Jason's demise. 'Stacey Adams, I am charging you with the murder of Jason Cole on the Seventh of September...' *Yeah, whatever*.

I was no longer listening, shocked to discover how shaky my hands had become as I held the detectives pen in my hand — an innocent length of plastic about to demand my penitence, once and for all. I scribbled my signature on the pre-typed confession, my palms hot and clammy, unwilling to read what they had printed on the charge sheet in black ink, for fear of what I might discover about myself if I did. It mattered little. The deed was done. Jason would never know another moment on this earth, breathe the fresh air I had dreamed for so long of sharing with him, our once-planned journey together, gone forever.

I took a breath as the memory of what he made me do sliced freely into my heart once more. I couldn't cry. Not here, in front of these strangers. It would be entirely inappropriate. They might assume an incorrect presumption of my feelings, *believe* I may actually be sorry. I wasn't. I loathed what that bastard had done to me — done to us all.

DCI Moor picked up the sheets of paper from the table and carefully scanned the contents. She didn't look at me. The lines on her face a telling reality she had witnessed too much suffering, many confirmed psychopaths with incurable issues — a lengthy career responsible for immeasurable failure to express genuine emotions under any circumstance. Her dynamic career was all that lay between the general public and people like me. A killer. A freak. She didn't know the half of it.

I was led along the corridor, back to my holding cell, to a place I would now be forced to sit and wait in silence, shunned by society, destroyed by the world in which I lived, my transfer to prison concluding this day and the rest of my life. These strangers would wash their hands of me for good. Forget me. Hand me over to someone else. I knew nothing of what would become of me now, yet, in the few seconds it took for them to take me away, something deep inside my brain began the painful process of shutting down, leaving behind an empty vessel that breathed good air, a heart barely beating inside a cold, dead chest. I touched my belly, the baby growing inside me simply along for the ride — nothing either of us could do about that travesty.

'DCI Moor?' I called back, the corridor around me feeling as hollow as my brain. The detective was standing in the open doorway, clutching my confession and charge sheet as if this day was the highlight of her career. She probably needed a cup of coffee now to complete it all, satisfied she had put another scumbag behind bars.

'Yes, Stacey?' Her tone was flat. Had I broken her spirit already?

'What will happen to my baby?' My words emerged cold, empty, as if nothing mattered beyond that simple question — the welfare of my unborn child being the only consideration to my otherwise miserable life.

'You don't need to worry about that for the moment.' Her reply was almost as icy as mine, emphatically telling the true extent of her emotions. How could someone like *me* bring a life into the world when so many innocent, *genuine* women couldn't have children at all? Did DCI Moor have children? Did she despise what she saw when she looked at me? *I* despised what she saw when she looked at me. It was an unfortunate truth neither of us could change.

I had all but given up hope, given up on justice, given up my freedom. So when a commotion from the front desk reached our ears, forcing the detective to leave my unwanted company and check what was happening, it felt — to me at least — like a sign. I recognised the voice immediately. *Mum.* I visualised her features, standing in front of an unsuspecting desk sergeant, hands on hips, a frenzied look on her horrified face demanding to know what the hell was going on. She would want to know if I was okay, how long they planned to keep me here. I almost smiled, the details of the last few hours overwhelmingly smothering — my mum's sudden appearance angelic to my rapidly deteriorating senses.

'Mum!' I yelled, tugging myself free from the immovable grasp of a police officer, our silent journey along that corridor interrupted brutally, thankfully. Mum's familiar voice was all I needed to bring me out of my growing despondence, back to a world I once knew and loved well. I'd almost forgotten. I lunged forward, my simple intention to race into the outstretched arms of my mother, towards comfort I felt I would never find elsewhere. I was desperate, dejected, my logic to blame for such a sudden outburst. Surely these people could understand my suffering?

Unfortunately the officer didn't allow much time for me to ponder any potential escape route as he grabbed me, forceful hands pulling flailing arms, gripping shoulders, restraining my attempted liberation with ease. I didn't mean to lash out. The poor guy was simply doing his job. But he was in my way. People who got in my way did not fare well. I don't recall kicking him, a wayward foot simply lunging out, although I caught him squarely between the legs. I couldn't have aimed it better. I heard the grunt as he let me go, no more than a split second, but long enough for me to race towards the reception desk, along the very corridor that had unwittingly become my closing coffin.

'Mum!?' I screamed again, needing her to hear me, race towards me, rescue me — tell me this was just a nightmare and I was safe once more in her embrace. She wouldn't understand the truth of what happened. Not yet. Nobody did. I couldn't help that. I simply needed to reach her before someone else did. Before unfiltered poisonous words were allowed the freedom to reach her attention, reach my dad's, change how they viewed me forever. It was unfortunate my pitiful attempts to reclaim normality were short-lived as the police officer with throbbing testicles was swiftly joined by protective colleagues that saw me grappled to the floor, firm hands pressing me into the ground with force, my cries for help going entirely unrequited.

'Be careful if she *is* pregnant,' the now familiar voice of DCI Moor caught my attention as she stood by and watched three grown men drag my wailing body to the floor. She was overseeing this entire event with little interest, probably wondering what the hell was wrong with me. 'The last thing we need is an enquiry if she loses the bloody thing,' she concluded.

*The bloody thing?* Jesus. Did this woman think so little of an innocent, unborn baby? A baby who knew nothing yet of this infected world? That was *my* child she was so coldly referring to. *How dare she?*

Her unsympathetic words instigated a torrent of emotion none of these people could have possibly understood about me, causing me to scream, kick, and yell my way towards potential freedom, my body held firm by strangers, yet my mind allowed to wander wilfully. I have always been aware that I can turn on a dial, able to create sudden chaos from apparent calm. My unfeigned one-hundred-and-eighty-degree turnaround was, in fact, wholly responsible for the position I was in now.

I hoped Mum could hear my cries, appreciate the genuine terror I couldn't dislodge. She might even be crying now herself. Her voice filtered loud and clear along the corridor, yelling that all this was Jason's fault, whatever had happened, whatever he'd done. They should let me go, she claimed. I was innocent in all of this. Poor Mum. She probably hadn't yet been told what I'd confessed to: that Jason was dead because of *me*. She couldn't have appreciated it was my fault his corpse lay in a pathology lab somewhere, the actual events leading to his sorry state still being deterred by experts, the state of my miserable mind undeterred by everyone.

I have no idea how long it took those people to force me into submission, my erratic behaviour slowly becoming subdued the longer I resisted. I kicked, thrashed, and screamed my way towards an escape I desperately needed. Yet, I wasn't concerned for myself. Not really. Everything I ever hoped for in life was long gone. No. It was my ageing parents I worried about the most. My niece. My unborn child. Nothing else mattered anyway, my personal wellbeing especially.

**4**

Sitting in the back of a police transport vehicle on my way to HMP Blackwood gave me a painful glimpse of what I assumed prison life would be like. Cold, stark, bleak. They already deemed me unstable, extremely dangerous. Nobody able to prevent my undoing, nobody who cared beyond the simple existence of my still-grieving parents. I wasn't sure how long I'd reside behind bars, my sentencing not yet awarded, though I was grateful, at least, we could all be spared the annoyance of a drawn-out court case, my confession seemingly all they required to close the door behind me, slam it shut, throw away the key. *Guilty*. To the world, that is what I was. A murderer. A killer. My file already stamped, my mug shot hardly a flattering portrayal of the person standing in front of the camera.

I was unable to see out of the tinted windows for my eyes to focus correctly, the world beyond too busy to notice, musing over all the prison dramas I'd ever watched on television. Orange jumpsuits, misshapen prison numbers stamped onto the nameless shoulders of women, acting as if they didn't belong on this planet, some of them barely acting at all. Did the prison I was about to call home house only women? Or a chaotic combination of men *and* women? How did they segregate them? How did they prevent unwanted communication, unwanted pregnancies? Ideas I didn't need inside my head washed my mind to near mush with acid thoughts and putrid potential. I would find out soon enough.

I was not alone on my journey, accompanied by two other women, neither of them giving much away of their current personal turmoil beyond the occasional sob they directed into their laps, probably for sympathy we all knew would not be given. A young woman with bruises around her mouth and on her arms, another not much older than me. The older of the two cried throughout the entire journey. I just wanted to shut her up, give her bruises to match the blundering wretch by her side, give her something to cry for. Instead, I tried to ignore them both, actually glad when we arrived outside an imposing building, its clinical, stark, barred windows set in rows like the teeth of a shark. I felt I was about to be devoured. Eaten by the system, never to be seen alive again.

We were led like cattle inside a high walled building where we were instructed to wait in a holding room until each of us were called in turn, the door locked, nothing in this place but a row of steel chairs nailed to the floor. I was allowed a phone call, so I called my mum. She cried when she heard my voice, her tone struggling to comprehend any of what the police already told her.

'They wouldn't give me all the details,' she sobbed, my eardrums threatening to burst beneath the suffering of my mother's tortured words. 'They say you killed Jason. It can't be true.' She needed me to tell her they had it all wrong, that I was innocent in the crime I was being charged for, innocent in everything she didn't wish to acknowledge about her youngest child. I didn't want to lie to my mum, yet equally couldn't tell her the entire story, the truth of this unfortunate matter. Not yet. It would change everything. I

30

wasn't prepared for that to happen. This day was changing my life swiftly enough as it was.

'Yes, it's true, Mum,' I whispered, still unable to believe he was gone. My amazing Jason. Dead. I closed my eyes for a second, hoping this place was nothing but a dream I didn't need to be experiencing. A nightmare, cold, unfeeling. I felt almost as dead as my man.

'But why, Stacey?' Mum asked, still unaware of my demonic reasons, the bitter actions of her daughter left to swirl around in the past — my untamed irrational emotions entirely to blame for it all. Why would I do such a thing? Why would I *kill* the man I claimed to love?

Why indeed? It was a question I knew I would need to answer at some point. Now was not that time. 'I can't really talk now, Mum. I just wanted to tell you I'm okay and that I love you. I love you all. Give Dad my love. Tell him I'm sorry. Tell Eva.'

My niece wasn't yet three years old, far too young to remember much about her parents *or* her aunt. It was a terrible shame. I hung up feeling sick, fully aware the next time we spoke my poor mum would know more, already having uncovered the actions behind her daughter's increasingly sickened mind, the police able to confirm it all. I left my mother to ponder over words unsaid, none the wiser as to why I'd been taken to prison so swiftly, no trial pending to prove this was all a terrible mistake, a confession of murder sitting in an unassuming folder at Newbury Police Station, probably already in a filing cabinet, already forgotten.

I was asked to check in my belongings at the desk but had nothing on me apart from my old mobile phone which was taken from my possession sometime earlier, along with my unaware, sleeping niece. The looks on the custodial officers faces told me everything I needed to know. I'd arrived straight from the police station, my crime too horrific for me to meet bail conditions, therefore I must be one of the bad ones.

I was taken to see a nurse, my general health checked, my pregnancy confirmed by a second test that mocked my very existence. I closed my eyes, recalling the day I'd sat alone on the toilet seat of Jason's ensuite bathroom, taking such a test alone, my man busy downstairs with guests who were attending his wife's funeral that very day. It all seemed so long ago now.

Once my baby's existence was confirmed, I was given a laundry bag, a plastic plate, a knife and fork, bedding, toothbrush, toothpaste, a fold-up comb, a "welcome pack" comprising of colouring pens and a colouring book. *What was I, five?* I fully expected to be strip-searched. I'd watched such things on television, the thought of someone looking at my private area too insane for my brain to acknowledge. Did they enjoy probing parts of the female anatomy with gloved fingers and searching eyes?

It was almost a shock when such an act of wanton violation wasn't actually carried out — almost a disappointment. Instead, I was kindly asked to sit, fully clothed, on a chair whilst a machine scanned my body for potential metal. Apparently, full strip searches are only carried out if the prison staff deem reasonable grounds to suspect an inmate is carrying drugs or other smuggled items on their person. I was carrying nothing but Jason's child, the poor thing not even big enough to equate to the size of a blueberry.

I wasn't provided with any prison clothing either. Such a requirement isn't deemed necessary in UK women's prisons. Only men are forced to dress like "prisoners". So there was no orange boiler suit for me, no baggy grey jogging bottoms, shapeless garments, numbered vests. I might have allowed an inappropriate laugh if this moment wasn't so profound. I was luckily able to keep my emotions to myself, for now. I was told a family member would be allowed to bring in some of my clothing, personal belongings, items to help make my stay a more exuberant affair — makeup, razors, my iPod, books, shampoo and such. I was asked if I wanted anything to eat, but I was too anxious, my morning sickness still lingering, the whole thing made worse by the day's unmitigated events, my mum's anxious tone still in my head. So instead, they allowed me to take a shower and led me to my "room", where I could gather my thoughts and settle in, the bedding and items in my arms feeling heavy, alien, somewhat unreal.

I hadn't yet been given the privilege of meeting any of the other prisoners. The only other people in the holding room besides myself were the two women I'd travelled here with, neither of whom seemed willing to say much or lift their sorry heads from their chins throughout our entire induction process. I fully expected my television drama visions to become a reality. A long walk along a desolate corridor ahead of heavy, encumbered footsteps, my brain creating impossible scenarios I had no place to put. It was entirely shocking the reality of the prison system greeting me now was very different. This place, it seemed, was more Sad Girls than *Bad Girls*.

It was as if I'd walked into a women's only refuge building, the inside of the unit I found myself in now, prison-looking from the outside only. The women on the inside told a completely different story to the one expressed by the dilapidated state of the building beyond, the high fences, steel bars, stringent enforcement. There were no tattooed dykes waiting to beat me into submission simply for looking at them sideways, no blank looks, no unspoken threats as I walked past, no burning rubbish in the middle of tired-looking cell block areas. Most of the women appeared average in appearance, many too young to be here, some past middle-aged, too old for locked doors. They all appeared sad, broken by a system they did not understand, sitting around chatting quietly, playing cards, reading books.

Although well worn, the carpet below my feet was something I hadn't expected to find. Walls lined with too many posters nobody probably ever read stood out against the grey backdrop. Soft furnished chairs and cushions helped depict a calm environment where inmates could serve a required sentence in relative comfort before the authorities tossed these poor sods back into the world. There was nothing here which matched what I'd envisioned in my mind, built up too highly for no apparent reason. There were no distinct sounds of fighting in the background, no screaming, no yelling. This place was almost calming. If you didn't mind being locked away from society, that is. An unfortunate side-effect of my day.

# 5

I sat on what would now become my bed, a single mattress set on a creaky metal frame, lumpy springs jabbing my backside occasionally to remind me I should not get too complacent, too comfortable. It seemed, for now, I would *not* be sharing this room with anyone else. *Thank god for that.* I didn't wish for companionship right now. I probably wouldn't be good company anyway. It was unfortunate this space was relatively small, not unlike my mum's box room, its single occupancy status not able to bring a smile to my lips. If it was a little larger, I might have pretended I'd checked into a shitty hotel room for a much-needed break from my life.

A thin, overly used, slightly stained mattress was set against a dirty grey wall, along with a chest of damaged drawers carelessly displaying something entirely illegible carved into its dated laminated top. I fully anticipated to find dried chewing gum pressed to the underside, should I choose to look. Uneven shelving lined the walls as if someone had hung from them at some point. A toilet and sink sat in the corner. It would have to do, of course, although I had entirely no idea what I was meant to be doing now I was actually sitting here, alone. It was my own doing that had brought me to this place, my own actions that would now be my actual *undoing*.

It had been a rather odd day, one that was not yet over, not fully concluded. I knew this was all coming, of course. The unassuming phone call made to my sister's unsuspecting cleaner became the very incident that kick-started this entire process. A phone call I now wondered why I'd made in the first place. I was hardly thinking straight at the time, my DNA busy infusing with Jason's, my man's blood all over the place, stinking up the house, staining my skin, fingerprints I'd never be able to wipe away cleanly left to mock my every action. The only thing I could think of was to go to my sister's grave while I still had the chance, my *last* chance to tell her how I felt, to repent for what I'd done to us all. Unfortunately, there was no other place for me to hide. Running would have made everything worse, I know. I'd woken up this morning beneath Jason's expensive Egyptian cotton sheets, only to find myself going to bed tonight wrapped in threadbare rags that smelled of something old, forgotten, wrong.

I once read somewhere that as of November 2020, there were around seventy-three people currently serving a whole-life sentence in the UK, meaning they would never be released from prison due to the severity of their crimes. Of those seventy-three, only two were women. One of those women was Rosemary West. The other was Joanna Dennehy. Both women were classed as cruel, calculating, selfish, manipulative serial killers who'd developed a taste for blood, a fetish for death. Both were twisted, violent women who could never return to society.

I wasn't entirely sure why such pub quiz trivia had taken this moment to pop into my head. I assumed murder of such magnitude as Jason's might place me in the category of deranged killer, cruel, calculating, probably just as manipulative. But was I deserving of a place in the same category as *Rosemary West*? I doubted that very much. Nobody yet appreciated that I was also a serial killer myself. Two victims. Three if you counted a dead cat, that equation firmly placing me in the realm of a *serial* killer. I wondered if a life sentence would now be passed down to me. I probably deserved it.

'In a world of your own over there, are we?' Someone popped an unwanted head around my cell door, forcing me to glance up, my thoughts elsewhere, my mind attempting an impromptu escape even if I wasn't going anywhere physically. The woman smiled at me. Her soft brown peppered grey hair only just managed to brush against her shoulders, looking as if it needed a damned good conditioning treatment. Her eyes were telling a story her mouth couldn't hide. The system had beaten the shit out of her.

'Sorry, I'm-'

'New. I can see that.' She held out a calloused hand, seemingly knowing my thoughts, able to read my mind. *What the fuck?* I didn't shake her hand. I didn't know where she'd been. 'I'm Paula,' she confirmed as if she assumed I wanted to know.

'Stacey,' I replied.

'Is everything okay in here?'

I wasn't quite sure how to respond. *No. No, I'm not okay at all, if you must know.* How can any of this possibly be okay? Yet, here we are — nothing I could do about that. I attempted a smile that probably looked more of an uncertain shrug than confirmation of the action I'd tried and failed to achieve. This woman didn't know me. How dare she presume to know my thoughts? I allowed a moment of self-gratification that, if I were to yell, scream, and throw a tantrum, this woman would probably not succumb to pulling out a knife, stab me to death where I sat, causing me any trouble other than the irritation of having to endure her presence a little longer than I wanted. However, luckily for us both, I did no such thing. Instead, I sat staring at this stranger as if I was trying to drill a hole through her cheekbone with my narrowing eyelids.

Paula sighed, completely missing her cue to leave me alone. 'A few things to remember, and you'll do just fine,' she offered, getting on my last nerve already. 'It's best not to ask what people are in for. It's genuinely not a done thing. Most women here don't want to talk about what they've been through.' I was glad to hear that. I wasn't sure I wanted to tell people why I was here anyway. It was none of their business. I certainly didn't give a damn what they'd done to land themselves in this place. It was *their* problem, not mine.

'Secondly,' she continued. 'The food is crap. Get used to it. You pick your lunch menu a week in advance and don't expect anything that tastes edible. You can trade things for items from the canteen, which are a little better, although only just. To be honest, most of the women in here tend to do that. Never call the staff by anything other than Mr or Mrs whatever, or more commonly just Miss or Sir.'

She regarded me for a moment, hoping I was taking it all in, not entirely caring if I was or wasn't. 'Whether ordering your weekly supplies, applying for prison jobs, doctor's appointments and such like, it's all done via an app. Once a week is canteen day. That's when you get your weekly supplies of shower gels, sweets, chocolate, tobacco, things like that. Of course, it's up to you what you spend your allocated funds on. They supply sanitary products for free, but even those you have to apply for in advance. I'm surprised you're allowed to shit without that bloody app, to be fair.'

Paula laughed, trying to diffuse the situation, diffuse

the tense atmosphere I'd accidentally created by staring at her for too long without offering anything that might pass for basic communication skills. 'Also, try and get a job as quickly as possible, or pursue an educational course if you can, to keep yourself out of your cell and earn some money. If your family can afford to send you cash, you are allowed to have a certain amount of that per week too. Laundry is collected at the end of every week on a Friday. If you don't want to lose anything or discover someone else wearing your clothes, place everything firmly inside your bag and tie it up well. Apart from sheets and towels, which are washed collectively, your personal items will be washed together inside your bag, so refrain from wearing any light clothing. White is a big no for obvious reasons.' She chuckled, not wishing for me to end up dressed in an array of sludgy pale colours instead of gleaming white clothing I would never entertain anyway.

I was struggling to keep up, the information aimed towards me too quickly, too sharply. I hadn't even put the sheets on my bed and already I was being given the low-down on daily prison life. I nodded, not entirely knowing what else to do. I wished she would just piss off.

'You don't say much, do you, Stacey?' Paula asked, folding flabby arms across her chest. I wanted to laugh. She was hardly giving me a chance.

'I've never been inside a prison before.' I didn't feel I needed to explain myself, yet I did so anyway.

'Most women in here haven't, and most are only here for a relatively short time,' Paula scoffed. 'It's okay. We don't see many hardened criminals in here. Murderers and such like. We are all just trying to get through this fucking system alive.'

She laughed. I swallowed. It was a throwaway comment meant to calm my emotions, put my mind at ease.

They didn't see many murderers. It was funny she should make such a statement. I wanted to smile, almost failed to refrain, yet, I assumed Paula wouldn't appreciate the hidden reasons for such an impromptu action at that moment. The woman was looking at one right now. I was glad my chances of being asked what I was in for were relatively slim. They probably wouldn't want to know anyway. They wouldn't appreciate who I was, *what* I was. Though I very much doubted they would care.

Paula left me sitting with my back against a metaphoric wall, listening to unfamiliar sounds around me that felt alien and uncomfortable. If I closed my eyes, I could pretend I was in a café somewhere, listening to the chink of teacups in other rooms, a low din of voices, chatting, laughing. Yet the smell of urine, recently disinfected floors, and constant slamming of heavy doors reminded me that I was actually in hell. I wondered about the real world. My parent's world would certainly be feeling anything but real at this very moment, no doubt. I wondered how long it would be before my mum brought me any clothing to change in to. Would she bother at all once she learned the whole truth of my crimes? Would she even want to know *me*?

# 6

I have no idea how I managed to muddle through that first night alone. Despite being surrounded by women in the same position as me, I'd never felt so forlorn and forgotten in my entire life. It was all-consuming, slightly unnerving, my brain borderline neurotic before they even turned out the lights. I assumed I would willingly accept my fate without question, the catastrophic error in how I'd handled Jason and his resulting corpse now entirely coming back to haunt me. I should have thought it through better, taken my time, handled things differently. As it were, I'd fully allowed my emotions to cloud my judgment, turning me into a crazed unhinged lunatic, the little time it had taken Jason to show his true colours all that was needed to uncover the very monster living inside *me*.

Each time I closed my eyes, I visualised his battered, lifeless face lying on that bloodied hallway floor. Or, at least, what was left of it by the time my fury had finished its unremitting indignation. Jason Cole. The man I once believed I loved more than life itself. The man I'd have done anything for. He seemed to mock me now from beyond the grave, able to appear more demonic in spirit than he *ever* could have as a man. How could everything I'd once deemed so incredible turn sour so violently, so regretfully?

It was unfortunate I had too much time on my hands to lie on my bunk now and think, the capricious sounds echoing behind paper-thin prison walls doing nothing for my objectionable, rather unwanted discomposure.

Everything had happened because of Jason and Emma. It was entirely their fault I was here, in this place, utterly alone with thoughts I couldn't get out of my head. I'd questioned for so long why everything always had to be about my goddamned *perfect* sister. Now, lying here unassisted in my thinking, unassisted in my existence, nothing seemed to have changed. I was still asking questions I had no answers to. Still assuming my life was what it was because of Emma and her prominent image of excellence. It was quite ridiculous to appreciate that as far as everyone who had ever known her was now concerned, myself included, the bloody woman would always remain perfect. Annoyingly so. Frustratingly so. I would never be able to change their minds about such a misguided consideration. At the tender age of thirty-three, her untimely death meant the woman would forever now be entwined in youth. Preserved in both youth *and* perfection. I'd meant to make my life easier, not harder.

It was a disgusting consideration I would now be forced to live with, my own mortality something that would devour me relentlessly — my subjective, somewhat less than perfect image disintegrating daily, the passage of time set to keep me suffering. Photographs of Emma would be permanently preserved in frames, on mantle pieces, in albums. Pictures of me would eventually display an ageing, bitter hag, staring out from some aged, bitter room, alone, forgotten long ago. I sighed, forcing cold walls to reverberate a hollow sound back to my ears in sharp focus. I hoped to God wherever Jason was right now, he was suffering as much as I was. He *deserved* to suffer. Such a confirmation might have the power to raise my otherwise subjacent spirits enormously, offer a dreamless, well-needed sleep I now felt would elude me forever. After all, I was suffering. Why shouldn't he?

I had no idea how long I would be forced to stay here. There was no point in denying my actions. Hideous frustration had already allowed unprecedented freedom to leave behind too much evidence for the police to discover. Yet, because of that, I would be stuck inside this place for the duration of my best years. My fertile years. I laughed into the silence of my single bedded cell for the hellish situation instilled onto me entirely by force. This place — my room. Possibly for the duration of my entire stay here. Or at least, until they moved me to some *bloody* mother and baby unit and forgot about me completely.

Paula was right. The food indeed was disgusting. I'd fed my cat Sylvester better meals than what I ate this evening. I had arrived, expecting all kinds of curious people to surround me, yet the women here seemed more destroyed by life than their actions. I knew exactly how they felt. We were all doomed, it seemed — none of us able to articulate a normal life outside our own personal demons. If tomorrow was going to be anything like today, I had no idea how I would deal with a potential life sentence in this godforsaken hellhole.

***

Breakfast consisted of a specially developed "breakfast pack", issued by a passing officer at the end of my first evening. It was meant for consumption the following morning. To be eaten in my cell before the doors were unlocked at eight o'clock. There would be no bacon, no eggs, no sign of any cooked offering beyond a single slice of white bread I knew would be dry as a dog biscuit by morning. I was so annoyed by the prospect of eating such basic food alone, I didn't bother listening when she told me her name. She'd pissed me off. It didn't matter anyway.

This so-called breakfast pack included nothing more than a small box of cornflakes that wouldn't feed a child, UHT milk in a tiny plastic pot, tea bags that took too long to produce actual tea, coffee whitener that clumped together on the spoon, granulated sugar, and a choice of brown or white bread. There was a small sachet of jam and some cheap margarine that had me slightly excited for around two seconds purely due to the fact I'd incorrectly assumed these items might have a taste. They didn't. It was all very regimented, the food designed to be cost-effective for the prison system, yet seemingly caring little for the stomachs and taste buds of the poor sods consuming the stuff.

I was given my own kettle and toaster, which was very kind of them, I guess, although my prison-issue teabags and cheap granulated sugar left a lot to the imagination. I assumed milk would become a valued commodity among the inmates, the small amount I was given already gone by the time the lights went out. I sat in the dark craving a bacon and egg roll with a pot of Jason's beloved Italian coffee beans, a Danish pastry, warm croissants dripping with butter. *Shit.* When had I become such a food snob?

I had already eaten most of my so-called breakfast pack before getting into bed, the evening dragging on relentlessly, boredom setting in fast. I was locked inside a darkened room from eight o'clock that evening with nothing to do but stare at the four walls around me, dramatically marked with reminders of damaged prisoners who came before me — frantically etched names and doodles, profanities best forgotten. Had the prison staff never heard of a tin of paint? It felt as if I were five years old again, ushered to bed swiftly so the "adults" in authority could spend their evening in peace. I would probably need to get used to the idea of being told what to do, and when to do it.

***

'Good morning, Miss Adams.' The female uniformed officer issuing breakfast packs the previous evening unlocked my cell door at eight o'clock sharp. Was it *legal* to keep human beings locked inside a tiny room for so long? She offered me a smile I didn't exactly feel the need to return. She was overly cheerful, probably glad her shift was about to end, freedom awaiting her. *Miss Adams?* Really? I felt as if I was about to be sent to the headmaster's office for a telling off.

'I trust you had a calm first night?' she asked casually. What the hell kind of question was that? *A calm night?* Have you heard the noises these women make in the middle of the night? I was starving too, yet I couldn't dwell on that fact, my belly filled with too much coffee that had the undesired effect of keeping me awake, an opened packet of processed strawberry jam with a finger mark in the middle, still sitting on the top of my laminated chest of drawers, the only thing left to consume if I became too desperate.

I nodded, not entirely knowing how I should respond without reverting to sarcasm, the resulting bitterness not very becoming of a lady. Maybe *she* should try spending a night in there. I hadn't slept at all, to be honest, the nightwear I'd been temporarily supplied with remained untouched on the chest of drawers next to my jam. The clothing was too big for me and rather unflattering. It sat where they'd left it. Unwanted. Like me.

The prison officer stared at me for a moment. 'I appreciate the first night is always a daunting one. But it will get easier. I promise.'

'Thank you,' I managed. I would have to get used to it. I had no choice.

'I believe your mum is dropping some of your things in today. Clothing and such like.'

My attention was caught. 'She's coming to see me?'

The woman shook her head. 'I'm afraid not. Visits must be approved and sanctioned first. I'm sorry. She won't be allowed beyond the main gate today. Maybe next week. I believe your solicitor is coming in tomorrow, though.' I wished I'd bothered to remember her name now. She seemed okay. I recalled what Paula had told me about how to address uniformed staff.

'Thanks, Miss,' I muttered as she motioned me out of my cell.

\*\*\*

As it was my first full day inside, I hadn't yet been issued anything to do, no job, no study programme to keep me busy and out of mischief, but I was required to attend an appointment with the prison psychologist. I was led along a corridor by the same officer who had issued breakfast, whose name turned out to be Mrs Carol Smith. I had to hide a private snigger, honestly feeling that she'd invented her surname name purely for anonymity. I hadn't spoken to any of the other women in here yet, apart from Paula, and that wasn't by choice, the bloody woman hell-bent on annoying the shit out of me. I just wanted to be left alone.

'How are you settling in, Miss Adams?' the prison psychologist asked me as I sat staring out of a window in his office. The only thing I could concentrate on was the call of freedom beyond, a life that had been taken away from me all too abruptly. I must have looked a right sorry state, still dressed in the clothing I'd arrived in, no makeup to disguise my darkening mood, my hair in need of a decent wash — a set of straighteners and a good hairbrush entirely out of my reach.

I glanced towards a reasonably young man dressed far older than his actual years, in a dark red tank top, sensible beige trousers, hair that needed a cut. If he was good looking, I might have shown a little more interest, but as it was, he was not that interesting in either visual context or intellect, so for me, I wasn't interested in conversation. His name was Farley. *Doctor* Peter Farley. All he needed to do now was to hand me a textbook, and the illusion of an average school day would be complete.

Farley's office was a reasonably large room, crammed with all kinds of plant life, including several in need of a good drink. A large picture window allowed light to flood the space, highlighting this guy's seemingly messy personality, terrible organisation skills. It matched his hair and the way he'd failed to tuck his shirt into his trousers well enough before leaving his house this morning. It felt weirdly calm here, though. Warm. Almost friendly. He was writing something in a notebook that reminded me of DCI Moor, the information I'd recently provided her willingly landing me in this hell now.

'Would you like a cup of tea? Coffee?' Farley offered, attempting to set a more relaxed tone. He glanced towards me, displaying a quiet, knowing smile that made me assume he had seen far too many people in my position. Maybe *that* explained his appearance? The women here had broken his spirit. 'You don't have to feel worried or nervous in this room,' he confirmed as he poured a cup of hot, black liquid from a nearby coffee pot. 'My job is simply to guide you through your experiences, talk about your problems and help you to understand anything you are currently unable to process.' Christ, this sounded long-winded, tedious, *boring*. 'Oh, I'm sorry,' he added. 'Do you take milk or sugar?'

'No milk. Two sugars, please,' I replied, stopping him before he poured milk into a mug. I didn't want dairy products slowing my rational thinking this morning. I only took milk in my coffee when I was feeling relaxed. Unfortunately, today was not one of those days. He swiftly topped up his own cup with milk, giving it a stir, handing me a large mug that felt oddly inviting.

'Help yourself to the sugar,' Farley pointed towards a chipped glass bowl on a table in front of us, crammed with sugar lumps that looked as if they had been stabbed to death at some point by an angry inmate or two. My overfriendly *schoolteacher-esque* shrink sat down on a cheap-looking leather chair and took a sip of his own coffee. His entire persona was kept professional, weirdly calming. 'I like to keep my sessions informal,' he smiled, allowing us a moment to sip our coffee in relative peace. It tasted pretty good. I noticed how the morning sun diffused light across the wooden flooring, bouncing off the desk, the plants, my skin, and I recalled how I'd once loved waking up in Jason's bedroom, in his arms. So very long ago now. God damn you, Jason Cole. God damn you for everything.

## 7

I wanted to close my eyes, absorb the innocence of this moment. Maybe that was the point. This room was designed specifically to dislodge built-up frustration, allowing emotions to emerge without remorse. I assumed this guy would launch into an immediate dissection of my state of mind, desperate to uncover the reasons behind my unravelling thoughts but, instead, we simply sat, enjoying a quiet coffee together, the warmth of the morning sun outside a welcome distraction to the nightmare I'd found myself in.

'So, how are you settling in, Miss Adams?' Farley asked as he placed his now empty mug onto the coffee table.

I glanced at him, allowing our eyes to meet for the first time, my thoughts forced to dissipate into much-needed solace. Did he see the sadness and the suffering behind my dilated pupils.

I sighed. 'You really don't want to know.'

Farley smiled, offering a knowing nod of his stiffened head. His hair was too long at the front, cut into a neat line at the back of his neck that made him look old, out of fashion, out of place. *What was it with this surname bullshit?* Even in college, I was allowed to call my lecturers by their first names. It created a relaxed environment for all. It made us feel grown-up.

'It's okay, honestly,' he laughed, unaware of my musing. 'In this room, you can tell me anything.'

I seriously doubted that was true. I automatically glanced around the walls and ceiling for signs of hidden cameras. Farley smiled again, shaking his head. It was quite annoying. Simply because he was a shrink with qualifications, it did not give him the automatic right to assume he knew what I was thinking.

'Do you want to talk about why you're here?'

That's more like it. *Let's get to the goddamned point.* I shook my head. *Nope.* I did not wish to discuss my private life with a total stranger, thank you very much.

'Another coffee then, maybe?' Farley rose to reaffirm his attention with the coffee maker in the corner of the room, happily minding its own business, totally unaffected by my presence or anything other than keeping freshly brewed coffee at an optimum temperature. This shrink was also seemingly unaffected by anything else. If only *my* life could be so straightforward.

I didn't mind the idea of drinking coffee in this room all day. I had nothing else to do, nowhere else to be. If he wanted to waste his time, I was more than happy to reciprocate. He certainly wasn't wasting mine. He was keeping me entertained. He replaced my empty mug with a fresh one, taking a seat opposite me, glancing in my direction, obviously wanting to unnerve me. To observe what he already believed he knew about me.

'Don't you people only have an hour to spare with each inmate?' I asked when I couldn't stand the silence between us no more. *You people?* Stacey, please. Remember your manners.

'Oh, she talks,' Farley laughed, causing me to narrow my eyes defensively. *Don't take the piss.* The guy smiled, waiting for me to say more. I didn't. 'Are you ready to talk to me? It doesn't matter what you say. Vent if you have to. Yell if it helps. I have very broad shoulders.'

I pressed my lips together, trying to suppress a smile of my own. *Broad shoulders?* I've seen broader green beans.

Farley appeared unconcerned by my ignorant mannerisms, my lack of enthusiasm for what he considered a quiet chat, my lack of manners at all. 'You're currently awaiting sentencing for murder. Am I correct?' The guy did not flinch at the sound of his own words. Neither did he appear unnerved to be in a room with a potential psychopath.

I shrugged. He had my file. It was hardly news.

'Jason. Cole.' Farley spoke Jason's name slowly, probably to see my reaction and witness how I might respond to the sound of that man's name. I swallowed, careful to give nothing away of how I felt inside — of how Jason *made* me feel. Farley began clicking his tongue against the inside of his mouth, opening a file on the table he'd already retrieved from a filing cabinet before my arrival. I'd only just noticed. He sat reading detailed notes to himself, muttering low vocals I couldn't understand, reviewing my freshly filled-out induction file with much enthusiasm.

'Wow, it says here you hit him several times with a golf club.' Farley raised his eyebrows towards me as if he was impressed by such an attack. I glanced away. *Seven*, actually. 'You also claimed he raped you.' I sucked in too much air, hoping it wouldn't choke me, wishing it had the power to choke him. Farley noticed. He stopped reading, glanced my way, focusing his narrowed eyes too long on mine. I had nothing to say about that.

'Hardly the act of self-defence? Wouldn't you agree?'

I'd heard it all before. I didn't need to hear it again. I shrugged.

Farley continued. 'What did he *really* do to you, to make you so angry with him, Miss Adams?' This surname shit was beginning to annoy me.

'It's *Stacey*,' I spat, taking a moment to glance his way before reconnecting to some bird I was busy trying to watch outside the window, attempting to ignore the man in front of me paid to evaluate my mind, metaphorically dissecting my composure with ease. I knew what he was doing. He was trying to push my buttons, see how far he could take this before I snapped. Confess to more shit.

'You don't like authority, do you, Miss Adams?' he wasn't giving this surname thing up easily. I didn't reply. 'What did Jason do to you? If he did rape you, I suspect he also did much more besides.' I stared at him. *How dare he assume to know what had happened between us?* He didn't know me. He didn't know Jason.

'Yes, he raped me,' I replied groggily, unable to stop myself. This guy was winding me up. He needed verification of what Jason Cole was really like. I was sick of hearing about poor *Mr* bloody innocent Cole.

'But, if that were true, why didn't you run away when you had the chance? Why did you not hit him the once and get as far away from him as you could? That's the normal response in these types of situations. To run.'

'How the fuck do you know what these types of situations include?' I had found my voice. It wasn't an ideal concept. DCI Moor had already asked the very same questions. *Read the fucking file.*

'Wish to tell me about it?'

I shook my head. This guy could seriously do one.

'Okay,' Farley shrugged, getting to his feet yet again, leaving my file open on the table as he turned around, raising his hands in the air, stretching his skinny spine with a crack. 'But you do know, Miss Adams, that if the judge is to pass an appropriate sentence, it would be in your best interest to tell us exactly what happened and why. Wouldn't you want to put your best case forward? Guilty or not, you wouldn't want to make things worse for yourself, surely? A distinct lack of remorse has the terrible side-effect of creating a wrong impression, forcing a lengthier sentence.'

Farley was right, of course. My crime was indeed way out of proportion to the incident I'd already professed had been committed against *me*. None of them knew the reasons behind my actions that night. Had it really only been two evenings previous? An otherwise healthy man was brought to his sudden end by the wrath of a seemingly deranged woman.

'What was your relationship like with Mr Cole? He was your brother-in-law, correct?'

I shot Farley a cold stare. *Oh, he was far more to me than that.* Or, at least, he used to be.

Farley continued. 'And, I see you're pregnant.' The statement sounded more like a question, seemingly uncertain if Jason was indeed the father of my baby, then at some point, we must have been in a close relationship. Either that or I had simply become his unwitting victim. I wasn't entirely sure which was the truth. 'Congratulations,' he added flatly.

I sighed. Farley took it as a cue to sit down again. 'Miss Adams. Stacey. Please. Look at this from my point of view.' He had called me Stacey. That was a starting point, at least. 'You didn't respond to Mr Cole's unwanted advances by lashing out. You bludgeoned the man to *death*. They found teeth embedded inside his skull, nothing left of his face to decipher anything of the man he once was. You must have been utterly outraged to do that. I'm having a tough time believing you would take such drastic action because he attacked you. Potential rape or not.' Farley was glaring at me now, unwavering. 'What did he *really* do to you?'

For the first time, I allowed a stray tear to find its way into the room, my cheeks slowly becoming reddened by a crime I had kept hidden for too long. How could I tell *anyone* the real reasons behind my anger? Jason had made a fool of me. He had pushed me to do things I would never have considered doing, taken my love, turning it into something bitter, revolting, ugly.

'You took away his face, Stacey. What didn't you want to see when you looked at him? What didn't you want *him* to see?' Farley was bloody good at this psychology shit. He was starting to get to me. We both knew it.

'He pushed things too far,' I couldn't help blurting out. I bit my lip, needing to shut the fuck up. Needing *him* to shut up. I was becoming hot, my cheeks flushing deeper with each passing second I was forced to sit here and endure his interrogation. I wanted the window to open up, to allow me to fall to the cool ground outside. If it killed me, so be it.

'How?'

I swallowed, wanting to say more, yet terrified of the revelation my untethered confession would provoke. I *did* take his face away, yes. I couldn't allow him to see what he'd turned me into. I didn't want to see the very reason behind it all. 'He made me do it,' I muttered. I was crying.

'Made you do what, Stacey? Kill him?'

He made me kill him, yes, but that wasn't the answer Farley was waiting for. 'No.' I shook my head. *Shut up, Stacey.*

'What did Jason make you do? Mr Cole was, by all accounts, a respected pillar of his community. He had no previous convictions, had never been in trouble with the police. So, what was so bad you felt you had to literally smash his face to pieces?' Farley sat opposite me, a calm look on his own face I didn't like. A quiet tone to his voice I

54

wanted to run screaming in protest from.

'He *pushed* me.' I couldn't help confirming such a truth. I hated what Jason had done to me. Farley could see my rising irritation. It wasn't pleasant.

'Pushed you how?'

'It doesn't matter.' Shut up, Stacey. *Please.*

'It does matter if it drove you to murder the poor guy.'

*Poor guy?* Was he taking the piss? 'He was no innocent. Neither of them were.' I shook my head with an indignant sigh.

'Neither of *them*?'

Bollocks. I closed my eyes.

'So, someone else *was* involved. Who was it, Stacey? Who else was involved in the murder of Jason Cole? Who are you protecting?' Farley now believed I had some kind of accomplice. Like DCI Moor, he now assumed someone else had hit Jason. That I was merely covering for a third party. He had *no* idea.

'There was no one else involved. It was just Jason and me. Alone.' Unfortunately.

'Are you sure?'

'Yes.'

'But he pushed your buttons. Made you do things?'

'*Yes!*'

'Care to share with me what drove a seemingly normal, excuse my assumptions, sane, quite attractive young woman to do something so despicable?'

'I can't tell you.' I was grabbing the fake leather of the chair beneath me, my teeth clenched, my fingernails digging into the tattered, crumbling material, my heart pounding as if the thing wanted out of my chest. Why was this man pushing me so much? He wouldn't want to hear the truth. None of them would. He called me attractive. Was that meant to lower my guard? Flatter me? Make me talk?

'What did he make you do, Stacey?'

'*He made me kill her.* That's what he did.' Something inside snapped, and I got to my feet in violent protest of words I couldn't bear inside my brain any longer. Jason was not a *good man*. He was no pillar of any community, no poor, innocent guy. 'Jason Cole was a sick, violent, twisted, manipulative son-of-a-bitch. He made me do it. He made me kill her.' It was true. It didn't matter that the stupid idiot had known nothing of my intentions, my actions. Jason was wholly responsible for everything I did.

'Kill *who*, Stacey? Who did Jason Cole make you kill?'

'*My sister!*'

Farley's eyes stared at me for a moment, fixated on my unexpected revelation — the shock of my unexpected words lingering in the air between us like smoke in a burning building. The room fell silent, neither of us daring to move or speak another word, an age seemingly passing before the man shuffled around his desk, a shocked look on his face coupled with surprise, excitement even. He grabbed his notebook from a pile of magazines and scribbled something he must have deemed suddenly necessary onto a blank page. There were papers, magazines, books, and dirty coffee mugs everywhere I looked. This man seriously lived for his coffee fix, it seemed. And now, he'd made me confess to a second murder. The one I assumed I would have happily taken to my grave, never exposing my truth to anyone.

# 8

I assumed my allocated one-hour session would be swiftly concluded after such an unexpected outburst. However, I'd actually been in Farley's office for over two, his underpaid time unimportant as long as he uncovered the truth. *The truth.* The very idea spat venom into my brain, laughing with mocked amusement that I'd been caught out, nothing better than a stray dog discovered sneaking sausages from an unattended fridge. I assumed he would shortly wish to relieve himself of my company, divulge to the powers that be, the full, uncensored version of what I had unwittingly confessed to him today.

I was still trying to convince myself I hadn't uttered those words, admitted to a second murder, the coffee in my system to blame for my sudden irreparable exposure. He had irritated me beyond normality, pushed buttons, the guy hell-bent on winding me up. *What the fuck?* What would happen now? I presumed his sessions were not as private as he initially indicated, my confession all but sealing my fate. It was my first full day in this place, and already my mouth had been allowed to run away from me — to flap frantically like an obliterated flag in a category five hurricane. *Bollocks.*

'Tell me about your sister, Stacey. Tell me about Emma.' Farley was sitting down again, his bony knees aimed in my direction, his notebook on his lap, pen in hand, his attention firmly caught. She was *dead*. They all knew that truth, yet beyond that, what was there to tell? My poor bloody sister was rotting in her grave, the very grave they'd found me standing next to, only yesterday. Everything had led to this moment, to this point in my pathetic existence. What else could I confirm that would shine any light on my apparent lack of sanity?

'What do you want to know?' I was still in shock, waiting for the fallout to catch up with me, scoop me from the floor and drag me to hell.

'What was she like?' Farley was calm, simply listening, unaffected by my previous unplanned moment, unexpected words. He was writing in his notebook, the sound of a cheap biro scratching lines into thin paper, etching torment onto my brain, painfully, pitifully.

'Perfect,' I found myself whispering, more to myself than the man in the room. 'Always, so *fucking* perfect.' I didn't mean to swear or confirm aloud what I really thought of her. It was simply in my head. My thoughts, my private considerations, allowed now to break free by the sound of Farley's incessant questions.

'I take it there was some animosity between the two of you?' Farley didn't look at me, instead turning a page on his pad, more interested in his own words than mine.

*Some animosity?* That was an understatement. 'She had it all.' It was untrue. I *assumed* she had it all. It was, in fact, a total, utter goddamned lie. 'Well, I thought she did, at least.' I hung my head, the world outside this window no longer holding my attention, the bird already flown to freedom some time ago. 'She never noticed me,' I automatically slipped into childhood, my thoughts allowed to drift unfiltered back in time. 'My big sister. The one I loved more than anything. Never noticed me.'

'Do you often feel unnoticed, Stacey?' It was as if Farley was able to unravel my thoughts, dissect the inner workings of my tormented mind.

I nodded. It was, in fact, simply amazing to discover that Jason *had* noticed me. He noticed my looks, my personality. Loved being in my company. It was why I loved him so much.

'And you felt that Emma didn't notice you because she was jealous of you?'

I glanced at Farley. Why would he say that? It was oddly the other way around. The realisation wasn't a good one. 'No. For reasons that have evaded me for quite some time, we genuinely did not like each other. It was just the way of things.' It was true. It was always true. I swallowed hard, trying to ignore the idea of a bank account full of Emma's money, my name printed on the statement, the unused bank card that was rightfully mine still sitting in my mum's kitchen drawer.

'But you hated the fact that your sister didn't notice your existence? I presume it had been that way since you were kids?'

I nodded, still hanging my head, unable to do anything else. I was a puppet on a string — Farley's puppet, nothing more than a sideshow attraction, a circus freak, all but ready for whatever they wanted to do with me, a toy in someone else's story.

'Do you see yourself as a killer Stacey, or a victim?' It was a simple enough question.

'Aren't we all victims, doc?' It was an uncomfortable truth. It wasn't the first time I'd thought such a thing, felt the painful sting of victimisation. Emma made me the way I am now. The way I ultimately became. She had no one to blame but herself for the way things turned out between us, for herself. My distressed emotions were entirely justifiable in everything that happened between this moment and the one that saw her life ebbing away in her car that fateful day. Although, I am still convinced my sister and I *must* have been close at one point. I cannot allow myself the concept of anything else. My childhood will always depend on that simple perception of love, togetherness. It is something I will keep in my heart forever, for the sake of our parents, for my own clarity. None of what happened afterwards was my fault.

Farley looked at me for a moment before rising to his feet, having finished recording all he needed to conclude our session, his pen probably running out of ink already, still too much left to confirm. He opened his office door, allowing much-needed air to drift inside.

'So, what happens now?' I asked uneasily as a uniformed officer came into the room to collect me. I was trying not to panic, no one other than Farley yet knowing my recent declaration. I might have deluded myself that it could be possible for me to deny full responsibility for Jason's murder, potentially classing the act as nothing more than coerced self-defence, the bruising on my body evidence to his bullying ways. Yet, my sister's murder was selfish, unforgivable, wrong. It was an act I would not find so easy to claim momentary diminished responsibility for. Potential mental illness or not.

'I'm afraid that isn't up to me at this point, Miss Adams, but I assume the police will want to re-interview you.' Farley gave nothing away of his emotions, his thoughts still on my confession, his coffee still warm on the table. So much for the *in this room, you can tell me anything* crap. He'd reverted to calling me by my surname. I presumed that was for the benefit of the uniformed officer standing by my side.

Of course they would want to re-interview me. What

60

else did I expect? 'I guess it would be too much for me to ask you to keep this between us?' I didn't mean to laugh. My entire persona was simply tangling at warp speed. I had no idea which end was up. I hoped Farley understood my failing composure because no one else seemed to.

Farley smiled blankly, shaking his head. 'I'm sorry. We can book another session next week. Talk more then.' It was his final word on the subject, our time over. I presumed it was hardly his last word on the subject of my murderous personality, my unprecedented deeds still to be observed by those in control of my life. A friendly chat and a cup of coffee were no longer required today, simply deferred for another day, to be resumed at some other time. I was led back along the corridor to my unit to await my fate, my belly doing summersaults that had nothing to do with the baby growing in my womb.

*\*\**

I lay on my bed with too many thoughts to tip me over the proverbial edge, my once assumed self-assurance now entirely misplaced, my cell no bigger than an eight by ten-foot box. I hated the concept this might become my home now for the duration of my stay. It was all so entirely different to how I'd expected my life to turn out, how I'd meticulously planned every last detail. I allowed my mind to wander to better times now long gone. To Jason. To Emma. A luxury house I fully expected to make my own, already having chosen paint colours and cushions in my head. Money I'd anticipated spending well. All lies. All gone.

I closed my eyes, the noise around me too much, these paper-thin walls too consuming. Nothing was private. Even the sound of someone urinating in the cell next to mine was loud enough to make me cover my ears in imposed frustration; doors banging, women shouting, footsteps every which way. I knew nothing of prison life, yet the surrounding noises were seemingly enough to drive a person insane. No wonder everyone looked so bloody depressed. I might have been slightly premature in my initial considerations of this place. This was only my second day here. If this day's revelations were to have anything to say about the issue, I would be stuck in this hell for a *very* long time.

I wanted to cry. I felt so stupid, so weak. Everything I once held dear was gone, nothing in the outside world now remotely reminiscent of the Stacey Adams I once thought I knew and loved well. Stuck in here, I would eventually become forgotten, lost to the duration of time, lost to a prison system I knew absolutely nothing about, nothing more to strangers than some odd demonic girl who went crazy and murdered her sister and brother-in-law for no reason. I wondered how people would react to such a tragic tale? How would my parents take the news that their youngest child is, in fact, a double murderer, wholly capable of unhinged behaviour?

I lay back on my lumpy mattress with a stench of disinfectant and piss in my nostrils, thinking of things I could not change, nothing to be done about events now complete. I hated *Doctor* goddamned Farley with a passion. How dare he have the power to rile me so swiftly that words flowed from my unchecked mouth without a single thought for the consequences? What the hell was I thinking? I would not be seeing him again so keenly, that much I was confident about. They would need to drag me to his office, kicking if necessary, screaming most probably. I didn't give a *shit* how tasty his coffee was or how inviting the view from his window looked.

I hugged my pillow, curling my knees into my body,

everything about my persona teetering on the edge of insanity. I wasn't confident I could do this. Prison life was not for me. If I couldn't get through the first couple of days, how did I hope to endure an entire decade, potentially two? I couldn't help it when my breathing became shallow, my lungs struggling to cope with oxygen that felt more like I'd been stuffed into a gas chamber by mistake instead of this unassuming cell.

I have no idea how it happened or when I actually snapped, but by the time I felt air might, by some crazed miracle, flood my chest again, my cell was utterly ruined. I had ripped the mattress from my bed, torn sheets now lying haphazardly across the dirty floor, mocking me, laughing at me. Cheap tea bags, coffee granules and sticky sugar was spilt everywhere, with no consideration for the person required to clean it up. Broken mugs lay in jagged surprise, my cell walls stripped of the posters I hadn't yet been able to bring myself to read, safety procedures, rules I needed to follow. I didn't need any of it.

When two officers came running, my emergency button pressed by a panicking fellow inmate, there was nothing left of my cell or my sanity, my crumpled body screaming in protest as they dragged me out into the cold corridor, to isolation and desolation beyond. My once carefully considered composure had been replaced now by a deranged figure that kicked, scratched, and spat into the faces of those in authority. An authority I detested with everything I had inside me, despised with every breath I took. It was entirely irrational. My actions now firmly ensured I was placed on the "at-risk" list, my mental health called into question, the newly acquired murderer in their midst no longer allowed any freedom of unfettered movement.

I found myself tossed into a bare cell, its cold, stark

walls befitting of the cold-hearted creature I had become. It mattered little. I would be in this place for a while, today's unexpected actions resulting in a need to let off steam, release pent up frustration that had been building since the night of Jason's untimely demise. I beat the bare walls with my fists until my bloodied hands throbbed, no one coming to my aid, my spirit and soul broken. I couldn't breathe. Everything had happened too quickly, sending me into a spiral I had no idea how to emerge. I needed help that no one could provide, my entire body aching for a love I felt I now would never know.

Jason didn't love me. Not really. He loved only the idea of what I had willingly allowed him to do to me. Of what he assumed he could get away with. My parents would no longer love me either once they discovered what I was, what I'd done. Eva would never get to know me, friends superficial, already gone, drifted away on the wind, tales of my repugnant deeds too much for their tiny brains to deal with. I thought of my niece's autism, help I could no longer offer my parents.

I slumped onto the unforgiving concrete floor under me and cried until my eyes felt as if they were about to fall from my eye sockets, sleep finally finding its way towards me after an endured suffering I probably deserved. *Emma did love me.* It was a truth I had only recently discovered. A discovery made too late, too painful to acknowledge, my infected hatred for my big sister entirely bringing this thing on myself.

I dreamed of her for over an hour. Of the two of us as children. Young, innocent, our entire lives ahead of us. Back when life was normal. Back when everyone assumed I was sane.

I stared into the glass of a windowpane too small to shed much light, yet too large to hide my demonic reflection that seemed ready to leap out and throttle me where I stood. I had wrongly assumed Emma only ever saw her perfect image in the mirror, nothing more, nothing less. Now I honestly had no genuine idea what my sister saw when she looked at her reflection staring back at her. What would she think of her little sister now? My face was so contorted, it resembled nothing of the woman I would have once hoped to become — what Emma always assumed I was, deep down, beyond an intolerable hatred for her that had seemingly come from nowhere. This whole thing had now brought me wholly to my knees. Justice. Karma. Call it what you like, it was coming to find me. I had nowhere left to hide.

# 9

I was awoken by the sound of the cell door opening, two officers storming in abruptly and lifting me from the floor, no words required, no offer of comfort to the woman in their care, already in desperate turmoil. To them, I must have appeared little more than a crazed psychopath, undeserving of their attention, their job to accompany me to an unsuspecting interview room. The awaiting police and pending justice were of no concern to them. I had no idea how long I had been inside that isolation cell, my thoughts allowed to wander frantically, my actions reaffirming events now complete. I wasn't quite awake, not quite of sound mind, my throat too dry, my thoughts twisting my gut into something really rather ugly.

I was led into a small, dimly lit room, the narrow window too high for me to see the outside world beyond, the bleak sound of heavy footsteps and slamming of prison doors providing temporary companionship I didn't want. I was ushered inside to the sight of DCI Moor, already sitting at a table, accompanied by another male I recognised as DS Cavendish. Their faces said it all.

'Stacey Adams,' she offered flatly, a look on her face telling me she hadn't expected to have to deal with me again so soon. 'How nice to see you again.' She wasn't pleased to see me at all. My swollen eyes and unkempt hair now made me look as if I'd recently escaped from a psychiatric hospital. It just added to what she already thought of me, what she already knew I was.

'DCI Moor.' I returned the greeting, unappreciative of why she was here. Farley probably couldn't wait to spill his guts at my expense, the revelation I'd made now altogether making things worse for everyone. I was pressed into a chair, cold hands on cold shoulders which felt too heavy, too forceful. If I had the capacity, I might have scoffed at such annoyance, given the irritating officer behind me a lingering glare. As it was, my treatment was now deemed necessary, required, my recent actions not exactly telling these people I was of rational sound mind.

'I assume you know why we are here?' DCI Moor looked tired, as if this entire case was becoming too much for her. As if *I* was becoming too much for her. I nodded. What else did she expect me to say? 'Care to elaborate on the death of your sister?' she asked, no small talk required. This entire meeting was meant to tick boxes, confirm my already documented guilt, stamp files. *My file.* She genuinely looked at me as if she thought I was a demented serial killer — my motives of no consequence to anyone.

'What did Doctor Farley tell you?' I asked, needing to confirm he had indeed shared the correct information. I did not wish to accidentally convict myself twice.

'Why don't you tell *me* what happened?' DCI Moor asked. A pen in her hand tapped gently against her thumb as she twisted it around several times. I detested how she did that. 'I understand you trashed your cell yesterday?' Was she asking or telling me?

I swallowed. Time was passing without my knowledge, sleep the only thing I found helpful. It was my unfeigned inability to retain a calm persona that had brought about this moment, my inability to keep my big mouth shut and my temper under control that now created such unavoidable questioning. I was more than prepared to receive my penance for Jason, his unexpected attack something I could hardly hide. Yet, I couldn't tell them what I had done to Emma, my sister's death entirely different. This place was slowly tipping me over the edge. Did anyone care?

'Miss Adams?' DCI Moor was waiting. Both police officers were staring at me now.

I nodded. 'It's not how it might look,' I began, needing these people to understand my distorted logic at the time, the way things were unfolding back then. It felt so long ago now.

'How *does* it look, Stacey?' DCI Moor asked, the pen still in her hand, poised, ready to record my declaration. She was too calm. I didn't like it.

'It probably looks as if I'm a cold killer with a serious anger problem. But I'm not.' I glanced at the woman in control of my destiny, a pleading look on my face entirely undeserving. Who was I trying to kid? I'd described myself perfectly. 'I honestly believed Jason loved me. I would have done anything for him. I only wanted us to be happy. Together.' Every word was accurate, yet none of the officers spoke. They simply allowed me to continue in my own time, hanging myself with the rope they had provided. 'I just wanted us to be happy. Was it so terrible for me to want to start a brand new life together?' I honestly believed my wayward thinking. Getting rid of Emma was a means to an end, part of an unfortunate plan that seemed justifiable.

'But you previously claimed that Jason Cole raped you, Stacey?' DCI Moor cut in. 'It hardly sounds like the actions of this apparent loving man you are now painting a picture of. A *married* man, by all accounts. A doting father.'

I glared at her for a moment, unable to put into words the truth of how our relationship was. How *could* I explain? 'He was a complicated man,' I muttered. *Complicated? Seriously, Stacey? That is some understatement.* 'Jason was so kind in the beginning. We'd known each other for over a decade. We used to laugh so much.' I closed my eyes, remembering. 'But, I also always knew, deep down, he wasn't happy with my sister.'

'Oh? And why was that?'

'The way he acted when he was around her. Always walking on eggshells, as if he knew she was capable of becoming upset by the tiniest of things he did. He couldn't do a damned thing right.' I wanted to add, *poor bloke,* but refrained, the real Jason far different to the man I'd initially imagined, wrongly invented.

'So, how did that lead to Emma's death?'

*Good question.* I could barely recall that day now. Too much had happened since then. 'I actually only wanted to save Jason from her. Honest.' It was true. It had consumed me once, turned me into something I wasn't. 'I believed that with Emma gone, Jason would be happy. Then, finally, *I* would be happy.'

'They had a child together?'

I nodded. 'Eva, yes.' My poor beautiful niece. All alone in the world now, my parents wilfully trying to do their best for the child.

'So you didn't assume anything wrong in taking her mother away from her?'

The truth was no. I hadn't thought about Eva at all in any of my plans. I thought only about myself. Always myself. And Jason, of course. *Obviously.* 'I knew Eva would be okay. I was going to look after them both?'

'Both?'

I pressed my belly. 'Both Jason's children.' Jesus, when

had everything gone so wrong?

'How did the accident happen, Stacey?' DCI Moor asked. 'The original police report did not find anything suspicious.' Oh, the irony of that truth. I had planned it perfectly, flawlessly. My temper, it seems, was entirely to blame for how things ultimately turned out in the end.

'I grabbed the steering wheel,' I confessed, closing my eyes to a memory of Emma screaming at me that day, the look on her face something I will never forget. There was no point denying any of it now.

DCI Moor nodded, writing down words I couldn't see. 'And Jason? Why did you then kill him? If you wanted to be with him? If you say, you *loved* him.'

I didn't know how to respond. I swallowed, a tear already forming. 'It was all lies,' I muttered, realising I'd never said any of this aloud before now.

'What was?'

'Jason. The house. The money. His relationship with my sister. All of it lies.' I closed my eyes, absorbing the enormity of such an uncomfortable truth. 'I thought Jason was different. But it turned out he was nothing more than a piece of shit lying pig. He loved rough sex, and he hurt me more than once. I initially thought it was okay.' I laughed at my stupid words, staring into the dark eyes of the unseeing detective, willing her to understand my logic, my suffering. 'I honestly assumed it was what love was meant to feel like. Urgent, desperate, eager. But then I discovered the debt, the house about to be repossessed, all those other bloody women he had on the side, just waiting for his phone call.'

I thought about the prostitute's phone number stored in his secret mobile phone, two other women, just like me, manipulated by the man they assumed they knew, no remorse, no consideration for anyone else. 'Jason was nothing more than a crazed sex addict who liked to hurt women for some weird gratification he'd wholly convinced himself, *and me*, was normal. A man who spent money he didn't have in order to look good, to fool others.' I closed my eyes. I almost sounded as if I'd done the world a favour by getting rid of him. Maybe I had. 'He certainly fooled me.'

'So you killed him out of pure anger when you discovered you had murdered your own sister for nothing? And everything you assumed to know about the man you planned to run away with was a lie?' The question hit me hard. *Yes.* Exactly that. I broke down and sobbed like a baby in front of DCI Moor and DS Cavendish, no apology, no plea for forgiveness. I had indeed murdered Emma for nothing. Who was I now crying for, exactly? For Emma, Jason, or *myself*?

I nodded. 'I believed she hated me. I certainly hated her.' I spoke the truth, words spilling from my mouth like poisonous darts aimed into the void of the room towards ears that did not understand — could never understand.

DCI Moor looked at her colleague as if she found me utterly incomprehensible. We both knew what my confessions meant. I would now be charged with double murder, my actions bringing me to this place — no one to blame but myself. I retained gratitude that there would be no trial to relive the painful events of the last few weeks. It was unfortunate none of these people would ever be capable of appreciating how I felt inside. Not really.

'You will need to sign a new statement, confessing to both murders.' It was not a request. 'We will need to revisit the original incident report, check previous statements, check her car. But I do not assume anything will disprove your confession,' DCI Moor explained, her tone as flat as the paper she was writing on. Why the hell would I confess to something I didn't do? I wasn't totally stupid.

I nodded, my head simply along for the ride. I was

doing a lot of signing recently, signing away my life, my freedom, my sanity. 'Tell my parents I'm sorry,' I breathed as I was led out of the room towards pending doom, eternal damnation. DCI Moor did not respond. I wasn't confident she was all that bothered *what* I was.

# 10

I didn't have to wait long to find out exactly what my mum thought about me. Just two days after my second police interview, I received confirmation that she had requested a visit. It was not entirely surprising. Of course, she would want to check on me to see how I was coping and ensure her youngest child was being looked after in this shithole. I wanted to see her, too. I honestly did. I needed to talk to her. I needed a *hug*. I wanted to know she was okay, that my dad and Eva were dealing well with everything recently thrust upon them too violently. I equally wanted to tell her how sorry I was. For everything.

It was unfortunate that I didn't anticipate the look on her face as I walked into the visitor lounge: as expressionless as my sister's corpse rotting regretfully in her grave. I was surprised at how pale she looked. Her usual bright eyes were now a disturbing slurry of crimson blood vessels, deep-set puffy grooves above her cheekbones. *Jesus*. When was the last time she slept?

We sat down, my mum offering no words of comfort that might appease my increasingly low mood, no desire, it seemed, to provide a hug she would have usually given without hesitation. I couldn't take my eyes from the prominent lines that had formed around her mouth, between her eyes. I smiled. It was not reciprocated.

'I'm so glad you came,' I breathed, fresh tears threatening to emerge at the sight of my mother sitting rather stiffly in front of me. She had thankfully dropped some of my belongings into the prison already, as requested by the staff here, a fresh change of clothing and a well-needed hairbrush, none of it a good substitute for my freedom or the love of parents I needed more now than ever — parents I took for granted too many times until being thrown into this desolate place alone. At least I didn't look like a random piece of shit anymore, my hair now washed, no longer appearing as if I'd been sleeping on the street for some time. She even remembered to bring in my makeup bag, moisturiser, cleansing cloth. Now though, looking at her blank features, I couldn't help wondering if she wished she hadn't bothered.

'I just *needed* to see the look on your face when I ask you the truth,' Mum spat, her tone black, her eyes darker than any starless sky I'd ever seen. I couldn't exactly see the emotions swimming in her thoughts. Yet, I didn't entirely want to. I furrowed my brow.

'Mum I —'

'No, Stacey.' Mum shook her head firmly. She could barely bring herself to look at me. 'I can't imagine you saying anything to me that I actually might want to hear.' She swallowed, her lips pressed tightly together, her eyes narrowing with each breath she took. It made her look old. I hung my head. She always seemed to have a way of making me feel like some naughty little girl without even trying. *How did she do that?*

'What exactly did the police tell you?' I already knew the answer, yet I needed to ask anyway. I hated being out of control, out of the loop, out of my goddamned mind. My voice emerged almost strangled, as if my mum already had

74

her hands around my throat.

'I honestly thought Jason must have done something terrible to you,' Mum confessed, throwing her trembling hands into the air wildly. 'That he attacked you, causing you to lash out so badly. You know how I felt about that man. What he put your sister and that poor little girl through.' She laughed. Not the funny, carefree type, but the sort of laugh that sounded altogether bitter, warped. 'How stupid must I have looked?' she said with a snort.

I nodded. I understood where Mum was coming from. I knew precisely what Emma was forced to endure at the pitiless hands of her once trusted husband. It made me feel quite sick, to be honest. I certainly did not believe my mum was stupid, though. She couldn't have known any different. Neither of us did.

'I even felt terrible for not being able to protect *you*,' she continued, ignoring my body language entirely. 'I'd already failed to protect Emma. I didn't know what to think.'

I could see the suffering my mum was going through, the hidden turmoil behind her disquiet, mistrusting eyes. I pondered for a moment how my dad was probably struggling to deal with any of this. He was a quiet man, kept his emotions in check, buried, often too deeply, in my biased opinion. It affected his health more than my mum would ever admit. I wanted to ask why he wasn't here now, why he hadn't come to see me, but luckily kept my mouth shut. My dad probably hated me more than my mum seemed to. It wasn't a comforting notion.

Mum scoffed, unaware of my troubled thoughts and festering reasons behind it all. 'So, imagine my surprise when the police turned up at the house yesterday afternoon to tell me that you have now also confessed to the murder of your sister. Your *own* sister.' Mum spat her words as if, at any moment, she was terrified she might actually choke on

75

them. Or choke me. 'A *double* murder charge now soon to be confirmed, a life sentence pending.'

I didn't know what to say, where to look. I certainly couldn't look at my mum. She would unravel my entire soul with a single flick of her arthritic wrists, a simple roll of her deep blue eyes. I wanted to explain, tell her that I was sorry, but the truth was, the unfortunate events I was wholly responsible for had unfolded in precisely the way I once assumed were the *correct* way. *The only way.* It was the only way my mind was able to make sense of any of what had happened. What was still happening.

How was I to know Emma had been saving money in a separate bank account to help me achieve a law degree? How could I have known my sister was living with a secret eating disorder she didn't want the world to know of? The entire thing was possibly brought about by the man she married, of course, the man she adored as much as I did. I certainly had no idea Jason was nothing more than a scheming pile of cow shit. It was a thought that now slowly threatened to destroy everything I once believed I was. What I once believed *he* was. I literally had no idea what I was meant to feel about Emma. I'd hated her for so long, I couldn't anticipate feeling anything else.

'Stacey? Look at me.' Mum was not asking politely. '*Look at me!*' she screamed, wayward spittle flying from her tightening jaw, several people turning our way in shocked, slightly muted response. How she was managing to remain in her seat right now was beyond me. How she hadn't got to her feet and punched me was actually quite admirable. I probably would have punched me, under the circumstances. Torn chunks out of my face.

I looked up. Mum did *not* look happy.

'Please, tell me they have this wrong? Tell me you did *not* kill your sister? I need to hear it from your mouth,

76

Stacey. I need you to say it to my face.' Mum was shaking now. It was entirely deplorable she hadn't quite conquered her earlier inability to look into my eyes, simply glaring ahead. All she needed was a gun. Her bottom lip quivered, her hands unable to retain any composure that might have otherwise presented her usual relaxed, friendly personality. The strangers around us were seeing the wrong version of my mum entirely. It wasn't pleasant.

I shook my head, glancing from my mum to the floor beneath me and wishing the thing would open up and swallow me whole. 'I can't,' I muttered, unsure the words leaving my mouth were my own at all. I didn't want to tell mum what I'd done, yet neither could I tell her a lie.

My mum let out a blood-draining cry, her entire body crumpling at the confession of murder I hadn't yet confirmed, hidden truths muttered from the mouth of her youngest child with seemingly no hesitation, no remorse. Carol Smith came to her side, asking if everything was okay, if she needed anything to drink, whilst offering me a *what the hell did you do now?* look of her own. Mum stared into the unsuspecting face of the officer, her eyes pleading for something she knew none of them could provide.

'Get me out of here,' Mum begged, clinging to the sleeve of my capturer as if her life depended on it. Mum had once again reverted to staring off into the distance. Anything that meant she didn't have to look at me. I'm sure she worried that if she did such a thing, it might be the last thing she ever did, dropping dead by the vision of sickening revolt in front of her. Smith nodded, helping my mum to her trembling feet.

'Mum?' I begged, needing to explain events I had no right attempting to make light of. *Please, don't go. Not yet.*

My mum was still clinging to Carol as she turned and raised her face to mine, sticky tears staining her makeup-less features. 'Just tell me why? *Why did you do it?*' It was an honest question, yet one I didn't know if I would ever be able to answer honestly. Would she want to hear the truth? Would I?

I shook my head. 'I don't know,' I managed to mutter, my words sounding as pathetic and weak as I felt. Of course, I knew. I just didn't need my mum to hear it.

'*You don't know?*' Mum couldn't believe my insensitivity, the nerve of me. I bit my lip. The truth was that I wanted my sister gone so I could have the life I thought she lived. The life I once believed had been devoid of my existence, cruelly, savagely, rubbing in my face in her success too often. It was all just stinging nettles and wasps, hell-bent on stinging me to death. Her husband, her house, her money. Everything that made Emma Cole who I *believed* she was. I couldn't tell my mum such things. Envy made me do it. Nothing more than pure and straightforward, vile jealousy. *That is what really made me kill my sister, mother dearest.*

'It's hard to explain —' I began, hoping to say anything that might somehow absolve me of my unforgivable crimes.

'You little *bitch!*' Mum yelled, cutting me off, taking me entirely by surprise. 'What is there to explain? I hope you rot in hell for what you have done to this family,' she spat, before spitting directly into my face. I felt a large glob of warm saliva land just above my right eye, dripping onto my cheek almost in slow motion, mockingly, tempestuously. My mum had never acted that way before, never expressed her emotions so coldly, so cruelly. We both knew she would never look at me the same way again.

*Oh my god.* 'Mum, please,' I sobbed, getting to my feet. I did not attempt to wipe away my mother's well-aimed bodily fluid. It would appear as if I was trying to wipe her away too. Wipe away her emotions as if they mattered nothing to me at all. It wasn't true. I needed the approval of my mother more than anything. I always had.

'Don't you *ever* call me Mum again. You're no daughter of mine. I do not even know who you are. Stacey Adams is *dead* to me.' With that, she was helped from the room, her heartbroken sobs all I needed to know of her broken state of mind. I had wrecked everything for everyone and would now receive precisely what I deserved. I understood why my dad had stayed away. Maybe he was outside in the car, heart already in his throat, face in his hands, waiting for his wife to confirm his daughter's incomprehensible, revelation.

'By the way,' she added furiously, removing herself from Smith's outstretched arms and storming towards me, leaning across an empty table as if she needed the thing simply to remain upright. She no longer looked fragile. I wasn't the only one to notice. 'You need to sign some paperwork to release Emma's funds into Eva's name. It's the least you can do for that poor child. For your sister.' It was an empty gesture, made to make me feel as if she felt nothing for me at all.

She was right. It was the least I could do. My sister's money meant absolutely nothing to me in here. It should never have been mine anyway. I didn't deserve any of it.

'Okay,' I choked as my mother took one last, cold look at my face. 'I love you, Mum,' I spoke into the room as she trundled away, not caring that everyone around us was listening. I needed my mum to hear it. *To believe it.*

'You don't know the meaning of love,' Mum bit back as she disappeared out of the door. Maybe she was right. I honestly thought Jason loved me, and look where that had led me. I had never been able to tell if my sister loved or loathed me, everything she did seemingly able to provoke a jealous emotion inside me that I knew I would have to own up to eventually.

'Mum, don't leave me alone in here. I need you. *Please*.'
It was my turn now to sob, to scream into the room as if
none of the other inmates or visitors in this place mattered.
To me, they did not matter. It was my turn to now act
considerably rude and out of place — the idea that my sister
and I were more alike than I would have dared contemplate,
not entirely sitting right with my rational thinking one little
bit.

## 11

I managed to get back to my unit unscathed, yet how I remained upright for the duration of that seemingly short walk, I have no idea. My heart was pounding so loudly I presumed the entire prison could hear every beat in my chest. Everyone had heard what my mum thought of me. *Her own daughter.* How would that make me look to these people now? It was unfortunate all the women in here would now discover that I was a killer. Tongues wagging, nothing else to do in this place but discuss the turmoil of others. I'd hoped to smooth things over between my mum and I, explain my position, demand the support she must have known I desperately needed. I was somewhat perplexed that she had mentioned nothing at all of my unborn baby, her youngest grandchild seemingly of even less importance to her than her youngest daughter.

I'd been kept in isolation since wrecking my cell. Smith led me back to my own room where I received my first official verbal warning, and told that I would find myself in isolation permanently if I trashed my cell again. She was not joking. *Joking* was not Mrs Smith's thing. As my unit's senior supervising officer, she had two silver stripes on the arm of her jacket to confirm her rank, a documented authority over us all. All other officer's uniforms consisted of a single strip.

It meant Smith could tell everyone in here exactly how things were going to be, every staff member and inmate alike. She certainly made it very clear today things would be different for me from now on.

I was slightly infuriated by the fact my cell was left just as I'd left it. I would need to clean it up myself, Smith told me. My mess, my problem. It was part of the punishment. How would I ever learn common decency and respect if someone else constantly cleared up after me? I couldn't help assuming she was including my mum in that equation, though she didn't confirm it officially. I have no idea why she needed to look so bloody happy about my predicament. Yet, it didn't matter what she thought. It fitted my mood, this place slowly becoming the very tomb I would probably end up dead in soon enough anyway.

I was told to take a broom from the nearby supply cupboard to sweep up a mountain of discarded sugar that had begun to weld itself in large deposits to the floor. Coffee grounds that had scattered to the far reaches of every corner were never going to be easy to dislodge, my mattress now a sludgy blend of sweat stains and little brown blobs. I had brought this entirely on myself. But what did I expect? My bedsheets were filthy, covered in dried, stinking milk splatters and stains I didn't wish to acknowledge. I was confident they had not been in such a state before I was thrown into isolation. I would have to sleep on these things now until Friday, a change of bedding no doubt a welcome relief for everyone within a twenty-foot radius.

I was glad it didn't take me too long to tidy my cell, this sparse box all but devoid of any tangible assets that meant anything to me anyway. I thought of the designer clothing probably still hanging in my sister's forgotten wardrobe. Unworn, unwanted.

When Paula came into the room behind me, I almost

didn't notice.

'Everything okay?' she asked, only trying to help, only wanting to connect with me and make me feel welcome in this unwelcoming place.

'Fuck off,' I spat, needing no support from her or anyone else in this dump.

'Suit yourself,' she muttered, leaving me to my mess. *My mess.* This entire thing was indeed my mess. Jason had ended up looking a mess by the time I'd finished with him. I now felt and looked like a complete mess. This room was a mess. My mum's emotions were now wholly messed up beyond normality. Everyone should sod off and leave me alone. I didn't need or want a damned thing from any of them. I was in this alone. My mum had made that very clear.

***

I wasn't allowed to wallow in my own wholly created self-pity for long. Once my room was tidied to a reasonable standard, my mattress, bedding and belongings placed back into passable order, I was taken to see a solicitor. He was a man I'd never met before, did not give a shit about, who knew nothing about me, but would be required now, it seemed, to tell me my fate. He sat in front of me in his fake designer suit, his cheap haircut declaring to the world this job paid relatively little. Despite his desperate revolt, his face a noticeable confirmation he enjoyed his daily tasks even less. We sat in silence for a few moments whilst he familiarised himself with my file, my case, a double murder charge still to be dealt with, no trial required by law — his job to discuss the pending judgment determined by the court. My entire life was now in this strangers hands.

'You confessed willingly to two murders, so the court

does not require a trial, as there is nothing for a prosecuting barrister to prove on their side. Does that make sense?'

I nodded.

'Okay,' the guy sounded grateful I wasn't about to give him any trouble. A smile wouldn't go amiss, though. Gratitude wasn't so entirely challenging to achieve, was it? 'I am required by law to verify all statements taken by the police and any witnesses involved,' he continued. 'Go through the legal procedures with you and, once a date has been set for your sentencing, explain the resulting conviction the judge will pass.' He wasn't even looking at me. His presence here was just required by law, neither of us able to change anything about that. I assumed I had made his job a little easier, though, my inability to cover my tracks as well as I probably should have, bringing me to this fitting conclusion now. He licked his lips, removing glasses that looked far better on his face than in his sweaty hand. 'I do have to tell you though, Miss Adams, because of the seriousness of the crimes, and, despite your willing confession of guilt, you will be looking at around twenty years, maybe longer.' I probably should not have looked so shocked by his words, but I was. I was quite dumbfounded. Twenty years? *Jesus Christ.*

I glanced his way for a moment, allowing my eyes to rest on the slight indentation between his eyes where his glasses had sat too long. 'Okay,' I muttered, nothing else to add, my throat tightening with each breath I took. What else was there to say?

The solicitor nodded his confirmation before carefully going through the police statements with me, including a formal statement taken previously from Farley, who, according to the file positioned upside down on the table, had no issues confirming my recent confession to them all. I was asked if I wished to add or retract anything recorded. I didn't. I just wanted to get the hell out of this room as fast as I could, out of the *hell* I'd now found myself in. After signing yet more papers, including a letter from the bank to transfer funds to a Miss Eva Cole, all I wanted was some fresh air. It honestly felt as if the entire day had passed before I was allowed some well-needed time out, my head threatening to burst by the volume of information dumped onto me, my stomach churning from thoughts left to their own devices.

I wasn't hungry, despite picking at my breakfast earlier that morning before my mum's visit, lunch already long gone by the time I was led back to my unit. If it were left up to me, I'd probably never eat again, my body only needing a week or two to break down, give up, leave this world behind me forever. Yet it wasn't up to me. I had a baby to care for now. It was a truth that sat uncomfortably in my twisted gut.

For as long as I can remember, I have wanted to be a mother, Jason providing everything I felt I needed to achieve such an incredible goal. Now, with said child proliferating inside me, I couldn't simply remove myself from this life so swiftly and with little thought for my unborn baby. It wasn't that simple. Yet, nothing would ever be simple again. *It wasn't fucking fair.* How ironic was it that I was now required to bring a life into this world, alone, destitute, totally forsaken by everyone? Into this very prison. My solicitor had probably given me some critical advice I was expected to conform to, adhere to, but I wasn't exactly listening. I very much doubted I would listen to anyone ever again.

# 12

I struggled to settle into the required daily routine, ensuring little engagement was given to anyone, much encouragement and persuasion needed to simply get me out of bed. I did my best to ignore the other women completely, doing as I was told, when told to do it, all the time feeling as if I was unravelling silently, remaining unnoticed by anyone who mattered — my entire world collapsing around me with volatile fury. I needed my mum. Although her behaviour towards me was understandable, it had left me hollow, shocked, depressed. She'd always been there for me. Now, she was gone, probably never to return to this harrowing place, never to utter my name in public again, or in private, come to think of it. Her daughter was dead to her and to everyone she met — the shame of what had happened, too much for the poor woman to contend with.

My morning sickness returned with a vengeance, forcing me to spend too long throwing up, head down the loo, my baby needing sustenance and attention I felt incapable of providing. I actually believed the indignant thing could sense my suffering, my inability to function rationally, unable to turn me into the mum-to-be I might otherwise have thrived on one day becoming. I attempted to placate myself with notions of a better future. I just had to hold on. *We* had to hold on. It was all I could do for my child now.

Because of my pregnancy, I wasn't yet scheduled to work in any of the more arduous departments of the prison. They didn't expect me to lug heavy laundry around, help maintain the grounds and gardens or, in fact, anything that actually required a skill I didn't possess. I was impressed to discover some of the inmates even contributed to the maintenance of basic plumbing and electricals, displaying abilities I couldn't have anticipated owning. They found it entirely annoying I showed no interest in those obtuse prison workshop programmes much talked about in here, either. In my opinion, rehabilitation was something the prison system oddly deemed far too necessary.

So, I helped out in the canteen. It was not a good combination, to be honest. The constant smell of food and disinfectant in my nostrils only aided in making my morning sickness ten times worse than it probably would have been if I was left alone to wallow in my cell. I swear the kitchen workers were convinced I was making the whole thing up to get out of participating in the required workload. Or, indeed, anything at all that meant I had to actually do something. *Anything.*

The inmates weren't exactly as I expected either, mostly just broken women who'd, unfortunately, ended up in the system due to some kind of abuse or another, be it physical abuse from loved ones or substance abuse to block it all out. I was careful never to ask questions, keeping a low profile where possible, staying out of everyone's way. Paula's early advice constantly rang in my ears, so I avoided all conversation where possible. There were, of course, a few so-called "hard nuts" inside this place, but they left me alone, for the most part. Most of those women were in a different wing of the prison anyway. However, I did wonder why, as a soon-to-be convicted double murderer, I wasn't already amongst them, thrown into the lion's den and forgotten.

Maybe because I was pregnant, the prison system was willing to give me a chance of redemption for the sake of my baby. Or perhaps they assumed my state of mind was too fragile to deal with anything else. I really didn't know. Whatever it was, it helped secure my low state of mind to the point where, most days, I ambled around, taking little notice of my surroundings, being prompted too often by the officers when I failed to achieve my required goals or apparent potential.

I no longer felt it worth my while to contribute anything else to society, prison life already far removed from the reality of the world in which I once knew. What was the point? Those in society had all but destroyed me, anyway, brought me to my knees. Of course, it would be so easy for me to blame everyone else, my mum included. She hadn't been in touch since she walked out of the visitor lounge with a bad attitude in tow. I'd received no further request for a visit, no letter, no apology for her unprecedented outburst. Even the phone call I was allowed to make to her went unreciprocated, my mum hanging up immediately when she knew it was me on the other end. She couldn't have known it at the time, but it only helped push me further towards the edge of something that even I didn't anticipate coming.

***

My thirtieth birthday came round surprisingly quickly. There was nobody in my life at that point willing to celebrate with me beyond a handful of random inmates I didn't wish to associate with much at all, the bank account set up by my unwitting sister sitting untouched, an apparent birthday gift unused, waiting for my niece to claim, mocking the very fact I had ruined it all. I was alone, isolated, the people I now shared living quarters with knowing nothing about me or my historical actions — nothing left but personal suffering I was now forced to endure alone.

In fact, the entire day passed with little interest, little acknowledgement. I couldn't even bring myself to sing a silent happy birthday, sobbing into my cell alone when I assumed no one was listening. As it was, I was slowly slumping into a depression I had little defence from. Of all the friends I'd made during my lifetime, I was shocked by how entirely non-existent such a concept felt. None of them *ever* came to visit me. None even seemed concerned by past events. It was as if I'd never existed at all.

The food was terrible, therefore I didn't always eat well. But the truth was, I was far too despondent to be bothered to chew and swallow on repeat, my baby hell-bent on sucking every last inch of life from my failing body. I was exhausted, every second of every day feeling like a punishment, my entire body aching to discover a solace I couldn't locate. So when I finally agreed to visit Farley's office for my second session, I was in no mood for his apparent pearls of wisdom.

'How are you today, Miss Adams?' he asked, rather too calmly, our previous meeting of little importance to him at all now. It was done, complete, his statement already sitting on some judge's desk, awaiting an ultimate conclusion to the rest of my life. I was staring out of his window, the only place in this entire prison with a decent view of the surrounding countryside. Even Governor Barrington's office looked out onto an unattractive neighbouring prison wall. I assumed that was the whole point. This room's location had been purposely chosen for well-needed counselling, long overdue mentoring, mental health made all the better by an apparent pleasant view.

'Fine,' I snapped. 'Apart from now being up on a *double* murder charge. Thanks for that, by the way.' The man was infuriating. I folded my arms across my chest, tapping my foot.

Farley sighed. 'Miss Adams, you can hardly blame me for that.'

He was right, of course. I couldn't. And yet, here I was, blaming him anyway. 'You told me I could say anything I wanted inside this room without reproach,' I spat, shaking my head. Plus, he had been seriously winding me up about Jason at the time. My confession was coerced, forced from me by the constraints of his pointed questions and the claustrophobic atmosphere of this coffee-infused room. Yet I couldn't hold it against the man, I guess. He was only doing his *job*.

'No,' he corrected solemnly. 'What I said was, in this room, you can tell me anything. Which indeed you did. But I had a legal obligation to the jurisdiction system —'

'To brand me a killer.' I thought I'd finish the guy's sentence for him. I almost bit a chunk out of my bottom lip in frantic pursuit of bitter words that left a nasty taste in my mouth. The very sound of them created nausea that lingered in the back of my throat, bile rising readily. *I was a killer.* It was hardly news. My legs were trembling now, jolting my knees up and down in swift pursuit, making me look as if I needed the toilet. I couldn't help it. I could barely bring myself to pick up my mug of coffee for fear of spilling the hot liquid into my lap.

Farley looked at me for a moment, thinking. 'And, you honestly don't believe any of *that* was of your own doing?'

I shook my head. I had no idea *what* I was thinking that

day. Could I claim temporary insanity? Diminished responsibility? 'Probably,' I muttered, hating the way he was able to turn all this around on me. I was the victim in all this. Why couldn't any of these people see that?

'The staff tell me you haven't been eating well. Do you feel that is good for your baby?' Farley was sitting back in his chair, cross-legged, seemingly unconcerned by my failing composure, asking questions meant to help tick more boxes. How the hell did he know *what* I was feeling?

'I'm not hungry,' I snapped. I wanted to tell him to try eating the food in this place himself and see how hungry he ended up. But, this entire thing wasn't about food. It was about my pathetic *life*, unwinding too fast for me to keep up. Jason Cole the entire reason behind it all. There was absolutely no way for me to make him pay for what he'd done to me now. The fact he was dead mattered little to anyone. How could I make him suffer from beyond the grave?

'You need to eat, Stacey, or they will place you under strict medical supervision. They can't allow the baby to be neglected. Do you want them to take your child away as soon as he or she is born?'

*What kind of a stupid question was that?* This baby was all I had left, my life nothing but a shell of what I once thought I was, what I once hoped I could be. I sighed, shaking my head. Did he know something I didn't?

'I'm fine,' I offered, knowing I was anything but, wishing to be anywhere other than here with this man. Peter Farley did not know me. He was merely paid to sit and dissect my brain for an hour each week. Doctor or not, I wasn't about to let that happen so readily again.

\*\*\*

I have no idea if it was Farley's blatant words, my solicitor's absent state of mind, or my mum's absence entirely, but that night I painstakingly slid a razor blade from the inside of my cheap plastic shaving equipment and cut my wrists. I gingerly pressed the used blade against my clammy skin, cutting across my pulsing vein as gently as I could muster the strength. I wasn't expecting it to hurt so much, to be honest, and I almost gave up halfway through, illustrating my embarrassing efforts for anyone looking on. The cuts weren't exactly deep, I hasten to add. I didn't *want* to die. I certainly didn't wish to hurt my unborn child or cause any more unnecessary drama. The idea of such a thing didn't even cross my mind, oddly. I wanted help, *needed* help, desperately reaching out beyond the dark place I was currently existing in, hoping to find the support I had nowhere else to search for. However, the resulting wounds did little more than create a mess on the floor of my cell, a slight panic erupting from a passing prison officer, along with a couple of nights spent under strict supervision in the prison medical bay.

I lay on my back in an uncomfortable, overly-starched bed, feeling sorry for myself, slightly sore and embarrassed, listening to strangers talking about me in the corridor beyond. I had shown very little remorse for my crimes, apparently. They were worried I might hurt my baby, my state of mind now deemed too fragile for me to be left to my own devices. They discussed transferring me to the prison's secure mental health unit. It would be a far easier option than keeping me in isolation or on permanent suicide watch. It would be for my own protection, they whispered, and for the sake of my unborn child. It was as if they were speaking deliberately loud enough for me to overhear them, their words designed to push every button I had. I didn't care what they did to me at that point. As my mum had put it so eloquently, Stacey Adams was *dead*.

# 13

It was entirely misplaced that my non-suicidal cry for help ironically saw me on full suicide watch for a grand total of two weeks until the understaffed, overworked officers were forced to relent, their time required elsewhere, underfunding a major contributing factor. My fragile state of mind meant I was subsequently paired with a cellmate, moved to a twin occupancy room, someone able to keep an eye on me, watch my declining mood in steady progression. They didn't yet have space in the mother and baby section, the secure mental health unit requiring paperwork not yet signed, both areas of the prison already overrun as it was. It told me all I needed to know about the current state of the prison system. I was moved into Paula's room, meaning I not only now had to share a space with someone else but also endure her continued quest for conversation. The fact she was older, already a peer worker for the newly acquired women here, meant I now had a chaperone wherever I bloody went. *Brilliant.*

It took a little over a month for my sentencing to be passed, for the judge to confirm the amount of time I would need to remain incarcerated. I stood in the courtroom dock, smartly presented to some undeserving, unappreciative judge, my appearance giving nothing away of how I was feeling, my parents noticeably absent from the viewing gallery. It was probably fitting I received a life sentence, although it was a shock to hear the numbers, all the same. My solicitor had got it almost spot on. Twenty-four years, almost a quarter of a bloody century. *Jesus Christ.* The double murder I'd committed deemed me a risk to society, so the judge was required to make an example out of me, she said. I tried hard not to look surprised, although I'm not entirely confident I pulled it off.

The one thing that did go in my favour, however, was the readily provided, firmly confirmed guilty plea I'd already submitted. It meant, oddly, my willingness to comply was taken into account when she issued the resulting sentence. I would have got far longer had I chosen to lie to them all, deny what I'd done, pleaded a false innocence. I received ten years for Emma's death and fourteen for Jason's. It would have been longer, the judge told me, had it not been for my willing assistance, my willing testimony. But my apparent unwillingness to show remorse or offer reasons behind my crimes wasn't taken lightly, either. A judge who did not know me was allowed to cast forth a life sentence and get on with her day unaffected. I was given the news as if my day in court was simply one in a line of many. The information presented, merely a requirement, a gavel slammed onto a wooden bench with force, the file in her possession one of several to be completed that same day. I stood in the courtroom, a shocked look on my face that twenty-four years of my life was taken away from *me* for the callous acts I'd done to *them*.

My baby was beginning to kick at this point, my belly swelling fast, baggy t-shirts and loose-fitting leggings all my sickness-ravaged body would tolerate. I hadn't worn makeup for months. Not since the day I'd been excited to see my mum; her short visit ensuring I lived every day since feeling like an unwanted orphan. It was quite ironic considering Eva was now an orphan because of *me*.

My phone calls continued to go unreciprocated, even on the very day I received my sentencing. I assumed they might care, show up at court even, but I clearly wasn't deserving of such attention. Eventually, my parents must have changed their number because my last desperate call to the house equated to nothing more than a *I'm sorry, your call cannot be connected at this time as this number is out of service* message lingering inside my troubled ear.

I stood with the phone receiver in hand, a queue of chattering women behind me, anger building in my body that suddenly came from nowhere. Without thinking, I slammed the phone hard against the wall, releasing a yell I doubted came from my mouth at all. Plastic and metal splintered violently against the brickwork, no match for my infuriated wrath, no cares I had caused trouble for those poor sods behind me who still hadn't made their well-deserved calls as yet. I screamed as loudly as I was able to muster the strength, crying for the parents I couldn't imagine living without, crying for my own sorry state of affairs. There would be no more phone calls for anyone else today, no vital contact made to loved ones until an engineer could be called to fix yet another mess I'd created. I was, once again, sent directly to isolation overnight to cool off, loud taunts of irritation behind me, my second verbal warning soon to become my first written one if I wasn't careful, this entire place responsible for everything I was now becoming.

And this is how things went on for quite some time. My unrestrained anger was constantly pointed towards anyone who assumed they could befriend me — nothing they said or did able to make any difference to my declining state of mind. I became a forgotten part of a system I had, at one time, known nothing about yet now formed my hated daily existence. I despised everything, myself included, my life having no meaning at all beyond breathing air that supplied oxygen for my expanding belly. Even the baby inside me could not sedate my prolonged suffering beyond a limited view of what he or she might look like, how they might make me feel once they actually made it into this world. I went to sleep each night with empowering visions of my new-born, waking each morning to the harsh reality of my uncertain situation.

Paula continued to be kind, even on those darkest days when I told her to do one, hiding beneath thin sheets I knew could never console me. She was older, wiser, her fifty-something years on this earth, meaning she had been in the system longer than most in this place, seen more than most, her personal traumas etched into her face for the entire world to see. Abused by authority and strangers alike, Paula's story was one of turmoil, abuse, her children taken into care many years earlier. They were all grown up now and living their own lives, the poor woman's alcohol dependency the very reason she had been in and out of prison for the last fifteen years of her kids' lives. I hadn't asked for any of this information, of course. She had willingly provided her colourful life story in some futile attempt to sedate my irrational emotions, make my struggles seem less problematic. It was okay to talk about your troubles, apparently, if you *needed* to. Yet, I didn't dare assume she would ever understand mine.

'Prison life has a way of tipping even the sanest of people over the edge, Stacey,' she told me during an innocent one-sided conversation. We were in our cell, the door locked, no way for me to escape, to run away and hide. I dared not tell her I probably hadn't been sane for some time — way before I found myself rotting in this place. I was on a self-destruction mission, and Paula knew it.

Many of the women I encountered were substance abusers, be it through drug or alcohol. Most days, I would watch them scoring in apparent secret, getting high behind closed cell doors, slipping little packets of innocent-looking white powder or dried brown wraps to each other in return for money, commodities, special favours. Even shampoo bottles were often filled with cheap, homemade booze and smuggled in by overly anxious visitors or prison staff on the take. The whole place seemed corrupt.

I hadn't been transferred to the mother and baby unit yet, although I was grateful that HMP Blackwood was one of a handful of prisons capable of housing pregnant and new mothers. It meant I wouldn't be travelling too far when the time came. I was not yet seven months pregnant, still plenty of time before my needs would need to be met, my circumstances changed forever. But, despite it all, I was glad I'd escaped the challenge of the mental health unit. Nothing about *that* place could have been more inviting than where I was currently forced to stay.

I should have been grateful I had company now, at least. Paula was able to raise the alarm, should I go into spontaneous labour in the middle of the night. We both knew when the time finally came for me to give birth, my fate would befall some other department, some other poor sods forced to deal with me and my increasingly turbulent mindset. Most days, I was happy to remain invisible, some of the women even nice enough if I were to take the time to notice, which I mostly did *not*. As far as I was concerned, their presence in my life confirmed I was rotting away in prison. They were a constant reminder, nothing more than that. Therefore I did not need or want their kindness, their friendship, their acknowledgement.

What was the point in befriending these people anyway? They weren't the type of people I would have mixed with on the outside, so why should I now pretend anything differently, because I was one of them? The fact that those I once assumed to be my friends were now long gone, did not register with me, ironically.

I equally failed to appreciate I had, in fact, a bigger need to be in this place than most of the women here. Their downtrodden lives had resulted in small-time criminal activity. Shoplifting to feed their starving children, sex work to pay a gas bill, drug-taking to block out painful memories. It was all part of a system that had failed them.

I was going through the motions, existing, struggling to move from day to day, my belly expanding too swiftly, leaving nothing behind of the figure I once knew. A figure Jason had once loved — couldn't get enough of. He would be mortified if he could see me now. As it were, I was happily ignoring everyone in here, the prison officers still mostly being called miss or sir because I couldn't be bothered to remember their names.

\*\*\*

One afternoon after an unwanted shift in the canteen, I returned to my cell to discover two women on my bed, sniffing cocaine from my pillowcase. When I walked in on them, sprawled out, completely off their faces, I saw red.

'What the *fuck* do you think you're doing?' I screamed, grabbing an open plastic wrap that was lying carelessly across my sheets. Both women were giggling, staring towards the increasingly dilapidated ceiling, trying to crawl out of their skin for apparent fun. I was actually impressed they still managed to lunge my way when they saw me, the only thought in their minds was to score and block out this entire place for a few hours, forget their names if possible. I understood their reasons, of course, yet doing it in my space was not acceptable. I shook the powder into the sink, both women racing to grab what was left, licking their fingers manically as if I'd taken away the very air they breathed. It was the most disgusting thing I'd ever witnessed, their entire bodies shaking violently with fear that they might lose a vital component to the innocence of a dripping tap.

'*You bitch*,' one of the women screamed at me. Her name was Ellie Dowle. She was only twenty-four, yet her skin looked haggard enough to help her pass for way beyond forty — *poor cow*. Dowle lunged towards me, her face red with turmoil, her panicked bloodstream screaming for sedation that would only come from blocking out the world around her with the aid of the powder I'd now thrown away. 'What the *fuck* did you do that for?'

Her friend, a new girl whose name I didn't yet know, was still in the sink, mopping up particles of swiftly dissolving cocaine, snorting it into her reddened nostrils as if her life depended on it.

'What the hell are you doing in my room?' I spat, grabbing Dowle by the arms. I didn't care that I was six and a half months pregnant, about to take on two intruders who wouldn't have noticed my unfortunate predicament anyway if they chose to fight back.

It was fortunate for us all that Paula took that moment to step into the cell, followed by a group of friends happily chatting amongst themselves. She yelled something that I was too outraged to hear, followed by a scuffle that saw me pulled swiftly from the room towards pending solace beyond, a chance to calm down, catch my breath. Angry words were exchanged, those drug-using bitches yelling something in my direction, my own fury rampant, insatiable.

I was marched to the common room lounge, where an inmate sat me down, draping her arm around my trembling body, telling me to take a breath, calm down, relax. I didn't want to calm down. I wanted those vile bitches as far away from my bed as possible. Paula was right. This place was enough to tip even the most rational person over the edge.

'Are you okay, Stacey?' Paula asked, looking flustered as she sat by my side with a cup of hot sugary tea in her hand. I didn't answer. 'Here you go, Honey, drink this.' I took the tea yet didn't feel like drinking it. The only thought in my mind was of the intrusion into my space. Prison life meant we had little enough as it was — the private space I'd been given, all I had. I hated the idea that it could, at any time, be invaded, taken away, pulling me into a dark world of drug abuse, additional time added to my sentence should a passing officer discover the location of such drugs in my cell.

'What the hell were those bitches scoring that shit in my room for?' I screamed. I was furious. *How dare they?*

Paula rubbed my shoulder for a moment, lost for words. 'Who knows why people do the shit they do, Stacey,' she confirmed with a flat smile. She wasn't wrong.

\*\*\*

It was a shame most of the women here didn't know me or know what I was capable of, my thoughts often drifting to a far darker place than most of these girls could have known. Although no actual harm had been done, my space had been invaded, the resulting cocaine infused pillowcase I now had to lie my head on was enough to send my brain into constant overdrive. My baby did not deserve to become embroiled with substance abuse so early, its life far more important than my own.

It was also a shame for those women involved that I worked in the canteen. Drugs were seemingly easily brought into the prison via this unassuming location. The staff either turned a blind eye or turned a profit from the continued demands of those unable to fend for themselves, the need for oblivion overtaking rational thought. I hadn't initially taken much notice of such goings-on, my inner turmoil meaning more to me than what was happening around me. Yet, after my cell was inadvertently turned into a drugs den, I couldn't let it go. There is always something going on in prison, comings and goings, people in and out of the kitchen and canteen areas, prison staff doing their best to maintain order. So, of course, it was easy for me to spend time in the storeroom alone, my job conveniently meaning I was exactly where I was meant to be — nothing out of the ordinary, nothing to see here, thank you very much.

Nobody even noticed when I stood quietly crushing a piece of broken glass into tiny particles in a mortar dish, ensuring they were small enough to mix with the readily available drugs packets now sitting hidden inside a large container of flour, waiting for its next customer, its next victim. I was meant to be counting the number of potted noodles, packets of dried soup, biscuits, tea, coffee and such, ready for a stock refresh the following day. I was grateful I knew where the canteen girls kept their stash, my disinterest in such surroundings ensuring I now knew precisely what to do. A large container of white flour had become the perfect hiding place. Only the canteen workers and kitchen staff were allowed in here, and, as far as I was concerned, I was doing them a favour, helping them turn their pathetic lives around for the good of everyone.

I want to claim that I planned it very well, yet even I was somewhat shocked at how easily my plan worked. The following day resulted in several women being rushed to the medical bay with bleeding nostrils and throats that were dangerously shredded by the absorption of glass fragments, including the very addicts who had intruded on my room. There was an internal investigation, of course, Governor Barrington doing all he could to refute claims of dangerous drug substances being smuggled into Blackwood, potentially deemed fatal, a bad batch the cause of much trouble for all. Drug abuse is rife in prison, always has been, probably always will be.

Unfortunately, the consequences of such goings-on are of little value to the outside world. This was no national news story. The general public did not care much for people like us. As long as we were out of commission, out of sight and out of mind, they were happy to leave us to rot. We could overdose all day long if we wanted for all they cared. It would mean far fewer criminals for taxpayers' money to support.

Of course, news spread quickly that a recently smuggled drugs stash had been tampered with, not just throughout my unit but the entire prison. The women involved in bringing the drugs into the place were beaten up, the main culprit almost beaten to death. Still, I couldn't help such things. If these people insisted on ensnaring themselves with substance abuse activity, no matter what format it presented, who was I to discriminate? I was thankful no one could prove what I'd done, my deliberately maintained quiet persona meaning I was overlooked by those seeking revenge. The incident in my cell had been dealt with, thankfully. None of the women were now able to link me back to anything that subsequently happened thereafter.

# 14

It must have been the stress of being in prison that caused my baby undue suffering because, at just thirty-four weeks pregnant, I began showing signs that I was going into labour. Initially, it was little more than a twinge, and I brushed it off, nothing more than indigestion, a cramp, probably just Braxton Hicks. But I lay in my bed at two o'clock one morning with a worrying feeling I couldn't shake. It was too soon. My child required more time to finish growing. The fact I was still eating very little, surviving on pot noodles Paula would insist I buy from the canteen to keep in our cell, purely because I was too self-absorbed in my private turmoil to eat a proper meal, meant I now worried I'd brought about an incredibly serious problem.

Was the baby coming early a punishment? The poor thing miraculously survived on the little nourishment I'd allowed, the exasperated prison nurses constantly providing me with supplements; folic acid, iron tablets I was forced to consume daily before going back to my unit, along with knowing looks of disgust they failed to hide. They did not imagine me fit to be a mother, and to be honest, neither did I.

I still hadn't been transferred to the mother and baby

unit, this unfortunate truth resulting from underfunding, understaffing. They said I still had plenty of time yet, a space becoming available within the next couple of weeks. Paula had been looking after me well, despite my continued inability to connect with a single word she said. I was glad she was here now, grateful I wasn't on my own, our cell door locked, nothing but a panic button by the door for company. Should I get her to press the thing? Would that create unnecessary mania?

I lay on my side, staring at the opposite wall, counting between contractions that seemed to be getting closer together. It felt like the most horrific period pain I'd ever encountered, pressing my insides together remorselessly, mocking the fact I hadn't looked after myself well at all. When my waters broke, I knew this was no false alarm.

Terrified, I jumped out of bed, landing on the floor with an unceremonious thud. She'd given me the bottom bunk, my constant middle of the night toilet trips to the corner of the room slightly irritating to us both. I now stood hovering like a wounded dog, unsure what the hell to do next.

'Stacey, are you okay?' she asked groggily, turning over to a vague shape of my featureless face next to hers in the darkness.

'I either wet myself, or my waters just broke,' I muttered, clinging onto my damp pyjamas as if I was still trying to figure it all out.

'Shit,' Paula scrambled out of bed, draping a warm arm around my shoulder. For the first time since my arrival, I was grateful for her company, thankful she was here. She swiftly pressed the alarm button, a resulting screeching sound echoing into the unit violently, waking the other inmates, their yells of irritation reaching my ears with force. Paula gave me her dressing gown, along with soothing words that failed to make contact entirely.

I had worried in secret about giving birth for months. With nobody to speak to about it, my mum wanting nothing to do with me, my only sibling dead and my friends long gone. I assumed I would be able to discuss my worries with the other new mums in the mother and baby unit at some point, heed their support, take their well-meaning advice. I'd completely forgotten Paula was also a mother, able to offer well-placed support, should I ask for it, my unwillingness to connect with anyone forcing my resulting turmoil to fester in silence. There was much banging on doors now, women yelling through the narrow-sealed windows of their closed doors. *What was happening? Who was hurt?* I was quite relieved when the door opened, and two night officers came in to rescue me.

I was taken to the medical bay, the voice of Paula behind me doing nothing to actually reassure me, my brain exploding with all kinds of fears I couldn't dislodge no matter how hard I tried. *What if the baby was in distress? What if it died? What if I died?* Was all of this my goddamned fault? I couldn't get the idea out of my head that, whatever happened tonight, it was all down to me, nothing more than I deserved.

The nurses were relatively good, I guess, the seemingly calm prison midwife even better. It was okay, they said. A thirty-four-week birth was not uncommon. But I still had six weeks to go, maybe longer, my body knowing something was wrong, my brain yelling at me violently from a place I didn't want to be. For the first time since my arrest, I thought seriously about my son or daughter, about to make an unexpected appearance into this volatile world. I had spent the last six months feeling sorry for myself, my world all but gone, my sanity taken along with it. My growing belly had felt little more than an inconvenience, something

106

to play on when I wanted to get out of doing much at all, my baby brain blamed for my imploding ignorance and low mood. It was a reason to escape to the medical bay when the overbearing company of the other inmates became too much. Now, I remembered with a jolt that this was an actual child, a human being with needs I didn't entirely feel I could meet.

I was slowly unravelling, my once prized steady focus now replaced with mixed emotions and panic. With each new contraction, my brain screamed at me I was about to make a huge mistake, my breathing matching the pace of my racing heart. I couldn't be anyone's mum. I could barely deal with my own emotions.

'Miss Adams, you have to calm down. This baby is coming whether you like it or not.' The midwife was trying to reassure me, failing, everything about me seemingly hell-bent on causing mayhem.

'But it's too early,' I yelled, my entire body trembling, the gas and air they'd given me thankfully doing its job well. It *was* too early. We all knew it. I wanted them to stop my baby from being born. I wanted them to stop everything.

*** 

Ten and a half gruelling hours later, I was lying in the medical bay, exhausted, my body feeling as if it had just experienced the most bizarre thing that could possibly happen to any human being. I was holding my child in my arms, my son, his tiny fingers curled around mine, his fragile face as beautiful as anything I'd ever seen. I'd honestly never experienced anything in my entire life as unique as the feeling that enveloped me now. He was premature, tiny, no hair, no eyelashes, barely any concept of where he was, but absolutely perfect in every detail.

I have heard about the profound love a mother has for her child in those early moments after birth, read articles about such matters, even rolled my eyes on the odd occasion. That all-consuming moment a new mum sees her child for the very first time and knows, without a shadow of a doubt, she has more love for this one human than anyone could ever imagine. After neglecting myself for months, cutting my wrists for poorly determined attention that wasn't forthcoming, and all but starving myself in a futile bid to be noticed, I now realised my one true purpose on earth — to be a mum to this tiny, incredible bundle in my arms. It was overwhelming.

At just over five pounds in weight, my son, who I named Elijah, would require a short incubation period, his fragile lungs not yet fully developed to breathe unaided, additional support needed. When the midwife carefully took him from my arms, still cooing over the name I'd given him, I could have screamed. What if they took him away and refused to give him back to me? What if, after everything I'd done recently, they presumed me incapable of even *being* a mother? It was ironic considering, only yesterday, I assumed I wouldn't have been all that concerned by such a concept.

'What are you doing?' I yelled, my eyes welling with tears I did not expect to sting so painfully, a profound love I did not expect to experience so forcefully.

'It's okay, don't worry. He's in safe hands. Nobody is taking him away.' The nurse sounded slightly irritated by my outburst, although she was probably used to such things, such accusations.

Despite desperately wanting to, I didn't believe a word she said, a sudden urge to protect my baby coming from nowhere. I'd heard much talk in this place of premature babies dying in prison due to lack of support, lack of ability, or both. I assumed it was all scaremongering, designed to piss me off, until now.

'Then where are you taking him?' I screamed as a total stranger placed my child inside a tiny clear-sided box.

'The NICU at Georgesmith Hospital.' Shit. The Neonatal Intensive Care Unit was miles away. I couldn't be separated from Elijah, not now. He needed me. It was entirely ironic. Only a few hours ago, I was quite happy to pretend he didn't exist. *What the hell was wrong with me?* I was given a sympathetic look, something in the nurse's eyes telling me she understood my suffering and that she had seen too many similar reactions previous to mine. 'It's okay. You're going with him, Miss Adams, don't worry.'

I swallowed hard, thankful, grateful that this place wasn't about to separate me from my child so rapidly. We needed to get to know each other. I also presumed they fully appreciated this baby needed his mother's warmth, his mother's milk. It was entirely irrelevant that my milk hadn't yet made an appearance, my body not prepared for such a swift arrival. The truth was, he needed me. I needed *him*.

Elijah was perfect, not a single blemish on him. Apart from having little in the way of developed hair follicles, his body covered in downy lanugo fuzz, every feature of my child had formed faultlessly. It was quite a miracle. I wanted to lie here and stare at him for hours, absorb his scent, lose myself in the little sounds his lips made as they slapped together quietly. As it was, he was swiftly wrapped in a nappy far too big for him, his little legs nothing more than delicate sticks that stuck out at an angle on either side, his naked body laid in an oversized, somewhat scratchy, prison blanket to help keep him warm. I had nothing for him yet, still believing that six weeks would be enough time to gather the baby garments and items I wasn't aware he'd need. I could still hear Paula's words now.

I was completely powerless as they ambled around me, my needs of far less importance than the innocent child in their care. By the time we arrived at the hospital, it was late afternoon, my private room made less so by the permanent intrusion of a prison officer by the door, handcuffs clicked over my wrists whenever I needed to use the goddamned toilet. They didn't trust me, of course. To them, I was nothing more than a convicted killer requiring continued supervision. They certainly did not wish to take responsibility for that indignant truth, should I try to escape. Yet, escape was the last thing on my mind.

My son was kept in the NICU for just under three weeks until he was finally brought to me in the arms of a stranger, her stark uniform the only premise that she had any authority over me at all. I'd been allowed regular time with him, thank God, sitting staring for hours at his tiny features behind the toughened glass keeping him warm, keeping him alive. The only thing I wanted was to hold my little boy. Now, thankfully, his lungs were stronger, the nurse said. He'd responded well to the oxygen they kept him on, his little body more than capable of dealing with life by itself. We sat together on a hospital bed, my arms wrapped carefully around his still tiny body, my love more profound than anything I'd ever known. He was dressed in a tiny pale blue baby-grow, buttoned to his neck, even the smallest of newborn nappies still too big for his delicate frame.

I was utterly obsessed with my son. It was a strange realisation. This was not the fatal obsession I'd developed for a man belonging to another woman. Neither did it in any way feel the same as the love I still held firm for my parents. No. This love was entirely different. Bizarre, incredible. I thought of my mum. Had she felt this same love for me when I was born? If so, then why the hell didn't she feel it now? I knew she would absolutely adore her youngest grandchild. I wondered if someone had informed her that he was here. Maybe she would want to come and see him? See us both?

I stroked trembling fingertips across Elijah's soft cheek, Jason on my mind, his son finally in my possession. What would he have thought of his youngest child? Would Eva have doted on her little brother? Would she have proudly shown him off to all who encountered them together? I thought about Emma for a moment, her once smiling face popping into my mind with a simple blink of a tear-filled eye. A sister no longer able to share my news. My incredible, beautiful news. Aunty Emma. That is what she would have been called. Elijah would have loved her, and she would have loved him. I closed my eyes. I couldn't imagine ever being without my son. I hoped no one would dare take him away from me. I dreaded to think what such actions might unexpectedly provoke.

# 15

It was a throwaway concept that saw me unable to shake the despicable idea that those now in charge of my life might deem me too unstable to care for my own child. I was certainly not expecting to be given just four days with Elijah before the authorities stepped in, removing him from my care forever. We had woken up together, happy, content, my son and I now in the potential safety of the prison's mum and baby unit, his health in good order, my heart swelling with pride I never expected to experience. My hospital bed required for some other new mum who probably didn't pose such an imagined threat as I did. It was okay. The sun was shining, a good day to be had by all, my mind lighter than it had been for quite some months.

So, when Governor Barrington came into my room, accompanied by two stiffened women with nametags hanging from threads around their necks, I was not expecting my morning to change so rapidly. Their mannerisms certainly did not provide me with a good feeling, yet I couldn't have known what was about to happen. Instinctively I scooped my baby into my arms, holding him against my chest, keeping him close, my once assumed good mood slowly ebbing away.

'Can I help you?' I asked, as if this thing was in any

way under *my* control.

'I'm sorry, Miss Adams,' the governor spoke softly, his voice as tight as the shirt around his throat, his balding head shimmering with nervous anxiety he tried and failed to hide. 'May I introduce Miss Porter and Mrs Davidson from social services.'

*Social services?* Why were social services getting involved? These people only got involved in child welfare when they wanted to take them away, proclaiming a mother unfit, nothing more than damaged goods.

'I don't understand,' I muttered. Elijah stirred in my arms as if he too was aware of the sudden change in atmospheric pressure.

'We don't wish for any of this to be uncomfortable for you,' the older female of the two told me. What precisely did they believe might be uncomfortable? What was she trying to say? 'But I'm afraid we need to remove Elijah from your current care. It's for his protection.'

I could not believe what I was hearing. 'What... what do you mean?' I muttered, stuttering slightly, my voice emerging somewhat strangled as if they had unwittingly removed my vocal cords in the process of making such a declaration. 'Protection, how?' I was scanning the faces in front of me, my frightened eyes darting between three potential monsters, nothing more than grotesque fat pigs who honestly believed *I* was the big bad wolf. I was far too terrified to ask questions for fear of answers that might never come.

'You didn't exactly look after yourself very well during your pregnancy,' the stranger continued to offer words of inconsequence. 'It was flagged with us a few months ago and kept on file to see if things improved. However, I'm afraid your son has now been placed in the at-risk file.'

*At-risk?* What the hell were they saying? He is not at

any risk from anyone, especially *me*. I love him. *I need him.* I stepped backwards, automatically recoiling from these people who knew nothing about me, nothing about the unconditional love I'd developed for my precious baby boy.

'What does *that* mean?' I managed to stutter, anger bubbling by the notion that I was now almost rendered speechless by these overbearing freaks. Powerless, it seemed, to change a damned thing.

'It means we need to place Elijah with foster carers in the short term, with the possibility of permanent adoption moving forward. Due to the duration of your sentence, your current state of mind, and your recent actions, we feel it's in your son's best interest —'

'*No!*' I screamed, not caring that I'd cut the woman off mid-sentence, the reality of my situation hitting home too fast. *Recent actions? What the fuck?* I thought of all the days I'd refused food, cutting myself in some vague, pathetic attempt to get noticed. Now, ironically, all I wanted was a nice cup of tea, a bowl of pasta with a cheesy sauce, maybe an apple, and to care for my child correctly, lovingly, left alone to figure this thing out in peace. Surely they could see that? They couldn't have been talking about the murders. I was already being punished for those. Elijah wasn't even born back then, not even a consideration in my mind. I certainly couldn't have known how much I was going to love him. They couldn't punish me twice, surely?

The older of the two females stepped forward, her visitor tag swinging from her neck like a noose that I felt she was about to hang me with. *Miss* Porter. Fitting. Her name was as pointed as her features. I visualised the woman going home to several cats, an ice-cold flat matching the ice-cold look on her iron-clad face as she darted anxious eyes towards my son, then to me. I flashed worried eyes of my own towards the governor, hoping he would see my desperation, help me, support me, give an actual shit.

I always knew, of course, that I wouldn't be able to keep my baby in this place forever. Eighteen months was seemingly the average age where the authorities would take him anyway. I assumed they now felt they were stepping up the timeframe, stepping in early, stepping on my toes. I felt sick. Never in my life had I felt such a pain at the idea of loss. Even the non-existent look on the face of my dead lover had not created such a volatile reaction as the one I was about to display now.

I rounded the bed, Elijah still asleep, miraculously unaffected by his mother's rising blood pressure, my arms tightening around his tiny body in automatic maternal response. They would need to prise him from my cold dead grip if they assumed they would be able to take him from me now, the need to protect my son stronger than anything I'd felt before in my life. For the first time, I understood the suffering my mum must have experienced at the sudden loss of her eldest daughter, her youngest undertaking the most unimaginable act of cruelly-planned vicious murder. She had lost both daughters, by all accounts. One to an untimely, unimaginable death and the other to a twisted path she could never contemplate being able to follow.

'Please,' I pleaded, picking a butter knife from the bed before I realised what I was doing. 'Don't do this.' I held the knife in front of me, no actual intention of using it, yet quite capable of inflicting pain should I be required to defend myself or my son. It did me no favours at all, of course, simply enforcing the notion that I wasn't entirely secure in either mind or body.

Governor Barrington stepped forward, his hands outstretched. It was a situation he wasn't expecting to arise so swiftly, hoping now to diffuse this moment with ease. 'Miss Adams, this is not the way to do things,' he told me, his firm tone matching the taut stance of my unfaltering presence. 'Give me the knife.' He truly believed that I was the deranged psychopath my file had already claimed. I could see it in his eyes. No wonder he looked so concerned. Did these people assume I'd willingly stab my baby? Stab them? Stab myself? All I wanted was for them to leave us alone.

'Give me the knife. *Now*,' he repeated, louder when I failed to acknowledge him, gesturing with his waving fingers for me to hand him the weapon calmly. I was meant to be spreading margarine on a piece of toast with it. Nothing more. *Now, look what they'd made me do!* The two women stood hovering to one side of the room, staring at Elijah as if they needed to snatch him away before he was injured in some horrific unprecedented crossfire. *I would never harm my baby.* He was my entire world now. He was all I had left.

'I can't,' I was crying now, tears already stinging my eyes at the idea of losing my recently acquired son. They threatened to land like acid on my sleeping child, the knife trembling in my grip, my suffering apparent to all.

'You *need* to do this, Adams. You have no choice.' Governor Barrington was still gesturing his hands towards me to give him the knife. I automatically swung it towards him violently, slicing the air between us in bitter defiance. He lunged backwards, sucking in his belly and arching his spine as if I was intending on slicing him wide open, killing him where he stood. *As if I'd do that?*

'Get away from us,' I yelled, drawing unwanted attention now from the other mum's in the unit who had arrived to see what was going on. *Nosy bitches.*

'Miss Adams, please,' the governor commanded, more uniformed staff now appearing in the doorway behind us, all three officers ready to tackle me to the floor as and when

116

required. I wasn't helping myself at all or the cause I felt I was defending, confirming to these people the sad truth they assumed they already knew about me.

I was sobbing. I couldn't help it. Elijah began to stir, his cries ready to erupt with the sound of my own. All he needed was his bottle, probably a change of nappy, a cuddle. Neither of us needed this stress. '*Please*, Mr Barrington. Please, tell them it's okay. Tell them they don't need to do this.'

Mrs Davidson, the younger of the two women, now stepped forward. 'Miss Adams?' she called out to me softly. 'Stacey?'

I glanced towards her, the sound of my first name alien to me now, this place hell-bent on treating inmates like prison numbers instead of human beings. She smiled. I could see she was only trying to calm me down.

'You don't want Elijah to get hurt, do you?' she asked calmly.

I shook my head. 'Of course not,' I snapped. 'I love him.' *Why could these idiots not see that?*

'Then do the right thing for your son,' she continued, holding her hands towards him as if the knife in my grip was nothing more than a soft toy, capable of bending in on itself innocently should I consider the idea of plunging it towards her.

She was right, of course. I needed to put Elijah's needs way ahead of my own. I glanced down at my stirring baby, one eye already open, a bright blue pupil looking up at me from the security of my loving embrace. It felt as if he was telling me to behave myself, motherhood far more critical than a selfish need for personal satisfaction. His needs came first, would always come first now. My own no longer mattered.

I let out a single scream, one last-ditch attempt to shake

off this impossible situation, to force them to leave us alone, leave my room. Mrs Davidson stepped towards the bed, closer to me than she probably should have been, obliviously unappreciative of my delicate situation. I assumed I wasn't her first rodeo, my suffering of no genuine concern to her. Governor Barrington was about to interject, but she raised a steady hand towards him, her apparent training in such matters confirmation that she had been in this situation far too many times before.

'I can't,' I muttered again, more to myself than those around me, the knife still in my grip, binding itself to my knuckles with force, my baby attached to my arms as if I might not be able to breathe without him.

'You have to,' she whispered, nothing more required in her tone. She placed two steady hands around my boy and gently scooped Elijah from my trembling arms, glancing at me for a moment, a look of pity lingering in her dull eyes. 'He *will* be okay. You have my word,' she confirmed as she cradled my fragile son in her arms. She stepped away, allowing the officers to race in, grapple the knife from my hands, grab my shoulders, forcing me to the floor. The whole thing happened so quickly I barely had time to react.

'Okay, okay,' Governor Barrington stepped in authoritatively as my body was lifted from the floor, firm hands already restraining any probable attempt to lunge forward or do anything stupider than I'd already managed. 'Everything is under control.' He glared at me, his tone as flat as I'd ever heard it. What did he *really* think of me, behind those cold black eyes of his?

With my lip quivering and eyes watering, I had little choice but to watch as people took my baby away from me, their presence in my room unnecessary, nothing more than a passing moment in time now gone. I caught a brief glimpse of the stranger holding my child as she retreated into the hallway, my screams going unheeded and unnoticed by all.

'Where are you taking him?' I blurted towards Governor Barrington as he stood in the doorframe, my body still held firm by stiffened prison security staff, my voice like jelly within their unrelenting grasp.

'Your mum has agreed to care for him in the short term,' he confirmed, his face a telling calamity he was trying to understand my pain, despite there being nothing he could do about the situation anyway. It was all down to me — my fault this was happening, my fault I was in this position at all. I physically felt my body crumble, the idea of my son being in the care of my parents seemingly able to diffuse an otherwise impossible situation. The very thought that complete strangers might raise him terrified me. At least, with my parents, he would be with his family, with his big sister.

I allowed my body to buckle, my legs turning to mush as the prison officers held me aloft. The last thing either of us needed was for me to face-plant the floor unexpectedly. I have no idea if it was the sheer shock of losing my baby so quickly or the idea of him being in the care of my family, but, in the moment it took for them to walk the length of the corridor towards a world awaiting my son outside, something inside my world collapsed. Every thought I ever had seemed to converge in that single instant, my brain imploding with impossible emotions no human being should ever be forced to experience. For just under eight months, my baby had been living inside me, my responsibility, my commitment. Now, he was gone, everything I needed to become a better person, dislodging my sanity in that one simple act. Of course, I wasn't the first mother that this had happened to, and I knew I wouldn't be the last. But it hit me hard, all the same.

119

I was alone again now, this place destined to devour me entirely, my son forced to grow up without me to cherish and support his continued development. I sobbed my baby's name over and over, my now limp body dragged from the mother and baby unit as if I was a piece of discarded laundry no longer required. I was thrown back into isolation, my actions today yet again bringing forth a warning of disciplinary action, the loss of my child seemingly not enough of a punishment for them. I was deemed unstable — everything I had done since my arrival was now responsible for the unfortunate events unfolding. The knife I'd wielded meant I was to be kept under strict supervision for the duration of my stay at Her Majesty's pleasure. What an utter travesty. What a stupid idiot I was.

# 16

I was in isolation for three days to cool down, calm down — find a way to deal with my rapidly unravelling emotions while those in charge took a painful amount of time to decide what was best to do with me. As a convicted double-murderer, they deemed me no longer able to hide behind the guise of pregnancy, motherhood no longer an issue, my mental instability still in question. Yet, nobody was able to conclude anything about the state of my mind beyond a vague notion of duty the governor appeared unconcerned was any of his actual business.

After a self-absorbed, uncomfortable stint in a locked cell with nothing for company but painful images of my beautiful innocent baby boy, forced to wallow in grief alone, I was once again thrown to the wolves, transferred into general population, no further protection given to the fragile oddity in their midst. It was a typical implication of what this place was like — my cell no longer my own, already given to a new inmate in my absence. Paula could now turn her attention to someone far less troublesome than I, much to her probable appeasement. I'm sure she must have been happy by such a revelation, yet I couldn't help feeling that I'd been cast aside, prison life as inconsistent as I'd always imagined. I was now required to share a twelve-foot cell with some other unsuspecting inmate. *Jesus Christ*. My earlier inability to connect with any of these women meant I was at the mercy of their wrath, my presence not fully acknowledged by anyone in this place at all.

To add insult to injury, nobody considered providing me with any updates regarding Elijah either. His overall health and welfare were something they all felt was no longer my concern. I visualised him crying into the night for a mother far away, his needs left unmet by a doting grandmother doing what she believed was her utmost best. I thought about Eva, who, like my son, was also alone in the world. Both their mothers long gone, brought about by a twisted act I had shown no remorse or acknowledgement of, their father taken from them savagely, wrongly. Yet, what was the point in dredging up the past, digging dirt on things I could never put right? If I were to tell them all how sorry I was, what would that achieve? It certainly wouldn't bring them back. The authorities had all but washed their hands of me now, leaving me to my own devices.

I found myself sharing a room with a gay woman called Braunie — her real name, Lesley Braun. She was thirty-two, looked more like a bloke of fifty, didn't like me very much, the permanent scowl on her face every time she looked at me, simply confirming she didn't give a *shit*. It did not take her long to tell me how she felt. In fact, the first day I arrived back on the unit consisted of much pushing, spitting, tossing my belongings into one corner because she didn't want me cluttering up *her* space. Without Paula's unappreciated support, I felt as if I was back at school, the playground bullies left to their rueful devices. Braunie probably fancied me, knew she didn't stand a chance, hated the concept.

She was in a "relationship" with Katelyn Williams, a slightly less-looking lesbian with a fetish for tattoos. Plenty of them. Especially on the oversized body of Braunie, their makeshift ink infused decorations often requiring urgent medical intervention. She had purposefully shaved her hair on one side, which of course, displayed her tattooed skull proudly, leaving the other side to grow long, as if to confirm to the world that she was still a woman, yet didn't "do" men, so they should fuck off and leave her alone — just in case they got the wrong idea.

It was an uncomfortable situation to find myself in, often slung out of my bed into the corridor whenever the two of them wanted intimate times together I wasn't invited to be a part of. *Thank God.* Those types of visions were the last thing I needed in my head. It was quite fitting I'd spent an entire six months in this place trying to ignore women who weren't all that bad, now to find myself in the profound company of these two. I was in a seriously dark place — too discomposed to notice, too busy decomposing to do anything about the bullying ways of Braunie and her followers. They didn't know why I was here or what I was capable of when pushed. None of them did. These unfortunate women believed I'd been transferred to this unit after losing my young baby to the care system, just some poor sap who'd found herself swallowed by the world and his dog — a common occurrence, nothing out of the ordinary. They probably thought I was scum. I was beginning to believe them.

I spent an entire week musing over Elijah's absence, everyone in this place bored of my unrelenting whining already. I asked the officers several times if they could find out for me, contact my mum, her old number no longer in commission. I knew they would have her new details somewhere, probably in a file with a note confirming her number should be kept far away from my prying eyes, never to be disclosed.

I felt that I had nothing left to live for now, so I stopped eating entirely, the resulting hunger strike I'd brought forth, leaving my body weakened beyond reasonable explanation. I went to bed every night with an uncomfortable pain in my gut that twisted knots around my internal organs, yet was too depressed and desperate to do anything about it.

I had always associated food with good feelings, happiness, comfort. I had nothing now to be happy or comforted about, my body still acclimatising to its post-pregnancy state. Although the last thing it needed was more stress, my brain was unable and unwilling to give a shit. It was ironic the prison staff did not seem to care either. My welfare was left entirely in my hands. If I didn't want to eat, I would go hungry. It was as simple as that.

I endured uncomfortable hunger for almost two weeks before stealing Katelyn's electric razor and shaving off every last inch of my hair, including my eyebrows, for reasons I couldn't fathom. I hated what I saw when I looked in the mirror, the stranger glaring back at me merely someone I didn't even know. Dark hair, dark eyes, a steadily decaying soul too diabolical in appearance for normal existence — nothing left of the woman I once was, nothing of my soul remaining intact.

I was found on the floor of my cell by Braunie, my once prized hair now gone, forgotten, lying in the sink, blocking the plughole, scattered across the floor around me in mocked surprise. It was my last plea for help — a pursuit for attention I did not deserve, my baby the only thing capable of keeping me sane enough to survive this hell. I did not assume prison life would be ideal for an adult, let alone a child, but I did at least expect to have a little more time with him. Our bond was only just forming, the love I had for him developing with each moment I looked into his beautiful deep blue eyes.

I don't even recall Braunie picking me up from the cold floor or sitting me on the bed, asking if I was okay, sounding concerned, acting as if she actually *cared*. Oh, the irony. It was as if, somewhere deep inside, someone had already turned out the light on my life, closed the door, threw away the key. I had already died, already left this building and those twenty-four long years behind me. As it was, Braunie was the one person who came to my aid, carefully clearing away unwanted hair from our cell, my shaven features telling of a woman finally tipped over that jagged edge. Although my cellmate had openly displayed a profound dislike for me, it was somewhat odd that she was now showing genuine concern, her previously unseen calming manner going unnoticed as I sat staring at a greying wall, nothing of my grey matter seemingly left intact.

It was as if the world had slipped into slow motion, taking my soul for a joy ride, my brain unable to understand anything of what was going on around me, my mental health declining rapidly. I just kept telling Braunie over and over I needed my baby, whispering his name into the void of the room towards ears I felt could do nothing about the situation even if they wanted to. I simply needed to ensure my boy was okay, safe. I must have repeated myself several times, the same words, again and again, my emotions all but destroyed with the loss of my once-cherished hair.

'I need to know that Elijah is okay,' I muttered, my focus on nothing now but him, my own needs hardly important, hardly deserving of anyone's attention. When Braunie eventually retreated into the corridor to get help, I was already waiting to die, in this room, alone. Nothing meant anything to me without my son's unwavering love.

\*\*\*

I do not recall how I managed to get from my cell with Braunie sitting by my side, to a high-backed chair in Governor Barrington's office. My sudden appearance in his private space meant something had gone seriously wrong in my unstable absence. How else would I warrant such personal attention from the man in charge? I hadn't *asked* to see him, so I assumed my presence here must have been requested on my behalf. He was sitting behind his imposing desk, as always, several brightly lit monitors on the wall behind him shining artificial light off his balding head.

Many different prison locations flickered in soft focus — innocent security cameras set to monitor not so innocent women, study our composure, confirm our compliance. He was speaking to me, but I wasn't listening. Either that or I no longer held the capacity to understand the English language. The last time we'd spoken, the man had savagely, *brutally*, taken my child away. It wasn't something I was likely to forget easily. It certainly wasn't something I was about to forgive. He had nothing to say that I wanted to hear now. When he mentioned my mum, however, my attention was immediately caught.

'Would that help?' he asked, his eyes on mine, my inability to function rendering me entirely speechless, powerless to prevent my destruction. Would *what* help? What had I missed? I glanced up, my blank eyes barely able to absorb my surroundings, my mind scarcely able to understand words aimed in my direction. All I needed was to allow an unexpected dribble to escape the corner of my mouth, and the governor's work here would be complete. He would have broken me completely. Well done, Mr Barrington.

Noticing my profound absence, the governor sighed, rising from his desk to pour me a cup of much-needed coffee from his personal machine in the corner of the room.

He handed it to me, seemingly as surprised as I was by how shaky my hands had become. I blinked several times, my brain quite unable to focus on anything around me, this poor man included.

'Did you hear me, Adams?' he repeated as I took an unsteady sip of black, rich, sugarless coffee that tasted bitter against my tongue. It was the first thing that had passed my lips in several days — *the only thing*, in fact. I gagged, the warm liquid slightly alien to my senses, my gut already becoming a shrunken, sludgy mess. I was surprised just how quickly the human body begins the process of shutting down when abused. Something had changed, deep inside me. I could feel it. Yet, unfortunately, it was not something I was fully able to understand. I wondered if Governor Barrington could tell I was suffering?

I shook my head. 'I'm not feeling very well,' I confessed, the last two weeks bringing me firmly to my knees.

The governor handed me a tissue that I took from him without hesitation, wiping escaping coffee from my cracked, sore lips. I must have looked a terrible state — no hair, pale skin, something that resembled eyeballs sunken into a hollow, seriously damaged skull.

'I *said*, I could speak to your mum for you. See if she would be willing to bring your son in to see you. So you can see for yourself that he's in safe hands.' The governor was looking at me patiently, waiting for a response.

I couldn't believe what I was hearing. *Was* I hearing this correctly? 'You would do that for me?' *Would he do that for me?*

The governor nodded. 'But I can't promise she will agree to my request. Of course, I can explain your current mental and physical health. Ask her the question. But other than that, the decision will be entirely hers.' He cupped his hands together, resting his chin against his closed knuckles.

I nodded, appreciating the governor's help, my mouth curling into a strange little smile that probably felt far better than it looked. The only thing I heard at that moment was that the governor was willing to ask my mum to come in. *To bring Elijah to see me.*

'Yes. Yes, please,' I replied, stumbling over words that had become alien to me, my mind making a desperate attempt to shift back into sharp focus, failing miserably.

Governor Barrington nodded, allowed me to finish my coffee, making small talk about how I was coping in general population. All the time, his eyes remained on mine, certain I was slowly losing the plot. He wasn't wrong. In his own way, I sensed he cared about the women in his care, this prison his responsibility, everything that happened inside these walls his burden, unfortunately for him. Poor sod.

# 17

It was painful waiting to hear the news that my mum might actually be willing to come and see me, her last words still lingering in my mind that I *did not know the meaning of love*. Well, I certainly did now. The birth of my son had verified that truth with violent, if not slightly painful, clarity. I wanted to tell her as much, express my sorrow for events complete, expel both our suffering, once and for all. Yet it was five agonising weeks before I received confirmation I had a visit from her due the following day. I couldn't quite believe it. I looked horrendous, my once cherished hair nothing now but stubble that peppered my misshapen skull, my eyes dark with savage emotion no one in this place could possibly understand — thoughts of suicide that I never expected to contemplate, allowed to swill around my troubled brain most days, keeping unwanted eyes firmly planted on my every move.

I was eating again, but only because I knew I needed to stay alive long enough to see my baby boy, to hold him in my arms once more, to smell him, touch him. I had lost a lot of weight. My clothing hung from my frame as if my body was little more than a collection of broken coat hangers that struggled to hold my clothes in place. I did not expect my mum to appreciate the suffering I was going through. Had she known my duress, of course, she *would* have come to see me sooner, told me she loved me, apologised for her previous unkind words. Given me a hug.

I sat in the visitor lounge waiting for her arrival as if she'd left me waiting at the school gates. My legs shook uncontrollably with anticipation, my savagely chewed fingernails tapping the table in front of me, two mugs of hot chocolate poured as a peace offering, waiting to be consumed. She was bringing Elijah with her, my son probably already growing rapidly, filling out nicely, his once tiny features now matching that of a full-term healthy newborn. When the doors opened, and visitors began filtering in, I almost lost hope she would arrive at all. Everyone in this room was readily greeted by loved ones, old friends, passing acquaintances. I scanned faces young and old, terrified she might let me down, force me to cruelly suffer some more. Yet, Mum wouldn't do that, no matter how much she protested her hatred for me. She loved me too much. She always would.

When I saw her enter the open door, a brand-new pram in her possession, I almost cried with relief. I got to my feet too quickly, my bottom lip quivering, my hands held aloft for an embrace I wasn't confident I'd receive. I glanced between my mother and my son, two generations of Adams standing in front of me, my mum's stiffened tone giving nothing away of what she was feeling. I'd suffered much taunting for my surname over the years, our Adams family status something that created much amusement for many. Now, seeing my mum and my son together, I was glad to be part of the Adams family. It didn't matter how we looked to outsiders. We could all be freaks together.

As mum wheeled my son toward me, I glanced inside his pram, my eyes searching for confirmation that he existed at all. Elijah looked well. Dressed in a warm one-piece coat, covered in a fluffy blue and yellow blanket, a woollen hat on his beautiful head, my baby appeared the perfect image of health. His cheeks had a soft glow, his eyes closed. I automatically reached out to touch him, to feel his beautiful angelic face against my trembling fingertips.

'Please, do *not* disturb him,' Mum snapped, needing no further words of confirmation this was not going to be the tender motherly visit I'd hoped. I removed my hand swiftly, a blank look in my eyes I didn't quite know where to place.

'Mum? How are you?' It seemed fitting to ask about her welfare first, ask about dad, Eva, the current state of affairs in a world I was no longer a part of, before getting to the real crux of why she was here. My boy.

My mum didn't initially reply, instead choosing to take a seat opposite me, seemingly too preoccupied with her grandson to notice my presence at all. There was a tense moment between us. Mother and daughter, now estranged, a wall between us leaving me out in the bitter cold. When she finally brought herself to glance my way, the look on her face said it all as her eyes widened in shock. *What the hell have you done to yourself, Stacey?* It was an excellent, unspoken question I had no answer to.

'I took the liberty of getting us a drink. Hot chocolate. Sorry, they didn't have sprinkles.' I tried to laugh, picking up my cup with a hand that wouldn't stop shaking, glad the liquid wasn't too warm to potentially scold me. Mum knew I loved hot chocolate. It had been our thing since Emma and I were kids. I swallowed as a random memory of my sister filtered into my mind without warning.

'They said I should come. That you haven't been coping very well.' Mum glanced at me again, staring too long at my non-existent hair, before looking at the floor with blatant embarrassment. She omitted to add, *I can see you aren't coping at all*, instead choosing that moment to pick up her own hot chocolate and taking a sip that she took far too long to swallow.

'Thank you for stepping in and looking after Elijah for me.' I genuinely was thankful. I couldn't express that fact firmly enough. I hoped she believed me.

'I wasn't about to see my grandson go into care,' Mum snapped, this entire thing obviously taking its toll.

'It was hardly my fault —' I began, fury beginning to burn inside me for the fact that my baby had been snatched away so cruelly, so quickly. I stopped short of blaming the authorities, blaming my mum. It *was* my fault. Everyone knew it.

My mum glared at me for a moment, something behind her dull eyes I couldn't read. She hadn't smiled at me once since my incarceration here, months previous now. I feared I might one day forget what it looked like. Forget how it felt to receive the love and unconditional support from a mother I desperately needed. After all, isn't unconditional love something that mums are supposed to possess without question?

'How's Dad?' I asked, a casual remark entirely unfitting of this moment.

'What do *you* think?' Mum bit back. She was quite unable to refrain from expressing her turmoil and pure unadulterated hatred, a paper cup trembling in her hand — nothing else to do but drink the stuff before she spilt it down herself or threw it over me. It was evident she hadn't yet forgiven me.

'Sorry,' I muttered, no longer wanting to drink my hot chocolate anymore either, actually feeling quite nauseous by the idea. I couldn't think of any other words to say. I glanced at my baby, still asleep, his tiny hand peeking out from beneath his coverings, blue and yellow bunnies peppering his fragile body that obscured most of him from my gaze. 'May I —?'

'*No,*' Mum stepped in sharply, knowing what I was about to ask. 'He's asleep. It took me all morning to get him to go to sleep. The last thing I need is for you to disturb him now.' I had never heard my mum speak with such cold disdain. She sounded flat, no words leaving her mouth remotely reminiscent of the woman I had left behind on that seemingly innocent morning, the day Jason lay cold and dead on his hallway floor.

I nodded, trying to understand her suffering, failing. Elijah was my son. Surely I was entitled to a cuddle with my *own* child? I shifted uncomfortably on my chair, the entire room feeling overbearing, everyone else around us unaware of the private conversation behind them — their conversations mostly kept light, discussing family life, sentence durations, pending release dates, declarations of love. As it was, the visit I had received today was nothing how I'd imagined it to be, how I'd hoped.

Instead, this entire thing felt staged, as if my mum was here purely due to an obligation, a simple request made by the prison service on behalf of a woman they had been brutally forced to endure. She hadn't even asked how I was. I could understand her initial outrage, of course. The earlier shock of my unexpected crimes probably something she would have been utterly distraught by. But months had passed since then. She had been given plenty of time to calm down a little, surely. I was the one suffering now. Stuck in this hell, no freedom, no luxury, no chance of experiencing the love I urgently needed.

I narrowed my eyes, my mum's gaze everywhere else but on the daughter who *needed* her attention. She noticed the other inmates, officers and visitors, even smiled at one, looked out of the window, spent too long reading posters

133

dotted around the walls, tapped her wedding-ringed finger against the tabletop too loudly. She spent too much of her time looking at Elijah, adjusting his blanket, stroking his cheek. I wanted to shout, yell — tell her to pay attention to *me*. I was still in the room, waiting to be noticed. Yes, Emma might be dead, and yes, it might be my fault. But I was still alive. I still needed attention. *I was her fucking daughter, too.* I managed to stop short of clicking my fingers towards her expressionless face, shaking my head, rolling my eyes, shouting at her, demanding respect. Yet, it would not be appropriate. I didn't wish to tip her over the edge entirely.

'Say goodbye to your son, Stacey,' Mum offered suddenly, getting to her feet, my perturbed feelings remaining entirely unbroached between us.

'*Goodbye?* What do you mean?' I shot to mine, already unsteady, prepared to pass out at any given moment. An unassuming prison officer behind us spotted the sudden composure change as she walked towards us slowly, arms folded across her neatly ironed uniform. What was she waiting for? A Riot?

'I won't be coming back here again. I will not be bringing my grandson back into this place. It isn't good for the child.' Mum was serious. I panicked.

'No. Mum. Please. Don't say that. I know things are difficult between us at the moment —'

'*Difficult?* Stacey, are you kidding me?' Mum looked as if she wanted to laugh, the seriousness of the situation preventing such an inappropriate occurrence.

I shook my head. 'I can make things right —'

'*How?*' Mum actually yelled. 'How on Earth do you think you can *ever* make things right?' She was glaring at me, her eyes so cold, so unfeeling. It was unnerving.

The prison officer walked over to us. 'Everything okay here?' she asked, quite ready for the situation to take a volatile turn, prepared if required, to grapple me out of the room by the scruff of my neck. Mum nodded, offering her a smile that I was disgusted to confirm she hadn't felt I deserved. Why would a total stranger warrant more affection than her own *fucking* daughter?

'Everything's fine, sorry. I didn't mean to kick off.' Mum sat down firmly, tugging her top across her trousers. She did not look at me. The officer nodded, glancing my way before she walked away. I sat down too, my legs like jelly, my head nothing more than a damp sponge, soaking up this moment along with every emotion I'd been forced to experience in this place since my arrival, far longer than that, even. Why did my mother always have to make such a scene whenever she came to see me? *Why couldn't she just behave herself?*

'You have to come back,' I stated boldly. I needed my mum. *I needed my son.* I wished I could have expressed such a truth.

My mum shook her head. '*Why* do I have to come back, Stacey? After what you've done to our family, I have no idea why I'm here now.'

I wasn't entirely sure how to respond. I'd already expressed how sorry I was for everything that had happened. I think. I could do nothing more than that. I wasn't able to rewind time. *I wasn't Marty McFly.* 'Because I need to see my son,' I confirmed, not able to back down now, even if I wanted to.

'Then take a good look because it's going to be a very long time before you're given that privilege again.' Mum was deadly serious. I swallowed a lump.

'Please —'

My mum got to her feet, placing a quivering hand flat on the table for a moment, turning around swiftly as if she wanted to say something that she couldn't bring herself to mutter. She reached into her pocket and slammed a photograph on the table in front of me before simply walking away. It was of Elijah, asleep on the rug of my parents front room, in front of the fireplace. It was a beautiful image. Probably the only reminder of him I would have now. I could do nothing but sit and watch as she wheeled my still sleeping baby away from me, not a word having passed her lips at how any of this was affecting *me*. I presumed she didn't give a shit. She hadn't even said goodbye. It was not a comfortable revelation.

## 18

The uncomfortable, unimaginable image of my baby boy leaving the visitor lounge was more than I could bear. Next to the parents I genuinely assumed would forgive me at some point, he was the only connection left of my pathetic existence on this planet that might, by some miracle, have the power to save my life. Elijah was the *only* evidence left of a relationship I'd once shared with his dad, a man I honestly believed had loved me once. Now, I didn't know what to do for the best, Governor Barrington's innocent request for my mum's visit ending differently from how either of us could have imagined.

It took twelve hours after her unrequited visit for me to decide to end it all. I could not anticipate enduring a second longer in this hellhole than I had to without my boy, let alone two decades. He would be a grown man by the time I got out of here, no longer needing the mother he wouldn't know anyway — a woman who adored him beyond rational thinking. My parents might even place unwanted ideas into his impressionable head, thoughts of a mother unfit for purpose, feelings they might tell him I did not possess. I couldn't live with that idea. I couldn't fathom a world without the very child I'd wished and prayed for, for so long.

I stole a knife from the kitchen, my canteen duties upgraded to full kitchen staff once my baby was no longer an inconvenient fixture. How I managed to get the thing to my cell undetected, I have no idea, the entire exercise done on autopilot, without any presence of mind. I wasn't just going to cut my wrists for attention this time. I was going to stab myself to death, slice my throat from ear to ear, whatever I deemed necessary to get the job done. It was an idea that was far easier to consider in my head than in real life, the actuality of such a painful concept rendering me unable to directly inflict trauma onto my body so aggressively. I was quite certain that I wanted to die this time, really I was. But I couldn't bring myself to deliberately pierce an artery or slice through several layers of skin to the muscle and veins below. I wasn't a complete masochist. I stood in the middle of my cell, Braunie busy elsewhere with Katelyn, a sharp knife trembling at my irreproachable throat, entirely unable to do anything but stand hovering, close to tears, waiting for courage that was now altogether failing me.

Eventually, I admitted defeat, dropping the knife to the floor, deflated, my mind an unprecedented jumble of ideas that were left now to swim undeterred. My hands were shaking violently, my body wretched with a dark suffering that consumed me. I couldn't spend a lifetime in this place without the occasional visit from my son to cheer my subjacent mood swings. I couldn't anticipate having to get through every day, not knowing when he'd achieved his first word, his first step, his first day at school, his first girlfriend, first *boyfriend*.

I snatched the bedsheets from my bunk in a hurry, using the knife in my possession to cut the thing into haphazard strips that I twisted together carelessly — the idea of making a rope an easier concept in theory than it was to achieve. I wanted to remove the decision from my own hands entirely, by kicking a stool from under my weight and allowing nature to take its course. I had no concept of how to tie a noose, the idea of hanging myself never entering my mind until my mum expressed her repulsion quite nastily to my face. As it was, my subsequent suicide would be forever on her head. *Her* fault. She would have to explain it all to my son. Live with what *she* had done to *me*.

I tied a rough knot at one end, looping it around the heating pipes in the ceiling that I hoped would hold my weight, the other end tied off in a random circular configuration that only just fitted over my head. I was standing on Braunie's stool. The one she used for watching television whilst Katelyn happily stretched across the length of her bunk, arms draped over her semi-naked corpse. It would be quick. I hoped. My time on this earth shortly to end, my emotions and struggles all gone in the instant it would take to kick the fabric-covered box across the room.

I tugged my makeshift rope, half anticipating the impending crash to send prisoners and staff to my room, to uncover my actions before I'd completed my crazy mission, creating yet another mess that would see me, once again, back in isolation, on more charges. I hoped I could get this over with quickly, avoiding such an annoying result. Thankfully, the noose remained in place, even when I forced all my weight against the thing, tugging the makeshift rope with both hands. *Did I really want to do this?* No, of course not. I didn't *want* to die. I was thirty years old. I still had plenty of time to live my life. Yet, at the same time, I saw no other way out. No other possible end to this unmitigated nightmare I was now forced to endure. I couldn't live without my son or the love of the parents I needed more than anything in the world. It was a consideration I never assumed I'd ever feel. I had *always* been loved. It made my life and what had happened recently, a somewhat complex affair that had staged my ultimate undoing.

I closed my eyes, ready. I needed to stop thinking, just *do* it and do it now, before I changed my mind, before my weakness was allowed to spill out, to mock me, leave me crying on the floor like a sapless, pathetic weakling. I held my breath. I honestly don't know why. I have no idea what I assumed preventing air from entering my lungs would achieve other than invoke added panic I didn't need.

I said a private goodbye to the world in general, to my boy, to my parents, salty tears already falling as I stepped onto my tiptoes, ready to kick away the stool. It was rather unfortunate my brain decided to choose that very moment to turn me into a coward, preventing me from actually doing it, my legs unwilling to move an inch, frozen to the spot, mocking me. I wanted to scream, cry, yell for help I knew would never find me. I wanted someone else to kick the stool away for me. Take away my choices.

I took a deep breath. *Come on, Stacey, you can do this.* I closed my eyes, allowing a wayward foot to kick the stool across the floor before I gave up on the idea. The incoming weight around my neck felt odd, unexpected, as if this entire thing was happening to someone else. I realised too late that I'd forgotten to write a suicide note, explaining to my beloved son that I loved him so much and that I was so very sorry for *everything*. Still, I couldn't overthink that now, my throat already being strangled by the incoming pressure of my weight, the rope around my neck doing its job well. *Shit.* Yet, I wasn't dying, merely choking to death too slowly. I hadn't expected to suffer, the irony of that concept now ready to make me pay — my final punishment, my just desserts. I was a murderer, after all. I deserved to suffer.

I fully expected the upcoming fall to break my neck, end this thing once and for all, blank it all out, but the stool

I'd used was mere inches from the floor, a foot at most. There was no forthcoming fall to break my neck, the bloody thing too low to the ground to do anything other than strangle me slowly, painfully, as my body dangled haplessly. I wasn't anticipating to feel my limbs convulsing beneath me, my legs and arms jolting back and forth, my windpipe slowly being crushed, cutting off my air supply, blocking much-needed oxygen from my brain. My eyes were wide open, yet I could no longer see a damned thing, my surroundings slipping away with the little life I had left in my body, the air in my lungs expelling at speed.

I certainly wasn't expecting to feel frantic hands around my legs, lifting me up, screams of terrified voices next to my head. When someone removed the noose from my neck, relieving the pressure from my throat, I wasn't expecting *that* either. I was lying on the floor, gagging violently, all but devoid of oxygen, ready to pass out, ready to die. I was colder than I'd ever felt in my life, my breath softly slipping away. If this was the end, I was happy to embrace it — glad to say goodbye to a world that had been nothing but cruel and unfair to me. I closed my eyes, fully expecting the end to come swiftly.

\*\*\*

I awoke to the feel of a stark hospital bed, scratchy sheets around my body, my brain throbbing, my throat aching. The idea of being found in my cell, some poor sod simply passing by and noticing my predicament, calling for help, saving my life, had not occurred to me. Yet, here we were. Another day dawning on a goddamned life I no longer wanted, my existence now meant as a punishment I wasn't sure I could endure much longer.

'Well, look who's awake,' a voice filtered from the side

of my bed. A nurse leaned in, took my temperature, checked I was still attached to the drip in my hand, checking I was still *alive*. I had no idea where I was or what had happened. I tried to sit up, but my body felt as if it had been stamped on, a whiteboard on the wall displaying a hastily written message that I was not expecting to read: *Constant Supervision Required*. I wanted to laugh. They should have added, *unstable patient in progress*.

'Where am I?' I croaked, my throat sore, my larynx damaged.

'You're in safe hands, Miss Adams,' the nurse offered. 'That was quite a call for help you performed back there.'

I hadn't done it for attention. I wanted to die this time. I lay back on my pillow, nothing I could have said to her making a shred of difference. It wasn't a call for help. It was my last-ditch attempt to reclaim control over my own destiny. 'Who found me?' I asked, wishing I'd simply been left to my own devices. My throat felt as if it had been cut with a blunt knife. The irony of that concept wasn't lost on me, either.

'An inmate. Lesley Braun.'

*Typical*. That was twice now she had come to my aid, the woman not even liking me all that much, apparently. I thought about how she might respond to those she *did* like. Maybe she would have wanted to fuck my brains out with something resembling a fake phallic shape. It was not an ideal consideration. My friends and family seemingly detested the sight of me, yet an almost complete stranger was able and willing to offer more support when I'd needed it than any of those people had ever shown. And on two separate occasions. I closed my eyes. I would be dead now if it weren't for Braunie. When the hell would this nightmare end?

Four days later, I was discharged from the medical bay,

142

yet I wasn't going back to my cell any time soon. I was now classed as *severely* mentally unstable, suicidal. My looks and recent actions provided urgent cause to have me transferred permanently to the mental health unit where I would be sectioned, shut away from the rest of the sane, rational world and forgotten. I would now be closely monitored, twenty-four hours a day, seven days a week. I would be required to eat with a plastic knife and fork, my bedding lined with a plastic backing, unbreakable, suicide no longer a viable option. If I wasn't going through such severe personal trauma, I might have sought Braunie out, thanked her, expressed my sorrow, my embarrassment. Yet, the idea of being moved into permanent mental health assessment had me wishing she'd left me hanging by that not so metaphoric thread.

143

# 19

I fully expected the mental health unit to be filled with women on the edge, haplessly banging their heads against walls, moaning in corners, existing on powerful medication, rocking back and forth. As it were, it wasn't the reality that faced me. The women here were just like me. Sad, confused, the world outside entirely responsible for turning everything they once held dear completely upside down — the collapse of their existence wholly blamed on society.

I was placed in a cell with another woman. Mia Young. She was indeed young, too young to be in this place, it seemed. Her skin as soft as a teenager, her huge brown eyes, warm, oddly inviting.

'What are you in for?' she asked. I hadn't even made my bed. We had known each other for less than five minutes and I was already being interrogated. Thrust together, I had no choice but to make the best of a bad situation.

'I thought we weren't allowed to ask questions like that?' Did I assume this girl, nosy, curious or merely filter-less? I liked the possibility that she might be the latter. If she had no filters to prevent random outbursts, I might come to like her.

Mia shrugged. 'Who *cares* what everyone else does,' she sat cross-legged on the top of a chest of drawers, watching as I grappled with bed sheets that looked as if someone had deliberately poked them with a sharp object, unable to break through the odd plastic backing despite several attempts. The result was akin to the surface of the moon, potted with craters and bumps that would feel uncomfortable to lie on. She had a point. I repressed an urge to grin. Filter-less she was.

'I tried to kill myself a few days ago,' I answered, my throat still making me speak as if I had been walking through a sand storm for weeks. It would have sounded quite sultry under any other circumstances. Sexy. Jason would have loved it.

'No. I mean, what did you do that saw you in prison in the first place?'

I wasn't expecting the question. No one else had ever asked, and I wasn't exactly forthcoming in providing details of my private life, my crimes existing in my head. I swallowed, glancing at Mia's innocent curiosity.

'I killed two people,' I replied without hesitation, unsure how she would respond to such a response, unconvinced I'd told her at all. It was, in fact, the first time I'd spoken such a truth aloud to anyone, the police included. It felt odd. "Filter-less Mia" seemed to have a way of bringing out the truth in me. Maybe that was a good thing.

Mia shrugged again. 'Sucks,' she said, disinterested in my unexpected revelations as she placed a piece of gum in her mouth, chewing loudly. 'Want some?' she asked, offering a half-empty packet of strawberry flavoured *Hubba Bubba* my way. I shook my head.

'And you?' I felt I had the right to ask, seeing as she'd already instigated this conversation.

'I stabbed my social worker in her back and neck when I was fifteen. She didn't die, luckily for me, but she did need urgent surgery to stop the bleeding from her carotid artery.

Oh, and she had to learn to walk again, too. She spent months in rehab.' Mia's words were casual, as if her throwaway remarks were little more than constructed syllables she tossed my way purely to gauge my response.

I wanted to ask her why she did it, what had provoked such a violent reaction? She looked so innocent, so gentle. What had happened to make her require a social worker in the first place? Why was she now living in the mental health unit of HMP Blackwood? I stood, mouth open, too many questions teetering on the tip of a tongue that had no right to ask a damned thing about anyone else's past — my murderous deeds and subsequent events that led to this moment far worse.

'Sucks.' I found myself repeating Mia's comment, trying to keep my overly keen nose out of this poor girls private business.

Mia smiled. 'I haven't been in a very good place for some time, to be honest.' I knew exactly how she felt. It was oddly comforting to have something in common with another human being, someone who shared a snippet of my turbulent past. I chose to ignore the fact we were both in a mental health unit. That was irrelevant.

'Why not?' *Shit, Stacey.* That was inappropriate. It was none of my business.

Mia shook her head. 'Good question. One I've been battling with for a while.' My new cellmate helped me tuck the edges of my sheets into the corners of the bottom bunk before she climbed on and lay down as if I'd made it purposefully for her to lounge across. 'This unit isn't like the rest of the prison, Stacey. They *try* to help you if you want it.' I could see she was trying to reassure me. She hadn't answered my question, though.

'So, why did you try to kill yourself?' she asked, replacing my question with her own, staring at me as if she could see right through me. 'Was it guilt?'

I glared at her. *Why would I feel guilty?* Oh, yeah, for the murders I'd committed. I sighed, realising I'd attempted suicide purely because I assumed I couldn't live without my son, my baby still none the wiser as to my actions or current state of mind. I had callously murdered two human beings, yet I was more concerned by my own suffering, the loss of my innocent child. It was something that had affected me far more than the atrocious crimes I'd committed against two people who I should have loved just as unconditionally.

'It's hard to explain,' I muttered, leaving out pretty much everything I was feeling about pretty much everything. Yet, I hadn't even tried to explain. It *was* hard to explain.

'I'm a good listener,' Mia laughed, a smile appearing on her face that I quite liked. It had been a while since anyone had genuinely smiled at me. It was as if she didn't notice the twisted person living behind the façade I portrayed. I wished I could tell Mia that I, too, was a good listener, but that would have been a lie. I spent the majority of my time thinking only of myself, my own emotions, my own needs. I rarely listened to anyone. If I had, I might have realised my sister was suffering. I might have seen straight through the false guise of Jason bloody Cole.

'Have you ever felt powerless to stop your entire world crashing around you?' I asked then, my question coming from nowhere, allowed to float around the room unchecked. I had no idea where this questioning Stacey had come from, yet I saw something in Mia that had been missing from my life for a very long time. Something kind. I saw Emma. Back when we were kids. I shuddered. I didn't need the reminder.

Mia laughed. 'Yes. Every day, since I was six years old,' she said, true honesty in her voice I wasn't expecting to

147

hear.

I smiled casually, leaning against the sink unit for support. 'Why? What happened when you were six?' I laughed, glad to be enjoying a light conversation, my thoughts in the clouds, the antidepressants prescribed the only reason behind it all. It was none of my goddamned business, yet my brain was willing to blurt out random questions, nonetheless.

'That was the first time my dad raped me.' Mia spoke as if such an event was completely normal in her mind.

'Your dad —?' I couldn't bring myself to repeat her words. Instead, I thought of Jason, his heavy body groaning on top of mine. It was hardly the same.

Mia's smile slipped a little, and she lowered her head to her chin. 'Too much?' she asked, needing to verify that I wasn't yet ready for such revelations. After all, we'd only just met.

'*For who?* Too much for you, yes, definitely,' I responded, my irritation beginning to prickle. Such a vile thing would have been too much for any little girl. It would be too much for an adult. I thought of Eva, three years old now, her birthday passing by with me stuck in this hovel. I hoped she would be treated well in life. She deserved to be happy.

'It's okay, Stacey. I've had a while to process it all. The shrink in here is pretty good. Doctor Farley has helped me a lot.' I thought of Farley, sitting in his cheap chair with his cheap trousers, cheap attitude, even cheaper coffee. Maybe I was being too harsh on him. He certainly had a way of bringing about my unplanned confession in a hurry.

'I'm so sorry,' I found myself muttering, this poor girl needing far more than shallow words of sympathy uttered from my imposing gob.

'Oh, you don't have to be. I have my good days. Bad

days are worse than most, of course.'

'Of course,' I mirrored. She looked thin. As if this whole thing had broken her. 'So, why are you —?'

'In the psych unit?' Mia laughed, finishing the sentence she didn't know I was going to ask. 'I suffer from bulimia, Stacey. Have done since I was ten.' I shot her a look, the painfully thin shoulders, lank hair, hollow cheekbones. I'd seen it before — my sister. I closed my eyes. Poor Emma. I had given her relatively little thought, even after I'd taken her life, even after finding myself rotting in this place. 'I received six years in prison after I stabbed my social worker, which ended up turning into eight because of my continued poor behaviour. The whole thing with my dad and my social worker pushed me over the edge. I began stealing, running amok, out of control, running all kinds of scams and rackets in the young offenders' place before being transferred here, where I've been struggling ever since.' Mia sat up, folding her legs beneath her. Everything she was saying was fact, nothing new. It was all part of her daily existence.

'It always felt if I didn't eat, I didn't have to exist. I could pretend everything was okay, eat a full meal, make believe I enjoyed it. Then go and bring it up in the bathroom afterwards. Nobody knew for a long time. They assumed I was thin for my age, weedy, a nerdy adolescent, still growing.' Mia took a breath, the memory of her short life too much. 'I guess, in the end, bulimia was a condition I used to hide behind the crimes I committed. Still do.'

I wanted to ask Mia about bulimia — how it started, how a person could hide it so readily. I wanted to understand the condition. I wanted to understand the sister I was embarrassed to admit I barely knew. As it was, I had no idea how to even ask or where to begin. Did I even have the right?

As she spoke, I glanced casually toward her bare arms. It was a momentary gesture, a passing glimpse. I certainly did not mean any harm by my impromptu actions or to make her feel uncomfortable in any way. Her skin was covered in tiny cuts, old scars that snaked around fragile wrists, inner arms exposing painful wounds never quite healed, dark marks where fingernails had torn viciously at unsuspecting skin. She self-harmed. Bulimia was a part of the same self-hating campaign she was undoubtedly still living with. Her criminal activity was nothing more than a by-product of the pain she couldn't escape from.

'I hate *men*,' I found myself saying, muttering the word *men* as if they were all tarred with the same brush. Pigs. Selfish. Deluded. It wasn't true. My dad was a wonderful man. Quiet, yes, and he probably hated me now. But he was still a good man, all the same. I still loved him.

Mia laughed. 'You and me both,' she chided, jumping up from my bunk and bumping my shoulder with hers playfully. She reminded me so much of Emma, my sister, long gone. It was strangely comforting, my need to feel something for a sibling I had once loathed behind rational thought. Memories curled around my mind like snakes inside a hollow tree stump. I needed to feel something, *anything*. I had been numb for too long.

'You remind me of my sister,' I muttered.

'What? *Black*? Or broken?'

Mia had a way of making me laugh at the most inopportune moment. I hadn't given the colour of her skin a moment's thought. I often found it perplexing why other people would. 'No. Of course not. You remind me of the time back when we were kids. Emma had a big heart. Like you.' I smiled. It felt normal. 'It was actually what made me want to become like her.'

'And now?'

'What do you mean?'

'Do you still want to be like your sister?'

I sighed. 'I probably always will be, to be honest.' It was an unfortunate discovery made the very moment I'd spoken the words aloud.

'Does she ever come to visit you?'

'No.' I felt a lump form in my throat.

'Why not?'

'She passed away.' The very words should have choked me to death right then.

'Oh, Stacey, I'm so sorry for your loss.'

I looked at Mia for a moment. She had no idea one of those people I killed was my very own sister. She was *sorry*. So was I. Sorry for the whole damned thing.

**20**

Mia and I fell into an oddly comfortable friendship. Her ability to chat about random things at random moments helped take my mind off my dejected, overly complex emotions. She was monitored daily, as was I, made to eat a carefully prepared diet and accompanied to every single bathroom trip. I, too, was closely monitored, also accompanied to the bathroom. I felt we might, under normal circumstances, accompany each other. No need for uniformed officers, no chaperone required. Yet, those in charge oddly assumed we might make a pact. Mia was confirmed capable of vomiting the last trace of nourishment from her body. Me, simply to do myself in. It wasn't true. I wasn't about to do that again. It hurt too much the first time around. I still had faint scars on my wrists from a suicide attempt I didn't actually mean, a dark mark around my throat from the one I did.

Mia did not seem at all bothered by my lack of hair, the resulting spiked haircut I'd inadvertently created producing a far more convincing lesbian image than I'd intended. She had no reason to question my personal sexual preferences, of course, no qualms at all in the choices I made. My appearance was my business. She couldn't have known how I used to look — no photographs in my cell as a reminder. I was glad we were sharing a room. Although our late-night chats often kept the other women awake at all hours, I felt like a teenager again, chatting in the darkness to my sister, despite being a thirty-year-old, slightly unstable, delusional woman with no hair — Mia's twenty-three years on this planet experiencing more suffering than I could have ever imagined possible.

What had never bothered me was the fact Mia was black. She was beautiful, absolutely perfect as she was, her deep caramel skin needing very little moisturiser to give her a potential natural glow, her personality ready to thrive, given the opportunity. She just needed a decent meal that didn't end up in the toilet and to come to terms with events of her troubled past.

It was a deplorable state of affairs that racism is as rife in prison as in the real world. Mia was no more immune to the occasional racist insult than any other person of colour, the often-despicable incoming reactions she had to deal with from other inmates on a daily basis, something I found profound, disgusting, unnecessary. I hated how they treated her because she was different to them. Of course, she wasn't the only black woman in this prison, not the only victim. But Mia was my *friend*. She was the only one I cared about.

How dare these women pass judgment on fellow human beings purely because of the colour of their skin? They should look in the mirror from time to time. See the demons living inside themselves. I would choose skin tone over shit personality any day of the week. Most of these bitches would kill for a decent skin colour that Mia naturally possessed. She didn't have to concern herself over such matters of tan lines or premature wrinkles. It was profound my new friend dealt with daily insults with ease, name-calling, the occasional physical assault that came from nowhere. However, after three weeks of silenced endurance,

I'd had enough.

'I'm *used* to it, Stacey,' Mia told me, dabbing a bloodied arm where someone had deliberately dug sharpened nails into her in the showers that very morning.

'Well, I'm not,' I spat. 'And you shouldn't have to put up with it.' I was pacing the shower block, the uniformed officer behind us uncaring of the incident that had occurred right in front of her face. *What the fuck?* I gave her a blank look. Miss Elaine Sharp was as sharp in nature as she was in stature, her cold stare quite willing to injure me too if I wasn't careful.

'Miss Sharp, please. Can't you do something about this?' I was beyond furious. Nothing in this place was ever taken seriously. None of the women here considered important. We might have been emotionally damaged prisoners, but surely we deserved some understanding and basic acknowledgement from those in charge?

'She isn't *dead*, is she?' Sharp snapped back, her arms folded across her broad chest, a set of heavy keys dangling at her waist. *Wow.* What a shitty attitude.

'Would you prefer it if she was?' I goaded, in the right mood now for a full-on confrontation.

'Leave it, Stace,' Mia stepped in, her arm now wrapped in a makeshift bandage. 'I'm fine.'

She wasn't fine, and we both knew it.

\*\*\*

That night, Mia asked me about the people I'd killed. What had driven me to such a thing? How had everything turned so sour in my life that I felt I had no other choice but to take someone else's?

'I do understand the anger,' she confirmed. We were lying in our bunks, the lights out, door locked, no one to disturb us or hear our private conversation if we spoke softly enough. 'I wanted to hurt my social worker, too. Badly.' Mia didn't look at me like everyone else did. She didn't give me that familiar *oh, shit, you might kill me, too* look, or act as if she wanted to race away from me as fast as she could. She didn't even seem to assume I was mentally insane, nothing more a deranged killer — the cold, calculated, twisted psychopath everyone else had believed me to be since Jason's unfortunate corpse was found on his floor. It was, in fact, the first time someone had spoken to me openly about the deaths since being interviewed by the police. Since my sentencing. I was nothing to anybody in prison. I was nothing to anybody on the outside now, unfortunately. I hadn't felt I needed to take responsibility for any past actions until now.

It was the first time I actually wanted to share my experiences with someone else, to explain why things had happened the way they did. 'I guess I got the wrong idea of things,' I told her, trying to be honest, trying to recall how I'd felt back then. I was staring at the far wall, my bottom bunk directly below Mia's body, her soft voice filtering through the mattress towards me.

'About?'

'About my sister.' It was true. I assumed Emma hated my guts. I had the wrong impression that her life had been designed the way it was, to wind me up. To make me feel wholly inadequate in my own pathetic failings. 'I believed she had it all,' I confessed, closing my eyes at the memories of my sister's life. Mia remained silent. Her steady breathing told me she was simply waiting for me to continue, happy to listen to my words, understand my motives. 'We hadn't been close since we were kids.' It was true. 'And I guess I was secretly in love with her husband.' I gulped. Was it such a secret?

Mia shifted position, leaning on her arms, waiting, listening. No judgment emanated from the darkness, her gentle breathing remaining steady. 'That must have been tough?' she asked, her calming words soothing to my senses.

'It was,' I sighed, remembering my short but passionate time with Jason. How he made me feel in those early days of a relationship I believed would last forever, go the distance, show them all. 'I honestly believed he was in love with *me*. I was certainly in love with him. He told me he did.' I recalled the first evening we had expressed our emotions in a physical display of heavy panting, tearing of clothing, much giggling.

'So, I take it he left his wife for you?' Mia asked. It was a simple question that should have resulted in a simple outcome, a simple *yes of course*. Jason *should* have left Emma for me. We *should* have begun our new life together in earnest. It was a simple plan at the time.

'Not exactly,' I closed my eyes. 'He tried to end things with me. Said he wanted a second chance at his marriage, telling me we couldn't be together after all.' The memory was still a painful event, one I would probably never get over. 'That's why I was forced to kill her. I needed to get my sister out of the way.' How was I able to tell Mia such truths so openly? My unfiltered words were allowed the freedom of this room, the freedom of Mia's calming manner, the darkness around us providing protection that might not have otherwise been available to my senses. 'Jason didn't know what he wanted,' I whispered. 'I had to make the decision for him. He couldn't have us both.'

Mia sighed. 'Aahhh. Got you.'

'Got what?'

'He wasn't prepared to leave his wife, and you couldn't stand the idea of him being with her when he should have been with you? I understand.'

What exactly did she think she understood? I sat upright, swinging my legs over the edge of the bunk. 'It all happened so fast, to be honest. I don't even know if I honestly *meant* to kill my sister.' It wasn't true. I'd meant every single carefully planned action I took that day. I did not confess to my friend that I was still struggling with the idea Emma had saved almost seventeen thousand pounds for me, for a law degree she planned to surprise me with on my birthday. 'Mia?'

'Yes, Stacey?'

'You don't hate me, do you?'

'Why would I hate you?'

'Because I did unforgivable things?'

'We've all been there. I promise you that.'

'How?'

Mia fell silent. I could hear her breath, slow, steady. 'When I stabbed my social worker that day, I *wanted* her dead. She didn't understand what I had been through. Nobody understood at that point. My dad was still abusing me. I needed help I didn't know how to ask for. I believed if I killed the woman, it would make everything go away. That it would help me hide the shame I'd carried around with me for most of my life. Yet, I wasn't able to show any remorse for my actions, the woman needing emergency surgery for serious injuries to her spine. I was only fifteen. Too young to be sent to adult prison, too old to be treated as a child. The only reason I only stabbed her twice was because someone intervened. What I actually wanted to do, was kill my dad.'

'What happened to him? Your dad?' I was leaning my head against the wall now, the surrounding darkness seemingly helping us both say things we might have otherwise kept silent.

'I don't know,' she whispered. I didn't believe a word

of it.

'Really?'

I heard Mia's audible, heavy exhale. 'He went to prison, eventually. But he was murdered in his cell during his second night there.' Mia sighed. 'They found out he was a kiddy fiddler. The worst part of it all was he got to end his suffering, leaving me to continue in my own personal hell, alone.'

I thought about Jason. The same thing had happened to him. When I killed him, I had unwittingly ensured he would no longer have to deal with the consequences of his actions. He had hurt me, scorned me, his raping, cheating ways, his lies, the mounting debt, all bringing me to that night, that moment. It had ultimately brought this entire thing on me now. *Jason* had really killed my sister, not me. I wanted to tell Mia that. I refrained.

'I was raped, too,' I confessed. I wasn't sure what Mia would make of such a revelation.

'As a kid?' Mia asked, slightly shocked yet not entirely surprised. She probably sadly assumed all girls were abused as children.

'No. Last year. By the very man I was meant to be spending the rest of my life with. By the man I had willingly sacrificed my sister's life for.'

'Your sister's husband?'

I nodded. Mia couldn't see. 'Yep. So I had to kill him, too. Ending that entire chapter of my life for good.' *Once and for all, it seemed.*

'I *really* hate men,' Mia muttered, my open confession seemingly not affecting the way she saw me or the men she'd been forced to endure, thank Christ.

'I know exactly what you mean,' I confirmed with a sigh of my own. I thought of Elijah, my baby boy, still too tiny to understand the ways of the world. The ways of men.

I hoped my parents would care for him well. Show him the right way to treat a woman. I couldn't bear the idea he might, someday, despite everything I had done to protect him, turn out like his dad. A man he would never know because of me. *I know exactly what you mean.*

# 21

Opening up to Mia wasn't something I initially anticipated. Yet, it oddly helped me come to terms with events I might not have otherwise been able to fully deal with if left alone. I attended the obligatory weekly sessions with Farley, grateful to be far more settled in my thoughts than I was when I first met him, the man no longer able to wind me up so readily. We'd sit in his office for an hour, drinking coffee, chatting about the weather, the state of the food in here, my overall wellbeing. I was under constant supervision now, Farley's job made even more turbulent by this absurd reality. My prison cell was monitored by CCTV cameras that could alert officers to any potential problem inside. It was slightly intrusive and unnerving to be watched, especially when dressing, yet I was no longer focusing on things I could not control. I was nothing more to them than a prison number with mental health needs, a surname in a file attached to requirements made of me each and every unrelenting day of the week.

Mia had spent every day since attacking her social worker, living on a knife-edge, her prison sentence continually extended via additional offence charges that wracked up quickly. She inevitably turned to drugs, stealing what she could to make ends meet, selling goods she stole from other inmates without remorse, existing in constant turmoil. By the time she was twenty-one, Mia's bulimia had seen her hospitalised four times, each recovery made by pure miracle, pure chance, leaving her no better prepared for life than she had been when she first discovered that throwing up in a toilet gave back some well-needed control. Now the poor girl was in Blackwood with me — nothing but two damaged women on a collision course with life and the very people we'd met along the way.

Bulimia was initially blamed for Mia's unmitigated actions, her apparent chosen way of life subsequently leading her to this place. The authorities did a terrible job of putting two and two together, as usual, failing to realise it was, in fact, her early abuse that created such a low self-image, low state of mind. I still had no genuine idea why Emma suffered from bulimia herself, hiding her illness from us all. Yet, I could no longer ask the question, my poor sister way beyond the capacity for holding a conversation.

It was uncomfortable to discover that Mia's dad often told her she was fat. She was only five years old when the abusive name-calling began. What five-year-old deserves such thoughts implanted into their impressionable, developing minds? I initially assumed it was coincidental that Jason had indicated such a thing to me once, my pregnancy not even showing at that time. *Don't eat too much, Stacey. Fat women aren't attractive to me,* he'd stated quite casually, quite coldly. What a bastard. I shuddered. Control is far better achieved, it seems, when taking on the guise of consideration for someone you are *meant* to love. I had, at one time, assumed he was looking out for me. Mia probably thought the same about her dad.

I had no doubt in my mind now, that Jason goaded my sister in the exact same way, especially after the birth of their daughter. Baby weight isn't easy to shift. It explained

Emma's sudden weight loss perfectly. I assumed she was, as usual, able to slip straight back into her pre-pregnancy size with ease. I now hid my unmoving baby belly under baggy clothing that went oddly well with my newly acquired boyish appearance. Jason would have been mortified by what I'd become. I certainly was.

Despite my friend's receptive attitude towards what had happened to her, Mia did not talk much about her emotional instability. Yet again, there aren't many of us who honestly do. The only thing I knew now was, whatever it took, I needed to help my newly acquired friend through her struggles. It was the least I owed her. The least I owed a sister I could no longer support, physically or emotionally. It might also help my own suffering, somehow. I hoped.

It was strange to admit I was happier in the mental health unit than I'd been in general population, even during the short time I'd spent in the mum and baby unit. It was unfortunate I lived most days in an apparent blur, my thoughts often drifting to dark places, my little boy, my overshadowing prison sentence. I initially assumed it was because I had more attention in this unit, but to be honest, most of the officers here were no different than those in the rest of the prison.

The anti-depressants contributed to my sudden rise in mood, of course, but Mia had given me a focus that had been missing from my existence for quite some time. Call it guilt, if you like. Guilt for the suffering of a sister I'd callously murdered. Guilt for a son who would now be forced to grow up without me. Guilt for a dead cat who had done me no wrong. Whatever it was, Mia and I fell into a carefree friendship that I hadn't appreciated for a very long time. We would touch on the complex history of our lives from time to time, Mia offering snippets from her past, with me allowing her the occasional insight into my own. We didn't dig too deeply, of course. Neither of us strong enough for all-out exposure.

I was in the canteen one evening, grabbing a few essentials for a relaxed evening planned to watch the little television we were allowed to view, Mia's much-anticipated chicken and mushroom Pot Noodles still in my arms as the security alarm sounded around me. Although the sudden intrusion was unexpected, I barely took much notice of the resulting panic, most days in this place consisting of some drama or another that bothered me relatively little. I was now immune to the traumas of daily prison life, numb to the reality of my pathetic existence. It was only when I heard Mia's name mentioned by a passing screamer, that my attention was caught, my thoughts anywhere but on the friend now presumed bleeding to death on the floor of our unit some distance away. *What the hell?*

I hated the way Mia had grown accustomed to the racist abuse, the sarcastic, intrusive names aimed in her direction, uncomfortable sound effects she did a far better job of ignoring than I did. It was a daily occurrence, something she'd been forced to endure for years. Nothing new, she claimed. The main culprit behind Mia's recent suffering was a woman called Rachel Rancock, known as *Double R* to her friends — a play on words, on account of the fact she had enormous breasts. She wasn't exactly the full ticket, though, a couple of sandwiches short of a picnic. The woman walked around as if she was top dog, top bitch, top of her tiny, pathetically deluded world. Addicted to heroin for most of her adult life, Rancock didn't just hate black people, she hated everyone who didn't fit her profile of apparent *normality*. It was ironic, considering the stupid bitch was in prison, shut off from the rest of the inmates in a mental health unit, trying to move from day to day via her next fix. *She* was the one sitting on the outside of considered normality, not Mia. She was the weird one — a complete freak.

I have no idea what happened to those noodles or packet of chocolate digestive biscuits I'd been salivating over for the last two hours. My mind focused on nothing now but locating Mia, getting her the help I wasn't even convinced she actually needed. I was terrified her injuries must have been severe, the ensuing panic erupting our unit into outright chaos, leaving me in a state I couldn't quite fathom. *Bloody Hell.* I didn't yet know what had happened, but I knew Rancock would have been involved somehow. It didn't take a genius to figure out what she had done, or why.

I arrived at our cellblock to see Mia on the floor, covered in blood, officers telling everyone to keep back, stay away. She wasn't moving, a nurse already accessing her wounds, talking to her, attempting to keep her calm. Was she conscious? I pushed through the growing crowd, the erupting carnage preventing me from gaining a clear vantage point, my friend dying in front of my shocked eyes, not a damned thing I could do about any of it. Mia had been stabbed in the chest, someone claimed. I didn't see this coming. Rancock must have chosen her timing perfectly, just outside the sight of the CCTV cameras. *Jesus fucking Christ.* I automatically glanced around, noticing one of the cameras was now facing the wrong way.

Rancock was standing some feet away now, surrounded by her hapless followers, her face calm, unconcerned by the unfolding scene creating such terror around her. The bitch almost looked *happy*. I glared at her, unable to appreciate that Mia was still unmoving, my racing heart launching into unprecedented consternation that Rancock could never have fully appreciated. They didn't *know* me. They didn't know what I was capable of when pushed, what I'd already done. They certainly did not know what I was about to plan now.

Mia was rushed to the medical bay, no information forthcoming on her current condition, despite my continued screams for attention. Would she need to go to the hospital? *Would she live?* The only thoughts on my mind were Rancock, what she'd done to my friend, and, what I could *not* allow her to get away with. I was already a killer. Convicted as one. Serving a hefty sentence. Why should I concern myself with the potential murder of a total stranger? A stranger I truly detested anyway?

I once heard that, for serial killers, the more people they kill, the easier it becomes for them to kill again. It's true. Technically I was a serial killer now, two humans and a cat equating to the required three kills that earned a person such a prestigious title. My killings were carried out under the guise of passion. Apparently most female killers victims are. I had no issues assuming Rancock's murder could also potentially be classed as such — my unanticipated planned actions brought about because of a genuine love I held in my heart for a friend I never expected to make.

I followed Rancock and her gaggling bitches back to their cells, my eyes locked in focused confrontation she didn't yet know was coming, her smiling features soon to be removed from her face, permanently. Other than myself, no one appreciated why she was smiling so readily, so freely, her appalling attack on Mia something she assumed nobody would ever discover. She certainly didn't notice me watching her, the commotion of the evening leaving most of the women shaken, some requiring sedation.

Despite what I had always believed, despite what I'd seen on television for many years, and despite continued media publicity, women's prisons aren't the violent places I expected. Most of the women here simply self-harmed, not hell-bent on harming others. Mia's attack wasn't unusual, of course, especially in an unstable mental health unit such as this. But most of the women here needed help, not locking away, the system failing them entirely — my own volatile presence being the exception to the rule, of course.

It was an unexpected, oddly all-consuming consolation that I could afford to take my time, work on a plan, get this right. Rancock wasn't going anywhere. Neither was I. I'd planned my sister's death faultlessly —an act that had seemingly worked in my favour for a while. It wasn't my fault I was subsequently coerced into making a later confession. Jason, of course, was a different matter. His death was entirely spur of the moment, a hard lesson learned that I should have thought it through before beating his brains to a pulp. *I might not be here now.* As it was, I was now a lifer, in this for the duration. No matter what it took, Rancock wasn't getting away with what she'd done to my friend tonight. I simply could *not* afford to get caught.

# 22

I endured a restless night, concerned for Mia, dreaming of Rancock's throat at my forthcoming mercy. I hardly slept, pacing my cell too long, staring at Elijah's photograph, Mia's empty bed — the darkening grey walls that threw shadows across my eyes like screaming demons. I mused over past events, wondering how things might have been different. Would Rancock have stabbed my friend if I were there to protect her? Were Pot Noodles and chocolate biscuits so *bloody* important? I knew Mia was unsafe if left alone, the racist taunts coming thick and fast. So, why didn't I stay in our cell? Why didn't I ask Mia to accompany me to the canteen?

When the cell doors were opened the following morning, I practically sprinted into the corridor, Miss Sharp's beady eyes noticing my rush for freedom as if someone was chasing me out of bed.

'Adams, what are you doing?' she demanded, still in the middle of unlocking cell doors, checking all was well.

'I need to see Mia. How is she?' I was out of breath, out of my mind. Someone randomly threw out a comment I was *worried about my girlfriend,* adding a wolf whistle for effect. I wasn't listening. It didn't matter what the other women thought about Mia and me. She was my friend. I hadn't had one of those for quite some time.

'Young is in good hands,' Sharp replied, unconcerned by my ranting or rapidly elevating heart rate.

'Is she alive?' It was all I wanted to know.

Sharp stopped unlocking doors and nodded blankly. 'She's alive,' she said with a simple shrug before turning her attention back to the other inmates.

*Thank god for that.* I sighed heavily, leaning against the wall. The cornflakes I'd forced myself to eat threatening to make a second appearance. 'Thanks, Miss,' I offered. It was terrible timing Rancock chose that instant to stride out of her cell, mocking my emotions, threatening my sanity. She glanced my way, our eyes locking in momentary acknowledgement. I glared at her, knowing what she had done, what she was, how much I hated the smug bitch.

I didn't know much about her other than the fact she'd apparently stabbed her brother in the top of his head with a six-inch kitchen knife because she thought he was a demon come to kill her family. She never displayed any remorse, even after her brother later died in hospital. Paranoid Schizophrenia ran in her family, going back to her great grandmothers time. Unfortunately, Rancock was not spared the indignation. According to her, *everyone* was out to get her. It explained the racism although it didn't condone it. She'd be lucky to ever get out of this place, her state of mind already keeping her retained at Her Majesty's pleasure longer than her original sentence. I narrowed my eyes. To be honest, freedom wasn't something the woman would ever have to worry her stupid fat head about if I had anything to do with it. The public could sleep safely in their beds.

Shaking off my unwanted attention as if my emotions didn't matter, Rancock turned her focus towards a fellow inmate before disappearing down a set of steel steps, my presence seemingly of no concern to the woman at all. *Mia was alive.* For that, I was grateful. Yet, things could have been very different, and I had no idea how my friend was, beyond the concept she was still breathing.

After a rather languid morning prepping lunch, I hung around the kitchen, wondering if I could get away with adding something *extra* tasty to Rancock's dinner. It was a simple idea, simple to do, a simple drug overdose not entirely unexpected of such a volatile woman. Of course, her unfortunate death was probably something the authorities expected to happen anyway, eventually. A confirmed drug addict, the tragic end of a lifetime heroin user and schizophrenic was never far from anyone's mind.

The inmates were required to fill out a weekly menu sheet outlining the meals they wanted each day. According to the governor, it was a far simpler way to maintain stock levels and keep things straightforward. I always felt the choices were limited, forcing us to consume the same tired, tasteless meals, day in, day out. Today, Rancock had chosen vegetable pasta bake. She literally could not have chosen a better option; this simple dish easy to disguise a heady blend of heroin, spice, anything I might get my hands on. Heroin and spice are two of the most accessible drugs available in prison. Weirdly, both drugs can leave the human system within just three days of ingestion. It is much easier to avoid detection during random drug testing than when consuming cannabis or cocaine. In fact, women in prison often end up on heroin because of this exact unfortunate truth.

It was, however, equally unfortunate that since my earlier moment with a pile of crushed glass from a jug that was *accidentally* broken in my care, the kitchen and canteen areas were no longer viable routes for drug smuggling. There were, thankfully, always new dealers ready to step up and step in, cashing in where the last chump messed up —

always new channels, new buyers. So it was entirely fitting I would have no issues locating an inmate willing to sell me a little clear wrap I could hide in my underwear until needed. I'd probably buy two, maybe three wraps, the forthcoming overdose I was now eagerly preparing for oddly raising my adrenaline and spirits enormously.

By twelve-thirty, I had my concoction prepared — a single wrap of heroin, two of spice. "Be careful with that," the dealer had warned. "Take your time with it. It's lethal stuff." Knowing I didn't usually use drugs, I'd unwittingly flagged myself as a potential risk factor, prison officers always on the watch for changing patterns of behaviour, the dealer now on the lookout for my unfathomed explosion. She didn't need to worry about me. I wasn't planning on causing her any trouble. I wasn't the one about to ingest the stuff.

I had to be careful, though, of course. I didn't want to hand the offending meal to the wrong inmate by mistake. I wasn't so deranged that I was comfortable for an innocent person to die at my twisted hand. I shook the idea out of my head that Emma was probably an innocent in my previous planning, Sylvester too. No matter. It was fortunate I worked in the kitchen, *un*fortunate for Rancock — my secret mission made far easier by a distinct lack of supervision. The officers did not assume meal times were cause for much alarm, usually allowing the women to eat together in relative solace, a time for reflection, relaxation.

I stood behind the serving counter, apron on, watching the women filter into the dining room for their lunch break, chatting, looking relaxed. My heart skipped several beats when I spotted Rancock grab a tray, heading towards the lunch queue, the list of pre-ordered meals already fulfilled, awaiting not so eager consumption. I handed out several meals, my usual calm manner seemingly eluding me now.

The pasta bake was behind me, a large pot of sticky goop blipping away in a pan. I had to move fast, prevent detection. I couldn't get caught. Not today.

I carefully tore open the packet I'd hidden in my apron pocket, secretly created from my hasty morning purchase, sliding a mound of the monstrous powder into a spoonful of pasta sauce, stirring well. I held the offending lunch tray in my grip as if the thing might, at any second, jump up and bite me. I merely needed to hand it to Rancock, my task complete. It should have been a simple action, yet my hands trembled as if I'd never actually *murdered* anyone before. Anyone would assume me a novice. *As if.* I couldn't take my eyes off the woman as she edged towards me, my mind quite unwilling to consider any other outcome than the one firmly planted inside my head.

I was actually quite relieved when she took the meal from my grasp, adding an apple and yoghurt to her tray, not so much as a thank you as she snatched the thing from my trembling hand. I smiled, grateful. Not directly at her, of course. Such an accidental display of affection would have been too weird. No. I smiled merely for the situation about to unfold. I couldn't help it. Dark thoughts had been left to linger, alone in a cell that should have been filled with laughter. It was entirely Rancock's fault. She had no one to blame for this outcome but herself. I wondered how long it would take for my plan to work, visualising the vomit induced, grey-faced bitch dead on the floor of her cell before this very day was out. It would be worth every bated breath I took.

I almost threw up a couple of times, watching Rancock pick around the edge of her lunch plate, far too much gossiping going on, far too little chewing. Eventually, she dug in and polished off the contents of the entire tray, seemingly on a mission to turn her attention to something more important than the tasteless meal in her possession. I had no idea if she would even notice the powder dissolving into lumpy tomato sauce, absorbing rapidly into her bloodstream. It was almost a relief the food here tasted terrible. She wouldn't expect her lunch to be anything other than utter shit. I held my breath in misplaced anticipation, altogether forgetting to serve several hungry women in my hesitant distraction. I didn't care. The deed was done. Rancock was now filled with deadly poison. It would only be a matter of time before her fate was complete. I merely needed to wait.

I was as patient as my racing heart would allow, waiting for my concoction to kick in, begin its journey into Rancock's bloodstream, to her vital organs — her ultimate death. Mia would soon be avenged. It was all I needed to maintain a calm semblance. I was happy to wait. My moment of triumph would soon be confirmed, my enemy about to get *precisely* what she deserved. It was almost worth the perpetual interval of boredom that followed, much lip and fingernail chewing commencing in private, holding back potential vomit as I washed lunch trays, scraped food scraps into a bin, mopped the floor.

I returned to my cell in turmoil, shaking like a proverbial leaf in a shit storm, unable to tell a soul of the deliciously devious act I'd flawlessly pulled off. I glared at my reflection in the mirror, unsure what I was looking at, disgusted to confirm the woman I once thought I knew was now long gone. Where once I would have witnessed long dark hair, full lips, full figure, I now saw only dark eyes, short, stubby spikes that stood out from a deranged head, gaunt cheeks, a much slimmer frame, my post-baby pouch needing bulky clothing to cover it all. It mattered little. I was still Stacey Adams. A detested, deserted daughter, failed sister, estranged mother. *Killer*. What else was there? What else mattered?

As Rancock ascended the steel steps to our cell area sometime later, two friends in tow, there seemed nothing out of the ordinary apart from the occasional complaint that the smug bitch was feeling a little *off*. Perfect. The drugs were beginning to work. I had to suppress a smile I wasn't convinced would not immediately give me away. Totally worth it, though, if it did. I couldn't overthink it now.

## 23

I couldn't see the woman directly, but I was glad to be within earshot, a sudden loss of limb function ensuing a commotion, a clatter, someone falling. I took a breath, swallowing hard, licking demonic lips that had become dry through consistent, absentminded gnawing. Hurry up. *Hurry up and die, bitch.* I leaned my head around the corner, daring a glimpse of an event I'd brought about, my face curling into an unprecedented smile I didn't try to subdue. I thought about Mia lying in a hospital bed somewhere, alone, her injuries serious, life-threatening. Rancock had brought this on herself. I had no reason to feel anything but smug satisfaction as she fell to the floor, convulsing violently, something white and frothy escaping her venomous lips. *Serves the bitch right.* She should learn some respect for her fellow humanity, no matter the colour of their skin or unavoidable personal circumstances.

An officer came running, Rancock's body now a cause of much attention, her hapless limbs thrashing in all directions, the violent seizure she was having, a perfect conclusion to my precisely planned actions. I hoped she would succumb to her death slowly, painfully, dying right there in front of a growing crowd, appearing the very monster I knew her to be. The prison would blame drugs, of course, this institution always rife with the stuff. Yet, there would be no inquiry, no investigation, a simple blood test telling everything they already knew. *Stupid woman.* What the hell was she thinking? If inmates chose to put such disgusting crap into their bodies, they deserved everything coming to them. The authorities could hardly be held accountable. This day would add to the growing number of drug overdoses the prison system had to deal with, the poor staff forced to watch the death count wrack up in earnest. It would be nothing unusual. I'd probably done them a favour.

They took a fully convulsing Rancock to the medical bay, her so-called friends panicking, everyone discussing what could have caused such an event. Yet, it was nothing more than an expected conclusion to a life *not* well lived. She spent most days off her face, high as a kite, the stupid bitch usually ambling around as if she was on a different planet. I hoped she would die on-route. No need for the prison doctor or nursing staff to waste their valuable time over this writhing bitch. I had ensured she would die today, and die swift enough, the plethora of drugs in her system fully capable of killing a horse. I'd seen the effects of a heroin overdose, my time in prison ensuring I'd witnessed the resulting deaths those toxins create. It isn't pleasant. Couple such a concoction with spice, and you'll have a wholly induced infusion of sheer hell.

I watched calmly from a distance, the commotion unfolding, the only person on my mind at that moment being Mia. I'd asked several times as to her current health status, receiving no valid answer that meant a damned thing to me at all. Somebody would find out, so they said. Yet they never did. As the first day without Mia turned my mind to mush, I feared my friend might *never* return. For that uncomfortable consideration, I owed her. I had already failed to protect her. I would not fail to avenge her. Today was nothing more than a necessity I couldn't have avoided, even if I wanted to — my efforts planned perfectly, performed flawlessly. Rancock would die today. Even if I had to go to the medical bay and press a pillow over her head directly, ensuring such an event occurred, cut off her air supply once and for all. End this thing forever.

As it were, I didn't have to wait long for an update about Rancock, unlike Mia's wellbeing, ironically. After taking her to the medical bay, Double R had drowned in her own relentless blood infused vomit, choking to death in front of the prison doctor and several nurses, despite futile efforts to clear her airways, flush her bloodstream, the poison destined to kill her, rendering them all *useless*. There was nothing the poor doctor could do. It was hardly his fault. He had no choice but to stand by and watch whilst she coughed her last breath. I was ecstatic. I almost wished I'd witnessed it first-hand.

All I needed now was to tell Mia, share this fantastic news with my friend. Of course, I kept out of the way of the other women, kept my opinions and feelings to myself. I was happy Rancock was dead, yet I could hardly spread such fantastic news around the unit, most of the women in this place *liking* the bitch for some bizarre reason. Confirmation spread wildly that yet another batch of dodgy drugs was going around the prison. Nobody was prepared to accept that Rancock had been careless, taken too much. Taken her own life.

It was as if, without meaning to, I'd set off a chain of events that led to the suffering of more than one inmate. Rancock was dead — *tick*. The usual channels used by the inmates to bring in drugs were now being questioned by the very women whose days depended chiefly on using the stuff to get off their faces — *double tick*. The ringleaders responsible for bringing drugs into this shithole in the first place found themselves beaten, both physically and emotionally, their income stream cut off sharply, their bodies bruised and battered by angry prisoners — *tick tick tick*. I wanted to rub my hands together in pure satisfaction. Maybe I was here to save them. After all, I hadn't been able to save myself. It was the least I could do.

***

Mia was released from the hospital two weeks after Rancock's untimely, somewhat shocking departure from HMP Blackwood. She was weak, still in considerable pain, but very much alive. She smiled when she saw me, our embrace much needed, our separation made all the worse by the simple fact we had nothing and no one else in our lives than each other, no external daily activities to keep us busy, distracted. She had been stabbed in the abdomen on the left-hand side, just above her navel, the resulting injury puncturing a lung, thankfully missing her heart, her stomach needing several stitches to prevent acid and blood leaking into her body. Much healing was still to be done, both physically and emotionally, but, at least, she was home. *Home.* The very concept made me cringe. The fact I now referred to a grey prison cell as home felt unnerving. Mia did not belong in this place, her unfortunate past bringing about events that ultimately created her resulting existence.

It was good to see her, though. Good to enjoy her smiling face again, her cheeky laugh. I made tea, asked how she felt, fussed too much, making her laugh more than was perhaps comfortable for either of us. Not that she expressed such suffering aloud, wincing whenever I told a terrible joke which made her roll tired eyes towards me.

She was allowed a few days of rest before returning to

light garden duties. I was assigned as her personal helper, the kitchen apparently more than capable of doing without me for a couple of days, they said. It was probably just as well. I don't think I would ever look at a pasta bake the same way again.

'Did you hear about Rancock?' I asked casually, eager to share the news with my friend. I could barely conceal my excitement, yet was careful not to express too much, too soon. I assumed she would be grateful, thankful, my actions ensuring her future security, once and for all. I would have been ecstatic had someone done such a kind-hearted thing for me.

'Yeah. A drug overdose, wasn't it?' Mia asked, sipping her tea, unconcerned, unaffected by the untimely death of a fellow inmate. *Good.*

I nodded, smiling, unable to hold back elated emotions I'd been forced to keep inside me for days. 'Indeed it was.' I sounded smug, all-knowing, the look I gave my friend firmly expressing a truth I expected she would understand immediately.

'What?' she asked, looking at me with quizzical eyes, tea in hand, brow furrowed.

I continued to smile, which turned slowly into a grin, then a grimace. I couldn't help it. 'The women in here *really* should be more careful with their lunch trays. You never know what you might find in your food.' I giggled. I hadn't giggled for a while, not since my time with Jason. I took a breath. I couldn't dwell on that. It was still too painful.

'*Why?* Stacey, what did you do?' Mia glared at me, her tea no longer wanted. She gave me a look. I tried not to notice. 'You didn't have anything to do with *that*, surely?'

I took a breath, allowing a sigh I felt might expose my less than steadfast composure, closing our cell door so no one would accidentally overhear. 'She stabbed you, Mia.

Did you honestly think I'd let that bitch get away with what she did?' My words were calm. It unnerved me how I was able to discuss an act of murder with such diffused clarity, such nonchalance.

Mia stared at me for a moment, her face giving nothing away of what she was thinking. 'Stacey, what are you saying?' Her hand was trembling, tea threatening to spill.

'I only did it for you,' I whispered. 'I will always protect you. I promise.' I sat on the edge of the bottom bunk, reaching out for my friend's hand.

'*Jesus Christ*, Stacey.' Mia had turned quite pale.

'What?' *Why was she staring at me like that? What the fuck?*

'Please tell me you're kidding?'

'Why aren't you pleased?'

'Shit. *Shit!*' She looked as if she was about to vomit.

'Mia?'

'Rachel Rancock didn't stab me. What on earth made you think she did?'

I laughed, unable to absorb my friend's words. 'Don't play silly beggars,' I chided, knowing Mia was being daft, winding me up. *Of course*, Rancock had stabbed her. Who else could it have been? 'Rancock was goading you for weeks. You should have seen the look on her face as you lay bleeding on the floor.' I shook my head, recalling her calculated presence, the way she was behaving. *Way too fucking smug.*

Mia swallowed, pressing a trembling hand over her bandaged stomach, the memory of that day still fresh in her mind. 'No, Stacey. It wasn't Rancock.'

I laughed, almost choked. 'Of course, it was. Don't wind me up. You probably didn't get a clear view of who stabbed you because you wasn't expecting it,' I cut in. 'It all happened so fast.' *I knew* Rancock had done it. Yet, Mia

179

continued to glare at me, her face unchanged, shocked by my confession. Mia had this wrong. I wasn't about to start killing random people for the sake of it, no matter how much I hated them. I always had a reason — *a motive.*

'Mia?' I questioned, still entirely unsure what she was trying to say. Who the hell *had* stabbed her then, if not Rancock? *Was this a joke?*

We stared at each other, Mia's tea going cold in her hand, forming a skin.

'Mia?'

Mia shook her head.

'Tell me who stabbed you.' I wasn't smiling anymore. Not even close.

'You don't need to know.'

I couldn't stand this much longer. I lunged forward, grabbing her arms, not caring I was digging my nails into her skin or spilling tea onto my own sheets. 'Tell me,' I spat.

'If you really want to know, Stacey, I came face to face with Mrs Smith when I left this room.' Mia pulled away sharply, spilling her tea, hiding a twinge I'd probably created as she got to her feet, dumping her cup into the sink with a crash. *Damn it.* I liked that mug. Mia continued as if the broken mug was of no consequence. 'I apologised, of course, stepping around her. That's when I felt something hit me. I thought it was a part of her uniform catching my top, her keys or something digging into me by mistake. I was about to apologise again when I noticed the blood. I looked at her, and for a moment, she didn't respond. It was as if she was glad. Glad she'd hurt me. Then, she walked away, leaving me to collapse to the floor.'

Carol Smith? *The prison officer?* 'No. You have this wrong, honey,' I confirmed. 'Smith isn't even on this unit,' I *knew* Mia had this all wrong. She had to have this wrong. Smith worked in general population. She was the one who had taken me to my cell that very first day here. She'd been *nice*. 'Surely you're mistaken.' Mia had to be mistaken. The medication in her system wholly to blame for her wavering recollection now.

Mia shook her head. 'I'm not mistaken, Stacey. There was no one else outside this cell at the time. Just Smith and I.'

'But I *saw* Rancock-'

'Yeah, well, she must have shown up afterwards.' Mia was staring blankly at me, unable to unravel my thoughts or her own, the feel of my grip still lingering.

'What are you saying?' Why the *fuck* would a prison officer do something like that? *What the hell was happening here?*

'I'm saying you got the wrong person.' It was not a revelation I was expecting. I assumed I would be the one to give Mia important information today, make her happy.

'Jesus Christ, Mia. You have to tell someone,' I stammered, no longer able to concern myself I'd murdered yet another *apparent* innocent person. She was a racist, a drug user, a pig. Surely that was enough? My motives were still confirmed, still justified, my state of mind still in the clear.

'Yeah, sure. And who's going to believe me?' It was a good question.

'Are you *sure*?'

'As sure as you're sitting in front of me now.'

*Bloody hell.* This was serious. I knew prison life was often corrupt, plenty of officers on the take, damaged inmates wanting an easier time of their stay, plenty of hell to be had by all. But the idea that a prison officer could do such a thing to one of the inmates in their care unnerved me.

'Why?' It was a simple question. I couldn't take this in. Did I look as deranged as I felt?

Mia shrugged.

'Why the hell would she do that to you?' I repeated, literally unable to absorb what I was hearing, frustration building by Mia's silence, her calm persona. 'We need to tell the governor,' I confirmed, scrambling to my feet, ready to leave. Barrington was a good man. He'd want to investigate. He would *need* to investigate. 'Something must have been caught on CCTV, surely.' I thought about the camera pointing the other way. Surely someone would have spotted the culprit as the image swung into the wrong position?

'It won't help,' Mia looked as if she had already resided herself to the idea of never getting justice for her attack, never uncovering the truth. Prison officers always covered for each other. Everyone knew this.

'But I don't get it. *Why* would she do that to you?' I was still waiting for the reason — the revelation.

'She hates me, Stace. Always has.'

'But-'

'No buts, Stacey. I've had to put up with racism and hatred my entire life. This is just another day in the existence of Mia Young. Welcome to my world. I'm used to it.'

I stared at my friend, unable to accept what she was saying. I didn't buy it for one second. I understood racism. Of course, I did. I'd seen it myself, first hand, Mia the target of many a volatile attack. But as a white British female, I couldn't possibly understand what really goes on in the minds of those affected, why people do the shit they do to fellow human beings simply because they appear different to them. I closed my eyes. We are *all* fucking different. We are all part of the same world. We should care more for each other. It was ironic. If *only* I had taken my own advice.

I had planned Rancock's death perfectly, precisely, leaving nothing to chance, nothing to lose. It was entirely satiric if I'd just waited until Mia's return, I could have learned the truth, taken this thing in an entirely different direction. Still, Rancock was one less racist bitch to deal with. I had to console myself of that authentic fact. But there was no way I was going to let this lie. Prison officers can't do this shit and get away with it. I simply had no idea how I would make my next move. Who could I even tell?

# 24

Of all the people I knew would help me in my quest, the one person I did not expect to turn to was Braunie. Yet, I needed to seek her out, persuade her to help me, explain in precise detail what Smith had done, work out how we, as a collective, could stop the repulsive bitch ever doing anything like this again. I knew there had to be more to the story than I currently understood, more to the reasons behind why a uniformed officer, paid to keep these women safe, would deliberately go out of her way to stab an innocent inmate in her care due to the colour of her skin. I didn't buy it for a single second. *What had Mia ever done to her?* The concept did not sit well with me. There had to be more to this than the racist attack Mia had claimed.

I managed to smuggle a message out of my unit with the laundry inmates, a folded piece of paper I'd entrusted with a fellow prisoner. It was for Braunie's eyes only, I'd painstakingly claimed. No one else was to see what the note said. I was fully aware my secret wouldn't be kept secret for long — my message a way for wanton gossip to spread freely around the prison, my secret note becoming common knowledge the very moment it left my possession. I couldn't have planned it better. Before the day was out, rumours were already circulating that Mrs Smith was somehow connected to an unprecedented attack on a prisoner, other officers equally becoming aware of the gossip, as was, I assumed, Carol Smith herself. I needed to create a buzz, a hype, get people talking, provoking much whispering in corners and sneaking around. If Smith was in any way planning a repeat attack, her probable aim to permanently shut Mia up once and for all, she was about to run into the wrong person.

Braunie replied to my note three nerve-wracking days later, her own hastily written message passed to me along with my clean washing bag.

*She's been acting odd, talking in corners. What the fuck has Mia said? B*

Mia hadn't said much at all. In fact, she'd been relatively quiet since her return from the hospital, my admission rendering her entirely mute. It wasn't like Mia to be so subdued. I couldn't shut her up usually. She hadn't been willing to discuss her attack at all, which was odd. If the incident was somehow linked to racism, as she claimed, surely she would want to see such despicable events become a thing of the past? This was no longer *just* about Mia. It was for all races in all society, minorities, disabled people, *women*. We had a legitimate and heartfelt need to stand up and say to the world, *no more of this bullshit* — your shitty behaviour is no longer acceptable in a rational, intelligent society.

As it was, Mia didn't wish to discuss it, my attempts to throw light on the subject remaining unreciprocated.

'I'm only trying to help,' I snapped at her. It was late, our lights long turned out. We were lying in our bunks, the entire place quiet for a change.

'You're not helping, Stacey. On the contrary, you're

making it worse.'

'How? I want justice. Don't you want to see that bitch struck off?' I wanted much worse than to simply see the woman handed a P45, yet I couldn't tell Mia about the dark thoughts twisting my nightmares to turmoil.

'It doesn't matter,' Mia spat, turning over in her bunk, seemingly so she didn't have to listen to me anymore.

But it did matter. I needed to understand why my friend did not wish to bring her attacker to justice. 'What have *you* ever done to Carol Smith?' I queried. I couldn't understand it. Mia was a lovely girl, quiet, pretty, hiding many problems she was still desperately trying to work her way through. I simply wanted Smith *dead*. It wasn't an option. I had no idea when my mindset shifted so violently — thinking of someone else's demise had the power to lift my mood. I'm sure I wasn't like that *before*.

Mia hadn't responded to my question, yet I knew she wasn't asleep. Her breathing changed when she was sleeping, becoming deeper, heavier, lost to dreams I often wished I had the power to share with her or remove forever. Whichever she needed. Now she was quiet. Too quiet.

'Mia?' I questioned, my irritation growing.

'What?'

'Talk to me.' I needed her to share how she was currently feeling, explain what I was missing. I'd failed to listen to my sister, her own battle with bulimia and an abusive husband going utterly unnoticed by the one person who should have spotted such a change immediately. *Me.* I wasn't about to make that mistake again. I wasn't about to let this go.

'Mia?' I repeated loudly, almost biting my lip.

'Go to sleep, Stacey,' Mia muttered, her voice becoming muffled, as if her face was already buried deep in her pillow, her only requirement being my silence.

I sat up, swinging my legs over the edge of my bunk, getting to my feet. 'Not until you talk to me.' I stood next to the top bunk, staring at the back of her head, straining my eyes in the darkness for a better view of my distant friend.

Mia half-turned, wanting to face me, seemingly unsure how to respond. 'I can't,' she confessed, something in her eyes I was glad I couldn't see in the darkness. I knew she was holding something back.

'What have you ever done to Smith to make her so angry with you?' My relentless questioning was becoming tiresome. Boring.

'You *killed* Rancock because of me,' she breathed.

'I did everyone a favour.' It was true. I wasn't about to lose valuable sleep over that bitch. Victim number three in the bag. *Tick.* Serial killer status, well and truly confirmed. There would be no investigation to prove such a fact, add more time to my sentence. No one would actually know I was a serial killer. It was almost uncomfortable. Yet, Mia should have been pleased. I was frustrated the prison wasn't currently investigating Mia's stabbing. A lack of CCTV footage was not enough to close the case, forget it happened. I assumed it was all down to Smith that the whole thing had simply gone away. *Bitch.*

'You can't keep doing the shit you do, Stacey,' Mia said, turning over to face me, her eyes glistening wet in the gloomy shadow of the solitary window overhead, her voice suddenly finding its confidence quite readily. She still hadn't answered me.

'Funny, I believe the exact same thing about racists, too.' If the situation had been different, I might have laughed at my potential joke. Yet, none of this was laughable.

'You say you killed your sister, then your sister's husband in order to try and fix issues you felt needed addressing. Every single time you kill someone, you manage to justify your reasons.' Mia was right. What was her point? Why was she catastrophising everything?

'And?'

'And, if you're so hell-bent on getting to Smith, she will become just another victim on your death list who you *claim* deserved to die.'

*Death list.* Oh my god. I liked that. *My death list.* I'd be using that phrase again. 'I still don't understand?' I wasn't grasping Mia's meaning, her profound words still ringing in my ears.

'You're not a serial killer Stacey. You've been nothing but kind and supportive to me. You're a good friend.' Mia was wrong. I was a serial killer. I was only just beginning to own that truth with appreciated gusto. Why couldn't she accept me for what I was? *I was trying to accept who I was.*

'All I'm doing is serving justice —'

'Serving justice to those who have wronged you?' I loved how my friend was able to confirm my emotions for me so freely.

'Yes.'

Mia scoffed.

'What?'

'Nothing.'

'Tell me?'

'You don't know what it's like to be wronged, Stacey. People who hate and hurt you your entire life because of who you are. You can't appreciate what it's like to be me. What it's like to be Carol. You can't keep assuming that killing people is a feasible way to solve your problems. You'll end up alone.'

'What it's like to be *Carol*?' I questioned, repeating Mia's words, my tone darkening. I'd managed to skip over everything else she'd told me, simply focusing on the name she casually threw into the mix. Why would she say Smith's first name so comfortably? What the *fuck* was it with Mia and this bloody woman?

'For fuck's sake, Stacey,' Mia sighed, turning over. 'Just ignore me. I'm ranting.' I grabbed her arm. I didn't want to ignore her. I suspected Mia had accidentally stated something she didn't mean to profess, a sudden intake of breath confirming her irritation had forced her to speak out of turn.

'Not a chance,' I whispered, my features contorting. I was glad of the darkness. 'Talk to me?'

'I can't tell you.'

'Tell me *what?*'

'About Carol.'

*What the fuck?* Why was Mia on such intimate, first-name terms with this woman all of a sudden?

'*Mia!*' I demanded, my hand still gripping my friend's arm, probably too forcefully. At that stage, I didn't care if I woke the entire prison. I was now seething by her unspoken words.

Mia pulled away, pressing her body against the wall behind us, the darkness framing a face I couldn't clearly read. 'You've helped me so much over the last few months, been a genuine friend when I needed one. I can't allow you to do something you're going to seriously regret. I can't see more time added to your sentence because of *me*.' She sighed. I still wasn't grasping her reasoning.

'But Mia —'

'Stacey! Carol Smith was my social worker.'

*What the hell?* 'I beg your pardon?' I stuttered. For a moment, I was stunned. 'The one you stabbed?' I couldn't take it in. *Surely not?*

I could barely make out the shape of Mia's face nodding in the darkness, nothing in her confirmation able to help me understand emotions that swam in her mind. 'She was fresh out of college, keen to help people like me. We struck up a friendship. Got close.'

'Close?'

'Yeah, you know.'

I literally had no clue. I shook my head.

'I was fourteen. She was thirty-two. She had recently changed careers, started over. A fresh start, she said. Though, of course, if anyone were to ever find out about us, she would have been struck off, , everything she had worked for, all for nothing. I was a minor, just a kid. She would have been jailed for paedophilia. Grooming a child. Whatever.'

*Oh, Fuck.* Now I got it. Wake up, Stacey. 'You're —'

'Gay. Yes, I'm gay, Stacey. Black *and* gay. What a perfect combination for the world to hate me just that little bit more.'

In all the time we'd spent together, sharing secrets, truths, laughing, building a friendship I'd come to depend on, Mia's sexuality had never been a topic of discussion. I literally don't know why. I wondered now why she felt she needed to keep such a thing from me. I would hardly have given a shit what she was.

'You and Carol Smith?' I think my mouth might have fallen open.

'Yes.'

'Bloody hell.'

'Indeed.' Mia sat upright, smacking her head against the wall in frustration, the whites of her eyes glistening sadly. 'But Stacey, you have to keep this between us. I need you to know that she *never* hurt me. We loved each other.'

'Never hurt you?' Did Mia even know what she was saying? 'She fucking stabbed you.' Oh, the irony.

My friend shook her head. 'I meant when we were

lovers.' She sounded pissed off with me now, annoyed I was making her say these things aloud.

'But I still don't understand why she would *stab* you,' I sighed. And, why, if indeed they had once been so close, would Mia stab *her*?

Mia licked her lips, taking a breath I felt might take the air out of the room entirely. 'We saw each other on a personal level for well over a year, sneaked around, hid from the authorities and that all too arrogant prying gaze of an ignorant society. I have never felt comfortable around men, as you can imagine. Especially after —' Mia paused. She didn't need to explain. 'Anyway, we enjoyed a loving relationship until she told me we had to end it. She couldn't risk her career anymore. Things were getting *complicated*. Carol seemed to place more emphasis on herself than me. I hated it. That's when my bulimia severely got out of control. I began stealing from the replacement social worker they sent. I wanted Carol back and would have done anything to have her.' Mia took a breath, old memories she hoped to keep buried forever, were now allowed freedom of this emotionless room, thanks to my relentless probing.

'Anyway, a few weeks later, Carol came to see me. She was so cold with me, so full of regret. She was married, Stacey. They had kids. She didn't want her husband to find out. She didn't want *anyone* to find out. She told me to leave her alone. That she never wanted to see me again.'

'And that's when you attacked her?' I remembered the very night Jason had told me something similar. The night he made a conscious decision to choose his wife over me. The same night I decided to kill my sister. *And my cat.*

'Yes,' Mia was crying, her unseen sobs threatening to break my heart into fragments.

'But I still don't —'

'When I found out Carol was a prison officer here, I

191

tried to reconnect with her. I was so excited, Stacey. I couldn't believe that, after all this time, she had miraculously come back into my life. I thought it was a sign, an omen. *Fate.* Have you ever been so deeply in love with someone that all rational emotion goes totally out of the window?'

Yes. Yes, I had.

Mia continued. 'Anyway, she didn't want to know me. Pretended I didn't exist. She still doesn't want to know me. She deliberately ensured she was never on duty during the day, the night shifts here paying more anyway. But it was just so she could avoid me. Avoid having to confront our relationship. She went as far as to tell me that I meant nothing to her, and if I ever told anyone what we did, she'd make my life a living hell.'

'So what happened?' I was beginning to form a bigger picture, establish a better pattern of those events.

'I threatened her. Told her I'd kill myself if I couldn't be with her.' Mia didn't sound comfortable sharing such a private thing.

'Seriously?' What had made my friend so co-dependent on anyone? I thought about Jason again, realising, unfortunately, I was no different.

'Yes. I eventually took an overdose. Cocaine. Yet, even then, Carol didn't bother to come and see me. She didn't acknowledge me or tell me how she felt. That all happened just days before I was transferred to this unit. They claimed I was unstable, volatile. Still do.' I knew what she meant. It was the very reason I was here, too. 'And...' Mia hung her head.

'And?'

'And then... last week, I saw her for the first time in months. She was standing outside, in the garden, like an angel in the sunlight.' I realised with a jolt that Mia had never got over her. 'Apparently, she was covering for an officer off sick. I was so overwhelmed to see her I threatened to expose us if she didn't give us a second chance, acknowledge how she felt about me. I didn't mean it. I was just so angry with her. I still love her, Stacey.' Mia was crying again. For the first time, I truly understood why we had connected so well in here. We were *exactly* the same. Neither of us were willing to accept rejection without a fight, convinced the people we loved must have felt the same way, simply too afraid to show their emotions, own up to their honest feelings.

'Shit,' I muttered. No other word would have fitted the moment.

'You have to call off the hit on Carol Smith, Stacey. She was just angry with me, frightened I'd do something stupid, ruin her career as well as her marriage. She already warned me to keep my mouth shut. It wasn't a racist attack. It was a cry for silence. My silence. I brought this all on myself. Please don't hurt her.'

'But she *stabbed* you.'

'Yes, and I stabbed her first. Twice.'

That might have been true, but it didn't make it right. Two wrongs and all that. Yet, who was I to pass judgment? I was no different. One unanticipated murder had led to another, then another, my potential fourth victim now nothing more than a need I'd convinced myself I had to fulfil — the protection of Mia something I felt my duty to undertake without question. There would have shortly become five victims if you included my cat in the equation.

'But why would she hurt you? If she loved you.'

Mia shrugged. 'Just covering her arse, I suppose. Like the rest of us.' She was right. That is all any of us *ever* do in life. We convince ourselves we are doing the right thing, making the world a better place. But what we are actually doing is making the world better for ourselves. Carol might have stabbed Mia, but she hadn't killed her. She probably never intended to, giving her ex-lover a taste of her own poisonous medicine, warning her off, living through her own deluded experiences. I concluded the human race seriously needed a damned good talking to. *I certainly know I did.*

# 25

I was slightly reluctant, yet swift enough to call off the impending attack on Smith, offering Braunie a somewhat weak, ridiculous excuse I had accused the wrong person, made a mistake. I was dealing with it, or so I claimed, the whole thing no longer her concern. I don't think she believed me. It didn't matter. Mia did not wish for things to escalate further, and I was happy to go along with her wishes for now. I understood what it felt like to be in love. To feel as if everything you do revolves around their ultimate happiness. I had no intention of adding more suffering to my friend's personal trauma. She'd been through enough as it was.

I have no idea if Carol ever knew how close she came to having her life cut short, an abrupt end all but rendering her family grief-stricken before their time, an earlier love affair something she'd probably profoundly regretted ever since. I felt for Mia. She wanted to be loved, understood, taken seriously, her confirmed lesbian status and dark skin tone creating problems in her life that should never have been an issue in the first place.

There is a term in prison called "gay for the stay". It means that, while inside the confining walls of a prison, during however long your sentence may be, being *gay* is wholly acceptable. You can be straight on the outside yet openly share a lesbian relationship for well-needed company, companionship and sexual gratification when serving time — the constrained walls of prison life allowing a circumstance that might not exist elsewhere. Of course, I can't speak for male prisons, yet I assume such a concept would probably follow a similar path.

Because of this acceptance, and because the principal racist *bitch* on our unit was now dead, I was comfortable presuming Mia would be allowed a well-needed respite from her otherwise daily existence of abuse. She and I could now go about our business in relative peace, the anti-depressants in our system responsible for creating a lighter atmosphere wherever we went.

I wasn't gay, of course, had no intention of becoming so for any length of stay. But, around Mia, I felt calmer, relaxed, happy allowing her to rest her head on my lap when watching television, often curling up with me in my bunk after the lights had been turned out. We were companions, more than friends. She had many issues still to work through, bulimia never far from her mind, her abusive father still haunting her dreams.

Things remained like this for months: settled, calm. Nothing more was spoken about Smith or Rancock, the occasional twinge in Mia's left side simply equated to indigestion. I hated what society had done to her, yet I couldn't hide inside the glass house that was already of my own making, my broken life lying in shattered pieces around me. Society had broken us both, it seemed, with men blamed for the overriding damage factor, leaving behind many scars where once lived two vital young women with much potential in life. Prison life was a forced situation in which we shared a mutual pain, abusive men linking our past, bulimia providing much personal suffering we had both experienced. I guess it was inevitable our closeness would develop further, our consistent togetherness eventually sealing our fate.

We were sitting together after the evening meal had been served and cleared, a couple of precious hours afforded to the woman during a "free time" period, where we were allowed to wander the common areas untethered, share conversations, a game of cards or pool, watch television, generally relaxed. As usual, Mia and I were alone in our cell. Nothing allowed on television that I wanted to watch anyway, but we were simply glad for the downtime, space to recharge depleted batteries. When Mia turned to touch my face, a smile on hers I always loved to see, I was momentary glad to be experiencing this moment with her.

'I'm glad you're here,' she whispered, running a casual hand along my leg. 'You make everything so much better in this place than it would be without you.'

I was glad of the compliment, glad for the smile I'd brought forward, glad for the gratitude of my presence. I smiled, about to say as much when, out of nowhere, Mia leaned over and kissed me. It was a full-on, tongue-twisting snog that took me totally by surprise — a kiss that saw me reeling backwards towards the wall. Nobody had kissed me like that for quite some time. Who was I kidding? No one had *ever* kissed me like that. I wish I could say it felt good, that I reciprocated, kissed her back, but it wouldn't be true. In fact, the shocked look on my face told my unassuming friend it was the last thing in the world I wanted. The last thing I expected.

'What are you doing?' I yelled sharply, pushing her away automatically.

'Oh, *fuck*, sorry,' she gasped, my lips still slightly unable to absorb the impact of such an unexpected intrusion.

I opened my mouth to speak, my brow furrowed, my eyes wide. 'It's okay,' I managed to mutter, wiping a chunk of Mia's lipstick from my bottom lip.

It was unfortunate Mia could see that it was anything but. 'I'm so sorry, Stacey. Shit. FUCK!' She got to her feet, pacing our cell, mortified by an event we both knew she *should* have avoided. 'Oh, for fucks sake. Shit. SHIT!' She was crying, unwilling to stick around to face her actions, fleeing our cell in a hurry and leaving me to ponder such an impromptu act alone. Yes, of course, we had grown much closer recently, and yes, obviously, I knew she was gay. But she equally knew I *wasn't*. I had made that very clear. Joked even. Made a song about it. *Gay for the stay? No, thank you, no way.* Such a thing was not for me. I liked male attention too much, no matter how much I protested otherwise.

'Mia, wait,' I called after her, needing to settle this moment, calm things down. Explain. We would laugh about it tomorrow. Yet, as I sat in our prison cell, the television on in the background, I realised Mia would take this as yet another personal rejection. I would now become someone else in her life who had willingly pushed her away, expressed a profound disdain for her existence. She, like me, was unable to appreciate the word *no*, unable to understand the things other people did weren't always about *us*. We both struggled to understand the viewpoints of others, unable to put ourselves in their shoes. It made us friends. As far as Mia and I were concerned, everything that happened in our lives *was* about us. Unfortunately, it always would be. It would forever be about how the world makes *us* feel, no one else able to factor into our tremulous emotions. Tonight, of course, would now be no different.

I rose to my feet, needing to find my friend, apologise, give her a hug if that is what it took to ease her emotions, ease mine. I wasn't about to let such a misplaced, wayward kiss affect what we had. It wasn't my fault I could never be willing to allow her to touch my lady parts or any other part of my body inappropriately, clothed or otherwise. I stood in shock, realising there could be no more passionate lunges made at inopportune moments, no more holding each other during the night. Maybe this was all my doing. I had encouraged Jason, made him *want* me. Now I'd done the exact same thing to a goddamned woman. I recalled what Jason had called me once, his words reaching my attention swiftly. *Stacey Adams, you little minx.*

## 26

I made a frantic excuse that I needed to take a shower before lockdown, knowing, if anything, Mia would probably be in the shower block, alone, washing away thoughts of my naked body along with the shame of such a lewd suggestion. Elaine Sharp was her usual sharp self, of course, confirming I should have showered earlier, expressing a notion of cold noncompliance. In the end, I was forced to confess Mia had run off, upset with me, troubled by something I'd done. By something I *hadn't* done.

'Please,' I begged. It was uncomfortable. 'Let me go and find her. You know how fragile she is at the moment.' Knowing of Mia's unstable history, probably hearing rumours of her suffering at the potential hands of a fellow officer, Sharp reluctantly allowed me access to the shower area.

'Yeah, actually, she did head to the showers a few moments ago,' she confirmed flatly. 'Told me she'd forgotten her shampoo.' We both knew Mia had lied. I wondered why Sharp had allowed her to go. Maybe she didn't give a shit. Whatever it was, it annoyed me. 'Two minutes. Hurry up,' Sharp snapped, unlocking the gate that separated our cellblock from the shower area. It was ironic those among us suffering from unstable mental health were usually not allowed access to such locations alone. Sharp knew how delicate Mia was, knew of her tendency to throw up when left alone. I mouthed a thank you, still slightly irritated yet grateful the woman was slowly softening. The longer we got to know each other, the more I was able to wear her down. I didn't believe she was as sharp as she made out — more paper cut irritation than machete death strike.

I raced along the now isolated corridor towards the shower area, my thoughts only on calming my friend's potential troubled mind, explain to her how I felt, tell her I was sorry.

'Mia?' I called, heading towards the bathroom. A shower was on in the background, the sound of running water already filling my senses with dread before I reached my destination. I visualised her sitting curled up in the bottom of a shower tray, gently sobbing, the incoming water jet and tears blending with cold water, cooling otherwise hot thoughts about her seemingly hot friend.

Something wasn't right, although at the time I couldn't put my finger on what. I wanted the nagging feeling in my brain to be nothing more than my oddly deluded imagination, but I could not ignore how it twisted my gut into a tight knot with each step closer I took. As I stepped into the bathroom, heading towards the showers, I was not expecting to come face to face with Mia, lying sprawled out on the wet tiles in the corner of the room, her wrists cut, blood everywhere, her beautiful dark curls lying flat and damp against her once joyful cheeks. She wasn't moving, her body hidden amongst a pool of blackened blood that flooded the floor on which she lay.

Without thinking, I raced towards her, grabbed her, dragging her lifeless body from the steady stream of running water, a ruse made to ensure any passer-by believed she was simply taking a shower. Nothing to see here. Nothing to worry about. I threw myself to the floor, her sticky wrists alien against the heat of my throbbing palms. Thankfully she hadn't been here long.

Mia had sliced herself badly, forcefully, the wounds deliberately deep, ugly, my own blood pumping violently around my veins in response to her suicide attempt. I thought I might be sick. I have no idea how long I clutched my friend's wrists as if my very life depended on saving hers, screaming towards anyone within earshot, needing help I feared might elude us both. I sat slumped on that cold stone floor, covered in Mia's blood, tepid water soaking steadily into my clothing, the gentle splendour of her once calming breath slowing down with each rise and fall of her failing chest. It was all-consuming, my body and mind elsewhere, my friend practically dead in my arms. She was extremely weak, already having lost a lot of blood.

'Help me!' I screamed. 'Someone, *please* help me!' I was holding onto her tightly, the smell of warm sticky blood in my nostrils too much, drowning my thinking, covering the floor. I was crying, unable to fathom the fragile mind of the young woman lying in my startled grasp. I have no idea how I managed to press the emergency button, thankful when a screeching sound rang through the place, sending heavy footsteps racing.

'*Jesus!*' Sharp yelled, seeing me on the floor of the bathroom, clutching the dying body of my beloved Mia. I was sobbing, her heartbeat fading fast, no way for me to stem the flow of blood from my friend's wrists. Where the *fuck* did she get a knife from? We'd been together all evening, hadn't left each other's sight. A mocking metal shape lay some feet away inside the shower cubicle, dotted with blood. A handmade shiv. *What the hell was going on?*

Sharp lunged towards us. 'Christ Adams, what did you

do?' she screamed, noticing the freshly used shiv behind me, believing me capable of such a terrible act.

'Nothing,' I yelled, still trying to stop Mia from bleeding to death. 'She did this to herself. Please. You have to help her.' You have to help *me*.

Realising the urgency of the situation, Sharp nodded her head, a colleague appearing in the doorway behind us. 'Get a stretcher, and Doctor Evans,' she instructed, removing her jacket and making a pillow she carefully lay beneath Mia's head. 'Hold her wrists tightly,' she yelled at me. I did not presume for a moment I was doing anything else. Sharp raced to the sink, tearing the sleeve from her shirt with no hesitation as she created a makeshift bandage that she wrapped firmly around each of Mia's wrists, pulling the material tight. *Why hadn't I thought to do that?*

I was sitting on the wet floor, shock quickly setting in, covered in blood, as Elaine raced around, making Mia as comfortable as this floor could allow, preventing more blood from leaving her fragile body. It felt like an eternity before the prison doctor arrived, followed by two officers carrying a stretcher. They lifted Mia from the floor, no sign of life left in her fragile limbs, no way for me to understand what had caused the ensuing chaos beyond a realisation this was all my fault. I couldn't help but feel guilty, mortified. She only wanted to *kiss* me. I should have let her. I should have allowed her to do other things, too, if that is what she needed. If such acts might have made her happy. I'd allowed Jason to do what he wanted. I practically let him *rape* me. *What the hell did that make me?*

I was taken to the medical bay along with Mia to get cleaned up and checked over for shock, wounds they felt they might have missed, details they needed to confirm. My friend lay in the bed next to mine, her body weak, the doctor checking her vitals, stitching her wrists, saving her life. It was lucky I arrived when I did, he said. I did not feel lucky. People around me ended up dead, it seemed — either by my hand or theirs. It wasn't a good feeling.

I glanced across the room towards the makeshift shiv lying on a nearby tabletop, evidence of my friend's actions, vital proof the governor would need to reach a problematic conclusion neither of us wanted to think about. It was nothing more than a used razor blade attached to a broken toothbrush handle. The two components were tightly wound with packing tape from the prison workshop. I recalled a pair of scissors I'd once tucked neatly in the inside pocket of an old jacket. I'd wished to cause harm too, that evening, irreparably, selfishly. My intention was not to spill physical blood, admittedly, but to create emotional pain. Being with my friend in this place now caused physical and mental pain I honestly had nowhere to place.

\*\*\*

The following day I was questioned in detail about where Mia had managed to get such a shiv from she was able to hide without detection, suspicion luckily deferred from me due to a genuine look of panic on my face the night before. Governor Barrington did not believe I had hurt her, neither did Miss Sharp. I'd witnessed a different side to her, oddly, a side that showed honest, genuine compassion. She wasn't as sharp as she tried to pretend. For that, I was eternally grateful.

The truth was, I did not know where Mia had obtained the shiv. Why would she even want such an item in her possession? Had it been lying in her pocket this whole time? Was she expecting me to reject her so severely, so entirely, and with such enforcement? Had thoughts of suicide lingered in her mind all this time? I realised I still knew very little about the woman I called my friend, despite the length of time we'd shared a cell. The irony was we were in prison, calling a mental health unit our home. This whole thing was hardly ordinary or normal.

Mia stayed in the medical bay for the next week, still very weak, still not saying much at all that made any sense. I was relieved, at least, she was alive. She had been through so much recently. I'd underestimated how fragile her state of mind was. It was the second time I'd been left to ponder the state of my friend's health, alone, her top bunk left empty once again. I'd miscalculated a lot in my life, it seemed.

I'd tried hard to push my own past to the back of my mind for a while, the unfortunate events of this last year meaning relatively little to me now. I could not change the things I'd done. I could never rewind time, go back, do things differently. It was what it was, as they say — as simple as that. Yet, during the time Mia resided in a supervised bed away from me, the one person who came to my mind more and more often was Emma. I spent many years secretly wishing she would disappear from my life, leave me alone so I could finally focus on myself for a change instead of living in her overbearing, under-compelling shadow. I wished her dead too often from the darkness of my private one-bedroom flat, inside a seemingly private mind.

Since her death, I'd allowed little time to focus on the woman I once called my sister, her husband becoming the impossible main aim of my secret desire — my only meaningful purpose in life. Now, every time I closed my eyes, my sister's soft features waited in the darkness, looming. I did not believe for one moment she had, somehow, come back from the grave to haunt me. I did not believe in ghosts. Such nonsense was alien to my way of thinking. No. I simply felt I was now being forced to acknowledge I didn't know the people I once claimed to love.

I failed to understand my sister's suffering, her struggle with bulimia probably brought about by a husband I'd unwittingly become far too obsessed with, to notice anything else. I wasn't able to see beyond that mop of mousy blond hair, his lopsided smile, the way he looked at me when he assumed no one else could see — impossible thoughts that lingered between us in private. Now, with a painful jolt, I realised I'd equally overlooked Mia's suffering too, her troubles of little concern to me until I was forced to witness the resulting carnage, first hand, up close. For days, the unrelenting stench of her blood remained with me, similar to the look on Emma's face the very day I forced her brand-new Mercedes into a ditch. Similar to the day I'd taken Jason's face from him entirely.

As part of my apparent reform, I was forced to visit Farley's office every week. Those mental health sessions we shared were required by law, set out by a prison system that didn't entirely know how else to help. Farley's warm, plant-filled room was the only thing about those meetings I ever looked forward to, his coffee the only thing I enjoyed. I'd all but shut down after carelessly allowing the man to rile me without warning, annoy me so much I'd accidentally confessed to the murder of my sister. Now, each week, we would sit, drink coffee, stare out of the window. It didn't matter to me he was trying to help me, *hoping* to help me, getting paid for such a potential event.

I was oddly far happier in recent months, attributing such an elevated mood to a barrage of anti-depressants and, of course, to Mia. I even managed a smile on the odd occasion, this place not as bad as you might think, once you got used to it. Now though, I was forced to sit alone with my thoughts once more, my mindset in question, my world in scrutiny. I have always been so collected, so gathered in my ideas and considerations. Nothing ever fazed me: stealing Emma's husband; cheating with him behind her back; killing her; subsequently killing him. Nothing affected my mindset or my mood. Everything I did was directed towards the assumption my reasons were valid, my rationale required, everything always so goddamned easy to achieve in theory. In each of those moments of my life, I had planned carefully, created absolute choices, despite absolute chaos, followed my unwavering heart. Now, I questioned that very same heart, chastised my thinking, hated such previously desired assumptions. I realised I didn't know a damned thing about anything. I didn't know Emma. I didn't know Jason. I certainly did *not* know Mia.

Farley tried to help, of course, but you can't help someone who doesn't want it. My friend had tried to commit suicide. I should have seen it coming. She did have an excellent point, though, and her words rang violently in my ears too long. I couldn't keep assuming killing people was a good way to solve my problems. It hadn't worked out well for me, up to now. And, yes, in the very process, I had indeed ended up entirely alone. What the hell had I become? *What on earth did that make me?*

## 27

I mulled around for an entire week feeling sorry for myself, Mia's disappearance from my life too swift, too uncomfortable. I hated the silence of our cell, the nights no longer filled with whispered girly chatter, laughter I couldn't imagine life without. And so, once again, I found myself disengaged from prison life, reverting to those much earlier days here, feeling lost, isolated, forgotten. When a new prison officer was introduced to the women, shown around the place, happily becoming familiarised with our stories and daily needs, I almost missed it completely.

I heard the commotion outside my cell, of course, fully appreciating this excited, hyped interest only usually came from the introduction of a new *male* staff member. It was quite unlike me to be unconcerned by such an event, yet here we were, welcome to the world of the *new* Stacey Adams. Most of the women here were like rampant cats anyway, ready to pounce, should the opportunity arise, their claws aimed firmly where they had no business being. Yet, such news wasn't appealing to me these days. Most of the males I'd come across in this shithole did nothing for my emotions or anything else — a potential lustful stirring in my underwear something I'd forgotten existed. It was a feeling I hadn't felt for a very long time.

'Adams, this is Mr Stuard,' Sharp tapped my open cell door as I lay on Mia's bunk staring at the ceiling, absent in both mind and body, willing myself to become absorbed into the concrete walls around me, already a vacant vessel. *Who gives a shit?* I sighed, offering a pre-rehearsed, automatic toothless smile that barely required any movement of facial muscles, turning my head towards the door casually, a gesture, nothing more intended, nothing more required. I wasn't expecting much anyway. *Fucking hell.* I sat upright, too fast, my mouth set agape in response to the vision that met my eyes. It did nothing for my composure or potential demure whatsoever. The guy was gorgeous, and I mean, *gorgeous.* I clambered from Mia's top bunk, straightened my hair, my top, giggled slightly, probably looking as pathetic as I felt. I always believed Jason to be good looking, but I'm sorry to say he didn't hold a candle to this guy. *Sorry, Jason.*

'Mr Stuard,' I found myself repeating his name, imprinting it onto my memory for future reference, embedding this moment into my psyche forever. 'It's very nice to meet you.' It was possible I had been devoid of male company for so long, I'd entirely forgotten how to act around them — *bloody hell.*

'Very nice to meet you too, Miss Adams,' the guy chimed in, a slight nod of his head denoting politeness I seriously didn't need. *No need for niceties in this room, Mr Stuard. I'm already yours.* He gave me a knowing wink that, for a moment, floored me. My mind wandered to a different time. To Jason. His once lustful eyes hid behind a privately created fake persona I'd once mistakenly adored.

The first thing I thought when I looked at him, the ONLY thing I thought was, *is this guy married?* Although, if I'm being candid, I didn't give a shit if he was or wasn't. It had mattered little to me that Jason was married, and he was married to my sister. *Mr Stuard.* I liked the name. I had a feeling I'd like his first name even more. Screw the rules on addressing everyone by their surnames. I'd even be more than happy to call him *sir* if that is what was required. *Yes, sir, no, sir, please don't stop, sir.* I must have stood next to my bunk staring at him for too long, just staring, nothing more. I wasn't even confident I was smiling now, simply glaring blankly into his face, tracing my eyes across his broad shoulders, that thick, luscious hair that I just wanted to —

'Thank you, Adams. You can speak to Mr Stuard again later,' Sharp cut in, her innocent tone bringing me out of my not so innocent musing. I glared at her, brow furrowed, perturbed by such a rude interruption. *Still Sharp by name, sharp by nature.* Did she notice my unexpected private musing? Did Mr Stuard? I could hardly contain myself as the two officers left my room, Mr Stuard offering a further smile as he glanced towards me over his shoulder. *Shit.* Stacey, for god's sake, *Do. Not. Overthink. That.* He was probably being, friendly, polite.

Still, I couldn't help the inappropriate thoughts that began swilling around my brain like the cheap wine I used to drink. Thoughts I hadn't experienced since my obsession with Jason now began creating havoc, rendering me entirely powerless in my private deliberations. I leaned against the doorframe, watching him walk along the unit away from me, unaware of how he was making me feel, still speaking to Sharp and, on the odd occasion, to the other women in his path. It was totally unexpected the ideas I began having seemed to shift something inside me I hadn't felt for a while. *Fuck off, you lot.* He's mine.

An odd feeling arose in my belly, not unlike the emotions I felt around Jason upon first meeting him all those years ago. It had mattered little to me he was dating my sister, although I was more reserved back then, careful not to offend. I couldn't imagine being like that now. I wondered how things might have turned out had I stepped in earlier, told Jason how I felt, turned his attention to me rather than allowing him to *marry* my sister. I released an unexpected sigh, my actions all but destroying that part of my life for good. No matter. Jason was a lying pig anyway. A scumbag. It might have been *me* in Emma's unfortunate position instead, suffering from an eating disorder, struggling with finances — dead in a ditch.

It felt weird to be lusting over an *actual* man after being stuck in prison with no one but depressed "gay for the stay" women for so long, and, excuse my rudeness, rather unattractive males for equally unwanted company. Governor Daniel Barrington was nice enough, but he was old, married for over a million years, his three grown-up kids older than *me*. He was also balding, had a pudgy belly he tried too hard to tuck inside his ever-expanding trousers without success.

Doctor so-called *Peter* Farley was a nerd, all tank tops and poorly ironed cheap cotton shirts that matched his cheap haircut and cheap attitude. I didn't mind a man in glasses. It could be quite sexy. But only if said glasses rested on a handsome face, which Farley's most certainly did not. Mr *Hunky* Stuard, on the other hand, was in a different league altogether. He was a god, sent from the heavens to save me from this hellhole. Or at least, in my mind, he was. Mr Hunky Stuard. I loved the name I'd aptly created for him. I felt I should keep my impossible considerations to myself, although for now, if my thoughts were all I had to keep me company, they would have to do.

I sat on my bunk too long, wondering what it would feel like to run my hands beneath his shirt, undoing his belt buckle as slowly as I could. Mmmm. Yes, please. I closed my eyes, actually forgetting for a moment what sex felt like.

*Shit.* I sat upright, banging my head on the metal frame above me in my haste. With Jason, it was all frantic and fast, too eager and desperate to create any lasting, lingering effects. It was somewhat unfitted I had equally, oddly, totally forgotten what sex before *him* felt like.

I sat for too long, thinking thoughts I shouldn't have been left alone with. I even managed to put Mia out of my mind entirely for a moment. I unwittingly spent a full thirty minutes thinking of the new prison officer instead of my poor friend currently lying in the medical bay with her wrists bandaged and pulse unstable. As much as I hate to admit, it was a good feeling to think of something distracting, even for a brief period. It had the profound effect of bringing me out of a bad place. I had a feeling Mr Hunky would become very useful to me.

It was unfortunate I was due back in the kitchen shortly — my presence required to prepare the evening meals, my mind required elsewhere. I wanted to lie on my bunk, dream of the new officer, touch places I hadn't felt the need to touch for some time, pretend they were his hands wandering freely. Yet, my daily life beckoned. *Annoyingly.* I assumed it might be the perfect opportunity to seek him out, speak to him some more, get to know him better. I also needed to know my eyes hadn't deceived me in a deluded fit of excitement and that, in fact, he was real. Not something I'd made up to amuse myself because I was alone.

## 28

My hair was still relatively short but had finally reached a length that could thankfully, potentially pass for an actual style. I allowed my hairbrush to glide through my tresses with ease, grateful for the presence of natural waves for the first time in my life. It gave my face a well-needed lift which probably would have made me look otherwise exhausted, defeated. I certainly didn't need to give the new officer *that* kind of first impression. I missed my long hair, of course, wishing I'd left Katelyn's shaver alone. Still, it was done now — no need to reminisce. My time in the mirror thankfully now allowed thoughts of *Hunky Stuard* to filter unchecked instead of the demonic, depressed woman that usually stared back. I even changed my top into something that allowed a little more cleavage.

It was unfortunate prison life permitted little beyond standard t-shirts, comfortable loose-fitting tops, matching bottoms if you're super lucky, jeans, flat-heeled shoes so nobody could be stabbed to death by a wayward stiletto. It was equally unfortunate I had a limited wardrobe to work with these days. It was actually somewhat ironic, considering all those evenings I'd spent staring into a wardrobe filled with clothing I once deemed less than perfect for Jason's eyes. Now, I'd give anything to have a fraction of the options I once believed unfit for charity shops. I wondered if my mum had thrown the rest of my clothing out by now. Probably. Shredded them to ribbons in a raging fury, no doubt.

I applied makeup, recalling a time when both sisters had used such cosmetic coverings to hide truths best left alone, bruises we did not want the world to see, bitter lies we told ourselves to make an otherwise heinous action feel somewhat better to bear. I could barely look myself in the mirror since my mum walked out of my life, my young son in her possession. Now, I felt as fake as my sister's once overbearing lipstick. So long ago had I expressed ideas above my station, designer clothing long gone, a designer home already owned by some other family, an otherwise expensive life I would now never know, long forgotten. Now, I'd simply give anything for the feel of fresh air in my lungs that did not exist inside the confines of a walled prison garden. *Sod luxury.* I would be grateful for a little one-on-one time with a man who actually liked me for who I was.

I straightened my t-shirt, glad it was a reasonably tight-fitting cut, the laundry girls responsible for accidentally creating such a garment when they set a wash cycle on a too-high temperature, shrinking several of my items in the process. At the time, I'd been irate, yelling at the prison officers my clothes had all been ruined. Now, I was somewhat grateful for the stupid idiot who set the washing machine to ninety degrees instead of thirty. *Thank you for that.*

Once preened and pampered as best as I could, I ventured out of my cell, having to follow the increasing noise of giggly chatter to locate the new officer at the centre of everyone's attention. It was a shame most of these women were unable to control themselves or their inappropriate connotations. As *if* someone like him would ever look twice at any of these bitches. *So pathetic.* I casually rolled my eyes as I rounded a corner to see the poor man swamped by several desperate housewives having a significant breakdown simply because there was a good-looking male in the building. Stop the press. Life just got interesting. I followed the wolf-whistles and sideways whispers, hoping for the opportunity to save the poor sod from becoming mobbed to death by this pack of wayward dogs. Excuse the unfortunate expression.

Hunky Stuard was obviously trying to fit into his surroundings, appear polite, talking to a few inmates he would probably have otherwise hoped to avoid. Yet, such an act might make him seem rude. I'm sure he wouldn't want that on his first day. Judging by her lack of presence, Sharp had already left him to it. Typical. I shook my head. How could these women be so forward that they couldn't allow the poor man a chance to settle in? Breathe a little, take his time? The idea made me smile as I made my approach. I had all the time in the world. I glanced down at my chosen attire. Did I look okay? *Did I smell okay?* The poor guy needed saving. I was an expert at saving men. Jason would have testified to that truth. Had he been able to do such a thing, of course, poor sod.

'Excuse me, Mr Stuard?' I asked calmly, standing behind the man, my soft, sultry voice emerging from nowhere. He turned innocently, noticing my approach, a genuine smile on my face, eyes purposefully painted dark, left to wander freely, probably inappropriately.

'Miss Adams?' Hunky replied brightly, probably wondering if he was recalling my name correctly. I nodded, my smile improving rapidly, my heartbeat easing. I surely didn't look *that* different without makeup, did I? Mr Stuard turned, expressing to two women currently hogging his attention he would indeed ask the governor about their request before turning his full attention to me. They both shared the name Jane, and, because of such a coincidence, had become quite inseparable. I glanced at them both, offering one of my *fuck off* looks. They took the hint.

'I expect you're feeling a little overwhelmed by this lot,' I chided, running a carefully timed hand through my recently brushed hair, glad it was clean, glad it was finally growing out. 'They're mostly harmless if you ignore them.' I laughed, licking my freshly glossed lips, knowing how to play a man. I loved this game. It had been far too long since I'd played it.

'It has been a bit full-on, I have to admit,' he confirmed with a smile of his own that would have flawed me, if it wasn't for the fact we were surrounded by too many people for me to give away my cards so easily. 'It is Miss Adam's, isn't it?' he queried.

'Yes, but when no one's listening, you can call me Stacey,' I offered with a wink that I instantly wished I could retract. *Christ.* I laughed, trying to diffuse the awkward moment I wasn't even confident had happened. *Stay calm, Stacey. Take it easy. You know how this thing works.*

'I'm quite sure I'm not allowed to do that,' he replied with a slight shake of his head. All I wanted to do was ask him his name. His first name. *Yes, sir, no sir. You can do that to me if you like, sir.*

'Don't worry. I won't tell a soul. What we get up to in private is nobody else's business,' I stated, wishing the ground would swallow me up and be done with it. 'Oh, god, sorry,' I laughed, pressing a hand over my unchecked mouth, my cheeks glowing hot, nothing I could do about that now. Was I blushing? 'That wasn't meant to sound so *wrong*.' I actually meant every word, but I couldn't tell him such a truth. Not yet, at least.

Hunky laughed, brushing off my wayward words with a casual wave of his hand. 'It's okay, I know what you meant,' he confirmed. He had absolutely no idea.

'So,' I offered, needing a genuine reason for loitering in the corridor when I should have been in the kitchen already. 'How are you finding your first day?'

'It's not been as bad as I initially expected,' Hunky confirmed, placing a hand over his key chain. 'The women here seem okay. A lot friendlier than I assumed.'

*That's because you're hot, and they all want to fuck you.* I smiled, coughed, almost choking on my inappropriate thoughts. I did *not* need him to know such a truth, now struggling to get the very idea out of my head. I didn't need the competition. I hoped I wouldn't suddenly call him Hunky by mistake and expose my position too soon. 'We're fairly normal in here if you can excuse all the mental health issues,' I said casually. At no point was I including myself in such a concoction, of course, the very fact I was one of them failing to register with me at all.

'Some of us just ended up in the wrong place at the wrong time,' I concluded, talking about myself now, hoping he hadn't read my file yet. I dreaded the idea of him reading my file. Would he want to get close to a double murderer? The serial killer, nobody knew of. Why the hell did I have to make such a statement? *The wrong place, at the wrong time?* Seriously, Stacey? I'm sure neither Jason nor Emma would have agreed with that admission. My smile slipped. 'Some of us are still having a difficult time processing everything.' It was true. I was having difficulty processing this very conversation.

'Oh?' Mr Stuard queried. He seemed the type of person a girl could talk to when needed, lean on for support, give a hug to on the odd occasion, amongst other things. I liked the idea.

'A friend of mine tried to kill herself last week,' I confessed, needing his sympathy, a hand around my saddened shoulders. God, I'd missed this flirting thing. I did hope that Mia was okay, though. I missed her too.

'I'm so sorry to hear that,' he replied, a sympathetic tone in his voice that I was already becoming very attracted to. 'Is she okay now?'

I shook my head. 'To be honest, Mr Stuard, I'm not entirely sure. She's been in the medical bay for over a week and nobody has been able to tell me how she's doing.' It was true. They had a knack of keeping me in the dark about such matters, as if they assumed it was none of my business.

'Well, if you give me her name, I'm sure I can find out for you, Miss Adams,' Hunky offered kindly.

'*Please,* call me Stacey,' I asked again, biting my bottom lip, wondering how my name would sound if whispered in the darkness of some cupboard, some closed storeroom. "Miss Adams" sounded as if this guy was my goddamned school teacher. I *never* wanted to fuck any of my school teachers. The very thought made me shudder. 'My friend's name is Mia Young,' I confirmed.

'Well, Miss Adams. *Stacey,*' Hunky whispered my name so as not to invite a telling off from his superiors. *Bloody hell.* I hoped my mouth hadn't fallen agape. Was I dribbling? 'I will ask about Miss Young for you and get back to you in due course.' He clicked his heels together firmly and made a tiny saluting gesture with his right hand that reminded me of Jason. I was instantly transported back to the days when he had been all I could think about. My obsession. My lover. Had Mr Hunky Stuard now become my new obsession? My new distraction? I could only hope to Christ he was able to become such a thing. I needed all the distraction I could get. If something could in any way be reciprocated, well, what more did I need to express about that incredible notion?

# 29

I endured my evening meal alone, thinking of Mia and Elijah, fantasising wildly about *Hunky* Stuard, what I wanted him to do to me, amongst other things I could barely contain in my head. The entire unit was buzzing with the thought of this new, rather sexy-looking prison officer in their midst, some of these women even sharing impossible ideas that the guy had given them a lingering smile. *Yeah, as if.* I rolled my eyes, stabbing at my overcooked jacket potato and stringy cheese, not hungry, trying to tolerate this moment until I could once again escape and seek him out.

Although our previous conversation had been relatively short, I felt it was a meaningful introduction. He had called me *Stacey*. How many of these bitches could confirm that? It was fortunate many of the women in this unit were too depressed to notice him anyway. Their mental health battles far more critical to their daily lives than what Hunky Stuard could offer them. Most of them, in fact, were unable to pull off a typical day, let alone pull a decent bloke.

I wasn't in the slightest bit hungry, so I made my excuses, leaving my kitchen colleagues to clear the plates, mop the dining room floor, anything to get me out of actual work. It wasn't a popular decision. I wasn't liked all that much anyway, my inability to connect with most of the women here always leaving me on the outside, looking in. I didn't give a shit about these women or their infected, poisonous viewpoints. I only had eyes for Hunky Stuard and how I could get him to notice me. So what if I was in prison for murder? I assumed, at some point, I would be able to speak to him honestly about my past, openly, help him understand most of what had happened to me was not my fault. Not really. No matter what my file and some judge claimed.

I went in search of Hunky Stuard, wishing to ask if he had heard anything about Mia. I was missing her. It was weird to experience a genuine connection to another human being, attaching sincere emotions to their existence. I acquainted such a feeling to the arrival of motherhood, everything about me changing in the very instant I'd held my baby boy in my arms. I also needed to apologise to her, smooth things over between us, the last time we'd spoken resulting in her running sobbing from our cell, suicide on her mind, embarrassment in her heart.

The two Janes were leaning against an air vent along a quiet corridor, enjoying a cheeky smoke, a cheeky laugh, hoping not to get caught. They were chatting, giggling, discussing something I couldn't initially hear. When I heard Mr Stuard's name mentioned, my attention was caught.

'Everything okay, ladies?' I asked casually, passing by, saying a fond hello. It didn't matter I barely spoke to them.

Jane number one, whose real name was Jane Tolly, aged fifty-seven, in and out of prison for most of her life, yet another poorly produced product of society, nodded, grinning a dilapidated row of battered teeth towards my ever-inquisitive ear. 'We're just discussing the new guy, Mr Stuard,' she whispered. 'Apparently, he's been giving one of the women the eye, if you know what I mean.'

I scoffed. I *doubt* that very much. Unless they were

talking about me, of course, and then, yes, I was very interested in what they'd heard and what they had to say about it.

'Who?' I snapped, my brow furrowing, hoping beyond rational logic to hear my name mentioned.

'Claire Bennett said she heard him whispering to Sharp about her.'

'*Fuck off, did he!*' I couldn't help snapping. Claire Bennett was overweight, under-educated, dull as dishwater. Ugly as hell. I hated the woman.

'I'm just telling you what I heard,' Jane number one replied, taking an uninterested drag of her cigarette that she aimed into the air vent.

Jane number two, whose surname I could never remember cut in, offering her two pence worth of readily available gossip. 'Claire claimed he winked at her this lunchtime as she took the laundry bins to the front gate.' Jane two was half the age of Jane one. They had a weird mother-daughter thing going on. They even looked a bit like each other. It was very odd.

'No, he did not.' Why the hell was I acting so defensive?

'Why are *you* so bothered anyway?' Jane one chipped in, making me want to ram her cigarette down her throat.

'Because the poor guy only started working here today. I don't think he needs stupid rumours circulating about him already.' It was true. If the governor caught even the tiniest indication Mr Stuard was considering a relationship with *any* inmate, he would lose his position before it had even started. I would probably need to be careful, actually.

'The guy has a reputation, Stacey. Surely you've heard?' Jane one folded her arms across her chest, shaking her head as if she couldn't believe I wasn't already party to this critical information.

'Heard what?' I honestly hated the way these bitches could create a drama out of pretty much everything.

'Apparently, he left his last post because of some scandal with a female inmate. Inappropriate behaviour, they claimed. Some woman he was supposed to be shagging on the sly. It was never proven, hence he was transferred here instead of being struck off.'

'I don't believe you.'

'Why don't you ask Claire, yourself?' Number two asked, swiftly losing interest in me and my accusations.

I nodded. I would. I was actually prepared to do that right now. 'I will.' I turned to leave.

'I'm only telling you what I heard. They say he's the kind of man who is only out for himself. Not that Claire cares about such things. She'd shag anything.' Number one was sucking the last dregs from her cigarette. I hoped she choked on the bloody thing. They knew nothing about Mr Stuard. How dare they create such disgusting rumours?

I left the two Janes to their once assumed private conversation, intending to seek out Bennett. She was an inmate I'd had relatively little to do with up until now. She was opinionated, bitchy, not *my* type of person at all. I needed her to calm her gossiping ideas, shut her wayward gob. Shut them all up. Hunky Stuard did not need such wagging tongues set about him. I was fuming as I rounded the corner, almost walking straight into Hunky in the process.

'Woah, take it easy,' he said, holding his arms towards me to steady my approach. I could have melted into his warm, inviting touch right there. 'Where's the fire?'

I sighed, offering a smile, feeling stupid. 'Sorry, Hunk-sir,' I said, almost accidentally calling him by the pet name I'd lovingly created. I breathed as slowly as I was able, allowing my lungs to expel air that had suddenly become too thick for me to catch my breath. I worried I might not be able to breathe at all if he didn't step away from me soon. His aftershave was intoxicating. 'I was looking for you.'

'Well, I am popular today,' he laughed. *Oh, more than you know.*

I sighed by mistake, needing to explain what I'd heard, warn him about the unchecked rumours that were already threatening to circulate. 'Sir, may I be frank with you?' I needed to sound as genuine as I could, no room in my mind for him to assume me a gossip. I didn't wish for him to view me badly.

'Of course, Miss Adams. What's the problem?' I was beginning to detest the sound of my surname, this place wholly ensuring my actual identity was all but wiped out.

I pulled him to one side and explained what I'd heard only moments earlier, the chat among the women about his apparent inappropriate advances towards a fellow inmate, both in this place and his last. I laid it on thick, making sure he believed Claire Bennett and the other women were seriously trying to cause trouble for him already, prepared to dismantle his brand-new career in HMP Blackwood. I needed him to believe I had his best interests at heart, had his back. *And his front, come to think of it, if he let me.*

Hunky looked at me for a moment, absorbing my words. I had all but branded myself a snitch now, a rat, my rebellious words left to fester readily in my mouth, burning a hole in the back of my throat, opening a door to potential hatred most of the women here wouldn't have any issues displaying openly.

'*Please*, Mr Stuard. This needs to stay between us. You know what these places are like.' He knew exactly what I meant. I now hoped he appreciated what I was willing to sacrifice for him. It was all that mattered.

Hunky nodded. 'I appreciate that. Thank you, Adams.

*Stacey.*' He smiled at me, emphasising my first name with a whisper, our eyes meeting in that single moment. *Shit.* He had called me Stacey again. If I was staring at him, it was entirely his fault.

'Oh, and while we are on the subject of looking out for each other,' he continued, completely unaware of how he'd made me feel. 'I spoke to the medical bay for you, and Young is due to be brought back into the unit this evening. I hope that helps.'

With that, he waved a free hand and carried on his way, his duties calling, the other women needing his attention more than he assumed I did, his lingering conversation with me no longer appropriate. I was glad Mia was coming home, although I had a feeling I would need to deal with Bennett before she became a serious problem to us all.

225

## 30

Mia walked into our cell just before lights out, her tiny features and huge curls an inviting sight for my sore eyes. I was lying on my bunk, arms raised above my head, misplaced solace allowing me a moment to dream about Mr Hunky Stuard. Mia glanced my way, her face one of embarrassment, her mouth set in a straight line, nothing of her tone expressing anything of the emotions hiding in plain sight.

'Mia?' I cried, rising from my bunk in a hurry. I raced the four-foot gap that separated us to give her a hug that I needed more than she did. 'Oh, my god, honey, I've been so worried. How are you? They wouldn't let me see you.' I was rambling, ranting, the last few hours of Hunky's existence in my life all but taking its toll on my ravaged senses.

Mia still had bandages around her wrists, a telling reminder of what happened between us. Of what I'd made her do. 'Stacey, I just wanted to say —'

'You don't have to say anything,' I cut in. 'Not until you're ready.'

'But what happened was —'

'Unfortunate. Nothing more.' It was true. I didn't wish to be reminded of the kiss she'd tried to smother me with. I certainly didn't need any rushed explanation as to why it should never have happened, unexpectedly prompting such a violent reaction she no doubt already felt terrible for. It was her business, not mine. Mia would tell me in her own time. I couldn't allow thoughts of my own failings to filter into the room, into my mind. I wanted to tell her about Hunky, although it felt a little insensitive to do such a thing so swiftly, even for me. So I made her a cup of tea and talked about nothing in particular, all the time wanting to express my increasing lust for a man she hadn't even met, hoping to avoid the real issue that was troubling me. Mia's unexpected suicide attempt.

'So, who's the new guy?' Mia asked, bringing him up before I'd even offered her a biscuit. I was glad she didn't seem angry with me for previously rejecting her so terribly.

'Mm?' I queried, pretending not to care, trying not to blush.

'Oh, come on. I might be gay, Stacey, but I'm not blind. The women have been talking about him all day. Yes, even in the medical bay, we got the memo.'

I glanced at my friend, knowing she probably knew me better than I gave her credit for. I smiled. 'His name is Mr Stuard. I call him Hunky. In my head, of course.' I allowed a slight chuckle to slip out undetected.

Mia laughed, which made me laugh, our friendship resuming regular duties. *Thank fuck*. 'Have you spoken to him yet?'

'Mia —' I almost groaned.

'No, no. Don't mind me. I'm obviously *not* your type. I assume *Mr Stuard* probably is, though.' She grinned at me. This last week, her personal suffering, all completely dissolved now by the idea of my new crush. It was good to have something to focus on to be honest. I was growing quite tired of everyone else's suffering.

I tilted my head, concerned she would think me ill-tempered if, after everything that happened between us, I was to start randomly chatting about some guy I'd literally met that very day. Had it really been only one day? It felt as if I'd known the guy forever already.

'He is quite nice, actually,' I confessed, sitting down by Mia's side on my bottom bunk, careful not to brush against a leg or any part of her body that might give her unwanted ideas.

'I knew it,' she laughed, poking a wayward finger against my arm with a grin. Was I so transparent? I really *would* need to be careful.

'Apparently, Bennett is already trying to get her claws into him?' I seriously had it bad. I actually sounded jealous.

'Oh, she thinks *every* man fancies her,' Mia laughed off my utterance, sipping her tea. She was right. She did. But I couldn't help feeling threatened by the idea all the same. I did not yet know Mr Stuard. *Hunky*. I didn't even know his first name, his presence in my life only occurring this very day. I had no right to be worried, jealous, anxious, or any other emotion I could think of. He wasn't mine. I thought about Jason. About wanting him so badly that nothing else had mattered. He wasn't mine either. I couldn't go down that rabbit hole again. Not for any man.

\*\*\*

I had to find out what Claire Bennett's intentions were, warn her off if needed, all under the guise of innocent concern I feared I might not pull off. I didn't want *poor little Claire* to become mixed up with random prison officers. I couldn't allow that to happen. She was vulnerable, poor cow. She wouldn't honestly have intended to place the new officer's career in jeopardy so readily, surely?

I found her in the laundry room, my presence in this

part of the prison only made possible by the pair of jeans I'd "forgotten" to place in my laundry bag before collection. 'I'm so stupid,' I confirmed. 'It won't take a moment. I don't want to put any of you guys out for my error.' Miss Sharp had softened slightly over the length of time I'd known her, her razor-sharp tendencies dulling now to a blunt point I knew couldn't inflict any lasting damage. Since we had saved Mia's life together, I felt we shared a connection that had left us more appreciative of each other. Plus, I had a rather profound way with people that seemed to confirm I was no threat, my charms able to surface on cue.

I shouldn't have been surprised Bennett was still discussing Hunky when I arrived, her *apparent* effect on him leaving the guy quite speechless. I rolled my eyes, hearing enough. *How deluded.*

'Do you think this is such a good idea?' I questioned, firmly putting on a "concerned fellow inmate" face for the benefit of the room as I stood in front of a group of women I didn't know, a pair of relatively clean jeans in hand, a slight noncompliant look in my eyes.

'It's no concern of yours, Stacey,' Bennett scolded back. We were standing in the laundry area, the machines around us loud enough to muffle any conversation, the officer by the door assuming I was trying to locate my laundry bag.

'I'm only trying to look out for you,' I lied, irritated by her infuriating stature, wishing I could plant her oversized head into the side of a nearby washing machine and be done with it.

'I'm a big girl, Stacey. I can take care of myself.' A few of the women sniggered. How dare they? *Bitches.*

My tone darkened, placing ideas in my mind that probably shouldn't have been allowed to develop. I had come here with the pretence of offering some friendly support, warn the stupid, deluded *bitch* not to do anything that could get her or Mr Stuard into trouble, the truth I wanted Hunky all to myself irrelevant. Now, these idiots had jumped on my last nerve, my buttons well and truly pressed. The bastards were daring to laugh at me.

'Oh, you think you can look after yourself, do you?' I was glaring at Bennett now, no longer caring about my fictional concern, my face close enough to hers so I could smell her breath, the sweat under her armpits. I sounded as if I was spoiling for a fight. I wasn't. She was just pissing me off.

'What's it to you?' she glared back, unwilling to back down. It was a shame the poor cow didn't know me. She didn't know what I was, what I could do when provoked. I'd managed to slip under her radar, the murderer in their mix remaining unknown to them all. Only Mia knew the truth, and luckily for me, she kept my past to herself.

'Mr Stuard is new here,' I warned. 'I don't think he would appreciate your lying tongue.'

'Ohh, I get it. *You* fancy him.' Bennett might have been spot on about that, but I wasn't about to let her know such a truth.

'Don't be so *fucking* stupid,' I snapped, shaking my head in defiance. 'The man's probably got a wife and kids. A mortgage.' It was probably true. The difference was, I knew how to be discrete. Play the game.

'And?' Bennett still didn't seem to care.

'And, if any of the shit you're hell-bent on spreading gets back to the governor, Mr Stuard will be out on his ear.'

Bennett seemed to soften for a moment, thinking. Then she laughed. 'Well, I can't help it if the man has it bad for me. I'll be getting out of this place soon anyway. We can be together on the outside.' She glanced at the other women, her apparent joke provoking a torrent of laughter coming from nowhere.

I couldn't believe the nerve of the woman, her feigned inability to see reality for what it was, fully responsible for my increasing anger. I automatically lunged forward, grabbing Bennett by the hair, dragging her chunky corpse towards an unused drier. I had no idea what I was planning. Nothing major. Just a nice, friendly warning. A little chat. Maybe I could get away with shoving her head inside the thing for effect? Bennett screamed out that I could fuck off, do one, bringing attention neither of us needed. Two officers raced over, forcing me to let her go, reluctantly. Bennett's hair was a mess, her top rucked up, exposing flesh that nobody needed to witness.

'Everything okay here, ladies?' It was Hunky Stuard. *Typical*. Perfect bloody timing.

'Fine,' I snapped, unable to prevent the glare I was still giving Bennett as I smoothed my own hair, ensuring I didn't appear as demonic as I felt.

'Okay, break it up then,' he confirmed, his recently acquired Blackwood uniform now put firmly to the test. Bennett glared at me, resuming her duties, yet not before offering Mr Stuard a lingering smile that, thankfully, he didn't reciprocate.

I walked out of the laundry room hot, irritated — all but ready to accidentally extend my time in here by the ridiculous thoughts that raced through my mind. Hunky would be worth every additional day. That much I was confident.

'Is everything okay?' Hunky asked me as I was escorted back to my unit.

I nodded, feeling terrible, hoping he hadn't noticed how shaken I was. 'I'm fine. Sorry about that, sir.'

He stared at me for a moment, holding his gaze longer than I would have assumed necessary. 'Stacey?'

*Fuck me. He'd done it again.* I swallowed, glancing into

the most beautiful eyes I'd ever seen. It was enchanting. 'I'm just worried for your career,' I confessed, closing my eyes and opening them again to see a wide grin spreading freely across his face. I wanted to laugh too, grateful I was able to refrain. 'You've barely started working here, and already some of the women are hell-bent on making things hard for you.' Why did I have to say the word, *hard*? I had a vision now I couldn't dislodge.

'You don't have to worry about me.'

'Somebody has to have your back in this place,' I stated with a smile, wanting him to see the lighter side of me, the gentler side. I visualised his front pressed against my back. Something pressed against my —

'So, Miss Bennett thinks I'm fit, does she?' Hunky asked, throwing out a casual remark as if we were just two casual friends, discussing potential conquest options. *Jesus.*

I swallowed, my mouth forming a grin. I couldn't help it. 'Most of the women in this place think you're fit, sir,' I confirmed, hoping not to inflate his head any further, hoping not to give away my emotions.

'Do *you* think I'm fit, Stacey?' The question came from nowhere.

Holy crap. What would I say to that? What kind of response would be deemed appropriate? Yes. *Yes, I bloody well did.* I shrugged. 'A little... maybe.' Shit. Was I blushing again? I couldn't tell. My face was still somewhat overheated from the overbearing air in the laundry room.

He tilted his head and tapped a free hand across the keychain on his belt. I wanted to ask if he was married? Did he have kids? *Did he fancy me?* What the hell was his goddamned name? Would he fuck me if I asked him nicely?

'Well, I will certainly bear that in mind,' he confirmed, unlocking the gate to my unit and allowing me to step inside. I still had my jeans in my possession. It didn't matter.

Bare *what* in mind? I swallowed, momentarily rendered speechless. Bollocks. That rarely happened to me. Usually, I had this thing all figured out.

# 31

I should not have read too much into Hunky's comments or thought anything inviting about the look I now convinced myself he'd given *me*. It would make me no better than Bennett. Yet, as it was, it had the rather impressive side effect of uplifting my mood so much, the doctor had considered reducing my anti-depressants.

'What has brought about such a sudden change to you, Miss Adams?' Doctor Evans asked me as he handed out the morning pills. 'You seem so different this morning.' It was an excellent point. One I couldn't answer honestly without inviting prejudice. This had been the worst year of my life, the worst eighteen months. It was no wonder I was now on powerful medication. I'd murdered three people; four, if I included Sylvester, which, of course, I did. My poor old cat an innocent in the journey that had become my rapidly unravelling brain — the most innocent of them all, in fact. My death list had increased since my conviction, my serial killer status firmly reached, exceeded. *So why the good mood, indeed?*

I wasn't expecting my life to turn out the way it had, to end up in a prison cell, a convicted double murderer. Yet, who would? I certainly did not expect to ever find love again after leaving Jason behind on his hallway floor, though I wasn't confident I would do such a thing now. I'd known Hunky a couple of days, nothing more. He was a distraction from my humdrum daily routine. He might not have even noticed me at all, yet, my brain was screaming at me, telling me to pursue him, take things further, that it was my right to feel something other than perpetual numbness that consumed me every single day. It was the same feeling I had when I met Jason for the first time, back when things seemed far more straightforward, more normal. I *really* needed to stop calling the guy Hunky. It was annoying. Yet, he was. It was a simple truth.

I hadn't allowed myself much time to think about Emma since my arrival here, my focus still occasionally wandering towards the actions of her volatile husband. I tried hard not to think of Jason much either, those events leading to his untimely death entirely unforgiving. The truth was, despite everything that happened between us, and everything I'd been subsequently forced to deal with since we parted company, I missed him. He was a pig — a selfish, greedy man with little regard for anyone other than himself, his needs the only thing in life that ever seemed to matter. But I missed Jason Cole, all the same. I missed his touch, the feel of him inside me. I missed the kisses, the stolen glances, the giggles we enjoyed in private.

If I was honest with myself, burying my emotions and pretending I wasn't affected by my past only added to my decline into depression and slow encumbered days that seemed to go on forever. I assumed the lingering, haunting memories of killing my sister and her husband might affect me at some point, provoke a darkening change in my behaviour, forge a pattern of guilt that would surface when I least expected it. But, the truth was, it hadn't. The authorities clearly stated on my record that I'd shown no remorse for the two deaths. They had a point. It was true.

The simple fact was I didn't feel anything at all for what I was forced to do to them. I couldn't bring myself to linger too long on events I could no longer change. It wasn't my fault they were dead. Those old events had happened without my knowing consent. Yet, nobody could understand that. Nobody seemed to care my emotions were far more delicate than I was willing to express.

Emma was dead because she failed to tell me the truth about her life. If I'd known she was suffering, that she wasn't actually living this incredible lifestyle I'd built up inside my head, *maybe* I wouldn't have felt the need to end her life in the tragic way I did. She certainly wouldn't have brought out the green monster in me. I might not have felt so inadequate in her seemingly *perfect* company. Jason was dead because he failed to end his cheating ways, proving that I had the whole thing so wrong in my head. I was wrong about him. Wrong about my sister.

Emma and Jason were not the fantastic couple they pretended to be in public. With no actual money to call their own, everything they possessed was made possible because of maxed-out credit cards, a colossal mortgage, long overdue loans. Jason loved rough sex. I believed it was simply because he couldn't get enough of *me*. Couldn't get away from his wife fast enough. If I'd realised earlier he was a serial rapist in disguise, pretending to be normal while grooming my wayward thinking, I would have stayed well clear, found myself a different pursuit, a decent guy. As it was, the stupid idiot brought his own death on himself. They both did. I even killed my poor cat because of the wrath I felt Jason was savagely bringing down on me.

However, meeting Hunky seemed to shift something in my mind I wasn't expecting. I could, of course, rot in this hellhole for the next twenty years or so, remain locked away, out of sight, out of mind, proving to the authorities now in control of my life I wasn't sorry for what I did, and therefore I would not be safe in the outside world alone. Or I could change things. Maybe even secure an early release if such a thing was possible. Rebuild my broken life. I chose to focus on a crazy idea of freedom. He didn't know it yet, but the appearance of *Mr Stuard* in my life had sent me into an unprecedented spin, helping me focus for the first time in a very long time on what I wanted to achieve from this mess I'd created. I felt, oddly, I could try and do something more, ensure the world viewed me differently. I had a son growing up in the outside world without me — a niece I needed to make things up to. Parents, I desperately craved forgiveness from.

\*\*\*

I woke up the following morning with a gem of a thought bubbling in my mind. I asked to see the governor, enthusiasm springing from nowhere, my hands tingling with an idea, just a simple concept, of how I could turn my life around.

'Miss Adams?' Governor Barrington was sitting behind his desk, slightly surprised to see me, slightly tired looking, as always, still sucking in his belly. The sunlight, as usual, was bouncing wildly off the top of his balding head, making me want to laugh out loud. 'What can I do for you this fine morning?'

'Excuse me, sir, but I would like to ask if it might be at all possible for me to begin a course. I'm very keen to learn, willing to turn my life around.' I felt that I'd been living inside a cave this last year, my head all over the place, my thoughts wildly misplaced.

The governor looked at me, a curious glint in his eye that I wasn't expecting. 'Wow. What a revelation,' he confirmed, getting up from his leather chair and twisting his window blinds to aim the morning sun in a different direction. It was indeed a revelation. I had, in fact, got out of the bed feeling oddly different this morning, enthusiastic, eager for a fresh start. 'What on earth has brought about this sudden desire for education?'

I couldn't tell him that the presence of a very sexy new male prison officer had prompted a sudden need to impress, to change the outcome of a life I now realised was firmly out of control, out of *my* control. I thought about Emma's money. The almost seventeen grand I'd already handed over to my niece, my mum's firm glare ensuring I signed it all away. Money that, rightfully, should have been mine.

'I want to do a degree,' I confirmed confidently, pressing my lips together at the very thought of the words leaving my mouth, unsure why I sounded so bold. Did I have the right?

'In what?' Governor Barrington sounded both impressed and shocked.

'In law,' I stated, feeling that, from wherever she was, my sister might have heard my request, my enthusiasm. I hoped she might even be glad for me.

\*\*\*

Despite the governor's initial uncertainty, he agreed to my request, telling me he would arrange the necessary paperwork and get back to me as soon as possible. He said it might give me a focus, a reason to exist for a change. He said he was impressed, proud of me, glad I had a positive notion of improvement. I left his office feeling lighter than I had in a while. Of course, the first thing I wanted to do was seek out Hunky. I was sick of calling him Mr Stuard, Sir — even the idea of referring to him as Hunky in my head was beginning to wear a little thin. Today was the day I was going to find out more about the new aim of my sudden desire. Find out his *fucking* name.

Mia was healing well, feeling better, calmer, our conversations still barely touching on that night, the reason she thought she had no option but to end it all. Still, I couldn't dwell on Mia's state of mind. I had my own life to deal with now, a new focus to concentrate my efforts. I found Hunky on duty in the kitchen, luckily for me, my request to see the governor taking me away from prison responsibilities for a while, away from Hunky's attention.

'Can I have a moment please, Mr Stuard?' I asked, gently touching his arm so he would turn and face me. He was keenly watching the kitchen girls mop the floor, ensuring they were not missing important areas, required to do a thorough job, my constant disappearance when menial work was needed, beginning to grow a little tiresome with them all.

'Good morning, Miss Adams. How can I help?' Hunky gave me one of his smiles. The very smile I looked forward to seeing now — the very reason for my visit to the governor's office. The reason I got out of bed with a spring in my step.

I gave him one of my "please, stop calling me *Miss Adams*" looks, provoking a knowing grin I wasn't expecting. He had no idea what he was doing to me or how he was making me feel.

'Sorry,' he corrected himself sharply, whispering, 'Stacey,' out of earshot, away from the potential prying ears of my fellow inmates.

I pressed my teeth into my bottom lip, nervous, manoeuvring myself so that we were facing away from the others. 'I wanted you to be the first to know that I've just requested permission to begin studying for a law degree,' I stated, feeling proud of my decision. As a teenager, I'd wanted to become a lawyer, dreaming of going to university, studying hard for a degree I felt might set me up for life. As it was, things don't always work out the way you plan, and for reasons that now eluded me, I didn't make it to university in the end. I can't remember why, but my once prized ambition of getting my law degree faded as I entered my twenties, working several shitty nine-to-five jobs, forgetting my dreams altogether for a while. Telling Hunky my plan was my way of making myself feel that I had a chance, that *we* had a chance. *Maybe.*

'Wow, Miss... *Stacey*. That is wonderful news. Well done to you.' Hunky looked pleased for me. I grinned, he grinned. I touched his arm, a gesture of gratitude, an expression of friendship. It was only a slight touch, nothing more than that. We had done nothing to warrant what happened next, the way things changed so swiftly between us. Without warning, he pulled away sharply. *Too sharply.* It caught me off guard, made me jump, made me blink. I stood in front of him open-mouthed as he recoiled from my unavoidable proximity as if I'd burned him, making a hasty retreat along the corridor, muttering something about needing to check that the gate between the two units was locked correctly. The bloody things were on automatic timers. He required his swipe card to get through. Of course, the gate was locked. This wasn't the year 1820. *What the hell?*

I tried to work out what had happened, what I'd done, retrace my steps, but could think of nothing that might have warranted such a shocking retraction, the look on his face telling of his embarrassment, the flush of his cheeks reddened with unprecedented unease. I hadn't tried to kiss him. I definitely would have remembered that. I hadn't squeezed his buttocks, or run my hand over his crotch, although believe me, I had dreamt about such an act far too often over the last couple of days. I scratched my head. All I did was tell him my good news, share my enthusiasm, nothing more than that.

I thought about going to find him, race after him, but the kitchen girls were already annoyed with me as it was, so I had little choice but to let it go, let him go. I resumed my kitchen duties, sorting the weekly menu sheets, checking stock levels of products the poor women were subjected to without anyone giving an actual shit about the welfare of these people, thinking of Hunky, as usual.

I was confident about one thing, though. Whatever had happened, Mr Stuard's face was telling me something I couldn't shake, couldn't get out of my mind. He was embarrassed by the simple touch of my hand. *Why?* Why would such innocent contact rattle him so much? Unless... *unless!* Oh my God! He fancied me as much as I desired him? It was a single, ridiculous concept that had me singing loudly until lunch was served, much to the annoyance of everyone. What a shame for them all.

## 32

Hunky seemed hell-bent on avoiding me for the rest of that day, the rest of that week, his presence conveniently required elsewhere whenever I came anywhere close to speaking to him. It was annoying. Within a few days, he had single-handedly managed to tip my mood from delighted elation to notable, potentially severe depression. Even Mia noticed, asking me if my mental health was beginning to tilt towards potential Bipolar Disorder, my manic state worrying to her. I snapped at her several times, having to apologise more than I should have, needing no excuse to draw unrequired attention to myself at any moment for fear of what I might accidentally admit to if left to my own devices. I couldn't express my feelings, tell her my hidden thoughts. Hunky's aggravating effect on my mood was hardly her fault.

As it was, I ambled around solemnly for the rest of the week, feeling sorry for myself, acting like a petulant child, my long face matching my long prison sentence, my expression confirming I was in a terrible mood and so everyone should keep away from me, if they knew what was good for them. They all knew me well enough by now to appreciate the consequence of anything else. Even Mia kept her distance, happy to disappear into some book she'd been meaning to read for months without much enthusiasm. I despised how men seemed to have such a profound effect on me. The more time I spent in the company of a man I found attractive, the worse I became. I was beginning to consider the possibility I might indeed have some serious undiagnosed mental health condition that needed urgent attention, my unfeigned need to be desired, wanted, admired, something I was unable to shake. Maybe Mia was right about me.

I was lying on my bunk trying to prevent my brain imploding in on itself, Mia on top of me, metaphorically speaking of course, the only sounds coming from her direction being the occasional rustle of a turning page.

'Miss Adams? May I speak with you for a moment, please?'

I glanced sideways, not expecting the interruption, not anticipating the concept of seeing Hunky standing in the doorframe of our cell, a hesitant, nervous look on his face.

'Sure,' I replied swiftly, confused as to why he would ignore me all week then suddenly require my undivided attention. My heart was in my throat, my legs unwilling to take my weight as I lifted my now excited body from my bunk to the floor. What the hell was wrong with me? Mia glanced my way as I straightened my wayward hair hastily, venturing out of our cell into the corridor beyond, struggling to hide how I was feeling to either of them. I didn't dare look at my friend. She would see straight through me, able to witness the impossible ideas that swam in secret behind now perplexed eyes. I was probably overthinking this thing anyway. The guy probably wanted nothing more than to update me on some trivial prison bullshit, tell me my law degree had been refused. Annoy me even further.

'I'm sorry to take you away from your free time,'

Hunky offered as he led me along the corridor towards the main recreation area.

'It's fine, sir, really,' I replied, trying to keep my tone neutral, needing him to get to the point fast before I passed out, causing yet more unwanted trouble for myself in the process.

Hunky unlocked the retaining gate between our unit and the kitchen area, stating loudly, 'Adams, I need you to check some of today's kitchen deliveries, if you don't mind. The governor needs the inventory amending.' Why the hell was he speaking so loudly? I was standing right next to him.

I didn't hide the widening confusion my face now displayed, slightly irritated by the thought of checking yet more packets of bloody cereal and noodles. He allowed me to step through the gate ahead of him, closing it firmly behind us, glancing around at a common room full of inmates who mostly didn't give a shit anyway and who mostly hadn't noticed a thing. I was about to answer his request with a simple 'okay, sir' but felt it unnecessary now he'd already told the whole unit.

We walked in total silence along the corridor, past the canteen, through a set of double doors into the kitchen and dining areas beyond. He stopped outside the main storeroom, unlocking it so we could step inside, talk in private, be alone. *Christ, if only things could be so simple.*

'Mr Stuard, is everything okay?' I asked when no forthcoming explanation was offered as to why I'd been summoned from my cell at seven o'clock in the evening, no confirmation given other than a statement he'd previously declared to the uninterested group.

Hunky looked slightly uncomfortable for a moment, glancing around as if expecting to be interrupted, caught, shot in the back, whichever came first. 'Please, call me Alistair,' he whispered, his words emerging out of nowhere.

I swallowed, staring at him. 'Sorry, what—?' *Had I heard that correctly?*

'No, Stacey. I'm the one who should be apologising. I noticed how I made you feel the other day, and I didn't mean for that to happen.' I didn't understand what I was hearing. To which day was he referring? He'd made me feel like shit for an entire week, ignoring me whenever he saw me, ignoring me when I spoke to him, pretending he didn't hear, didn't care less. I opened my mouth, changed my mind. 'You looked so happy when you shared your fantastic news with me about your potential degree. But then,' he paused, trying to find the right words. He took a breath. 'But, then something changed. It was my fault, I know. I didn't handle it very well.' *What the hell was he talking about?* What didn't he handle very well? 'I have been watching you all week. You've looked so depressed since we last spoke.'

'I —'

'Please, Stacey, allow me to say this while I can.' Hunky — *Alistair* — glanced at me, something behind his dark brown eyes confessing a truth I wasn't convinced was real. I was still reeling slightly from the concept he had willingly told me his first name. Alistair. *Alistair Stuard.* Bloody hell.

'I'm a married man,' he continued. 'I have two kids and a mortgage that I can't always meet the monthly repayments on. This job was meant to change all that. Change things for the better for my wife and I. Help the kids have a better future. Help us all.' Why the hell was he telling *me* all this? I wondered if it might have had something to do with his last job, his last post. I dare not ask. 'Then I met you, Stacey, and,' he paused again, running a trembling hand through his hair. 'Everything changed.'

*What the fuck?* What was he trying to tell me? I did not wish to create something in my mind that wasn't there, invent a sudden love affair that could never be real. 'What do you mean, sir?' I couldn't have heard this right. Had the innocent touch I'd given him last week triggered some lustful response in him too? *Oh, Jesus, please let it be true?* Had he felt the same way about me since we first met? All those days ago. All *nine* of them. Or was I deluded, deranged, devoid of any rational reality?

I didn't know how to respond. So many questions lingered on my rapidly drying lips. It was lucky for me that Alistair did, though. Instead of saying anything further, he simply chose to lean in and kiss me. Properly. Passionately. He slipped a throbbing tongue inside my shocked mouth, searching, his heavy breath designed to tip me over the edge once and for all. It worked. I kissed him back, the storeroom door blocking us from any potential prying eyes; no one allowed back here at this time of the day anyway without reasonable, justified need. I was probably dreaming, inventing this entire moment because I was a sick, twisted, deluded woman with even sicker delusions of grandeur. I must have fallen asleep, the sounds of relentless pages being turned above me enough to drive any sane person to distraction. I momentarily recalled what the two Janes had mentioned about Alistair's last prison post. The female inmate he apparently saw in secret, behind his wife's back. I didn't give a shit about any of it.

We stumbled backwards across boxes of breakfast cereal, tins of baked beans, dried pasta, our passion and muffled laughter igniting in an instant, restless hands running over wrestling bodies, fumbling with buttons, tugging underwear. Alistair's hands were telling their own engaging story as we kissed, eager lips seeking eager contact, our bodies slowly becoming one. Was he going to have *sex* with me? Right here on top of the morning breakfast products? *Jesus Christ.* Yes, please. *Stacey Adams, what have you done to deserve this?* Breathe, Stacey, breathe.

I lay back, allowing Alistair to peel clothing from my trembling body, freely exposing what I'd kept hidden for so long. He slipped off his jacket, allowing me to undo his shirt, his trousers. I recalled that first night with Jason, the way we had torn at each other, leaving behind painful welts in our desperation for attention, our "passion wounds" left on display without apology. It was odd that Alistair, although just as keen, just as willing, wasn't quite as willing to hurt me as Jason was, instead choosing to take a little more time over this unexpected moment. He allowed his trousers to fall to the floor, his growing penis all too enticing for my senses to fully appreciate what was about to happen. It had been so long since I'd felt a man inside me. I certainly had not expected this day to turn out quite like *this*. I probably would have laughed if someone had predicted such an outcome.

Alistair found my warm place with ease, without any consideration of being caught, the condom he dug out of his pocket somewhat surprising to me. I don't know why. Jason never cared for such items. Yet again, rapists usually don't. I tried not to overthink why I'd chosen to think of Jason *now*. Had Alistair got out of bed this morning anticipating this very moment? Was he simply waiting for his chance for us to be alone? Did he, like me, take one look at my face and realise he just had to have me? I hadn't even told him how much I liked him. *Fucking hell.* Was this honestly about to happen?

'Alistair,' I breathed quietly as he pressed himself against me, ready for entry. I wanted to ask him if this is what he actually wanted, what he truly needed, yet all words failed me the moment he glanced into my eyes, my entire body and soul at his mercy. He ran a hand across my cheek, cupping my head with the palm of his hand before sliding slowly inside me, two into one, our lovemaking taking place. I wanted the world to stop, closing my eyes at the feel of his erection entering me. We breathed each other deeply, feeling the moment, tasting each other without remorse or fear. Shit and double shit.

Get me. Stacey Adams. Having actual *sex* in a prison kitchen storeroom cupboard with the hottest prison officer within a million-mile radius. Who would have thought that a possibility? Certainly not me. *Fuck me.* Quite literally. Excuse the pun.

# 33

I was lost in the moment, free to allow this situation to take a firm grip on me, rendering me totally without rational thought. It had been so long since I felt the emotional embrace of a passionate lovemaking session. Jason Cole was ironically a man I now wished I could erase from my mind and past completely, his embrace not so considerate, not so intense. How I allowed him into my life and my bed so readily, I do not know. Alistair Stuard, however, was a different type of animal altogether. When he finished, he didn't immediately rise to his feet, no longer interested in what I had to offer. Neither did he dress swiftly, removing himself from my side, as Jason often did. No. Alistair continued to touch me long after his own orgasm had surfaced, allowing mine to break free almost without apology.

It was as if I'd been saving the thing for this last year and a half, waiting for the gentle touch of a new man, a man I didn't know existed until just over a week ago. Now, here he was, having sex with me, making me moan like an experienced whore, albeit as quietly as I was able, in secret, our passionate affair only just beginning. He couldn't have known what he'd begun. Neither of us did. This moment was all that existed in our minds.

I wanted to ask him openly, honestly, *what the fuck was that?* but I was rendered entirely unable to speak or think straight, instead opting to stare into his huge eyes with an equally huge grin imprinted onto my much-satisfied face. *Bloody hell.*

'Was that okay for you?' he asked softly, still lying semi-naked, semi-erect, on top of me, still breathing heavy, tracing wayward fingertips across my pulsating body.

'Are you *kidding me?*' I giggled, resuming a habit I hadn't participated in for quite some time. 'You were —'

'So were you,' he interrupted, not allowing me time to confirm how unforgettable that moment had been for me. For the both of us. He rose to his feet slowly, reluctantly, pulling on clothing, removing his condom, wrapping it in a tissue before placing it into his pocket to be discarded later.

'*Wow.*' I couldn't help expressing such a word. What bought that on? Did I want to know? *Did I care?*

'Please tell me if this isn't what you want?' he questioned, buttoning his jacket, helping me up from a now squashed bulk box of cornflakes. Shit. I hoped no one would notice a haphazard backside shaped dent in the thing. It would be quite funny listening to the impending whines of inmates forced to eat obliterated breakfast cereal.

'It's a little late for those types of queries, don't you think?' I laughed, making him laugh — both of us lost to this impossible moment. A moment of incomprehensible madness. What was it with men and their impromptu need to fuck my brains out at the most unexpected moments? 'Of course, it's what I want,' I confirmed firmly, still shocked, the warmth of the session we'd just shared still fresh in my unobjectionable mind, my body not yet calmed down from such an unexpected expression of lust. 'But what made you want *me?*' It was a good question. Alistair Stuard was gorgeous. He could have his pick.

'When you innocently touched my arm the other morning, I realised I couldn't deny my feelings for you, Stacey,' Alistair confessed. *Oh my god.* I should have known he wanted me as much as I wanted him. I smiled.

'I assumed something was wrong. I thought I'd done something to upset you,' I replied, straightening my top whilst attempting to deal with the crushed box at my feet. It was futile.

'There was nothing wrong, Stacey. I promise you that. I just didn't expect to feel —'

'Neither did I,' I confirmed, smiling at the man I had now fallen utterly head over heels in love with. Neither did I.

***

Alistair walked me back to the unit, back to my cell, thanking me for my much-needed time in the kitchen, essential stock checking that couldn't wait for another day. It was a silent message only the two of us appreciated — pure emotional bliss developing inside my heart at the very moment I lay on my bunk with time to think, to ponder. I couldn't get the thought of Alistair's used condom, currently in his pocket, out of my head. It made me smile. Of course, this was *not* how I might have wished to begin a new relationship. We both knew Alistair couldn't pop into my cell at any given time of the day or night for a quickie, lying in bed with me all night long, watching television, eating junk food, lying to his wife. No. Our time would be limited to the occasional stolen glance when nobody was looking, a simple wink, the touch of a wandering hand, a smile.

For the next few weeks, I walked around as if I was living on a cloud, secret stolen moments with Alistair now vital to my overall mental health, crucial to my continued personal preservation. Of course, Mia noticed my rapid change in mood, again questioning my state of mind on several occasions. Was I confident it wasn't bipolar? Maybe I should see the doctor, just to be sure? I didn't mind. My mindset was far too elevated to concern myself with her fears now. Even the humdrum boredom of daily prison life seemed easier to bear now I had something to look forward to, to focus on. It made my need to study for a degree all that more critical, too. It meant that, at some point, they might *actually* put me up in front of a parole board. They might someday let me go. The very idea made me shudder. It was just a shame I couldn't tell Mia about any of it.

My potential studies and rapidly improved spirits might at some point, secure an early future release. It was all I could think about, all that consumed my every waking moment — that, of course, and Alistair. I wished I could tell Mia my news about the two of us. I'd even managed to keep his actual name to myself for several days after our first encounter, convinced it was our little secret, proud no one else knew it. That was until someone saw it written on a file in the supervisor's office, and Alistair Stuard became a topic of fresh conversation for a few irritating days that threatened to see me ruin everything. Nothing was *ever* kept secret in prison for long. It was an unfair truth. One I would need to be extremely mindful of now.

Alistair, of course, ensured I understood what would be at stake should we ever be discovered. I wasn't foolish. I knew how dangerous such a thing would be for both of us. The last thing I needed was to see the man transferred, suspended from duty, taken away from me forever. I needed him as much as he needed me. It was uncomfortable to admit our relationship wasn't unique to the prison system, of course. There was often much talk of random prisoner/prison officer relationships happening in secret, behind closed doors. Each person in question using the other for self-gratification, unearned privileges, drugs, special favours.

Such inappropriate sex acts were not always confined to the male staff either. Anyone in here could become a prime target for the women if it suited a purpose, both males and females. I thought randomly of Peter Farley and Elaine Sharp. *Maybe not.* Thankfully for me, Alistair was different. We were getting nothing more from our arrangement than the incredible passion we shared in private. I was elated my fantasies were no longer an existence forced to reside inside my head and that the man was, in fact, as attracted to me as I was to him. It was real.

Of course, as with everything I ever did in my life, as far as I was concerned, it was all or nothing. I was permanently unable and unwilling to wait patiently for our next "session", Alistair eagerly accompanying me unnecessarily to the garden, the boiler room, the kitchen storeroom. I spent less and less time with Mia, the poor woman wondering if I was experiencing a nervous breakdown, often watching me when she assumed I wasn't looking. Alistair even managed to get himself appointed as my peer worker, my continued welfare and mental health of great concern and importance to him. Of course, there were other inmates to whom his peer worker status also extended, including Claire *fucking* Bennett, but I wasn't in the slightest bit concerned about her. Alistair only had eyes for me. That much was evident in the way he made me feel whenever we were alone.

\*\*\*

How we managed to sneak away one morning to the boiler

room to check a "problem" with something unimportant, I have no idea, but we hid in secret, pulling each other's clothing, giggling, chewing bottom lips and other things, desperate to feel each other's increasingly urgent touch. It was now exactly a month after our first unexpected encounter. The kitchen storeroom was never quite the same for me after that first evening, my thoughts often causing an impromptu smile to spread across my face without warning. We had fucked five times since that night. Yes, I kept a firm count. Each subsequent time was as carefully planned as the last. Today would be no different.

Nobody ever came to the boiler room — the decades of dust in this place testimony to that fact. I was learning much about Alistair, and he, in turn, was learning the things about me I allowed him to know. He must have read my file by now, already aware of the reasons behind my twenty-four-year prison sentence. Yet, it didn't seem to matter to him that much. It was in the past, over and done with, gone. It was fantastic he didn't judge me for actions I now had no control over anyway. Not that I ever did.

We were lying together on a pile of old laundry bags that Alistair had managed to locate for our planned moment in private. I was on my back, Alistair inside me, holding me, stroking my hair. I used to believe that slow sex was fake, stupid, the images and scenes in movies merely invented for viewing purposes. Now I realised how wrong I was. The man on top of me now, readily making up for those ill-formed assumptions I'd misplaced so inaptly.

'Tell me something about yourself,' I asked as Alistair moved his body on top of mine, pressing himself deep inside me unrelenting. He kissed me, still breathing hard against the weight of his incoming thrusts.

'What do you want to know?' he whispered, the darkness around us a protective cocoon from the horrific world outside this desolate space. I didn't wish to break the moment, interrupt our passion, but we had little time elsewhere to discuss these important things.

'Tell me about your wife?' I needed to understand more about her, what made her tick. Why would a man such as Alistair be with *me* if he were in an apparent happy marriage?

Alistair sighed. 'Do we have to talk about that right now?' he asked, nibbling my ear in an attempt to change the subject, still mid-way through our much-needed session, not yet ready for it to end so swiftly.

'We do if you want to keep *fucking* me,' I replied playfully, licking my lips as I lifted my hips towards his willing body, grinding against him, rubbing his back, digging my nails into his skin as deeply as I dared.

Alistair seemed all the more turned on by my sudden probing, causing him to deny everything but my existence until he'd completed his eager mission. He rolled off me begrudgingly, lying by my side, stroking a hot hand across my bare belly.

'Her name is Charlotte,' he told me casually, seemingly far too distracted by my breasts than the name of his elusive spouse. I waited patiently in the darkness for more to come, wanting to understand his life, his marriage, his kids. 'But we don't exactly have, what you might call, a *good* relationship.'

*I knew it.* I knew he wouldn't be lying semi-naked with me now if he was happy with his wife, his life. I guess they were all the same, men. Quite willing to accept a comfortable existence, more for convenience than true happiness, true love.

'So, why don't you leave her?' I asked. It was an honest suggestion. I assumed he must have already considered it.

'I guess it's just easier to stay, for the sake of the kids,' he confessed, leaning his head against my neck, kissing me tenderly. It tickled.

I understood that. I assumed it was the very reason Emma stayed with Jason for so long instead of taking her baby and running as far away from the cheating pig as she could. I closed my eyes. It wasn't a thought I needed in my head. We kissed again, this time without any urgency for repeated sex. Alistair Stuard was so different to Jason Cole in every way possible. For starters, he didn't leave painful, noticeable marks on my skin that hurt for days. Although, in fairness, that might have been so we could remain undetected. Yet, neither did he ram into me as if his life depended on it, leaving me sore, opting instead to ease inside me gently, almost teasingly, agonisingly excitedly. *This* relationship was so different in so many incredible ways.

Eventually, we had to admit that our time was up, the world calling us back to our real lives, back to our suffering. I sat upright, handing Alistair his trousers, still slightly giggly from a recent orgasm, happy to be with my new man in this impossible moment, no matter how short-lived our time together would always need to be. As I leaned over towards him, a faded photograph fell out of his pocket into my lap. I picked it up. It was of a woman, standing between two young children, two boys.

'Is this your wife?' I asked, sounding more irritated than I intended, the dimly lit room only just providing me with a glimpse into the private life of a man I barely knew. 'Is this Charlotte?'

Alistair sat up, taking the photo from my hand, its crumpled edges telling me it had either become forgotten, or he looked at it often. 'It is yes,' he confirmed, a slight saddened tone to his voice that I couldn't read. 'This is Anthony, and this is Jonathon. Ant is eight, Jon is six.' He didn't say anything more about Charlotte. He didn't need to. However, I did not fail to notice how pretty she was, all the same.

'And you keep them in your pocket because —'

'Actually, I keep this photo in my wallet. It must have fallen out.' Alistair picked up his trousers, checking that his wallet hadn't disappeared, grateful for the hard bulge that met his grasp. I knew how he felt. 'I often need reminding of the reasons I do what I do, every single day,' he continued. 'To give my boys a better future.' Alistair sounded a little subdued, the moment of our lovemaking firmly over. He removed his wallet from his pocket and tucked the small photograph inside a leather flap.

'And what *are* those reasons, exactly?' I questioned, hoping such a revelation didn't imply our limited time together was Alistair's way of passing the time to endure a career that might afford his kids an apparent brighter future.

'The reason I stay with Charlotte instead of asking for a divorce. The reason I pay the mortgage on a house too bloody big and too expensive. The reason I send my kids to a good school.'

*Oh, thank god for that.* I sighed loudly, glad he wasn't about to express some profound regret for our insufficient time together. Glad he seemed to hate his wife as much as I was beginning to. I didn't even know the woman. I didn't want to. It was enough she existed. Enough that she seemed to make him miserable.

I reached over and touched his cheek, bringing his attention back to me, wanting desperately to tear that photograph to pieces, stab out the eyes of the woman he went home to each evening, probably kissed, fucked in private.

'I love you, Alistair Stuard,' I confessed, out of nowhere, yet needing him to appreciate I wasn't screwing around

257

with his emotions. I never would. *Shit, Stacey. What the hell is wrong with you?*

Alistair glanced at me, tilted his head, lowered his chin. 'I think I love you too, Stacey Adams,' he confirmed. *Jesus.* Had that just happened? Did we just declare our love for each other without question or hesitation? Alistair rose to his feet, pulling me to mine, holding me in an embrace that I wasn't prepared for. 'I love being with you. I love everything about you.' He touched my thankfully growing hair with his fingertips. I wished he could see me how I used to look. 'Fuck me, Stacey Adams, I. LOVE. YOU.' His declaration was made loud and clear, almost loud enough to be overheard by an unsuspecting passing ear. I giggled. *Fuck me backwards with a feather.* If that was even a thing, which, if Alistair Stuard had anything to do with it, it might very well have been. What an impossible incredible day I'd had.

# 34

It took several agonising months before Governor Barrington called me into his office to confirm I had been accepted as a student to begin my Law Degree studies. I'd all but given up on the idea, grateful Alistair was luckily providing me with enough sustenance to occupy my otherwise festering brain matter. I had thankfully already achieved the two A levels required for minimum entry on the course — Maths and English now becoming the very qualifications I was suddenly extremely grateful to my parents for forcing me to complete. They were the ones ensuring I attended college in the first place, knowing full well I was already becoming highly strung, my low attention span and eager desire to possess anything that wasn't currently mine, often keeping me entertained elsewhere. *Somewhat like now, in fact.* It seemed that nothing much had changed.

The news was so incredible they could have told me I would need to study for the next decade, and I still would have agreed to their requirements, still acted just as keenly and excited by the prospect. As it was, a degree would take around three years to achieve if I put in the work, got my head down, studied hard. I wasn't officially allowed to become a solicitor or barrister directly. I was just granted permission to study for a degree, so I was not required to take further examinations or pass any bars. I'm sure they have rules about convicted killers representing other potential killers. As it was, I had all the time in the world, and with Alistair firmly by my side, I felt I could achieve anything. It was as if the entire world had fallen keenly to my feet. For a while, prison life didn't feel as impossible to bear as I'd previously anticipated.

I settled into my new daily routine with ease, three hours spent on kitchen duty, five hours allowed to study. The rest of my time was endured hoping Alistair would find a moment in his day to seek me out, fuck my brains, keep me happy. The library was so quiet. I'd all but forgotten the feeling of solace, my mind usually overrun with the increasing demands of a women's secure mental health unit. It's funny how quickly you can get used to something.

Along with my law degree, I was now studying psychology in my spare time, a subject the governor found most impressive, if not a little unfathomable. He had no idea where my sudden change of direction had come from, my willing need for driven structure. I obviously couldn't tell him it was all due to his newest, most impressive male staff member, my thoughts and opinions forced to remain inside my head. Luckily the prison library was a wealth of knowledge, allowing me access to far more than I ever expected. I was a zealous hungry caterpillar, devouring all information set in front of me, book after book consumed keenly, relentlessly. Alistair helped, of course. He satisfied my insatiable appetite for sex, which in turn drove my inner desire for knowledge.

Knowledge is power, so they say, and I have to admit that, initially, I was somewhat drawn to the idea of studying to impress the authorities. I heard somewhere that prisoners who undertake education or work placement programmes, generally willing to keep their heads down, proving to those in control that they are hard-working and ethical, can often be granted early parole. Ironically, the very idea of an early release would have never crossed my mind had I not met Alistair. My time in this shithole suddenly required a carefully planned end date. There was no other option for me now.

I would have decayed and withered to nothing but dust had it not been for the arrival of my new man, the guy inadvertently giving me a purpose, a reason to tackle this unfortunate obstacle in my life that was aptly named "prison". This place was nothing more now than a roadblock I needed to overcome before I could begin a brand-new life, somewhere far away from here. There were even books in the library suggesting ways to survive prison life, purposefully placed to help us poor buggers work through any issues the authorities might assume us afflicted with.

I was not expecting it to happen, but I began to see the women around me differently, my attention now elsewhere, my need to be loved well and truly sated. I even noticed Mia's struggles properly for the first time, her suffering still very much apparent, bulimia still very much an active part of her daily life. It was hardly my fault that, although we spent a lot of time together, I hadn't allowed myself much time to sit down and see the real woman behind the person I classed as a friend. We were going through the same thing — prison. She had the same condition as Emma. Bulimia. That, however, was where I assumed my responsibilities ended. Since taking a slower route through my day, feeling less stressed, primarily due to Alistair's unwavering affection and wandering fingers, I was oddly able to see my fellow inmates with fresh, enthusiastic eyes.

My private studies in psychology showed me the often-uncomfortable inner workings of the human condition, unravelling thoughts I might never have otherwise understood. It uncovered emotions and struggles we all go through yet primarily hide away from, myself included. I have to admit it was a rather odd situation to find myself in. I have always felt the need to put *myself* first. I see no problem with that. *Don't we all?* However, this new state of mind I'd uncovered allowed me to notice issues the prison system was failing to address.

During my time in the prison library, or at least during the time I actually chose to notice, I began witnessing women who had, for whatever reason, like me, lost their children either to the care system or, if serving a long enough sentence, to permanent adoption. Regularly, I would witness this inhumane course of action forced upon women who had nowhere else to go but downhill, nothing afforded them that might have the potential to make any lasting difference to their lives at all.

Unsuspecting mothers were often forced to say a bitter goodbye to their babies during a single visit, knowing they would never see their children again. All this happened with biased, unfeeling solicitors present, pens ready for undeserving signatures, faceless files tucked inside cold leather briefcases, held by hapless suited humans who did not give a shit anyway. If those same women subsequently lost their homes due to unavoidable rent arrears, they would also lose their possessions because they couldn't afford to put them into storage. A woman could enter this place for a minor offence and lose absolutely everything in the process, her kids, her sanity, her entire existence.

It wasn't just the frequent loss of children and personal lives I began to notice. One of the biggest problems in this place seemed to be the continued self-harm approach to dealing with the fallout left behind. Many women who lose their children eventually lose themselves, including everything that happens along the way. Self-harming often, unfortunately, becomes the only area of their lives they can control for themselves. On a far too regular basis, I witnessed inmates swallowing batteries or anything they could get their hands on, the concept of hurting themselves, something that went unnoticed until urgent medical intervention was needed. It was a cry for help, not attention. I knew exactly how they felt. I'd been there myself.

The unprecedented level of self-harm in this place was awful. I had already witnessed Mia cut her wrists out of rejection. I'd even attempted to do the same thing when I saw no other way out. I was forced to watch one poor inmate, a young mum, desperately deprived of anything she could hurt herself with, still manage to self-harm so severely that she was left requiring blood transfusions every week for over four months. It was terrible. The consistent cutting of skin, swallowing batteries, drug overdoses, makeshift ropes — anything to take away the pain of inner turmoil they had no idea how to otherwise appease. To me, these poor sods did not need the added punishment of being locked away. Their entire life was punishment enough as it was.

To make matters far worse, when their enforced suffering finally came to an end, many of those women serving short custodial sentences were subsequently thrown out of prison, nowhere stable to go, very little money to their name, zero self-esteem left behind by a system designed to apparently rehabilitate them. They often ended up in hostels, halfway houses, unstable, volatile shared housing, places rife with drugs and scandal, beginning the entire cycle all over again, reoffending, heading back to prison on a loop. These women were not out shoplifting or sex working because they got a kick out of it. They did it because they would starve to death if they didn't.

I spoke to Alistair about my observations, something, he said, he'd seen for far too long. Nothing would change, he told me. It was just the way of things, the way the system worked. I disagreed. I couldn't prevent a woman from landing herself inside a jail cell, but I was learning the skills that might allow me to help change something fundamentally important — a healthy state of mind. Alistair initially thought I was crazy. *I* thought I was crazy. Yet, once again, I requested permission to see the governor. I was in a good place. An exceptional place. A place I hadn't considered existing in for some time. I certainly never expected to feel so confident about my own future. If I could share a little of what I was learning, I felt I owed it to the poor wretches I was locked away with to help them change a few things in their own lives. Firstly, significantly, their overriding mindset about everything they believed they knew about mental health.

***

'You want to do *what?*' Governor Barrington was grinning at me from behind his desk, his office far more oppressive to me now than the freedom of the library with its garden view and large picture windows. A view I now thankfully enjoyed daily, took for granted. He clearly thought I was as insane as Alistair did.

'I want to start a programme to help the women cope better with circumstances beyond their control and their subsequent troubled state of mind. I feel it might aid their future release. I honestly believe, sir, if they have the tools to better deal with their emotions, they might come to realise they can make clearer decisions once they are released back into society.' I was sitting upright, back straight, my tone calm, my eyes alight with a sparkling gem of a minuscule idea. An impossible idea. 'I want to call it the EIP.'

'The what?'

'The EIP, sir. The Emotional Insecurities Programme.'

Governor Barrington regarded me for a moment as if an over-enthusiastic alien had invaded my body, replacing my usual state with something he wasn't convinced was genuine. 'Miss Adams, I do believe your studies are slowly tipping you over the edge,' he chided, shaking his head in apparent amusement, a smile lingering across his lined face that I hoped to turn into a satisfying conclusion before I left this room.

'On the contrary, sir,' I chipped in, feeling confident in my idea, knowing at some point, I would be able to convince the governor of its value. 'I've seen too much suffering in this place since my arrival. Mine included. What do you have to lose?' I raised beseeching hands towards him before pressing my palms together, appealing to his better nature. 'It isn't going to cost you anything, and I get to do something positive for a change instead of wallowing in my own pathetic self-pity.' I knew that would do the trick. If nothing else, it might sway the governor's decision, although I wasn't entirely comfortable referring to myself as *pathetic*. It didn't matter. He did not need to know I was partially doing this thing to gain some well-needed traction with the board, force the prison service to see that I was becoming a changed woman — a better person, a potential valued member of society. I wanted a straightforward way out of here. A way to be with Alistair. It was as simple as that.

'And you honestly assume the women will get something from it?' the governor had stopped smiling now, at least, taking me a little more seriously.

'I *know* they will.' I sat and stared at the man's features, unwavering, unwilling to compromise, my thoughts focused only on what I needed to achieve. I *did* want to help them. It was a strange side effect of the actual reason behind my request. It wasn't a feeling I could shake. It was entirely bizarre.

'Okay,' Governor Barrington raised his hands in absent defeat. 'Let's try it out. You have one month to prove that this isn't all just a waste of prison time and resources.' He dismissed me with a nod of his head, a grin on my face he wasn't able to dislodge for anyone.

'You won't regret it, sir,' I concluded, leaving the room with a spring in my step that saw my feet practically bouncing back to my unit. I assumed he felt my antidepressants might need reducing. I didn't care.

'Let's hope, for your sake, that I don't,' he muttered, returning his attention to more important matters than me.

## 35

Alistair was equally shocked and delighted when I told him the impressive news that my EIP request had been granted. But he wasn't as surprised by the governor's decision to allow my crazy idea as he was by the very concept that I wanted to do such a thing in the first place.

'But why?' he asked me for the fourth time, a puzzled look on his face that matched Governor Barrington's.

'Because I want to do something good for a change,' I confirmed, rolling my eyes, a weird buzz in my body I hadn't felt in some time — or *ever*, if I was being perfectly candid with myself. It was an odd feeling. I was shocked to discover that by placing his ill-founded confidence in my apparent abilities, Governor Barrington had unwittingly entertained something that now niggled deep inside me — a concept that might have the fundamental ability to make a real contribution, a real difference. I, of course, could not express the truth that I'd initially wanted nothing more than to do everything in my power to secure a potential early release someday, my thoughts initially set on my own needs, as usual. I certainly didn't wish to get Alistair's hopes up about such matters any more than I hoped to raise my own. Now, however, something else lingered in my thoughts. Something I wasn't expecting. *Hope.*

We had been in a "relationship" for just over a year by this time. I use the term lightly because we were only ever allowed limited stolen moments away from the ever-watchful eyes of this godforsaken place, nothing of an actual *relationship* existing. I would have given anything to wake up in his arms, share a morning coffee, pop to the shops. Just an ordinary couple in love, an average day in paradise. Yet, despite everything, Alistair's presence in my life had given me a focus I wouldn't have otherwise been able to achieve without.

My degree course was also well underway. I was studying hard to ensure I passed with a good grade. I was aiming for a First Class Honours, showing the world that Stacey Adams wasn't a woman to be trifled with. I would have settled for an Upper Second Class, of course. Although to me, second class meant second best, and I'm not convinced I would have been comfortable with that. I was now also studying for a diploma in Psychology, my spare time keeping me busy, content. If my mum and dad could have seen me now, they wouldn't have recognised the change in their youngest daughter. Their *only* daughter. I was a brand-new woman, and it was all because of Alistair Stuard.

\*\*\*

Alistair was kind enough to help me organise a vacant counselling room for my first official EIP session, arranging a row of chairs that I continually re-positioned, constantly discontented with the results. A total of four separate units in this place – including the much-needed mental health unit, of course – were initially offered a weekly hourly session with me. I assumed the governor wasn't expecting much. Four units equated to well over a hundred women, the new programme capable of generating at least *some* interest if he spread the word far enough. Alistair personally oversaw the design, and printing of, leaflets which were handed out, the new therapy sessions available to anyone wishing to seize the opportunity, see what this thing was about.

I was so grateful to him. He was my rock when I needed him the most. I honestly do not know what I would have done without him. Probably hurt myself again, no doubt. But, deeper this time, ensuring the resulting damage produced a completely different outcome, my call for help made permanent. It was the very reason I wanted to do this EIP in the first place. Well, mostly. Like the women here, I too had been through the worst times of my life. Losing my son, my parents, my freedom. I needed to do something positive. Give something back.

I was as much a part of the system as any of the women around me, more so because, upon my release, twenty-four annoying years could have passed me by. I would be fifty-four years old. *Jesus.* I literally couldn't imagine that. I would be an old woman. The EIP group sessions were a way for me to achieve something, tick boxes, maybe even help a few wayward souls in the process. It might also do *me* some good. Yet, I hadn't exactly anticipated how it might affect me. I'd turned from suicidal maniac to calm, degree-studying pillar of the prison system. If I could impart a little of my newly found knowledge onto some of the women here, teaching them how to better cope with their own emotional responses to a world that had wronged them so severely, it would certainly make a good impression with the prison authorities. Plus, I was learning the law, fully able to offer much-needed advice on legal matters, should they require it.

I committed myself to pursuing the idea of getting out

of this place while I still had a little *life* left inside me —
whilst Alistair and I had a chance of a fresh start together, a
brand-new life away from locked doors, prying eyes, our
constant secret rendezvous status growing quite tedious. It
was a miracle we'd managed to keep our relationship secret
thus far. I guess I just needed to keep my head and tongue
in check a little longer.

\*\*\*

The EIP was officially set up in an unused group counselling
room that had all but become a forgotten part of a depleting
prison system. It smelled of decades-old dust, disuse,
mistrust, this entire room needing a damned good clean and
some much-needed ventilation. Alistair confirmed the once-
prized prison counselling sessions were abandoned a while
ago due to a lack of funding. Doctor Farley was
subsequently left alone to do the best he could with limited
time and resources. Poor sod. It was typical of prison life.
Despite much talk of rehabilitation and reform, most of us
were forgotten, left to fend for ourselves, society simply
glad of our incarceration.

   Alistair was proud of me, he told me, stealing a kiss in
private when no one was looking. There was no CCTV in
this room. We were safe. I felt sick, nervous, unsure what
the hell I thought I was doing, my enthusiasm wavering
slightly the closer it came to my allocated hourly slot.
Would anyone show up? Would I be expected to *cure* every
deep routed issue these women had? Or would they all just
sit and laugh at me? Poke fun, making me the butt of some
private prison joke?

   I was allocated a time slot between two and three
o'clock every Thursday afternoon. After lunch, any women
wishing to participate would be allowed free time away

from their usual duties to attend. Plus, they would be more relaxed at that time, hunger-sedated, irritation a far less vexing issue for me to contend with. It was a good plan.

'I feel sick,' I said, nothing Alistair could say or *do*, able to make a difference to my shredded nerves, no matter how much he protested. It was just after two o'clock, and I was yet to see a single attendee. The governor would shake his head in disgust if this didn't work out, roll his eyes, laugh. Alistair might shake his head too, glare at me as if I was a blithering idiot for even suggesting such a stupid idea in the first place.

'Will you please relax,' he whispered, running his hand across my shoulder blades, pressing well-positioned fingers into my tense muscles, massaging gently. My hair had thankfully grown again, finally looking and feeling more like the actual hair I'd owned before I lost my way, lost my mind. Oddly it was thicker than it used to be, an unanticipated upside of shaving the whole lot off in frustration. It still wasn't as long as I would have liked, but it was getting there. Alistair traced his hand along my shoulder-length bob, tugging the ends gently, teasingly, attempting to straighten my unrelenting waves with his warm fingertips. 'You've got this.'

*Did I, though?* Did I seriously *get* a damned thing that I was trying to achieve? My brain was already turning to mush with each infuriating tick of the clock on the wall behind me, each second passing by with no one to actually share my pearls of apparent wisdom with. Wisdom I now felt I'd invented out of pure deluded self-importance, empty chairs staring at me from the void of an empty room. At four minutes past two, I was ready to quit, race back to the library in tears, barricade myself in, set fire to the whole place if necessary. Shut myself firmly inside, those old, stale smelling books capable of making my exit from this bloody world as swift as possible.

I was about to admit defeat when I saw a figure looming in the doorway, a look of quizzical hesitation spread across her beautiful face, a blank expression unmoving, uncertain, unconvinced of my apparent motives. It was Mia. I smiled, gesturing her to come in, sit down, save me from this potential debacle, thankful she was willing to support her deranged friend in need. I knew my best friend wouldn't let me down. I was, however, surprised to discover she was followed by three more women, two of whom I'd never met. Alistair glanced my way, smiled knowingly. Shit. This was really happening.

The four women strode casually inside, chatting amongst themselves, unaware of my rising nerves, the prison officers happy to stand by the door just outside the room. I was grateful they deemed it appropriate to give us some well-needed space, privacy, time to talk openly about issues plaguing us for too long, share our experiences, express untethered emotions. I insisted the chairs were set out in a semi-circle configuration, providing a more relaxed environment. I'd seen it done many times on television. It seemed to be a *thing*. I was glad I'd only placed ten chairs out, yet there still appeared to be six chairs too many now. I was focusing on the negative. Four chairs were filled, at least. That was something. I hoped to Christ I wasn't about to make a massive fool of myself.

'Thank you for coming,' I began, sounding more school teacher than fellow inmate, my apparent shared knowledge of what these women were going through still unconfirmed by all. Alistair mouthed 'good luck' from the back of the room as the women chose their seats, my nerves threatening to render me speechless, ensuring I looked as stupid as I felt. I needed to relax, so they, in turn, would relax with me, talk to me, tell me how they felt. After all, they must have read the leaflet, knew what the EIP sessions were designed to do. Being run by a fellow inmate allowed these four individuals to come to me of their own volition, no coaxing, no forced requirement needed. It had to be a good thing, of that I was confident. Yet, maybe they would see me as nothing more than a fraud, laughing at my futile efforts?

I sat down, trembling, Mia offering a smile and a wink that helped calm my nerves, if only for a split second. I wasn't sure if she was here for moral support or felt I could help with her issues. Whatever it was, I was eternally grateful. I would need to thank her later.

'You honestly don't know how thankful I am that you all took the time today to come along and see what this EIP thing is all about,' I laughed, trying to create a relaxed atmosphere, terrified that I was failing already. *All?* Who was I trying to kid? There were literally only *four* women here. Yet, it was a starting point. It was four more attendees than I had expected.

'I wasn't even sure the governor was going to allow it, to be honest,' I continued, needing to be as honest as I was able. 'A bunch of fragile women in a room together, talking about their *emotions*. Imagine that?' Everyone laughed. It was precisely the response I needed to help me relax, physically, mentally. My shoulders, already a tight mess with the stress of the whole thing, were allowed now to ease a little, my tongue uncurling itself from the grip of my panic-stricken tonsils.

I began by explaining why I decided to set up the programme in the first place, why I felt it was in *all* our best interests to talk openly to a fellow inmate, someone who had gone through the exact things as them. I, too, had lost my son, I confirmed. Technically, I also tried to kill myself. Twice. However, the first attempt was a superficial cry for help that, had I been a little less careful with my cheap, somewhat already dulled razor blade, things might have ended rather differently, tragically. Like them, I too, had felt all the anger and pain associated with being in this hellhole. We were in the same boat. I understood them. I could help.

It seemed to have the desired effect because by the end of that first hour, all four women had spoken to me openly about their once hidden troubles, Mia, included. The poor girl wished somebody could help her bulimia beyond a strict daily meal structure, strict supervision, ongoing medication plan. Of course, Peter Farley had helped in his limited way, but she needed to open up on her own terms, not purely because "talking therapy" was a requirement of her current incarceration.

Julia French, a woman in her late thirties, was sentenced twelve-months for stabbing her husband in the back. He had abused her for seven years without a single repercussion being served to him. It was ironic. She lost her daughter to the system in the process, that single act of mistimed self-defence landing her in a jail cell, rotting, forgotten. She was lost, broken, beaten by society as well as the man she believed had loved her once.

Tania Thomas was a drug addict, a shoplifter, in and out of prison for well over ten years, a pattern of self-destruction keeping her in a loop of broken promises, broken dreams. Even Katelyn Williams, Braunie's jail-bird girlfriend, had shown her face, curious, open to new ideas, interested to see what I had to say. All four women desperately wanted to break the cycle that had become their unforgiving lives, change the pattern, create a better future they did not otherwise know how to achieve.

By three o'clock, I was exhausted, my throat dry, my ears burning with relentless stories of pain unfolding before me. Women in prison do not like to talk about their crimes, despite what you might assume. Women are meant to chat a lot, I know. We are supposed to be nothing more than idle gossips who love a good natter. *Wrong*. Imprisoned women tended to be lost, alone, frightened. Paula Jones had expressed this fact to me on my very first day. *Don't* ever *ask what people are in for*, she'd told me, firmly. I now understood what she meant. I wanted the EIP groups to change this factor of prison life, to show the women most of us are in the same boat, in it together. We should be helping each other through this, helping each other at every turn, not holding it all in, self-harming, sadly self-preserving.

'Well done,' Alistair told me as we cleared away the chairs, my ears ringing with other people's emotions. He was proud of me. I could see it in the wink he afforded me, the nod of his knowing head, the passionate thrusts he gave to me a short while later, lying together behind a stack of decaying books in the darkening prison library, the lights out, everyone gone back to their cells.

*Well. Done. Me.*

## 36

That week saw me become an accidental celebrity, those initial four women attending my programme oddly keen to share their experiences with the rest of the prison. The entire place began discussing the profound inmate who was doing something *positive* for a change. The following week, twelve women showed up, all nervous yet keen to speak to me, eager to seek my advice. The week after that, twenty-two. The governor was even forced to allocate more chairs to the counselling room, spending money he didn't have, apportioning time he couldn't spare. The EIP became so popular that my single weekly session was eventually upgraded to a twice-weekly option on Tuesday and Thursday afternoons.

I wasn't exactly expecting to do much beyond tick boxes, ensuring I looked good in the eyes of a prison system I continually struggled to understand. Yet, as it turned out, I loved every single one of those sessions. It gave me something to look forward to, to focus on. By the end of the fifth month, seven of the women attending regular weekly EIP sessions were granted early release, free from drugs, free from a poorly acquired mindset, free to live a new life away from this place, a fresh start pending. A further three inmates were subsequently placed on a regular day release programme, their newly acquired good attitudes equated firmly to me. I was grateful to have helped them with potential work and housing options upon their release. I was doing a good thing, the governor told me. For the first time in my shallow existence, my self-serving ideals had created a positive outlook for others. It was no longer just about *me*. I actually got something out of this. I had a *purpose*.

I wasn't, however, expecting to be told that, because of my efforts, I would soon be rewarded with a transfer back into general population. Good behaviour and a consistently elevated mood ultimately meant I no longer posed a mental health risk. They were happy to reduce my medication, reduce my supervision. I was beside myself. As much as I wanted to be deemed normal, healthy, sane, to me, this seemed yet another punishment thrown at me purely because they could. *I hated the idea.* I was unstable, they'd once confirmed, written as much in my file, stamped the thing in bold ink. I honestly believed the EIP sessions were as much my therapy as they were for the other women. Surely they couldn't throw me back to normality, back to the dogs, so to speak?

The simple truth was, I didn't wish to be parted from Mia *or* Alistair. The mental health unit had become my home, as strange as that might sound. I was finally getting to know the women in here. I understood them, appreciated their needs, and they, in turn, now understood mine. It was somewhat tricky persuading the governor to leave me precisely where I was. I enjoyed sharing a cell with my friend. I enjoyed my time here. I didn't want things to begin unravelling for me. I didn't need change. I was still having a hard time, still fragile beneath my bravado. It would be ironic if all this hard work had the exact opposite effect on *me.*

It was ludicrous to appreciate that I had a far less chance of an early release whilst residing in the mental health unit. Yet, I couldn't assume I would cope well without Alistair or Mia. Thankfully, Governor Barrington bought into my continued pleas, needing me to shut up, calm me down. He allowed me to stay where I was, for now, impressed by the work I was doing, my changing attitude towards prison life enabling him to take my personal needs into account rather readily.

Mia continued to get better, she told me due to my unfailing, unwavering support. No longer did she vomit into the toilet, hiding food she ate in large quantities, purging herself to the point of bringing up traces of blood. I never claimed to understand the condition, offering an overriding psychological viewpoint, teaching her how to love herself again. She wasn't damaged. Her past didn't equate to her whole life. She needed to learn to appreciate she too was special, important. It gave my friend a fighting chance for survival. I loved her for that.

***

The following year, I finally graduated as a law student, my studies awarding me a First-Class Honours. I was beyond elated, ecstatic to the point that, when Alistair gave me his *present* that very evening, locked in the prison library together well hidden behind several ageing bookshelves, I almost yelled out in premeditated glee. I was grateful our time together was more relaxed lately, very few people using this space anyway, and those who did either happy to turn a blind eye to the antics of the couple in their midst, or extract a *reward* for continued silence.

My life in prison had taken a strange, if not, impossible

turn. I had been here for just over four years now, settled into the system well. I still thought about Elijah often, of course, alone in my cell, once the lights were out, no one and nothing to distract me from that single photograph of him on my mum's rug, a tiny baby that my parents would by now, almost have forgotten he once was. I would hold it in my hands for hours, tracing his features, trying to imagine what he looked like now. He would be running my parents ragged, no doubt, talking back to them, getting into mischief, starting a new school this coming September. Everything was happening without me, without my much-needed influence in my beautiful son's life. I wanted to tell my parents about my degree, about how proud Emma would have been of my incredible achievements. I wanted them *all* to be proud of me. The EIP group sessions were now a standard part of my week. Surely they would be impressed by what I'd done.

As it was, no such visits were ever awarded, no confirmation ever received from my family to substantiate they even cared about me at all. It didn't matter. I was dealing with it. Yet, despite everything, I couldn't help detesting how Alistair went home to his wife and family each evening, leaving me alone in the darkness to dream of a life not my own. It was always the same dreaded time of day that forced me to face my own reality, face my demons in the blackness around me — a time that, despite it all, often left me on the brink of sanity. I would be lying if I said prison wasn't affecting my own mental health. It affected everyone's. Yet, the more time I spent with Alistair, the more I wanted a normal life beyond what I had come to know. I hated to admit that he was the longest relationship I'd ever had, although, inside these walls, none of it felt real.

We had never spent an entire night together, had never been to a restaurant, the cinema, bowling. We had never booked a naughty weekend break away, never ate pizza in bed, watching crappy old films and making love all night long. I wanted those simple things. I *needed* them. We both knew if the truth of our relationship ever got out, it would be a disaster. He would be transferred, struck off, his kids placed in severe financial crisis. I would be punished, losing the privileges I'd earned through sheer hard work and dedication. Alistair would lose his job, his family, although we had discussed this requirement in detail already, and he was planning to leave his wife soon anyway. He loved *me*. I believed him. Nobody had ever treated me as well as he did. No one ever understood me as much.

Alistair knew about my crimes, the murders I'd committed long ago, although I was careful in my detailed explanations, always maintaining a profound innocence in it all. *None* of it was my fault. Not really. Nevertheless, I was painfully sorry for what had happened, so desperately sorry for it all. Or, at least, as far as he was concerned, I was. The truth was I still had no genuine idea of what I should be feeling about any of it. It was in the past. Long gone. Mostly forgotten.

Despite the success of the EIP sessions, I still attended my required weekly sessions with Farley, still forced to sit and share my emotions with *him*. It was ironic, considering what I was doing for the other women. Women he had failed to help. He joked I might be after his job. *As if.* All I wanted was to get the hell out of this place. Every year that passed me by was one more year away from my son, and my man in the uncomfortable arms of his overbearing wife.

## 37

The day Mia received news of her upcoming release was the day I saw my world fall apart all over again. My EIP sessions had all but turned things around for my friend, helping her uncover deep routed emotions she'd buried for so long — feelings she didn't realise she was hiding. She blamed herself for her dad's motivation, confessing she'd spent years believing if she were ugly, repulsive, he would not have wanted to go near her. He wouldn't have hurt her, wouldn't have raped her repeatedly for several years. At such a young age, Mia couldn't have appreciated it had nothing to do with her appearance or attitude that made her dad the way he was. Bulimia subsequently became a way of controlling her own body image, all but destroying the person she was in the process.

Now, thankfully, she had finally put on weight, finally looked healthy, happy, her desire for self-destruction no longer an issue, food tasting somewhat normal to her again, thank Christ. I was happy for her, really I was, but it stamped an unfortunate truth onto my troubled brain that I would be stuck in this place alone now, my cell requiring a new inmate for company I wasn't convinced I wanted.

'Thank you for everything,' Mia said, leaning in for a

hug. We were standing in our cell, our arms around each other, my much-needed embrace unwilling to let the poor girl go. We'd been through so much together, so many emotions, good and bad. I couldn't imagine life in here without her smiling face awaiting me in the mornings, helping get me out of bed.

'Just you make bloody sure you don't *ever* come back here again, do you hear me, girl?' I scolded, trying to hold back a stray tear. This was a good day. Mia didn't need my shit.

'I promise,' Mia added, kissing my salt infused cheek. 'And make sure you keep up the good work. I'm so proud of you. Elijah would be, too.' My friend was trying to be nice, trying to console me, but her words sliced a fresh wound into my already breaking heart. I couldn't allow her to see how I felt. It wouldn't be fair.

I nodded, my *only* friend about to leave my life for good. 'Don't fucking do anything stupid,' I laughed, needing her to go before I screamed, held her captive, did something idiotic that would destroy us both in the process. I wanted her to be happy, find a better life for herself. She deserved it.

'Likewise,' Mia told me, jabbing a wayward index finger into my shoulder blade, trying to keep our last moment light, upbeat. 'You keep out of trouble, and you'll be out of here in no time.'

I nodded my head, knowing she meant well, knowing she was trying to be kind. Mia didn't need to worry about me. She had a new place to go now, somewhere safe where she could begin the slow process of rebuilding her life. I feared without me for continued stability, she might slip into old patterns, old habits, but I hoped she was strong enough now to forge a new path for herself. I was probably just thinking of myself, my own inability to cope without *her*. A better future awaited at least one of us. She had new friends to make, new memories to create without me.

In all the years we shared a cell, I'd oddly never been able to speak about *that* fateful night when I could have lost my friend forever. Finding her on the bathroom floor, covered in her own blood, death moments away. It was a memory that had stayed with me ever since. Every time I closed my eyes, in fact. I hadn't told Mia, of course. That would have been unfair, but I felt now was as good a time as any to mention it. After all, if things became awkward, she was free to leave this cell and my life, never to see me again if that is what she wanted.

'Just one thing?' I said, hoping to Christ I wasn't about to make a colossal mistake, lose my best friend, my *only* friend, forever.

'Yes?' Mia was smiling, a glow on her cheeks that made her skin look so incredible, so healthy. If I ever realised I was gay, Mia would undoubtedly be my type.

'We never actually got to talk about that night.' I held my breath, hoping I wasn't overstepping the mark. I was now quite good at talking, sharing thoughts, expressing emotions. We'd already shared so much, so why the hell was I finding this moment so confrontational? So utterly confusing?

Mia glanced towards the floor, biting her lip, recalling a painful memory neither of us needed. 'Shit, yeah. We never actually got round to it, did we?' My friend looked at me as if she wanted to say something yet wasn't sure where to begin. 'Please, don't be angry with me, Stace,' she stated, placing a warm hand over mine. Why would I *ever* be angry with Mia? I loved her, platonically, of course. 'But there is something about that night I never told you.' Mia closed her eyes for a moment, thinking back.

'It was all my fault—' I began, wanting to apologise, make the past a better place for both of us.

Mia shook her head. 'No, honey,' she sighed. 'It wasn't.' Mia stepped away from her bunk, away from me, lost in thoughts I wasn't aware of. 'Oh, shit,' she sighed, as if recalling something she hoped would eventually become lost to time.

'Mia?' Why did she look so downtrodden all of a sudden?

'I didn't want to tell you because I knew it would damage your chances of *ever* getting out.' She looked skyward for a moment, staring too long at a blob of dirty grey chewing gum that had been stuck to our cell ceiling for longer than anyone could remember. *Tell me what?*

'What are you talking about?'

'Everything has been so much better lately, for both of us. And, the more time passed, the less it seemed important to say anything to you at all.' Mia was chewing her lip, an uncertain look in her eyes. She sighed. 'If I tell you now, you *must* promise me this will *never* leave this cell? Promise me you will not do anything with the information I'm about to share with you?' I wrinkled my brow, literally no idea what she was talking about. I couldn't promise what I didn't know.

'*Promise me?*' Mia repeated firmly, loudly, grabbing my hands in hers, holding tight.

'I promise,' I muttered, still no idea what my friend was about to tell me. Nervous by words I couldn't yet understand.

'That night, in the showers, after we —' Mia closed her eyes, poised. 'After *I* ran out of here.' She took a breath. 'I didn't slash my own wrists. Someone made it look like a suicide attempt.'

*What?* What the hell was I hearing now? I glared at my friend, unsure what I was hearing. 'I beg your pardon?' I gulped loudly. Mia opened her eyes, the look on my confused face unable to sedate the simple fact she was telling me she hadn't hurt *herself* and instead, someone else had. She offered no immediate reply, no longer willing to look at me. *What the fuck?* 'I don't understand,' I muttered, shaking my head. I genuinely didn't.

'To be honest, I *never* wanted you to learn the truth. You would have gone after them, made things even harder for yourself in this place, added time to your already ridiculous sentence. I'm only telling you now because I'm confident you have the emotional intelligence and clarity of mind to avoid trouble, keep your nose clean, get the hell out of this place while you can.'

'Who exactly are you talking about?' I questioned, my throat dry, my friend's words entirely unexpected. 'Gone after *who*?' I couldn't take any of this in.

'Ellie Dowle and Cheryl Blake.'

'*Rancock's* old mates?' Why were those names so painful to hear? What the hell?

Mia nodded, a look on her face I couldn't read. 'They were waiting for me in the shower block that night. It was a pure coincidence they were there at that time, obviously. They didn't know I was already upset with you, already heading their way. I didn't even see it coming until they grabbed me. I felt something hit me from behind. Then everything went black.'

I couldn't take it in. 'I don't understand.' I'd willingly, *rightfully*, murdered Rancock because I believed she had stabbed my friend. I couldn't have known I had it so wrong. I certainly had no concept revenge was something her friends would have planned for weeks afterwards.

'They found out what you did to Rancock. Getting to me was a far better way to hurt you directly, Honey. They knew how close we'd become.'

*Bloody hell.* This couldn't be true. How did they even

know I had anything to do with what happened to Rancock? I stared at my friend, unable to grasp the fact she'd kept this from me for so long. Yet, at the time, I was hardly displaying any sympathy by the woman's sudden departure from the world. It probably wouldn't take a genius to work it out, even for stupid people like Dowle and Blake.

'Shit,' I whispered, the truth sinking in too sharply, too painfully. 'I'm so sorry.' I couldn't believe that I was responsible for what happened. I assumed Mia was upset with me because of the rejection I'd given her, forcing her to attempt an easy way out. *How deluded was I?*

'You couldn't have known.'

'If I had, then—'

'Then you would have gone after them, too. Just like you did with Rancock and Smith.' She was right. I retaliated badly after the very same bitches had snorted drugs from my pillowcase. It was so long ago yet I could still hear the sound of crunching glass shards, how it made me feel to consider their downfall. 'You would be rotting in this place for the rest of your life, Stace. Your boy would never have the chance to know his mum. I couldn't allow that to happen. I *can't* allow that to happen.' Mia looked perturbed to think of my suffering.

'So you kept quiet all this time?' She certainly had more restraint than me. It might have been impressive had it not been such a serious issue.

'Just long enough for Dowle and Blake to get out, so you couldn't get to them. I knew they would never attend the EIPs, would never come clean about what they did. They probably assumed I would have told you at some point. They probably assumed things were even.'

*Even?* Jesus Christ. 'But they—'

'Didn't succeed,' Mia cut in, finishing my sentence with a shake of her head, stroking my now trembling hands, needing me to understand. 'Like I've always told you, Stacey. You can't keep assuming killing people is a good way to solve your problems.'

She was probably right, but to me, my murders *had* solved problems. Emma was out of the picture, finally, no longer a shadow over my existence. It would have given me the chance of happiness, had things been different. Rancock was never going to cause Mia any more issues. It was a shame that Jason's death had the unfortunate side effect of landing me in this shithole.

'I'm so sorry,' I breathed, quite unable to express any other emotion.

Mia shook her head. 'It's all in the past now. Oh, and before I forget,' she added, changing the subject rapidly as if what she'd just told me was unimportant, picking up her belongings from her bunk, ready to leave our cell for the very last time. I glanced her way, hardly able to bring myself to watch her walk away from me. 'This is for you.' Mia placed a large bar of chocolate onto my bunk. *Cadbury Dairy Milk*. My favourite. 'I honestly do not know where I would be now without you, Stacey Adams,' she confirmed, blowing me a kiss, heading out of the door, tears welling in beautiful eyes I would sadly miss.

I didn't say a word or follow her out. I couldn't speak. The irony was she would probably be dead now if it weren't for me. The fact I found her in time was irrelevant. The last thing I would ever remember of her now would be a bar of chocolate I wasn't sure I could ever bring myself to eat. Doing so meant I would be removing her from this place forever, my friend's last words cutting sharply into my cold dead heart.

I listened to distant footsteps, women talking, everyone wishing Mia good luck, telling her to look after herself, keep in touch, stay out of trouble. I smiled, knowing my friend would be okay, hoping she would find a far better life than the one she had in here.

'I'll come back and visit,' she yelled, aiming her words in my direction. Then she was gone, the unit gate closed, the rest of the women dispersing just as swiftly.

'You'd better,' I yelled into the void of the now empty room, knowing Mia couldn't hear.

'Are you okay?' I looked up to see Braunie standing in the doorway. I opened my mouth to ask her what she was doing here when, behind her, Paula Jones appeared, followed by several other smiling women. It had been so long since I'd seen either of these two. I had no idea what was happening. In turn, they walked into my cell, placing items on my bed, offering me a nod, a wink. Shampoo, chocolate, coffee, delicious cakes and biscuits usually only reserved for treats, special occasions. My bunk became crammed with all kinds of luxury items, each inmate thanking me as they left my cell.

'Thank you, Stacey, thank you,' they each said in turn.

'What's all this?' I asked as Braunie grinned widely from the doorway.

'Just a little something we've all been allowed to do, seeing as Mia was leaving today and all.' Braunie stepped back to expose Mrs Smith, Miss Sharp, Alistair, and several other officers, all standing in the unit together, surrounded by women from different locations, including general population and the mum-and-baby unit. They each walked into my cell and out again, no trouble pending, no need for concern. I even received a bottle of unopened baby lotion from one of the new mums. *What the hell?*

'We wanted to thank you for the EIP sessions. Cheer you up. You have helped many women in this place, Stacey. You honestly don't know how much,' Braunie stated, stepping forward, handing me her radio. The one she always had in her possession, never left her side. The one she would have beaten anyone to a pulp if they so much as breathed on it sideways.

'Because of the EIP groups, I'm going home tomorrow,' she continued, sounding a little shocked yet happy by the concept. Katelyn was already waiting for her on the outside, already released a few months previous, thanks to the efforts of my EIP meetings. I wondered if she was planning some big celebration dinner for the two of them, a lustful much-required first night together pending. 'It's all down to you, Stacey. Thank you,' she confirmed before leaving my room. I couldn't believe what I was hearing. I was not worthy of their gratitude. I was not worthy of anything. I stared at my bulging bunk, Mia's secret ringing uncomfortably in my ears.

## 38

I stood in the middle of my cell, shocked by the sudden appearance of possessions that would no doubt be of great personal value to most. Consumables usually retained for special occasions lay spread across my sheets along with prized items many would miss. Mia was gone, yet in her place lay a plethora of personal effects capable of keeping me entertained for the next decade. Yet despite such a kind gesture, I couldn't dislodge my friend's words, her ultimate confession today bringing an unexpected disquiet directly into my thoughts. She had *not* attempted to end her life. I couldn't fathom such a truth, unable to absorb the information. Why the *hell* didn't she tell me all this before now? She conveniently left it until today, the very moment she was leaving this place, leaving me behind to deal with the fallout of her unexpected disclosure.

Mia was right about one thing, though, as always, because, if I had known these facts previously, I would indeed have gone after both Dowle and Blake, ensuring they received far worse than anything they could inflict on my best friend. I still had no idea how they even knew it was me who'd ensured Rancock's untimely demise in the first place. I thought I had planned it all perfectly, carefully. Her death was ruled as an accidental overdose, nothing more. It was, of course, fitting that Mia's time in the shower block was equally judged as a suicide attempt, both women simply victims of their own actions. Mia was correct in assuming it would have hurt me far more by killing my friend than if they had attacked me directly. At that time, I couldn't care less what happened to me. I shuddered. Why did they not come back and finish the job? Finish my friend, once and for all? Finish me?

'Mrs Smith?' I called into the corridor, my thoughts threatening to twist my mind into a tightly knotted ball of string. 'May I have a moment, please?' Smith glanced my way, nodded a disinterested head, strolling over to where I stood as if she had far better things to do.

'What is it, Adams?' she asked, her attention focused more on the women she was trying to escort back to general population than my unheeded requirements.

I motioned the woman to follow me inside my cell, needing this moment kept private, no accidental ears able to ruin my forthcoming confrontation. Smith complied with a disgruntled sigh, not expecting my following words.

'I know about you and Mia,' I stated boldly, needing to confront her directly now that the poor girl was no longer able to prevent me from doing so, an alternative motive floating around my head, this opportunity the perfect moment to kill two metaphoric birds with one stone. I glared at her, hoping she wouldn't need much clarification.

'What *are* you talking about, Adams?' she snapped, in no mood for games.

I smiled. I hadn't expected her to respond any differently. She was so predictable. Yet, neither had I expected to see the woman today. It had to be a sign.

'And, I know what you did to her,' I said, folding my arms across my chest, my eyes set on Smith's, unmoving, unforgiving. I needed a glimpse of remorse. *Something* to confirm the woman standing in front of me now wasn't the total and utter *bitch* I had created in my head for several years. That's all I needed. It would have been enough. I was somewhat amazed at how calm I remained, grateful to my psychology studies for maintaining my inner dialogue, my inner peace.

Smith scoffed, shaking her head. 'Adams, you're making no sense, whatsoever.' She turned to leave, bored already, oblivious to my simmering emotions.

'She loved you, you know,' I confirmed firmly, hoping something would resonate with the woman, click into place, press a few buttons, hit home a compelling truth we both knew existed between them. 'She probably always will.' It was true. Mia was a complex young woman who wore her heart on her sleeve. She probably never got over Carol Smith — the only person Mia believed had ever shown her any genuine affection after the cruelty thrust upon her by her twisted father.

'Adams, what the hell are you talking about?' Smith wasn't backing down, still unable and unwilling to confess to past secrets, past mistakes.

I shook my head. It didn't matter how much she protested her innocence. 'Why did you stab her?' It was an honest question, heartfelt. Easy to answer.

Smith faltered for a moment. 'I have no idea what—'

'*Spare me the bullshit!*' I yelled, needing something more from the woman than continued denial. I was unable to dissipate the dark thoughts I knew Mia lived with every single day. Did the poor girl not deserve a little closure? 'What did she *ever* do to you?' My berating tone echoed through the cell, penetrating walls that held no secrets.

Smith stared at me for a second, something in her eyes that didn't exist a moment earlier. 'What exactly do you *think* you know?' she spat back, her lips tightening along with shoulders that seemed to tense with each word.

'Did you seriously believe Mia wouldn't tell me about that day?' I swallowed, standing my ground. I couldn't dwell on that.

'What day?' Smith wasn't giving this thing up easily.

'Jesus. Do you have no feelings at all?' Was this woman already *dead* inside?

'Adams, you really are deluded—'

'Carol, please,' I breathed, using her first name as if we were old friends. I shook my head. 'Mia loves you. She's gone now. Why can't you just help me give her closure she's waited years for you to provide? She can't hurt you anymore.' She wouldn't.

Smith faltered for a moment. 'I never meant for any of it to happen,' she confessed suddenly, her words erupting from nowhere, a blank expression stretched across her face. She closed her eyes, visions allowed to form that she didn't need, stinging her eyes, hurting her brain. I know how she felt.

'Which part? Stabbing her in the corridor, or falling in love with her in the first place?'

Smith opened her eyes, staring at me, mouth agape, her mind swimming. 'Both... I guess.' I wasn't expecting such a swift confirmation.

'Then why did you do it?' I was impressed by how calm my words sounded, how casually I was able to form such painful sentences. Inside I was anything but calm. I was screaming. I wanted revenge, *needed* it, owed my friend some well-meaning justice. Yet, I also owed her the honest, genuine truth.

'I was only planning on warning her off,' Smith whispered, closing my cell door, standing in front of me. 'I *never* meant to use the fucking knife. But Mia was threatening me. Telling me she would expose us, expose *me*, if I didn't take her back. If I didn't pick up where we'd left off.' Smith looked pale, shell-shocked, as if my knowledge of such truth was a shock to her system.

I waited as patiently as my racing brain would allow, needing to know more, no more forceful words required to persuade her to continue this personal quest for redemption. 'And?' I added softly.

'And, then she walked out of her cell, straight into me. Straight into the bloody knife. Neither of us was expecting it to happen.' Smith shook her head, a flash of something passing over her now ashen face. Was it guilt? 'I was holding the knife in my hand at the time, expecting to just threaten her with it, give her a warning, make her back off. Nothing more than that.'

'You punctured her *lung*.' How dare she sound so blatant?

'I didn't mean to stab her. Honestly. She just walked right into me. Right into the knife-edge. I *loved* her too.' Smith was looking directly at me now, tears welling in emotional eyes that seemed to show a genuine response neither of us was expecting. I believed her.

'Loved?'

'I'm a married woman with kids and responsibilities. Mia was just—'

'A bit of fun? A passing phase? A kid?'

'No. She was, *is*, a good girl. One of the best.'

'Then why the *hell* did you treat her like shit?' It was a good question. My voice was less than a whisper now, my friend's awkward secret barely retained within these wafer-thin walls.

Smith took a breath, swallowing a lump that seemed to stick in her throat. 'I guess we have all done things we wish we could change.' She didn't say anything else. She didn't need to. She'd said it all.

'Don't worry. I won't say a word about any of this,' I breathed, knowing I'd extracted what I needed. At least I could now provide my friend the confirmation she had waited so long to hear. Reasons she lay awake at night pondering over, dreaming of, crying into the darkness around her when she assumed I was asleep. I'd faithfully promised Mia that I would leave it, leave Carol Smith alone, forget it ever happened. I would continue to keep that promise. *That* is how much Mia meant to me.

'However,' I spat, my tone as cold as the grey walls surrounding us. 'There is one thing you can do for me, *miss.*' I spoke coldly, my alternative motive for getting her into my cell in the first place, now readily coming into fruition.

'I would deny it all anyway, Adams,' Smith confirmed with a scoff she had no right to express, wishing only to claim back the power she wasn't about to allow me to have over her so easily. 'What *exactly* do you want?' She probably expected me to demand favours, extra privileges, smuggle things in from the outside. She need not worry. I wanted none of those things.

'I found out this morning that Mia did *not* try to kill herself that night in the showers.'

'*What?*' Smith looked as confused as I'd been feeling for the last twenty minutes.

'She told me it was a set-up. Made to look as if she had cut herself to defer blame from the real culprits.'

'What the hell are you talking about now?' Smith was shaking her head, glaring at me as if I'd finally lost my mind, this place finally taking its toll.

'Let's put it this way. If Ellie Dowle or Cheryl Blake *ever* find themselves back inside this place, you damned well make sure they suffer. For Mia.' I refrained from adding, *If you really love her.* Of course, I would have already taken care of it myself, given the opportunity. But I was working hard towards my release, my future far more critical than those two bitches ever could be. I couldn't allow yet more people to decide my destiny, conclude my fate.

'Are you seriously trying to tell me they had set Mia up?' Smith's features had darkened.

I nodded.

'Why?'

Why indeed. Did I tell her? Confess my murderous deeds to a prison officer who had the power to extend my life sentence with a simple visit to the governor's office? A simple statement made on my behalf that Rancock did not die of an overdose? No. I think not.

'Who knows why people do the shit they do?' I said, those very words reaching my unfeigned attention as Paula's much earlier comment sprang into my mind. It had a lasting impact I couldn't shake. 'I can't take care of it myself, obviously. I've kept my nose clean for too long.' It was all I had to say on the matter.

'But I still don't understand,' she muttered, unwilling to accept that someone had tried to kill Mia.

'You and me both,' I confirmed, my expression telling that I knew nothing more than she did. Nothing to be done about any of it now.

Smith nodded, knowing we were done here, our conversation complete. 'Okay, Adams. If I *ever* see those two back in this place, don't worry, I'll take care of it.' She motioned a knowing nod my way, a private confirmation of the secrets we would now forever keep for each other. I tried not to notice the slight tremble in her hand as she opened the cell door, stepping outside, leaving me alone. Was she as angry as I was? I assumed she still loved Mia, too, in her own way. Their much earlier relationship something neither of them would ever forget. Life can be cruel, fickle. *It was all so fucking unfair.*

# 39

## *Ten years later*

It's quite surprising where time goes when you're not watching the clock. Once Mia was gone, I settled into a regimented slump, a further unrelenting decade passing before I received the news I'd waited so long to hear. I was up for parole. I'd served just over fourteen years of my twenty-four-year prison sentence, eventually being forced back into general population around a year after Mia's release, much to Alistair's initial dismay. As peer worker for the mentally unstable, his continued service was needed in the mental health unit, so he was unable to swap his daily duties to the central unit to be close to me, unfortunately for us both.

It was somewhat lamentable our needs were unimportant to this place anyway, yet it was just as well. If our relationship became anything other than secret, the resulting chaos would have been disastrous. It only bothered me for around a week until we found a way around our separation by meeting twice weekly in the prison library. The EIP had inadvertently ensured we still got to spend time together, the women's mental health extremely valuable to us both. If anything, it strengthened the bond we had firmly formed.

My continued good work meant I'd been in the prison's good books for a while — my time was now served, they confirmed, my punishment complete. I was oddly classed as reformed, able to re-join society without any potential fear of reoffending.

They did not assume I would kill again. They did not see me as a threat. Should my parole be granted, I was even asked to consider continuing my EIP work, returning each week to HMP Blackwood to continue the group sessions. The women had come to rely heavily on the source, its abrupt end potentially unfair for all. They also asked if I would be prepared to extend the programme to other prison locations if the governor could get the idea passed by those in charge? They would pay me, of course. I would have immediate employment via a specifically designed back-to-work prison scheme the government were trialling for ex-cons. Plus, they could keep a close eye on my continued reformation. I couldn't turn it down. I was now forty-four years old, the majority of my adult life already spent behind bars. What else could I do? I didn't exactly have a glittering career to fall back on.

Mia came to visit me often, of course. She had settled well into her shared accommodation, the other girls of similar age, of similarly troubled pasts. We spoke for weeks before I confessed to the private conversation I'd shared with Carol Smith, just moments after my dear friend had walked free. I do not know if she appreciated my interference. If she did, she didn't tell me, sat quietly with thoughts I wished I had the power to take away from her. I'd lowered her mood, untethered her subjacent spirits, upset the balance. Still, at least she could live her life now with the knowledge that Smith never truly intended on causing her any actual harm, and privately she loved her too. I assumed, deep down, Mia already knew. I presumed she had already forgiven her. Unfortunately, we never saw Blake or Dowle again. What happened to them? I don't know. I privately hoped karma would find them someday, deliver the justice Smith and I had been cruelly devoid of.

I enjoyed my time with Alistair more than ever, still being loved in stolen moments, still giggling in secret. It was, in fact, he who delivered the shocking news of my upcoming parole hearing, his tone expressionless. It was the news we'd talked about for so long — the news that would all but change our lives forever. His children were growing up fast, needed him less, his wife no longer requiring the support of the *cheating* husband she didn't even know she had. I couldn't help that. I didn't know the woman. It wasn't my fault.

It was unfathomable that, despite waiting so long to hear word of a potential release, when it finally came to pass, I couldn't help feeling slightly anxious by the concept. I'd been away from the world for a long time, and my only visitor was Mia. My much earlier, somewhat unforgettable, visit from my mum was now all but forgotten, my family long gone, my once assumed friends hardly there for me in the first place. The women inside had weirdly become my friends, my family. I would have a hard time settling into life beyond these walls.

I thought about my old flat, my old job, gone now, taken by someone else far more deserving than I ever was. If Sylvester's body was still out there somewhere, he would be a decaying fur-covered corpse in some landfill site by now, nothing but roadkill, no longer resembling a cat. My poor sister would be a pile of dusty bones in her coffin. It wasn't an ideal consideration. I did not know if Jason even had a grave or whether his parents had chosen to burn his body to ash. Judging by the state I'd left him in, I assumed they wouldn't wish to be constantly reminded their damaged son lay six feet beneath their shoes, his skull bashed in, his identity removed. Cremation would have been a kinder option for them all.

The world I left behind was probably long changed. Stacey Adams, long forgotten by a society who barely noticed anyway. It was a strange consideration. Elijah would be fourteen now, becoming a man, his voice already deeper, potentially sounding like his dad. I hoped he hadn't turned out like him. The irony of such a concept would probably haunt me forever. Did he hate me? Would he be unwilling to reconnect to his absent mother after all these years? Eva would be almost seventeen. I couldn't imagine her all grown up. I wondered if she looked anything like her mother. I hoped she did. Emma was beautiful. I thought long and hard about my parents and how they had left their youngest daughter to rot in prison, their eldest rotting in her grave, both so very much alone to their miserable fate.

With too many unaddressed emotions left to linger, my initial elated mood had already turned quite melancholy as I was led along a corridor towards awaiting parole officers, to a room ready and willing to hear my story — the whole thing designed to confirm a notion I was ready to re-join society. *Was I, though?* Had I really changed? Do any of us? I just did what needed to be done for the sake of my survival.

My days were only made bearable due to the love of a good man — a man I probably didn't deserve. Yet, I had achieved so much here. The lives of many women were better because of the decision *I'd* made to do something positive. I would be leaving prison with a first-class honours degree in law and a diploma in psychology, the last twelve and a half of those fourteen years offering a gleamingly clean record that had led to this very day. A full ten years ahead of my scheduled release, in fact. An entire decade that I would potentially now have to enjoy freedom I felt I might never experience again.

'Your behaviour over the last few years has been exceptional, Miss Adams. Exemplary, even.' I was being addressed by one of three panel members in the room. They were sitting in a row, their low-backed chairs set in front of mine, my solitary chair set down in the middle of the room as if I was about to feel the full force of some prison interrogation — more *firing squad* than *fair hearing*.

'You have received a highly commended recommendation for release by both the prison governor and your psychologist.' He pointed to Farley, also in the room, who offered me a smile I did not reciprocate. I was too nervous to smile. I felt sick. 'Tell me, Miss Adams, what do you feel you have gained by your time in here?' the guy in a black suit continued. He shuffled in his chair, straightening himself stiffly, failing to remove unwanted creases from his jacket that matched the ones on his face. He looked as if he might be happier attending a funeral. It was a reasonable question, though.

I took a breath, remembering Alistair's advice to speak purely from my heart. *My heart?* Did I even have one? It was debatable. My parents would undoubtedly refute such a thing.

'I was given the most profound opportunity to help others like me,' I began, needing to make the best impression I could. I would never get another chance like this. 'I wanted to study for my law degree, initially.'

'Yes. And why was that?' another board member chipped in, breaking my train of thought by throwing a further question my way.

'I always wanted to study law. Even as a child.' It was true. 'The prison system has thankfully been able to afford me such a fantastic opportunity. I am grateful.' Perfect. Well done, Stacey. These people love being sucked up to, told how great they are.

'Okay, thank you,' the woman confirmed, nodding a seemingly satisfied head. 'Carry on.'

I swallowed, almost forgetting the first question entirely. 'I noticed women coming in and out of this place who were broken by society and the people they often wrongly placed their trust in. Most of them were not able to survive in the real world, reoffending because of a misjudged pattern they had found themselves locked in, not able to deal well with their personal traumas or emotions.' I almost sounded as if I *wasn't* one of them, not included in the statistics, not meant to be here at all. I was impressed by how professional I sounded — almost authoritative. 'I guess I wanted to do something positive, change things for the better.' I refrained from adding, *to change things for me*.

The black-suited man nodded. 'Yes, your Emotional Insecurities Programme. I have heard impressive talk about the sessions, Miss Adams, and the help they seem to provide.' He glanced towards the other panel members, seeking confirmation, they agreed. 'If granted parole, what do you plan to do on the outside?' He lifted his chin, stone-faced, waiting.

'I've been offered a wonderful opportunity to continue the programme, sir,' I replied, feeling immensely grateful to have been offered such a position. *Thank you, Governor Barrington.* 'They want me to continue working in the prison system with more EIP groups rolled out to different locations.' I felt as if I was in a job interview.

'And do you now feel that your initial crimes are no longer something that was your fault or out of your direct control?'

I swallowed. I had fully expected this question, always maintaining my continued non-compliance in my earlier behaviour, avoiding responsibility for my actions. I guess that's why I spent so long in the mental health unit. Nothing that happened was ever *my* fault. Yet, did these people see me as a reformed character or a deluded psychopath trying to break free? A killer. Nothing more. Forever capable of inexplicable deeds.

'I regret everything I ever did, sir, every *single* day of my life. If I could go back and change the course of my actions, believe me, I would. As it is, I now have to live with the truth of my crimes, the pain I caused, fully appreciating that my parents will hate me until the day they die. Understandably, of course.' Most of that statement was true. At least, the last part was. My parents did hate me. I could never change a damned thing about that. It was unfortunate that I still did *not* understand why.

The parole board continued to throw questions my way for another hour, the entire room closing in around me, choking me, mocking my very existence. By the time I made it out into the hallway, I felt as if I might faint, my legs like jelly, my head in a spin.

'How did you get on?' Alistair was keen to know.

'Good, I think.' I hoped. *Prayed.*

\*\*\*

For the rest of that week, I walked around on eggshells, waiting daily for news, anything. Even a *no, fuck off, Stacey, we saw right through your lies* would have been better than the silence I was consequently forced to endure. So, when Alistair walked into my cell one afternoon, I wasn't expecting his confirmation.

'You got it,' he told me, leaning casually against the doorframe.

'Don't take the piss,' I chided, scrambling to my feet in a hurry, the book I wasn't really reading falling to the floor.

'Seriously?'

Alistair nodded, offering me a smile that didn't seem to reach his eyes. I didn't notice.

'No way,' I cried, throwing my arms around him in the same hurry as I'd rushed to my feet, the pages of my poor book crushed beneath my sudden excitement. I was crying. Alistair was hugging me. Yet something in his tone was off. Usually, he shared my good news with great enthusiasm. He was usually the first person in my corner, the first to bring me word of good fortune, good grace. However, standing in front of him now, my parole confirmed, my release date pending, something felt odd. I couldn't put my finger on it. There was something in Alistair's smile. Something not quite right. Although I tried not to overthink his lowered mood, I didn't like it one bit.

# 40

I wanted Alistair to be happy for me. Happy for *us*. It was perplexing that I was literally walking on air whilst waiting for everything to go wrong. I did not intend to take any unnecessary risks or do anything that might affect my pending release. I was overly kind to everyone, sickeningly so, ensuring they had no reason to *ever* become upset with me, refuse my parole, laugh in my face. I even purposefully distanced myself from Alistair, just in case we were found out, karma firmly coming back to smack me in the face.

Since I began the EIP groups over a decade earlier, I was oddly viewed as some authority figure on all things mental health. The women now came to me instead of asking to see Farley, much to his often openly displayed annoyance. I was seen as a motherly figure to many, my advancing years and prolonged prison sentence raising my status from annoying inmate to person of much appreciation. Because of this, I worried my release would, unfortunately, create a problem for some of the more unstable women here. I worried they might try to jeopardise things for me, do something stupid to extend my stay, ensure I stayed with them a little longer.

As it was, I need not have concerned myself with such trivia. Governor Barrington had stated I was a credit to the prison system, a true figure of reformation, testimony to the very idea that a once deemed damaged person can genuinely turn their life around. I had agreed, on a trial basis, to continue the EIP groups that would be increased to four sessions per week. I would, of course, need to slot them around my parole office visits, the world outside nothing of what I'd left behind or what I remembered. I didn't mind. I was glad to have a reason to return to the very walls that had become my unwitting protector.

It was all very frightening, to be honest. Fourteen years locked inside the walls of a prison had rendered me uncertain of the world beyond. I had, as they say, become fully institutionalised. I was glad Alistair was by my side, though. I doubted I would have made it this far had it not been for him. I couldn't wait for us to finally be together, a brand-new life waiting. I was happy to keep my head down, keep our relationship quiet for a while longer if that's how things needed to pan out in the short term. I was about to become a free woman. We would soon be free to begin something incredible. I was happy to allow everything to unfold precisely how it was meant to. There was no rush.

'I can't believe it,' I breathed into his ear, my voice almost childlike, excitable. We were outside in the prison garden, not alone, yet not in full view of the others. To them, we were simply having a heightened conversation. Probably discussing my upcoming release, my excitement unrelenting, something I hadn't shut up about for days. 'Tomorrow, we finally get to begin that life we've talked about for so long.' I wanted to kiss him, hold his hand, tell him I loved him. Tomorrow, I could do that. I was grinning somewhat painfully, my jaws not used to such exuberance, this chapter of my life due to end very soon.

'Alistair, did you hear me?' I scolded playfully, leaning into him, careful not to do anything to arouse unwanted suspicion, provoke undesired attention. We had been so cautious for so long. It would hardly do now to undo all our good work, uncover the secret we'd shared for the last thirteen years. There were, of course, a small number of women who knew we were a couple, covered for us on several occasions, made our time together far more enjoyable than it would have been without them. The EIP had helped me in more ways than I could ever have believed possible. I owed those women a lot. It didn't matter I often overheard false stories of Alistair's so-called misplaced relationships with other inmates, many of them told to me via apparent concern. None of it was true. None of it bothered me.

'I heard you, Stacey,' Alistair whispered back. He wasn't looking at me. He didn't seem to want to engage in this conversation at all.

I smiled, my cheeks still glowing with the idea of what awaited me beyond these walls. 'Are you okay?' I asked, a look on my face that should have told him instantly how in love with him I was. I couldn't help it.

Alistair nodded, still unwilling to offer anything further, still not looking my way.

'You must be as nervous as me, hey?' I chided, nudging him on the arm gently when no eyes were aimed our way. 'Alistair?'

'Not here, Stacey,' he snapped unexpectedly, nodding a firm hello to a passing inmate who wanted to see the governor about something or nothing. Later, he told her. She could wait.

'What's wrong?' I asked, once the poor scolded woman had moved on.

'Nothing.'

I could tell there was something. I knew him too well. I rarely saw Alistair's frustration, his gentle side the only thing I needed. 'Tell me?' I queried, needing to know what was on his mind. My smile had slipped, along with the good mood I thought I was in.

Alistair sighed, moving away to position himself behind an old disused greenhouse that no one had bothered growing anything inside for some time, much to the governor's annoyance, especially when prison funding was so stretched. We should be more self-sufficient, he'd once claimed, give the prison a reason to flourish. Alistair was worrying me. Was there something wrong with my release date?

'Oh my god, what is it? Is it my parole? Oh shit, they changed their mind, didn't they?' Without warning, my heart lunged, sending my head into an unexpected spin. I should have known it wouldn't be this simple.

'No, it isn't that.' Alistair stood unsteadily in front of me, his feet shifting from one to the other as if he needed the toilet, his hands not sure what to do for the best.

'You're scaring me,' I pleaded, unable to do anything now but stare into his blank eyes. What the hell had happened? 'Just tell me, what's wrong.'

'You're getting out of this place,' he spoke quietly so nobody would overhear.

'I know that. Shit, for a moment there, you had me worried.' I smiled, realising he was as nervous as I was. I understood for the first time how much our new life beyond these walls obviously meant to him, too. It wasn't just about *me*. I reached out to take his hand. Nobody was watching. Alistair pulled away. *What the fuck?* I stared at him, my smile slipping further, my brow furling into a tight knot that probably showed my age. '*What?*'

'Our time together has been amazing, Stacey. I honestly want you to know that.'

I smiled, feeling the same way. He had no idea how

vital his presence in my life had been. So, why the hell was he acting so cold?

'But—' he continued. Shit. What did *that* mean?

'But, what?' Suddenly I wasn't so confident about anything.

'But... I'm married.' Alistair glanced at me for a moment, his eyes meeting mine, anxiously.

*Fuck me. Was that all?* 'Jesus Christ, Alistair, for a moment there, I thought you were about to end it,' I joked, knowing he would never do that to me. He loved me. I needed him now more than ever. 'I *know* you're married. I've always known it.' We'd discussed this unfortunate fact many times. I knew how much he adored me, the life he lived outside these walls nothing more than a front, a sham, something he maintained to look, to the outside world as if everything was carrying on as usual — nothing to see, nothing to notice. He needed nobody to stop and point fingers, cause unrequired mayhem, ruin his career.

'No, Stacey, you don't get it.'

'Get what?' I was still buzzing by the idea of the two of us together, a new life, a fresh start.

'What we've had in here has been great, like I said. But I'm sorry, Stacey. We can't do this thing on the outside.'

'I beg your pardon?' I turned to face him. I needed to see the look in his eyes as he told me he no longer wanted what I'd spent the last fourteen years of my godforsaken life waiting for. He was winding me up. He had to be. I attempted a smile, wrapping my arms around his waist. Alistair pulled away.

'I have a wife. A family. My boys need me, so does Charlotte.' He was chewing his lip, knowing I wouldn't dare kick off in front of the entire prison, cause a scene, jeopardise my release.

'*What the fuck?*' Did I say that out loud? My smile was

long gone.

'I'm so sorry. Honestly, I am. Please don't hate me. I couldn't bear that.' Alistair had a look in his eyes that told its own secret. A dark tale of shame and betrayal. It was his nerves talking, nothing more. I understood that more than most. He was unsure how things would unfold for us on the outside, our real-life more concerning to him than I'd initially noticed.

'I could *never* hate you,' I smoothed a hand over his shoulder, knowing he was simply telling me what he thought he needed me to hear in order to make my new life on the outside easier to handle. Yet, I didn't want or need anything other than *him*. I was more than happy to go along with whatever plan he deemed easiest. I thought I had made that perfectly clear. If we needed to sneak around for a few more weeks whilst he sorted a place for us to live, leave his old family behind, I could fully understand that. I could wait.

'Don't be nice to me, Stacey,' he shook his head. 'I don't deserve it.'

'Nice? Alistair, what are you talking about? I love you.' I laughed, speaking the truth, his pathetic attempt to try and break things off with me completely missing its mark. I wasn't going *anywhere*. He didn't need to worry about such things. I did love him. He needed to know it. Our relationship wasn't a passing phase. I'd invested years. I was in this for the long haul.

Alistair looked at me, noticing a growing ignorance lingering behind my adoring eyes. Did he honestly not understand what he meant to me?

'Shit, Stacey. I'm not playing around. I'm ending this thing. Now.' Alistair had developed a dark expression that extended beyond simple anxiety.

'What are you talking about?' I repeated, still not

entirely understanding the magnitude of this moment, the reality of the situation.

'We're done. Finished. Once you leave these walls, we won't be able to see each other again.'

I stood staring at him, the blank look on my face telling him nothing of what I was actually thinking. 'Are you serious?' My tone had matched the darkening shade of his cheeks. No more grey areas for my brain to contend with.

Alistair nodded, turning away from me, wanting to leave. 'Good luck on the outside,' he whispered, leaving me with the burning sting of his words and tears that spilt onto my cheeks like poison as he walked away. *What the hell was that?* My brain unable to absorb the enormity of the situation, understand words that struck me like shards of glass. *Good luck on the outside?* Was he fucking kidding me? I span around, my head spinning, my throat tightening. This wasn't happening. Let this be nothing more than a stupid joke aimed to make me laugh — one last prank. The women had obviously conspired with Alistair to create one final send-off hoax as a meaningless farewell chuckle. *Seriously not funny!*

I stood in the garden, glancing around at women I'd shared my life with for so long, none of them truly understanding the real authentic Stacey Adams at all. Alistair did not understand the real Stacey Adams. He couldn't have done. He wouldn't have just done what he did if he fully appreciated who I was, deep down. *What* I was. How could I let this go? I surely didn't expect me to walk away after all this time? Surely he wasn't *that* stupid?

# 41

Something wasn't adding up. Alistair adored me. He told me often, had proven it many times, verbally and otherwise. We'd shared an intense love for thirteen years. *Thirteen*. It had to mean *something* to him too because it meant the absolute world to me.

I couldn't shake the notion that what I'd been told many times about Alistair's "other" relationships in here, must actually hold some truth. No. I was being stupid. He wouldn't do that. He wasn't *Jason*. I searched for him for a while until I gave up, dejected, the man hell-bent on avoiding me, his firm declaration one he did not seem interested in arbitrating. I went to bed that night feeling as if I'd been shot in the chest, bumbling around my cell the following morning feeling slightly sick, an odd feeling in my belly knowing I would never sleep here again. For a brief moment, I feared I might never sleep again. What the hell was Alistair doing to me?

I gathered my belongings slowly, carefully, the world beyond my accustomed existence now immense and frightening. Alistair was the one thing getting me through all this, the *only* thing. He was the very reason I'd worked so hard to secure an early release in the first place — my one single chance at moral redemption. Now, I had no idea what to think. My brain creating painful scenarios as I left the remnants of a jar of coffee, Braunie's now ageing radio, half a bar of *Dairy Milk* chocolate that I felt too sick to eat, along with an unopened bottle of shampoo on my bed for whoever wanted them — for whoever next called this room home.

I stared too long at Elijah's photograph, faded now, crumpled at the edges, time slowly removing my boy's earliest memories from my life, greying in parts where the sun had filtered readily through the barred window onto his tiny features, relentlessly removing every last trace of colour and joy from my past, mocking me painfully each night before I went to sleep.

Although I was desperate to see him, I was somewhat surprised when Alistair finally popped his head around my cell door. I was ready to leave, psyched up, pumped up, this place no longer home. *I could do this.* I took a breath when I saw him, allowing a tiny smile to break free, knowing his previous words were not his real feelings. It was okay. I understood. Once I was out of this shithole, we would finally have a chance to claim the much-needed perspective we needed, have an honest conversation, forge an eagerly-desired clarity that had been devoid of our lives for so long. Only then could we find a way to focus on what was truly important. *Us.*

'I'm so sorry.' Alistair sounded genuinely sorry. He certainly looked it. I was so relieved I almost burst into tears.

'It's okay,' I reassured him, knowing he hadn't meant anything of what he'd claimed. 'Honestly, I get it.' I really did. I understood more than most what this place does to a person. It isn't pleasant. How could we possibly discuss our authentic relationship when we were still stuck behind these harrowing walls? How could we be honest with each other, honest with our feelings? I knew he was afraid. I was too. It was normal, expected — this entire thing *brand-new*. I held out a hand, needing the warmth of him against my body once more before, like Elijah's photograph, the memories of these walls faded forever. Alistair stepped forward, allowing a much-needed embrace, the man I loved more than anything releasing a heavy, impressionable sigh as I held onto him for all I was worth.

'I will always love you, Stacey Adams,' he said, kissing me gently on the cheek.

'I know you will,' I replied, knowing precisely what he meant, unravelling the words he wasn't using, appreciating a hidden tone only these walls would ever understand. I knew him too well. He hadn't given up on us at all. He was waiting for me to settle into my new life before commencing the future we both deserved. A future we had waited so long to experience. Alistair was afraid. I guess it made him human, humble, amazing. Such a concept now ensured I could remain calm. I needed to be. I was holding him against me, drawing him into my embrace, needing him close. Just a moment longer. I looked into his eyes, witnessing a profound love hidden behind darkening, unreadable pupils.

'I will *always* love you, too,' I confirmed. 'Never forget that.' I needed him to know that we would be together, no matter what happened after this day. He didn't need to worry or concern himself with matters yet to unfold. After fourteen years in prison, I had learned to allow time to take its natural flow.

'No hard feelings?' he asked me, seriously, curiously. I shook my head. Why would I *ever* be angry with the one man who had made everything so much better for me than my existence would have been without him?

'Of course not,' I promised him, a genuine smile reaching my mouth that seemed to help his cheeks flush wildly. I wondered if we had time for one final forbidden sex act, the door firmly closed, as usual, my panting kept to a minimal volume.

He pulled away, almost too soon, almost as if reading my thoughts. I wasn't finished. He couldn't have known what I had already set in motion, what I now needed to do to secure our much-needed future together. 'Are you ready?' he asked, standing by the door. He sounded sad.

I nodded. 'Just give me a moment, would you?' I needed a minute or two by myself. There was one final mission I had to complete before I left this place forever, one last claim to the old Stacey Adams I couldn't dispel. Alistair smiled, stepping out into the hallway towards a group of excitable women who had gathered to say their goodbyes, some of them I now even called friends.

I didn't need long inside my cell, thankfully. I was left alone for what everyone else would happily assume a mere private musing, one final glance around a tiny room I'd called home for too long. One last goodbye to my old, unwanted life.

'Good luck, Hun,' Tania Thomas waltzed into my cell and grabbed me, holding me in an enthusiastic embrace, her muffled sobs of joy and emotion emanating from a rapidly juddering chest. 'Don't you dare forget about us,' she laughed, a tear already making a break for it down a reddened cheek. As *if* I could ever forget any of them. In their odd little way, they had all shaped who I ultimately now was. I owed them all more than they realised.

'Never,' I sighed, wiping Tania's stray tear from her cheek.

I was eternally grateful to this woman that she was amongst those initial four curious inmates attending that very first initial EIP session. We had since become firm friends, more so once Mia walked free. She appreciated I needed cheering up, helped me more than I realised I needed. I hadn't anticipated just how valuable and vital such connections to these people would become until that first night without my cherished friend. It was a shame that poor Tania was probably always doomed to spend a life in and out of prison, but at least, now, she was better equipped to cope with it all, thanks to me. Thanks to the EIP. I could leave this place with gratitude that I'd helped her in some way.

I was due back here next week for my very first *externally*-run EIP group, so I would see everyone soon. It made my departure a far less emotional event. The difference now was that, once my hourly session was over, I would be free to leave this place, gladly hand my name badge into the front desk, walk outside, breathe fresh air, order a pizza.

Many fond farewells were aimed in my direction that morning as I headed out of the unit, Alistair by my side, many words of encouragement lingering on saddened lips. Even Miss Sharp wished me luck. It was an odd moment. I was afraid of being stuck in prison forever, terrified of so many locked doors, yet I was now far more fearful of what awaited me on the outside.

I was grateful that, at least, I now understood Alistair's valid fears. I had listened to his concerns, appreciated what would need to happen next. Of course, he wasn't breaking things off with me. *I knew that.* I understood. He was telling me what he thought I wanted to hear, what he believed I *needed* to hear in order for me to begin a brand-new life on the outside. It wouldn't be easy, I know. Many challenges lay in our path. He came with baggage. I'd always known it. Yet his boys were older now, no longer in need of their full-time dad, and he certainly couldn't stay with his *wife* forever. My man was trying to protect me, aid the potentially uncomfortable transition into a normal life that felt anything but. Yet, I didn't need an easy transition. All I needed was him.

We stood by the main gate, my nerves jangling, my hands trembling at the overwhelming thought of freedom, at last. The gate was not yet even unlocked to the world beyond, not yet allowing me the potential to walk through, unrestrained, unhindered by the invisible chains that had shackled my life to this place for so long. I appreciated what it must be like for butterflies, emerging from their protective cocoons, finally able to unfurl wings they never realised they possessed. *Shit.* I felt sick. Was this actually happening? I automatically slipped my clammy hand inside Alistair's, grateful when he squeezed it tightly, reassuringly.

'Goodbye, Adams,' he told me flatly, patting my tense fingers with his free hand, clasping them together firmly in a final bid for compliance. I almost laughed, knowing his deflated tone was purely for the benefit of everyone around us. I would have given anything for him to express how he really felt, kiss me wildly, right there in front of them all.

I turned to him, smiling, desperately needing him to know that this *was* going to be all right. I would make everything okay in the end. We were surrounded by prison staff, officers, security guards. Even Mr Barrington and Farley had come to see me off. I couldn't say too much to Alistair or lean in for a kiss, of course. Neither of us were free to do that, unfortunately. Instead, I glanced around, smiling at those all too familiar faces, knowing a friendly goodbye hug would be okay for everyone to witness. After all, hadn't I earned a final embrace? One last act of composed compassion for those people who had helped turn my life around, before I walked away, a free woman.

I turned to Alistair. 'Thank you for everything, Mr Stuard,' I stated clearly for the benefit of those around us. 'It's been a genuine pleasure knowing you, sir,' I laughed, pulling the man I adored towards me for a much-needed hug, a colossal embrace I didn't care who saw, confidently slipping something into his back pocket before he had a chance to notice. I even patted his bum. It was something I'd earlier taken from his unwitting wallet when we were in my cell, when he was trying to be nice to me, trying to smoother secret emotions he didn't want me to see. He would find my gift soon enough, carefully tucked inside his trousers. Only then would he realise my true intentions, appreciate what I was wholly prepared to do for him now. What I would *always* be prepared to do for him from this day forward.

Alistair didn't initially notice the hastily folded piece of paper and "special gift" awaiting his discovery. I nodded, excited for the acknowledgement I knew would come soon enough, for the understanding we had both undertaken in secret, in the darkness, wrapped in each other's arms, naked, together. We had planned this moment for so long. I'd spent so many nights alone in my cell, just waiting for this very day to come. It was almost overwhelming. I licked my lips as the gates began to slowly slide open, the incoming clatter of metal rollers slightly alien to my senses, a gentle breeze tugging my hair. Goodbye prison life, goodbye dark lonely nights. Hello, incredible life with Alistair Stuard.

'Thank you, Miss Adams, and good luck to you,' Governor Barrington held out a hand for me to shake. 'See you next week. Do not be late.' He laughed before tapping Alistair playfully on the shoulder, leaving us to it, glad my former peer worker was able to send me on my way. The governor was probably quite proud of himself right now, proud his prison made a difference, occasionally. I glanced into the eyes of the love of my life, winked at him, the gates opening to a bright, sunny morning. It reminded me of the very morning I'd stood by my sister's lonely grave, both sisters lost, streaks of sunlight burning my fragile eyes. The day of my arrest. I couldn't believe how long ago that was, this day now signalling the beginning of something incredible. I chewed the side of my bottom lip, a smile curling automatically around my anxious, chattering teeth.

'Look after yourself, Miss Adams,' Farley confirmed with a nod, his glasses perched on the edge of his nose, making him look nerdy, as usual. I smiled, wanting to tuck his wayward shirt back into his trousers, like his mother would have done, before he turned his attention back to the prison and awaiting madness.

'Goodbye, Stacey,' Alistair stated. The gates were now fully open, exposing a world that felt so alien to me now, frighteningly colossal.

I winked at my man, knowing his tepid words were for the purpose of the staff around him, their faces nothing but unrelenting stone pillars that meant nothing to me anyway, this moment a daily routine for them.

'Goodbye, Mr Stuard,' I nodded to my man, secret words left to linger unspoken between us. *I will see you very soon.* I stepped away from Alistair, the whole world suddenly feeling cumbersome and uninviting. Did I honestly have the strength to head out into the morning sunshine, to freedom beyond? I wanted my man to come with me, hold my hand, help me, save me. My heart fluttered a little at the idea of being alone after so long, yet there was so much now that needed doing, so much to plan for, to prepare for.

I was free. I'd spent fourteen years locked inside a women's prison, forced to retrace my unfortunate steps, take a different route, become a different person, a potentially better one given the chance. Now, everything felt strange. Even my echoing footsteps on the tarmac below sounded distant as I headed away from the main gate, Alistair still staring at my slowly disappearing body, my possessions in a carrier bag, my throat dry. He was probably watching my bottom swaying, liking what he saw — wanting me all that little bit more now that he could finally have me all to himself.

## 42

Ironically, I didn't appreciate my newly acquired surroundings at first, the sheer fact I was a free woman taking a somewhat indigestible amount of time to sink in. The prison walls loomed aggressively at my back, clawing my sanity, reminding me of what I was, of what I'd done. Still, I couldn't look back now. Forward was the way I was heading, and forward must forever be the way I walked, emotionally, physically, everything in between. A slow clink of metal threatened to rattle my brain to pieces as the gates began to close steadily behind me — an uncomfortable, distinct reverberation that almost witnessed me race screaming backwards, pound on the closing steel frame, run straight into Alistair's outstretched arms, tears blocking my view, preventing my escape. What the *hell* was I doing out here?

I wanted to turn around, comfort myself one last time by the sight of familiarity, even if that came in the form of doomed confinement, punishment, much personal suffering. Fourteen years is enough time to change a person's perspective. It shifts how you view pretty much everything around you, distorting your once carefully protected comfort zone. If the human mind is capable of creating metaphors from situations, places, people, this moment should have shown me something important. Something vital. I should have already created an image in my mind of who I was. What I had become. Instead, I felt nothing at all now but misguided personal sacrifice, an empty shell where there must have once lived a rational, sane human being, still, unfortunately, answering to the name of Stacey Adams.

It took a few moments of adjustment before I noticed someone standing several feet away; two people, actually, their backs casually pressed against an open door of a low purring taxi, chatting anxiously, their voices indistinguishable. Who the hell was *that?* I couldn't exactly see their faces or read their expressions. Age had reduced my vision slightly, annoyingly, my short-sightedness becoming something I chastised myself often over, fought the need to wear glasses, blaming such an infliction on the limited light of my cell, including fourteen years of endured private hell. I squinted, the low autumnal morning sunlight doing nothing for my sense of awareness of this new, alien environment. I made my way unsteadily along the path towards the street beyond, just as one of those two strangers noticed my not so careful approach. They stood upright, skinny jeans and floppy hair only just visible to my blurred line of sight. Who *was* that? I stepped closer, slowing down, my pace unsteady, uncertain, my facial expression muted.

It appeared to be a young man, a teenager, his baby face reminding me of someone who, initially, I couldn't tell. Ironically. *Stupidly.* He stepped towards me, his trembling legs appearing equally as uncertain as mine, the young girl by his side equally as obscure to my jaded memory.

'Mum?' I heard a voice, clear, loud, emerging from this lanky young man standing right in front of me now, his adult tone not yet fully developed, still in the trappings of youth, the lad not long entering his teen years.

'Elijah?' *No way.* I couldn't believe I was speaking my son's name aloud. I never thought I would ever see him again, hardly assuming I would be given such a priceless gift. The last image I had of my boy was of some beautiful rosy-cheeked baby wrapped in a blue and yellow blanket, my mum's voice telling me firmly to say goodbye to him, his photograph forever in my pocket. I blinked hard, screwing my brow tightly, knowing it made me look older than my years, entirely unconvinced that the boy, *my boy*, was here at all. Was my sudden freedom simply giving me unwanted hallucinations? Was I going crazy? I glanced towards the girl by his side, her long, dark hair so much like Emma, it was impossible not to recognise her beautiful face immediately.

'Eva?' Oh my god. *Was this real?* Were my babies genuinely standing in front of me right now? How did they know I was getting out today? *Why* would my mum even allow them to meet me? Questions I had no answers for raced through my brain as I reached out a shaky hand to touch my beautiful son's face. Jesus, he looked so much like his dad. It was almost painful. He smiled, a half-smile, but a smile I was willing to take as a win, all the same.

'You came,' I muttered, unsure of everything, startled by such an unexpected event, feeling more like a child than either of these two ever possibly could.

'I wanted to see you,' Elijah muttered, his insecurities as imposing as mine. He glanced at Eva. 'We both did.'

I shook my head, tears automatically spilling from my eyes as I pulled my son and niece into a robust, much-needed embrace. I didn't care how manic I looked. It was as if, in the brightness of this morning, I'd been given a second chance at life. A fresh start, forgiveness for crimes I no longer had *any* control over.

'Does your grandma know you're here?' I questioned, my voice sounding like someone else, a stranger. Did they even call her grandma? Or did mum prefer granny, nan? I couldn't imagine my mum being comfortable that her grandchildren even *wanted* to see me today or any other day, come to think of it.

Elijah nodded. 'She knows,' he confirmed, something telling me I wasn't wrong in my assumption that she wasn't impressed by the concept. Still, it was something to work on. If my boy and my niece were prepared to meet me out of jail after all these years, my parents would surely come around at some point. I needed to bide my time, wait. I hoped dad was well, *still alive.*

I smiled at Eva, unable to grasp this moment. The last time I saw her, we were sitting by her mum's grave. The poor child was too young to remember that day or to appreciate the truth of her aunt's malignant identity. She was too small for the magnitude of that moment to reach her honest understanding, too tiny to appreciate the events unfolding. I couldn't believe she was here. Actually standing in front of me. Tall, slim, beautiful. Exactly like her mum. Simply perfect in every way.

I refrained from asking too many questions, for now, instead taking this moment to glance towards the prison, hoping Alistair had noticed this incredible moment unfolding in the street beyond. I was relieved to see him standing next to the gate, still half-open, still watching me, still waiting. I wanted to smile at him, wave, point out my now fully-grown son as he acknowledged my continued presence, the beautiful scene happening beyond the darkness of that lonely place. He raised a hand, nodded his head. I nodded back.

We smiled at each other confidently as Alistair casually reached his arms back to stretch, glad to confirm I was okay as he rested a wayward hand against the lining of his back trouser pocket. Had he found my gift? His attention caught on something as he pulled a folded piece of paper from his pocket, along with my parting gift to him. Alistair momentarily looked confused, glancing my way, unsure what he'd just found. I smiled knowingly, eagerly, as my man unfolded paper that smelled of my perfume, carefully reading the note I'd hastily derived that very morning. He was staring intently at the ageing photograph he always kept inside his wallet. I couldn't read his facial expression as he scanned the text in front of him. I was too far away. No matter. I knew what it said.

*Dearest Alistair. I want you to know that whatever happens from this day forward, we are in this thing together. I will always love you. I will always be here for you. You can depend on me. We will be together soon, I promise. Leave this to me. Yours forever. S*
*xx*

That old photo, the one showing his two boys when they were young, standing with their mum, now had a slight difference that I hoped would confirm my intentions with pure irrefutable clarity. His soon to be *ex*-wife's face was scratched out, no longer needed, no longer critical. It was my personal, private promise to him. An ultimate pledge to my beloved that, no matter what happened from this day forward, we *would* be together. I would make damned sure of that. She no longer needed to exist. He no longer needed to worry. From now on, it would be just the two of us, his boys, my boy now as well, it seemed. Eva, too. We would become a family, a perfect little unit.

He would never again need to worry about finding the courage to leave his wife, telling me things needed to cool down between us because he was too wrapped up in wedded suffering to do anything else. He was a good man.

Jason had equally wanted to save the marriage he assumed he had a duty to fight for. I knew how this thing worked. Charlotte would be gone soon enough, gone from our lives. I'd done it before. I could do it again.

However, this time, there would be no mistakes, no inflamed passions driving my insatiable actions, no stupid errors leading to any unfortunate arrests — no more jail time for me. I had studied psychology. I now understood the law. I knew full well how better to serve my emotions, both legally, morally. Prison had oddly made me a better person. It would ultimately make me a more prolific killer.

Alistair glanced my way, staring, a slightly shocked expression appearing on his face that I couldn't read yet appreciated. It didn't matter. I continued to smile and nod as the gates closed too swiftly. This moment complete, my lover understanding my carefully planned next move. He didn't need to worry. Everything *would* be okay. I would make it easy for him. Easy for us both. I'd make it look like a tragic accident, sparing our boys from the unfortunate, unbearable truth, the whole thing firmly out of my hands now anyway. Alistair already knew what I was, knew what I was capable of. He *understood* me. Nobody had, in fact, ever appreciated me the way Alistair Stuard did. I mused over my name for a moment. *Mrs Stacey Stuard.* It had such a lovely ring to it.

I couldn't overthink the look on his face as the gates closed, interrupting our perfect moment. I had so much to do, so much to plan for. Excitement bubbled as I wondered about his wife, what she would say when she saw me for the first time, how she would react — our first encounter becoming her last. I stepped into the taxi with my son and my niece, a knowing smile on my face I couldn't hide from either of them. My new life awaited. *Our lives awaited.*

I guess there will always be something dark living

inside me — something twisted. I believe a good person can be pushed to do bad things, but a bad person will always be a bad person, no matter how hard they try to convince themselves of anything else. I was no different. I understood that truth more than most. *I was what I was* — what I was always destined to be. Stacey Adams. Serial killer. I'd had fourteen years to get used to the idea, come to terms with such a truth. It was ironic that I only did what I did for the love of those people in my life I deemed important enough. Those people I needed to protect. The people I needed to save.

If Jason had chosen me over Emma, he would still be alive. Emma would still be alive, Sylvester too. He would have left her behind, started his new life with me. None of what happened needed to happen. None of it was my fault. Now Alistair equally had the same choice. He could leave his wife, begin a brand-new chapter with me, or suffer the consequences of what we both knew would need to happen next.

I stared calmly out of the taxi window, watching the passing world beyond, the warming sunlight guiding me towards a brand-new existence I never assumed I'd ever truly become a part of again. I closed my eyes for a moment, recalling how I'd asked myself all those years ago if I honestly believed that leopards had the potential to change their spots? I guess, thinking seriously about such a concept now, the honest answer is no. No, they cannot. The only genuine ability such a creature has is to become a far better hunter, a far better manipulator.

*A far better killer.*

SRL Publishing don't just publish books, we also do our best in keeping this world sustainable. In the UK alone, over 77 million books are destroyed each year, unsold and unread, due to overproduction and bigger profit margins.

Our business model is inherently sustainable by only printing what we sell. While this means our cost price is much higher, it means we have minimum waste and zero returns. We made a public promise in 2020 to never overprint our books just for the sake of profit.

We give back to our planet by calculating the number of trees used for our products so we can then replace. We also calculate our carbon emissions and support projects which reduce $CO_2$. These same projects also support the United Nations Sustainable Development Goals.

The way we operate means we knowingly waive our profit margins for the sake of the environment. Every book sold via the SRL website plants at least one tree.

To find out more, please visit
www.srlpublishing.co.uk/responsibility